THE BRAZEN SHARK

A Novel of the Clockwork Legion

DAVID LEE SUMMERS

Hadrosaur Productions, Mesilla Park, NM

The Brazen Shark
Hadrosaur Productions
Second Edition: March 2022.

First date of publication: January 2016
Copyright © 2022 David Lee Summers
Cover Art Copyright © 2022 Laura Givens

ISBN-13: 979-8-9851120-2-3

Hadrosaur Productions
P.O. Box 2194
Mesilla Park, NM 88047-2194
www.hadrosaur.com

To Dean Summers
who wrote letters from Japan when I was seven years old
and introduced me to the simple beauty of haiku.

ACKNOWLEDGEMENTS

A challenge of writing historical fiction is that you have to imagine places that have changed and people who no longer exist. Although this is alternate history with a solid dose of science fiction and a sprinkle of fantasy, I hope to create a past that nevertheless feels authentic.

Thanks to Dean Summers for pointing me to the writings of Lafcadio Hearn, who in turn helped to transport me to Meiji Era Japan. Thanks to Ronald Mastaler for discussions which have given me insight into Alexander II's Russia. Also, thanks to Bob Arnold who suggested that if the Japanese built airships, paper would be a major component.

Thanks to the Tucson Steampunk Society and the Arizona Steampunk Society for providing opportunities to dress up and actually be a mad scientist or an airship pirate for an afternoon. Such events are both a well needed diversion and an important source of inspiration.

Jeff Lewis, Kumie Wise, Doug Williams, and Myranda Summers all read early drafts of this novel and gave me valuable feedback that made it stronger. What's more, thanks to Myranda Summers for proofing and correcting my Japanese.

Thanks to Phyllis Irene Radford for working with me to polish this manuscript. She has given me many tools to be a better writer. For that, I'm most grateful.

This book was created with the generous support of my Patreon supporters. Among them are Robert E. Vardeman, John D. Payne, Anthony D. Cardno, the Creative Play and Podcast Network, and Madame Askew and the Grand Arbiter. I'm pleased to have received their support and comments through the process of revisiting and updating the Clockwork Legion Series.

Other Books by David Lee Summers

The Solar Sea
The Astronomer's Crypt

The Space Pirates' Legacy Series
Firebrandt's Legacy
The Pirates of Sufiro
Children of the Old Stars
Heirs of the New Earth

The Clockwork Legion Series
Owl Dance
Lightning Wolves
The Brazen Shark
Owl Riders

The Scarlet Order Vampires Series
Dragon's Fall: Rise of the Scarlet Order Vampires
Vampires of the Scarlet Order

THE BRAZEN SHARK

CHAPTER ONE
A LEGION IN HIDING

Shinriki hefted a twelve-foot long marek and sighted his quarry. With a practiced thrust, he drove the spear's hooked tip into soft flesh and lifted the squirming body, streaming water and blood. He turned and dropped the flopping salmon onto a mound of its kin and nodded, satisfied.

"A good haul," said Pasekur from the boat's stern.

Shinriki looked to the river where salmon still schooled. Although plenty of daylight remained, the boat lay low in the water and the catch needed to be cleaned and prepared for the smokehouse.

His gaze drifted to the Russian village called Poronaysk on the river's far bank. A year ago, the smoke would have alarmed the fisherman, who would have assumed a nearby forest fire. Now, he knew it came from Russian factories. At least the Sakhalin Islanders left his village alone. According to travelers, Japanese soldiers harassed Ainu villages in Hokkaido to the south.

He took a deep breath of pine-scented air. At least the wind blew the smoke out to sea, away from the river. Aside from the smell of salmon, which indicated a satisfactory catch, the air near the village remained fresh.

Shinriki lay the marek down in the boat, then settled into the bow and retrieved an oar. Together, he and Pasekur rowed against the current to the Poronay River's far shore. As they reached the bank, Shinriki spotted his wife, Ipokash. From a distance, the dark ink around her mouth looked like a smile. Once he pulled the boat onto the beach, he saw a genuine smile within the tattoo. She summoned several young women who helped them haul the salmon to a work area in front of the smokehouse.

1

After a few minutes to refresh himself with some water and to wrap his weary arms around Ipokash, Shinriki settled in to help gut the salmon. As the messy work drew to a close, long shadows darkened the land. The women hung the cleaned salmon in the smokehouse and rekindled the gentle fire while Shinriki went to the river to wash up.

As he knelt by the water, horses thundered in from the northeast. He stood and turned, water dripping from his long beard. Russian soldiers would ford the river nearby.

These soldiers wore lacquered metal armor and helmets. Vertical, rectangular sashimono flags adorned with a flower in a circle fluttered from poles mounted to the backs of four riders. Horn-like maidate adorned the leader's helmet. Shinriki blinked a few times. Samurai!

The Meiji Emperor's army outlawed the samurai in Japan. These samurai must be bandits, driven northward. Of course, raiding a city as big as Poronaysk with a contingent of Russian soldiers would be futile, but the small Ainu village on the Poronay River's far bank must seem like easy prey.

Shinriki ran to the boat and grabbed the one weapon available, his marek. As he rushed toward the village, the samurai fired pistols and at least six Ainu fell backwards. Women ran around, shouting and herding children into the huts. Men rushed at the samurai with knives and clubs only to be rebuffed by the mounted warriors.

Pasekur appeared from his hut with a bow and arrows. He loosed an arrow, which ripped through a sashimono flag. A mounted samurai fired a second pistol. The bullet caught Pasekur, whirled him around, and he flopped to the ground.

Shinriki ran forward, cursing the long, narrow marek. Not made for combat, the spear wobbled with each step.

The samurai stirred up a dust cloud as they brought their horses to a stop, dismounted, and dispersed through the village, unleashing a fresh cacophony of screams, shouts and cries. One group of warriors made straight for the smokehouse. Ipokash charged out and shouted at the warriors in Japanese.

The leader whirled around and pointed at her with a curved, gleaming katana. Shinriki sprinted a dozen steps, planted his feet, and prepared to drive the spear's hook into a joint between armor plates. The leader spun and knocked the spear away with the flat of the katana's blade. As Shinriki back-pedaled, he noticed the leader wore a face guard, adorned with a fearsome horsehair mustache. The leader took a step forward and crouched, spine straight, and glared at Shinriki with dark, brown eyes. The posture seemed unbalanced, but the fisherman didn't have time to consider it further before the samurai brought the katana back for a blow.

Shinriki dove inside the strike and tackled the leader. With surprising agility given the armor, the leader rolled out from under Shinriki, dropping the katana. Shinriki lunged for the sword, but the samurai kicked him backwards. The fisherman gasped for breath and fought to focus on the swirling pinks and blues of the twilight sky above. The samurai retrieved the sword and rushed back to the village center.

Shinriki's vision cleared enough and he lifted himself onto one elbow, then reached up and touched his moist forehead, not surprised by the blood on his fingers. No doubt, the samurai's armored boot cut his scalp. Perhaps the warrior thought Shinriki had been dealt a fatal blow. Dizzy as he was, he considered it possible. He lay back for a moment swallowing gulps of air.

Soon, breathing came easier and he sat up again. He reached out and ripped a strip of cloth from his sleeve and wrapped it around his head wound. The samurai tied salmon bundles to their horses. A woman's scream brought Shinriki to his feet. Ipokash yelled curses in Japanese, Russian, and Ainu as a samurai shoved her onto a horse between a rider and a bundle of salmon.

"Ipokash!" Shinriki reached down and grabbed the marek. He stumbled forward as Ipokash struggled, causing the horse to dance around in a circle. Shinriki circled with the horse, found an opening and drove the marek home. The samurai whirled and dislodged the spear's hooked head.

Another samurai rushed in from the side and shoved Shinriki to the ground as the rider regained control of his horse. The leader barked a command and the samurai ran for their horses. The fisherman floundered on the ground, his joints screaming in pain as the samurai mounted their horses.

Ipokash had fallen silent. Shinriki tried to focus as he pulled himself to his feet. The samurai rode away. He finally caught sight of Ipokash, lying between a bundle of salmon and the rider. He ran after the horsemen, but they soon outdistanced him. He stopped, panting.

After a few minutes, Shinriki caught his breath and turned around to face the tattered and broken village, so beautiful and idyllic just moments before. The samurai bandits hadn't burned anything, but they'd ripped out door curtains and burst through walls, taking anything they thought held value. Friends lay on the ground, dead or wounded. The horse corral stood empty, the Ainu mounts stolen or run off. Shinriki unleashed a yell of rage which set his head throbbing.

Just then, Shinriki remembered Pasekur, cut down by a bullet. His friend lay near his hut, blood pooled under his ruined shoulder.

Shinriki knelt beside Pasekur, and examined the wound, which seemed small and bled little despite the darkening pool of congealed blood. Shinriki tried to revive his friend, but his gut lurched as though falling from a great height when he felt the cold, waxy skin. Pasekur would never wake again.

Shinriki leapt to his feet and ran several steps after the samurai. He needed to rescue Ipokash. They killed Pasekur. He sank to his knees when he realized he held no weapon and the growing darkness swallowed the bandits' trail. The night's first stars seemed to mock him. The samurai had his wife, but how could he hope to fight for her. His village had been decimated and might not recover. Men, women and children all wailed into the darkening night. Did anyone remain to fight?

Shinriki shot an angry glance at Poronaysk. Lights winked on, defying the darkness. More than once, Russian soldiers had come across the river to demand the Ainu's fealty to the emperor a continent away in St. Petersburg. Perhaps the time had arrived to determine that fealty's worth.

The next morning, far to the east of Shinriki's village, Ramon Morales awoke to bright sunlight streaming through a round window in a metal wall. He lay in a comfortable bed next to the most beautiful woman he knew—Fatemeh Karimi, his wife. He supposed that made her Fatemeh Morales now. Onofre Cisneros, a one-time pirate, swept them away for a honeymoon aboard his freighter called the *Ballena*. The Spanish word for whale suited the sturdy, powerful steamship. The name belied the ship's speed, but served to keep people from associating the new vessel with Onofre's sleek pirate frigate, named *Tiburón*—Spanish for shark.

Cisneros turned pirate to demonstrate a small submersible boat's potential in warfare. The Mexican government shunned him because of ties to the former Emperor Maximillian. He gave up the career in piracy when Fatemeh showed him the submersible boat may have more uses in peacetime than in war. Since then, Cisneros had purchased shares in the seaport at Ensenada, Mexico and ingratiated himself with President Diaz.

Now, the captain traveled to the Hawaiian Islands to sign a trade agreement with a British sugarcane plantation owner. The captain thought the islands would be the perfect vacation getaway for the couple.

Ramon leaned over and kissed Fatemeh gently on the cheek. She squirmed a bit, but remained asleep. He climbed out of bed, pulled on trousers and washed up. A Bible sat on a table next to a chair. Ramon wasn't sure whether Fatemeh had brought the Bible or whether it belonged to the cabin's previous occupant. It didn't matter. It allowed him to check the faint memory of a Bible story which had been gnawing at him.

He sat down and thumbed through the book. Less than a month ago, in Sausalito, Ramon spoke to an invisible creature—or were they creatures?—that came from a distant star. The creature, called Legion, helped the Russians invade America, but Ramon persuaded it to let humans solve their own problems. The creature soon departed, which allowed the American army to push back against the Russian invasion. At last, the two countries negotiated—a distinct improvement over fighting.

Ramon found the passage he sought in the Gospel of Mark Chapter 5, verses 8 and 9: "For he said unto him, Come out of the man, thou unclean spirit. And he asked him, What is thy name? And he answered, saying, My name is Legion: for we are many."

Legion described itself as a creature from the stars, but Ramon saw parallels with a mischief-causing demon. Certainly the "heavens" the creature showed Ramon seemed more hellish than any angelic realm he'd ever imagined. Ramon pictured Legion as a swarm of tiny clockwork automata.

A knock at the cabin door interrupted Ramon's thoughts. He looked back and made sure a blanket covered Fatemeh, then cracked the door open. A steward held a tray containing two breakfast plates and a carafe filled with coffee. "The captain's compliments," said the man.

Ramon thanked him and brought the tray inside and set it on the trunk at the foot of the bed. Fatemeh stirred and sat up.

"Well, good morning, sleepy-head," said Ramon.

"If you hadn't kept me awake so late, I would have been up earlier." Fatemeh gave a sly grin. "Did I hear breakfast arrive?"

"Thanks to the captain." Ramon handed her a plate with eggs, beans and chile, then poured the coffee and handed her a cup. She took a sip, sighed contentment, then dug into the hearty breakfast.

Ramon gathered up the second plate and cup, but felt uncomfortable and lazy as he returned to the chair. He'd been many things including a sheriff and a ranch hand. He enjoyed working, but Captain Cisneros insisted Ramon and Fatemeh were guests and must enjoy their time together. Despite his lethargy, Ramon's stomach rumbled. He gulped down breakfast and sopped up the leftover egg yolks and chile with a tortilla.

"Slow down," said Fatemeh. "You'll give yourself a stomach ache."

"I don't know why I'm so hungry."

She shrugged. "Must be the sea air."

Glancing over at the tray, Ramon spotted a folded paper. He set the empty plate on the small table next to the Bible and read the note. "Captain Cisneros has invited us to visit him on deck after we finish breakfast."

"Does he say what he wants?"

Ramon shook his head. The captain had been occupied since they boarded the ship and they only visited him once as guests for dinner. The newlyweds dressed and made themselves presentable then left the cabin. Ramon eyed the steamship's steel girders with suspicion. Even though Fatemeh had explained it to him, Ramon found it counterintuitive that a steel vessel could float.

The two reached the companionway to the ship's afterdeck. There, beside the rail, a man wearing denim trousers, a teal waistcoat and a white, peaked hat looked off into the distance. He turned around and removed his hat. "You look lovely today, Señora Morales."

"Why thank you, Captain Cisneros." Fatemeh curtsied. Ramon noted her grace, and tried to recall if she'd made the gesture before.

"When we first met, I had the privilege of taking you aboard the *Legado*." The captain referred to a submersible he'd built based on a Spanish design. "Not only do I have a new ship, I have a new submersible as well."

The captain led them to the ship's stern, where he lifted the protective lid on a control pedestal. The captain pressed a button and a hatch slid aside. A mechanical rumbling sounded from below decks and a white, egg-shaped mechanism arose. Four fins, each resembling a ship's rudder, encircled the stern. Round windows lined the vessel's sides. Near the front, four long, arm-like cylinders protruded with finger-like claws. Ramon thought it resembled a stubby, pale squid with four tentacles instead of ten. The machine seemed ready to grapple some unseen foe.

A chemical reaction steam engine that vented into the cabin itself powered the captain's prototype. If the steam engine had burned coal or wood, such venting would be fatal for the crew, but the captain's craft used oxygen-producing chemicals.

Cisneros strutted alongside the strange craft and banged on its metal side. "I've made this new submersible much stronger than its predecessor." He climbed up ladder rungs welded to the craft's side, opened a hatch and then disappeared inside. With a whir and a hiss, the arms moved out to the side. The claws opened and closed. Afterward, doors opened near the

craft's keel. Hydraulics hissed and squeaked as a pair of continuous track treads similar to those on a steam tractor emerged.

The captain's head protruded from the submersible's
hatch. "I can use the arms to repair ships under water. I can use
the treads to work on a ship close to land or push a grounded
craft into deeper water. I call this new submersible, *Calamar*."

Ramon smiled, thinking the Spanish word for squid was
indeed an apt name.

"It's marvelous," cried Fatemeh.

"You gave me the idea," said the captain.

Ramon's brow furrowed. "And the execution? This looks
quite sophisticated, not unlike the Russian airships. How did
you figure out how to build this craft?"

Cisneros pursed his lips. He left the submersible, then led
Ramon and Fatemeh to the rail and looked out over the sea.

"I gather you know about the creature called Legion," said
Cisneros. "He split into multiple parts. Part remained with the
Russians. Part traveled with Maravilla…"

The captain referred to an exiled Mexican professor who
invented craft that flapped their wings to fly and an automaton disguised as a wolf. He'd also invented a mining machine
called the Javelina, which wreaked havoc in Apache country
southeast of Tucson. "Part of Legion went with you," surmised
Ramon.

"Legion has been a good companion." Cisneros's voice
held a sorrowful note. "He guided me as I built my business,
helping me choose good investments. He showed me better
ways to build machines. He even helped me build better ships,
such as the *Ballena*. A few more years under Legion's tutelage
and I could imagine Mexico surpassing the United States as the
Western Hemisphere's commercial leader."

"Except if Legion's influence continued—and he succeeded in his plans—there might be just one country and our emperor would be Czar Alexander." Ramon folded his arms.

Cisneros nodded. "I wonder if one world government
would be so bad."

"I think it would be a good thing," said Fatemeh. "However, I think humans have to build that government on their
own."

"Do you know what happened to Legion?" asked Cisneros. "I just caught a glimpse of him reunifying before he vanished from my mind." His smile grew wistful. "I have to admit I had grown used to his incessant chatter in my brain. It's lonely with him gone."

Ramon shook his head. He didn't like the idea of an alien creature knowing his thoughts and poking around his memories. He was glad the interfering, invisible alien had vanished. "I have no idea where he is. No idea if he'll even return." He hoped the alien had left for good.

Legion lingered on Earth, observing humans in a contrite silence as he pondered his actions. He'd chosen the name Legion millennia ago because he was a swarm of microscopic self-propelled automata. Although the name also could mean an armed contingent, he possessed only a limited ability to alter the environment around him. Long ago, he had been a single, self-aware organism who discovered he could upload his memories, consciousness, personality—everything that made him alive—into a machine which had the ability to modify itself. The machine evolved and grew stronger until it achieved its present form. No longer encumbered by a planet or mortality, Legion wandered the universe, observing, learning, and gaining knowledge.

Since arriving on Earth, Legion had encountered beings who referred to themselves by names such as Duncan, Gorloff, Morales, and Cisneros. One called himself Maravilla—marvelous in the Spanish language—a name the being assumed to identify himself, much as Legion created his own moniker. Legion remembered assorted names. Most were simple combinations of letters and numbers which identified the different machines he once occupied, but some held ancient meaning. Perhaps one had even been his name as a corporeal life form.

For millennia, Legion had never once cared about any names he'd held. Now, he looked back on his long journey and wondered how his knowledge changed him. Perhaps if he knew his earlier names, he might remember what he'd been like in times past. He searched volumes of data, but couldn't tell which name had once been his. One early machine he'd occupied had deemed the information irrelevant and erased his early names from memory. If Legion had tear ducts, he might have wept for the memory of the organic being he had once been.

His. He. What did personal pronouns mean when you were a swarm of microscopic machines that reproduced asexually? Since he arrived on Earth, Legion gravitated toward male hosts. He wondered if that meant anything. Humans ascribed much meaning to gender. According to his observations, men tended to cultivate power more than women. Legion never cared about power before arriving on Earth. He was an invisible being, content to observe whatever he came across. Power only mattered once he developed an agenda.

Over the millennia, Legion had observed much. He'd watched solar systems form. He'd watched supernovae destroy thousands of species in a microsecond. On one planet, simple multicellular organisms had frolicked among algae forests. In a distant, barred spiral galaxy, a star empire once held sway over a million worlds. He'd occupied a green and tentacled space explorer's brain to understand the reason for a lonesome voyage and had found a kindred spirit who thrilled in being the first of his kind to visit a system of planets orbiting a pulsar. Legion had examined a five-gendered animal species to find out what they sought in mates. He'd ridden tachyons from one end of the universe to another. He'd placed himself in a slingshot orbit around a black hole and listened to the whispers of information retreating with the radiation. It all fascinated Legion, but he'd never once involved himself, except as a spectator.

Never once, though, had Legion come across another creature identical to himself—a merging of organic and machine intelligence.

What compelled Legion to get involved with humans? He supposed it came from encountering them at just the right point in their history, when machines moved beyond tools. He hoped, perhaps, to influence human evolution. Perhaps they would avoid the suspicion some species held about machines and form a true kinship. Over a few thousand years, they might evolve into creatures like him.

Was he lonely?

There was no logic in the idea that a swarm could be lonesome. Nevertheless, when he'd integrated with Maravilla, Cisneros, even Gorloff, he'd enjoyed interacting with other beings who might interpret the same data in different ways and had seen meaning beyond the physical. He'd also known their loneliness when he'd been quiet in the back of their minds and observed.

Legion had been tempted to fully integrate with Maravilla and Cisneros. He could have lived out their mortal existences as them, sharing their consciousness. It would have been a flicker in his existence, but what a joy it would have been to understand the world as they did and bring the experience back to the swarm. Then he'd realized they had a right to their own existence, no matter how fleeting. He must not trifle with their lives.

The human called Ramon Morales also helped him see the inherent danger in attempting to manipulate the entire species. Instead of unifying the species, he might cause them to destroy each other. Legion had seen civilizations self-destruct. He could fix the problem by occupying every human on the planet, but then humans would just be puppets. Their free will and their perspectives made them interesting potential companions who could help him evaluate and find meaning in the knowledge he'd gained.

Legion decided to pull back and see what the humans did. If he could prevent destruction, he would. If they asked for help, he would evaluate the situation and take the most beneficial action. He wanted them back on a track to meld with their machines. He looked forward to a day when he would have a companion. He could wait. And if humans failed, he would seek other beings, elsewhere.

Shinriki worked late into the night helping those who survived the raid clear away the dead and restore order to the village. Only forty of the one hundred twelve villagers remained and most were bruised and bleeding. After the elders counted, the only Ainu missing was Ipokash. Despite their wounds, the few surviving men made brave noises about tracking the samurai to their lair. The village elder, Akiki, shook his head as he cradled his splinted arm. "We are too weak to fight the samurai. Fighting now would just bring more tragedy."

Shinriki trembled as he stared into the campfire, tears streaming. He agreed they didn't have the manpower to hunt the bandits, but he needed to take action. "I'll go to Poronaysk tomorrow and ask the Russian mayor for help," he choked out at last.

Akiki looked up, a faint glimmer of hope warring with resentment. "What do the Russians care for us?"

"The Russians might not care for us," said Akiki's wife, Katkemat, "but they will surely care about a Japanese incursion on the island."

Shinriki nodded, then trudged off to his hut and fell into a troubled sleep.

The next day, he sought a simple breakfast but found the samurai had taken all the grains he might use for a porridge. Stomach rumbling, he dressed. Fog had rolled in overnight and poured through the holes in the hut's walls, adding to the day's dismal, dreary feeling. Shinriki strode to the river, pushed his boat into the water, and rowed across to the far side.

Men in tattered coats and trousers eyed him as he reached the far bank. A few spoke in hushed Russian, but didn't speak to him. The Russians who worked along the riverbank were accustomed to the Ainu fisherman, neither hostile, nor congenial. None seemed concerned about the village's condition. Had no one witnessed the samurai raid?

Shinriki slogged up the riverbank onto the village's cobbled streets lined by gray boxy structures. Sometimes, the Ainu villagers crossed the river to barter for food or supplies. Shinriki knew his way around. Along the main street, men strung white, red, and blue banners between windows. Beyond the city hall, workers raised a long, narrow tower. Poronaysk poised for a celebration.

Shinriki climbed the city hall's steps and entered a bare, gray corridor. Although a steam radiator stood in the hallway, the Ainu fisherman shivered and wondered how the Russians could work in such a sterile place. He entered a small office. A clerk wearing a coat, trousers, and waistcoat only a little less tattered than those belonging to the men on the riverbank sorted papers. Shinriki waited for a moment. When the clerk continued to work, the fisherman stepped forward and rapped on the tabletop. The clerk looked as though he'd eaten something sour. "May I help you?" The words came out in a huff.

"I wish to see the mayor." Shinriki spoke serviceable Russian.

The clerk shook his head. "I'm afraid that would be impossible. The mayor is much too busy right now."

"Raiders attacked our village last night," said Shinriki. "My wife abducted. Many killed. Our horses stolen."

"I'm sorry to hear that." The clerk's words sounded rehearsed rather than sincere. "But what you Ainu do to one another is of little concern to us." He leaned forward, ready to return to work.

Shinriki barred his teeth, frustrated. The Ainu were not mere savages who raided one another. "Not Ainu," said Shinriki. "Samurai."

The clerk looked up and blinked, showing interest for the first time. "Samurai? From Japan?"

"Where else would samurai come from?"

The clerk sat back as though evaluating Shinriki anew. "When did this raid occur?"

"Last night. Many men killed. My wife... taken."

The clerk removed his wire-frame spectacles and rubbed the bridge of his nose. "Wait here." He stood and disappeared through a door behind the desk.

Shinriki noticed the clerk had not offered him a chair. As he waited, raised voices came from the other room, but not quite loud enough for him to make out the words. After a few minutes the clerk followed a man with silver hair and a neat goatee through the door. Taller than Shinriki, the new arrival wore a tailcoat and a purple waistcoat.

"You say samurai attacked your village?"

Shinriki recounted the previous night's raid, but sensed he was losing precious time. "They took my wife. Will you send soldiers to find them?"

The mayor waved his hand. "You're sure these people were Japanese?"

"They wore samurai armor," insisted Shinriki.

"Does it matter if they're Japanese?" interjected the clerk. "If this raid occurred, it's clear we have troublemakers on our hands."

The mayor nodded. "And we don't need trouble. Especially not now." He met Shinriki's gaze. "Return to your village. I'll send a patrol to check out your story and follow up."

"The raid happened." Shinriki opened his robe and revealed his bruised shoulder.

The clerk stepped forward, took Shinriki by the elbow, and led him from the office and down the hall. "I can assure you this matter is of the upmost importance to the mayor. You should return to the village and wait for the soldiers."

Shinriki frowned, but couldn't think of anything better to do, so he returned home.

As the day wore on, the fog dissipated, but a high overcast remained. The Russians' half-hearted response disheartened the villagers and they again debated whether they should attempt to follow the bandits' trail on their own. Despite their brave words, only Shinriki's cousin Resak seemed up to the task. He'd survived the battle with just a few bruises and scratches. While Shinriki had pleaded with the mayor, Resak followed the samurai trail a few miles upriver before returning home to report what he'd learned.

Before noon, two barges ferried a squad of mounted Russian soldiers across the river. The soldiers examined the village, questioned a few of the men, then walked around the perimeter while the horses grazed on the lush grass. Completing their circuit, they convened near the remains of the smokehouse. "Whoever raided your village rode off along the river," declared the squadron leader. Shinriki didn't know Russian military insignia well enough to know his rank.

"Why does the mayor doubt us?" asked Shinriki.

The soldier sneered, as though simple questions from peasants annoyed him. When Shinriki refused to back down, the soldier explained further. "It's not that he doubts you. He just doesn't want soldiers tied up with everything that's happening right now."

"What exactly is happening?" pressed Shinriki.

The soldier's eyes drifted along the tree line. "You'll find out soon enough. All I can say is that it's an important time for Poronaysk." He returned his gaze to Shinriki. "Don't worry. If the bandits are still around here, we'll find them and we'll deal with them."

"We want to come along. At least a few of us." Shinriki brandished his bow and arrows. Resak stepped up beside him.

The Russian soldier raised his hand in an unspoken signal and the scouts mounted their horses. "You'll just slow us down." The soldier's words held no malice. "We're better equipped to deal with these bandits." He mounted the horse and swept his hand forward. The soldiers rode off, following the samurai's trail.

Akiki approached and grabbed Shinriki's elbow as though he needed a little extra support. "So is that it? We just wait for the Russian soldiers to return?"

"I may not be as fast as them, but I can follow their trail and report what they find."

Akiki grunted approval.

Shinriki strode after the soldiers. Resak followed but Shinriki held up his hand. "Stay here and help the elders. The Russians may detain me if they catch me following. If I don't return, it'll be up to you to rescue Ipokash and the supplies."

Resak gave a sharp nod as Shinriki set out.

CHAPTER TWO
HAWAIIAN HOLIDAY

R amon leaned across the ship's rail, breathless as the *Ballena* steamed into port. The land rose up to his right into a single great mountain topped by a billowing cloud. To the left, swaying palm trees and vegetation carpeted the land. He'd seen palm trees before in Southern California, but never as numerous as those on this island oasis in the middle of a vast ocean. Growing up in the New Mexico desert, he'd never seen greenery so wild and uninhibited. Ahead lay a village, quaint by the standards of sea ports like San Francisco and Los Angeles. He sensed a presence behind him and held out a hand. He sighed at Fatemeh's tender, but firm grip.

"You've traveled the world, corazón," said Ramon, "have you ever seen a place as beautiful as this?"

She shook her head. "Nothing as lush as this. People have left their mark, but not as much as most places I've been."

Two ships swayed at anchor in the harbor. One flew an American flag, the other a Union Jack. Not exactly a bustling port, but the two ships reminded Ramon that Russia wasn't the only country with imperial ambitions.

Captain Cisneros tromped up the deck, allowing Ramon a moment to squeeze Fatemeh's shoulder before taking a step to the side.

"Welcome to the Island of Maui in the Kingdom of Hawaii. I hope you like it. It's my present to you both," announced the captain.

Ramon's eyes widened as Fatemeh gasped.

Cisneros laughed. "Oh, not the whole island, of course. My friend, Sir Elias Pennington-Smythe, owns a sugar plantation up the beach a few miles. He has a small bungalow on a quiet inlet. It's private and I thought you would enjoy some time in paradise."

Ramon nodded as he turned around and shook the captain's hand. "It's perfect, Señor. Thank you!"

"It's the least I could do." The captain's eyes drifted to Fatemeh. "You set me on a profitable—and legal—course." With that, Cisneros turned away. He called orders to his executive officer. Mr. Gonzalez, in turn, relayed the orders via speaking tube.

Ramon moved away from earshot while watching the activity on the docks. "Here's the thing I never understood," he said to Fatemeh under his breath. "The captain was penniless after the Mexican Revolution. He stole money when he raided ships. Did he not return the money?"

Fatemeh sighed. "Sometimes it's best not to pursue those lines of inquiry. That's between God and the good captain now."

"For one who seeks justice, you seem awfully ready to turn a blind eye to dirty deeds, corazón."

She put her arm around Ramon and gave a gentle squeeze. "I also seek peace. Often times a blind eye is necessary to that goal."

Ramon turned his head and kissed her. She melted into him. Two weeks ago, she would have resisted, hesitant to show too much intimacy before they married, but now she resisted no longer. Ramon anticipated the bungalow's privacy and time alone with the woman he loved. The ship lurched, causing them to break the embrace.

Crewmen tossed ropes overboard to dockhands on the pier. Ramon's eyes followed the ropes, surprised. The dockhands wore little, even for men working in such a torrid climate. Some only wore trousers, while others wore a floral wrap around their lower bodies. Ramon gathered they must be native Hawaiians. He wondered if the Hawaiians had any ships of their own, or if this port just existed for Europeans and Americans. Fatemeh stared at the workers unabashed.

"Enjoying the scenery?" asked Ramon.

Fatemeh blinked, but smiled rather than have the good grace to look embarrassed. "I'm imagining what you would look like in traditional Polynesian dress."

Ramon glanced at the men on the dock, muscles rippling and glistening as they tied off the ropes. His stomach lurched and his face heated. He hoped Fatemeh wasn't too serious about trying to get him into a native costume.

A crewman slid a section of the ship's rail aside and lowered a gangplank to the dock. A horse and carriage pulled up at the pier and a man in a top hat and tailcoat emerged. He looked out of place among the topless dock workers. A shrill boatswain's whistle set Ramon's teeth on edge. The man in the top hat boarded the ship followed by a Polynesian man, also in a tailcoat. The Polynesian man ran his fingers under his shirt's long sleeves, as though trying to give himself more air. Captain Cisneros stepped forward and shook the new arrival's hand, then beckoned Ramon and Fatemeh over.

"This is Sir Elias Pennington-Smythe."

Fatemeh held her skirt and curtseyed while Ramon thrust out his hand. Pennington-Smythe shook it and smiled. "It's a pleasure to meet such charming newlyweds."

"Thank you for allowing us to use your bungalow," said Fatemeh.

"It's my pleasure, young lady." Pennington-Smythe fluttered his hand as though loaning out a house were a trivial matter. "In fact, I imagine as ship traffic increases, there will come a time when more people will make Hawaii a travel destination once they're married. It's such an idyllic setting. If you care to gather your things, I'll have my coach driver take you there at once. I have some business I need to discuss with the captain."

The captain betrayed surprise just as Ramon and Fatemeh left for their cabin. They gathered their belongings and returned to the deck, where the Polynesian man in the tailcoat led them back to the coach. "I am Haku," he said. "I oversee Sir Elias's properties here on Maui."

"Pleased to meet you," said Ramon.

Haku loaded their baggage onto the coach, then climbed in after Ramon and Fatemeh. She looked back toward the village. "May we purchase supplies for the bungalow?"

"Sir Elias has put his staff at your disposal. The cooks will prepare food for you as you wish. Just let me know what you would like."

"What would you normally prepare for visitors on their first night?" asked Fatemeh.

Haku smiled and patted his belly. "We like to welcome visitors with a luau."

"That sounds perfect," declared Ramon.

Shinriki was a fisherman, not a hunter, but even he had no problem following the tracks left behind by the samurai, the village horses, and the Russian soldiers. They traversed a line alongside the Poronay River's meandering oxbows. The terrain rolled uphill and by nightfall, he reached the point where the Kamenka River flowed into the Poronay.

Fire rings and trampled brush all indicated a campsite. Shinriki guessed the samurai paused to take stock of their loot after the raid. No bodies lay beside the trail, so Ipokash must have spent the night here. His hands trembled in outrage as he wondered if she'd been tied up, forced to work, or raped. He grabbed one of the rocks from a fire ring and hurled it off into the trees, venting his anger enough to continue the pursuit.

The trail continued along the Kamenka River, toward the hills. Despite the clear trail, it would be difficult to follow after the sun went down. Shinriki found shelter by a tree, pulled his arms inside his woolen jacket and closed his eyes while waiting for the moonrise.

When he awoke, the moon was already high, but still behind him in the east. He clambered to his feet and resumed tracking the soldiers and samurai. A few hours later, the sky lightened further as sunrise approached, but the terrain grew more rugged and wooded. He could only tell the horses had continued upward into the mountains. By now, following the samurai and the soldiers alone seemed ill considered. He crouched beside the trail and took a drink from his water skin to moisten his dry throat and calm his racing thoughts.

He saw just three possibilities. The Russians had caught up with the samurai and they'd already fought. The Russians still pursued the samurai, but both groups were so far ahead he couldn't catch up. Finally, the Russians might have lost the trail themselves and given up. The Russians would be better trackers than him, so if they'd lost the samurai, he didn't expect to succeed where they failed.

A thrumming in the air interrupted Shinriki's thoughts. Unable to pinpoint the sound, his heart raced. He guessed he heard horses and scanned the surroundings. Even though the thrumming grew louder, he caught no movement. He looked skyward. A great, silver craft drifted southward like a wind-blown cloud, following the mountains, on a course toward Poronaysk. The water skin slipped from his fingers. He quickly grabbed it and sealed it before too much seeped into the ground.

He was tempted to see it as a craft of the gods, except he recognized it as the work of men. It made a veritable racket like all the Russian machines and left a fine smoke trail just like their factories. What's more, white, blue, and red bars, the same as the Russian Imperial flag, adorned the fins at the back—a Russian ship of the air.

Shinriki's gaze followed the hoof prints into the trees, then moved skyward and followed the airship's path. He climbed for another hundred yards before he heard hoof beats and shouts behind him. Russian soldiers rode along the valley floor, taking the shortest path back to Poronaysk.

From this distance, Shinriki couldn't tell whether they were the soldiers who pursued the samurai, but he thought they must be. He had to learn what they'd found. He waved and shouted, but they either ignored him or couldn't hear. With heavy heart, Shinriki abandoned the trail and climbed down to follow the Russian soldiers. It consoled him somewhat to realize he might learn who flew the marvelous machine.

Shinriki reached Poronaysk late in the afternoon. Sunlight glinted off the silver airship tethered to a tall tower among the army barracks behind city hall. Up close, the sheer size took his breath away. He couldn't imagine how something bigger than the Poronaysk city hall could float, swaying like a flag in the breeze.

He trudged into town, tired, stomach rumbling, and disheartened. He walked through the streets to find a crowd gathered before city hall. Soldiers guarded the steps. A podium sat at the top.

Shinriki pushed through the crowd until he came face to face with a Russian soldier in a pressed black coat with buttons down the side. The soldier sneered at him.

"I wish to speak to the mayor," said Shinriki.

"No one sees the mayor today."

"Why?"

The soldier walked away.

Shinriki turned to a woman standing nearby. "What is happening?"

"They're getting ready for a speech," she said.

"A speech. Who's speaking?"

"A scientist called Mendeleev. They tell us this is a historic day for us on Sakhalin Island."

"What about the mayor? Is he speaking?"

The woman shrugged and pushed further into the crowd, whether to escape Shinriki's questions or get closer to the speakers, he couldn't tell.

Frustrated, Shinriki ground his teeth, then looked around at the crowd. He had no patience for speeches, but he was here and the alternative was to admit defeat and return home empty handed. He might just as well stay and see what this Mendeleev had to say.

Captain Cisneros watched as Sir Elias's coach carried Ramon and Fatemeh away, then turned to his guest. "I plan to be in Hawaii for a week, perhaps two," said the captain. "I'm pleased you brought your coach for Ramon and Fatemeh, but I confess I'm surprised to see you so soon. I expected we'd meet in a few days."

Pennington-Smythe pursed his lips and gave a slight nod. "I have the agreement with me and saw no need for delay." He patted the tailcoat's breast pocket. "But, first, I would like a tour of your fine ship. I have heard the *Ballena* is quite the engineering marvel."

Cisneros forced a smile, then instructed Mr. Gonzalez to

oversee the resupply operations. He suspected the English-
man was up to something, but knew he'd reveal his hand soon
enough. He led Pennington-Smythe on a tour. He showed him
the cargo bays with cranes which could lift sugar pallets into
the holds. Cisneros led him down into the engine room and
showed the plantation owner improvements he'd made to
increase the engine's efficiency. "We made the crossing from
Ensenada to Hawaii in just four days at an average speed of
twenty-one knots." The captain folded his arms and cast a
glance to the chief engineer who wore a smug grin.

Pennington-Smythe nodded and his brow furrowed. "And
your costs are lower. This makes you quite competitive. What
happens if your ship is damaged en route?"

"Although natural enemies, this whale has a squid for a
helpmate." With that, the captain led the plantation owner
back to the deck. He activated the hydraulic system which lifted
the submersible *Calamar*. The captain explained how the arms
could repair a ship. They climbed inside and Cisneros opened a
hatch, showing off the chemical reaction steam engine.

"It's so small," declared Pennington-Smythe. "It's hard to
imagine such an engine could propel a craft this size."

"Professor M.K. Maravilla used this same type of engine to
propel ornithopters in America," said Cisneros.

"You mean those flapping, flying machines they've used to
fight the Russian airships?"

Cisneros nodded. "I've flown one myself."

"Indeed! I have heard remarkable things about your engineering prowess. It seems the stories are no exaggeration.
Where do you get the fuel for the ship and the submersible?"

"I make it myself in a laboratory in Ensenada. The raw materials are rather inexpensive, but it's time consuming to make
the fuel in the quantities I need. I have a small lab here on
the ship and can make smaller quantities en route." The captain folded his arms. Pennington-Smythe seemed interested in
more than commerce. Time to get to the bottom of the merchant's new-found interest in engineering. "Are you worried
about me running out of fuel?"

"Oh no, nothing like that." Pennington-Smythe waved
the question away. "I'm convinced you can maintain a regular

shipping schedule to North America. Any doubts I had about a contract with you are firmly banished."

"I'm glad to hear it."

"I may have an additional job for you, though—one which would require your engineering expertise."

Although confident in his own engineering abilities, the technical know-how for many of the recent improvements came from the alien, Legion, who had gone silent almost a month ago, now. He swallowed, but pushed ahead. They were coming to the point. "Tell me more."

Pennington-Smythe held up his hand and glanced around to the porthole, then up at the open hatch above. "We should discuss this in greater privacy."

The captain's eyes drifted around the small vessel. What did Pennington-Smythe fear? Lip readers on deck? "Shall we adjourn to my cabin?" Cisneros led the way back to the *Ballena's* deck, then strode down the nearest companionway and entered his cabin at the vessel's stern. "Would you care for anything to drink? If so, I'll summon the steward?"

"Not just now." Pennington-Smythe eyed the door.

The captain turned the key in the lock and strode to the desk. He indicated a chair opposite, then sat down. The plantation owner removed his top hat and hung it from a hook by the door, then retrieved two envelopes from his inside coat pocket. He lay the first one down on the desk. "This is our agreement. It's already signed. Read it over at your leisure. If you agree to the terms, sign it and return it to me."

"If I don't agree to the terms?"

"We can discuss them when you return."

"Return? Return from where?" Cisneros leaned forward. "I planned to stay in Hawaii for the next two weeks."

Pennington-Smythe held up the second envelope. "This may tempt you to reconsider." He looked around, as though checking to see if anyone unexpected had entered the room. "As you may know, England has been negotiating an alliance with Japan. This is critical to both nations' security, with the Russian airships and all."

"By all indications, their American invasion failed," said Cisneros.

"The Russians overextended themselves." Pennington-Smythe leaned forward. "I don't think they'll be so foolish next time. Those airships represent a real danger to world security."

Cisneros nodded. "I can see that, but how can I help?"

Pennington-Smythe opened the second envelope. He unfolded a piece of paper, which showed a diagram of a dirigible similar to the Russian ships. A wooden exoskeleton held a single gasbag. Cables suspended a gondola beneath the exoskeleton. A large engine drove two side-mounted propellers. Based on the gondola's scale, he estimated the ship must be much smaller than the Russian craft—a scout or a trim fighting ship. "It's amazing," he breathed.

"The interior cabins are made of lightweight wood and paper, if you can believe it. It's much lighter than those heavy Russian airships. The Japanese could use help developing effective ship-to-ship weapons and would like to lighten the steam engine. You can see it's rather large. They also want to test the ship's range. As it turns out, you have a port in North America which would be perfect for the test."

"You mean they've already built an airship?"

"Two, in fact."

Cisneros nodded. "What's in it for me?"

"The gratitude of the British Empire... and a quarter million pounds sterling."

Cisneros ran a quick mental conversion and decided it would recoup his losses from the Mexican Revolution. He would be a rich man again. "You can keep the British Empire's gratitude. The quarter million pounds interests me. How do we make arrangements?"

Pennington-Smythe shook his head. "The Japanese want to consult with you, and make arrangements for a trans-oceanic flight. That way, they can ask questions, figure out parameters, that sort of rot."

"Makes sense. When should I go?"

"As soon as possible. Of course, your friends Mr. and Mrs. Morales are welcome to stay until you return."

"How do you know you can trust me?"

The plantation owner shrugged. "You already possess the

knowledge we wish to share. You haven't been paid yet and won't be unless you return with a letter bearing the Japanese Imperial seal. If you attempt a forgery, you can expect all your prospects around the Pacific Rim to dry up, unless you think you can convince the Russians to join you as trading partners."

Without comment, Cisneros stood and walked over to the chart table. He measured the distance from Hawaii to Japan. "Six days one way, if the weather is good and we can maintain full speed. I should be able to restock and be ready to depart day after tomorrow. I'll speak to Mr. and Mrs. Morales tomorrow. I imagine they'd be happy to stay here for two weeks, more or less."

"Outstanding." Pennington-Smythe folded the airship diagram and placed it back in the envelope. "I look forward to working with you, Captain Cisneros. I think this would be an auspicious time to summon your steward for a drink."

Poronaysk's mayor took the stage. Shinriki's Russian served well for basic communication, but he struggled to follow all the mayor's words. He gathered the newest building in town had something to do with the airship docked on the tall tower to the north, and it would mean more jobs for Russians in the local mines and at the natural gas works.

Shinriki wrinkled his nose. The latter building smelled of farts and made his eyes water. He had been cautioned never to strike a match nearby. Ainu were often encouraged to work in the coal mines, so they could rent a flat in town instead of living across the river in the village. The Russians promised them money and luxuries. Later, those Ainu dressed like Russians, but often looked drawn and haggard. Shinriki had no desire to become a coal miner and wondered why the Russians were so pleased at the prospect of more mining jobs.

The next person to stand behind the podium reminded Shinriki of those Ainu who worked in the mines. He had long hair and a wild beard, but he wore a Russian suit. Unlike the Ainu who worked in the mines, his cheeks appeared ruddy and healthy. The mayor introduced him as Dmitri Mendeleev.

Even from a distance, Shinriki noted a certain sadness in the man's eyes, as though he suffered a loved one's loss. Mendeleev spoke in a deep, sonorous voice about the future.

Mendeleev said Russia led the world in something called "tekhnologiya." Shinriki didn't know what that meant, but found it interesting the Russians now led in this area. He wished Ipokash were there to translate for him. "We have built the world's first airships." He gestured to the great behemoth floating behind him. "We can improve overland transport. We can improve sea transport. Perhaps we can even send men to the stars."

Shinriki's brow furrowed. Ages ago, oil arose from the great ocean and formed the heavens and the land. A mist formed into the first gods. The mayor and Mendeleev spoke about drilling for oil and harvesting strange gasses. This sounded like men tampering with the fundamental firmament of the universe to challenge the gods themselves in their own domain. Shinriki couldn't imagine such a challenge ending well for humans.

As Mendeleev continued to speak, Shinriki's attention wandered to the crowd. Most watched enraptured. Russian soldiers skirted the crowd's perimeter. Shinriki recognized one as the leader of the soldiers who came through his village the day before. The Ainu fisherman pushed toward the soldier. Applause erupted. Mendeleev's speech came to an end and the crowd began to disperse.

Shinriki had to peer around the throngs of people returning to work and their homes to keep the soldier in sight. At last, he caught up with the man. "Sir, please. You led the expedition into the mountains following the samurai. What did you find?"

The soldier frowned and narrowed his gaze. "Poronaysk is secure," said the soldier. "You need not worry about raiders from the hill country."

"What about my wife? What about the samurai? Did you find them?" Shinriki fought to keep desperation from his voice.

"There are no samurai since Emperor Mutsuhito restored military authority in Japan," declared the soldier.

"Samurai, bandits, it matters not what you call them! Yesterday, you hunted those who raided us. What did you find?"

"We determined the bandits are long gone. You have

nothing more to worry about," declared the soldier.

"I'm not worried about the bandits. I'm worried about my wife. I'm worried about our horses." Shinriki's voice turned shrill.

The soldier snorted. "If you want more horses, go work in the mines. They will pay you enough to buy new ones." With that, the soldier spun on his heel and walked away.

Shinriki stood wide-eyed, his hands clenching and un-clenching. He considered running after the soldier, but shook his head, realizing it would do no good. He now understood the soldiers' orders were to assure no one disrupted this day's festivities. He cast a glance up to the podium where the may-or and Mendeleev had been. He thought about telling them bandits remained in the woods, but despair crept over him as he realized the Russians had every reason to keep their sol-diers close. Shinriki's only hope was to return home and mus-ter what help he could from his own village. Resak would help and perhaps others could, now that they had time to recover.

Returning to the river, he spied Resak on the far bank. He waved and a short time later, he climbed aboard his young cousin's boat. "Did you have any luck?" asked Resak.

Shinriki shook his head. "I saw where they followed the Kamenka River into the woods, but then I lost their trail."

Once they reached the far bank, Shinriki thanked Resak, then trudged back to the village where the surviving men and women repaired the thatched huts.

The village elder looked up from his work and spoke the traditional Ainu greeting. "Let me touch your heart."

"My heart is heavy," said Shinriki. "I could not find the bandits. I would like to gather the men to search the woods for them."

Akiki looked around, deflated. "I know the men are all willing, but they would all die if you encountered the samurai. They must not go. It's not worth it for food and horses. Other-wise, the rest of us would have no choice but to cross the river and work in the Russian mines. It would be the end of our village."

"It's not just food and horses. It's my wife." A deep weari-ness settled into Shinriki's bones. "I fear our village has already met its end." With that, Shinriki trudged to his own dwelling, lay down on his mat and fell into a restless sleep.

Ramon sat in the bedroom feeling ridiculous.

"Are we going swimming or not?" called Fatemeh.

"Are any of Sir Elias's people still in the house?"

"No," said Fatemeh. "They've all returned to the main house until tonight."

He crept to the door and peeked out. "This is ridiculous! You're fully dressed. Why do I have to go out in something that looks like a pair of short long johns?"

Fatemeh sighed as she pushed the door open. She planted her hands on her hips. "You know, your suit looks much better for swimming than mine."

Ramon looked down at himself. Even though the suit covered him from shoulders to knees, it was so tight it left little to the imagination, even decorated in broad white and blue stripes. Fatemeh's ankles and forearms may show, but at least she wore a proper dress with exaggerated lace.

"What if someone sees me?" Growing up in the desert, the closest Ramon had ever been to water were the rivers of the Southwest. He'd fished the Rio Grande numerous times, even waded in, but he'd always been dressed in a shirt and pants with the cuffs rolled up. The only time he'd worn so little in the water was alone at bath time.

"So what if they see you? They'll probably be wearing a suit similar to yours."

"That doesn't exactly help."

Fatemeh pushed past him to the window and opened the curtain wide. "Look, we have the beach all to ourselves. It's a beautiful day out there."

"I don't know how to swim."

She shook her head. "We won't go all the way in. We'll just wade out a short distance." She held out her hand.

Fatemeh's confidence convinced Ramon he wasn't going to win this. He'd rather look silly and be with her than spend the day cooped up in the bungalow. He took her hand and gave it a squeeze. "All right, let's go."

The two went down the hall, through the front door and out onto the beach. Ramon hopped back on the porch. "The sand's hot!"

"Let's run for the water. The wet sand will be cooler."

Ramon gave a sharp nod, then followed her to the point where the waves lapped the shore. Fatemeh unbuttoned an outer, billowy garment and dropped it to the sand. The swimsuit underneath still covered more than his did though. He breathed a sigh when his naked toes cooled off. A moment later, a wave came in and swirled around his ankles. He swiveled his arms, afraid he would fall. She reached out, took his hand, and smiled at him.

"It always feels like it's pulling on you, drawing you in, but it's not. Not unless you wade much deeper."

"There's so much of it," whispered Ramon. "If you get drawn out, you'd never be found again."

"Well, let's just go show the ocean who's in charge." Fatemeh led Ramon further into the water. She paused when they were shin-deep, then stopped again when the water reached their waists.

A wave splashed Ramon's chest. He blinked back surprise and spat out briny water. He turned to Fatemeh who sent more water splashing at him, then bobbed under the surface. He tried to run after her, but the drag from the water limited him to a trudging walk. When she reappeared, Ramon cupped his hands and sent a shower of water at her. She threw up her arms to protect herself and laughed.

Another wave came in and caught Ramon unaware. He toppled forward a couple steps, but remained standing. When he looked up, he stood next to Fatemeh. Her wet suit clung to her curves and Ramon found the sight intoxicating. He pulled her close and kissed her. A moment later, distant singing distracted him.

They both turned toward the sound's source. A short distance up the beach, the white sands blended into fertile, black volcanic soil. Polynesian workers sang as they harvested the sugar cane plants some distance away. Beyond them stood the sugar mill, its tall stack billowed smoke. Fatemeh's flesh pimpled out in goose bumps.

"It feels like one of Blake's 'dark satanic mills' in this paradise, doesn't it?"

"It is paradise." Ramon forced himself to sound cheerful. "The mill produces sugar, not weapons. The workers sound happy."

Fatemeh gave a wistful half-smile. "Working for Mr. Pennington-Smythe."

"Well, he knows how to treat his guests. What about the luau last night? I'm still full." Ramon rubbed his stomach.

Fatemeh's gaze narrowed. "I don't know. This may be the Kingdom of Hawaii, but it sure feels like a colony of the British Empire... at least this part of Hawaii."

Ramon hated to see her mood turn dark. "Let's go in and get dressed. We can go for a walk and see some more of the island before Captain Cisneros comes to dinner."

She sighed, then looked over at Ramon with a twinkle in her eye. "All right, but you know, it may take some time for me to peel you out of your wet swimsuit and who knows where that will lead?"

"I like the way you think, Mrs. Morales." With that, they ran back across the hot sand to the bungalow.

CHAPTER THREE
HIJACKED!

F atemeh Morales meditated on her new name as she sat on the bungalow's porch next to Ramon, holding his strong, callused hand, watching the waves roll in and out. As a young girl, her father said she shared a name with the Prophet Mohammed's daughter and the name meant she who abstains. According to Ramon, the surname Morales meant "moral." The moral abstainer. She wondered how well the name suited her.

As a young girl, she'd met a French trader who did business with her father. He'd resembled no one she'd ever met. He had a bare chin and wore strange clothes. He'd spoken with a heavy accent and he'd given her a music box. When she wound up the clockworks, a little ballerina on top whirled while music played. The ballerina seemed free in her tutu with lithe, muscular legs and bare arms. She'd wanted to see the place which produced such wonders and see women who danced ballet to lovely music.

Her father had smashed the music box and told her such dreams were improper for a young girl. She must have jumped at the memory because Ramon turned, brow furrowed. "Are you all right, corazón?" His nickname for her, which meant "heart," expressed who she wanted to be much more than her given name. Perhaps even more than her new married name.

She smiled and nodded even as she struggled to shake off the painful memory. "I think the breeze just gave me a slight chill."

"It smells like dinner's almost ready," said Ramon. "Captain Cisneros will be here soon."

"What a wonderful present he gave us in this honeymoon." The words sounded insincere. Hawaii was beautiful, but the real adventure of travel came from meeting new people and

31

learning about their cultures. This bungalow seemed designed to keep her safe from real Hawaiian culture. If she stayed, she and Ramon would need to explore and learn more about the islands and their people. She wondered what Sir Elias Pennington-Smythe would think of such an expedition.

Years ago, her father may have destroyed the music box, but he couldn't keep her from dreaming. He probably exacerbated the situation by sending her to school. She'd learned poetry and housekeeping, things that would make her a good wife, but poetry had also made her long to see the places poets celebrated.

Her grandmother had taught her about herbs and showed her how to heal many common ailments. Her father had approved because those skills would attract a good husband. She'd approved because people everywhere paid for a healer's skill.

Captain Onofre Cisneros rode up the beach on horseback interrupting her thoughts. He dismounted a short distance from the bungalow and led the animal to a rail, where he tied off the reins. As he did so, he reached into his coat pocket for an apple and fed it to the horse. "Good evening, my friends," he said.

"It is a good evening." Ramon inhaled the sea air. "I haven't been this relaxed in a long time."

Fatemeh knew he told the truth, even if she didn't share the feeling. She enjoyed swimming in the ocean and the quiet time with Ramon, but it felt strange to have others cook and clean for her, especially when those others were natives working for a foreigner.

The three went inside as a Hawaiian woman set the last plate on the table. She smiled at them and indicated they sit. "Dinner is almost ready."

"Thanks, Lelani," said Fatemeh.

Captain Cisneros hung his hat on a hook by the door. Ramon held the chair for Fatemeh, then seated himself as the captain sat across from them. "How are your negotiations with Sir Elias proceeding?" asked Ramon.

"Extremely well," said the captain. "He's impressed with the *Ballena* and has already signed an agreement for us to carry sugar back to North America. This could prove quite lucrative."

"I'm guessing you'll need it to pay for this." Ramon gestured around at the bungalow. "We won't ever be able to thank you enough."

Lelani appeared a moment later with a platter containing a beef roast and potatoes. Both Ramon and the captain smiled with delight. Fatemeh fought to hide her disappointment. She enjoyed the previous night's luau and sampling Hawaiian cuisine such as poi and lau lau. Tonight's dinner seemed all too British.

"Don't worry about it." The captain stood and sliced the roast, then served portions to Ramon and Fatemeh. "Sir Elias is getting his money's worth from me. In fact, he will owe me more money after I complete a short mission for him."

"Oh? What sort of mission?" As Fatemeh asked the question, Lelani brought a bowl with chopped papaya, pineapple, banana, and mango. The native fruit piqued her appetite.

"He wants me to go to Japan." Cisneros served himself a slice of beef and two potatoes. "He has... a client there who would like to consult on some engineering matters."

Fatemeh reached out for the fruit bowl. "So when will you go?" She wondered if the captain could get them home and travel back to Japan before winter.

"I leave tomorrow."

"Tomorrow?" Ramon's fork stopped halfway to his mouth. "How long will this venture take?"

The captain shrugged. "Somewhere between sixteen and twenty days. It's a pretty simple errand. Sir Elias says you're welcome to stay here on Hawaii for the duration."

Fatemeh frowned. "I hoped you'd take us around to the other islands while we're here. Maui is beautiful, but it would be difficult for us to explore on our own."

Ramon shrugged. "I admit, it's a little hard to imagine getting bored with you, corazón, but yeah, twenty days sitting around on the beach is a long time." He poured a glass of wine and offered to pour some for Fatemeh. She considered for a moment. As a Bahá'í she shouldn't drink alcohol, but she didn't feel constrained to rules this evening. She indicated he should go ahead and pour.

"I could speak to Sir Elias. I'm sure he could arrange for a tour of the islands," said the captain.

Fatemeh took a drink. "Would it be possible for us to go to Japan with you?"

Both Ramon and Captain Cisneros gaped at her.

The captain recovered first. "That's at least two weeks aboard my ship. I'm proud of her, but do you really want to spend your honeymoon aboard a freighter?"

Fatemeh turned to Ramon before he could speak. "You've always said you want to see new places. This would be a chance to experience the Far East."

Ramon's eye twinkled and she could tell she'd hooked him, but he looked down at the plate. "I feel like I've hardly had a chance to experience Hawaii."

"With apologies to your friend," Fatemeh cast a sidelong glance at Captain Cisneros, "I think the Hawaii Sir Elias wants us to experience is an extension of Great Britain. Japan has no intention of being anyone's colony. America is setting itself up to be a world power. So is Japan. If you want to be a diplomat, don't you think you should see a place that's front and center on the world stage?"

Ramon took a drink. "If we go to Japan, will I have to wear that swimsuit?"

"Now you're giving me second thoughts." Fatemeh smirked, then turned to the captain. "So, what do you say? May we travel with you?"

The captain sighed. "Why not?" With a shrug, he lifted his glass. "The more the merrier."

Shinriki's gut churned and writhed in conflict. He feared Ipokash had been killed. If so, Akiki was correct and the village's survival came first. He helped bury the dead and repair the huts, but it provided no relief or closure. If the samurai lingered nearby, another raid could render any effort rebuilding the village futile.

Shinriki fished without enthusiasm. The airship gently swaying over Poronaysk's army barracks seemed less a marvel and more an evil omen. Ipokash's loss clung to him, but unless he helped, the villagers would need to enter Poronaysk and find jobs or face extinction. Those two options seemed equivalent to Shinriki.

No troops strayed far from the city to scout the countryside. Neither did he see any sign of the bandits' return. Of course, they had stolen a winters' worth of food. He looked up at the clouds forming above. The next day would be a poor one for fishing.

As night fell, he found the elder Akiki by a cooking fire. Autumn winds blew, chilling the air. "I have to follow the trail again. I have to find out whether or not Ipokash is still alive."

Akiki frowned, but scanned the surroundings. "We are a village of farmers and fishermen. Most of those who could have fought are dead. Even if you found the bandits, could you free your wife?"

Shinriki jabbed his finger at the elder. "I have to try! If I can rescue her, I will. If not, perhaps I can find evidence to spur Russian soldiers into action." He sat back and folded his arms. "Much as I worry about Ipokash, I wonder how we will survive with all our supplies gone."

Akiki nodded. "I sympathize about Ipokash, but I worry she may already be dead." Shinriki stood to leave, but Akiki held up his hand. "Damaged as the village is, we'll find a way to survive. If you must go after the bandits, please take someone with you."

"I thought of bringing my cousin, Resak."

Akiki looked to the ground, thoughtful. "I hate to lose him, but I agree, he's the best choice."

"Thank you." Shinriki stood and bowed, then found his young cousin. Together the two made plans and packed supplies as the wind blew outside the hut.

Dmitri Mendeleev awoke in his stateroom aboard the Airship *Nicholas Alexandrovich*. He'd gone to bed during a wind storm and his sleep-addled mind attributed the jostling to turbulence, but the ship bounced up and down with no side-to-side shimmy. What's more, the ship canted to the stern. He closed his eyes and listened. A faint rustling followed a door's click and whisper. A dull thud followed.

Someone had invaded the ship.

If only the being which called itself Legion had not departed, he would know the invaders' identities. In fact, Legion could have alerted the crew well ahead of time and prevented an incursion. Then again could they afford to get so used to Legion's help that they no longer relied on their own wits? Mendeleev shook his head to clear his thoughts of these early morning ramblings.

Mendeleev slipped out from under the covers. He slid trousers on, then found his boots. He eased toward the door, attempting to match the invaders' stealth.

The door latch turned. Mendeleev reached behind him and activated the electric lamp as the door opened revealing a man in lacquered armor. The man threw his arm in front of his face and Mendeleev kicked out, slamming the door closed and knocking the invader backwards. Heart pounding, the scientist rushed to the door, opened it, pushed past the stunned invader and ran down the hall toward the gondola's entrance hatch.

He threw open the hatch, slung himself against the ladder and slid to the deck below. His joints complained and again he wished for Legion's assistance. He whirled around and faced two warriors wielding swords. The shorter one stepped forward with a certain lithe grace that reminded Mendeleev of jungle cats in the emperor's zoo.

The warrior scrutinized him from behind a face shield, then asked a question in a language Mendeleev didn't recognize. He wasn't sure whether the warrior directed the question to him or the other warrior, but the voice, although gruff, sounded decidedly feminine. The other warrior answered, saving Mendeleev the trouble of responding.

The woman thrust her sword at Mendeleev, then barked something at him. When the scientist didn't reply, she called up the ladder.

Mendeleev analyzed the situation. The armor suggested these were samurai warriors. Last he had heard, though, the Japanese emperor had disbanded the samurai. Perhaps they were mercenaries attempting to capture the airship in a covert operation.

A rustling sounded from the ladder. Mendeleev risked a glance over his shoulder. Another samurai entered the gondola, followed by a woman in a long, flowery dress and a black, painted clown-like smile. Looking closer, he realized her lips had been tattooed. She must be a primitive of some sort. If Legion were still available, Mendeleev could have requested more information.

"I am called Ipokash." The tattooed woman spoke Russian.

"Are you a prisoner, too?" Mendeleev narrowed his gaze.

She nodded. "I am from the Ainu village across the river from Poronaysk. It seems the samurai sought someone who could speak both Japanese and Russian."

"Do you?"

"Better Russian than Japanese."

"How did they pick you?"

Before she could answer, the samurai woman released a sharp hiss, then spoke to Ipokash, who bowed in submission. "The samurai want you to show them how to fly this great sky whale."

"That is not something easily taught. It's even more difficult through a translator," said Mendeleev. "Soldiers from Poronaysk will investigate soon."

Ipokash provided a halting translation. The samurai woman considered for a moment, then answered. "She says they are not going far. They just want to leave the city, then land in a valley nearby."

"If I refuse to help?" Mendeleev asked the question even though he thought he knew the answer.

Ipokash translated the snarling reply. "There are ten people aboard. Some can be made to help."

The scientist considered his options. He could fight to keep the airship from these raiders, but suspected he would die quickly, even if other Russians joined him. However, if he stayed alive, he might learn more about these samurai and take more effective action later. "I need two Russian airmen here," said Mendeleev. "I can train people later, but I need people who can already fly the ship if you want to make a clean getaway."

Ipokash relayed the request. The samurai leader replied. "Name two who are not…" Ipokash's brow creased. Mendeleev guessed she must have been given a difficult word to translate. "Leaders," she said at last.

Mendeleev sighed. "Officers," he suggested. Officers would possess the most general knowledge, but would also be the most likely to resist. He named a mechanic and the helmsman. Although the helmsman was, in fact, a junior officer, he hoped the samurai would agree. Perhaps "leaders" meant "senior officers." "Should we go get them?"

"Iie!" called the woman. Mendeleev had no doubt she disagreed with the proposition. She sent the man behind Mendeleev back up the ladder.

"Just who is our captor?" asked the scientist.

"She is Imagawa Masako," explained Ipokash. "She has been fighting the Imperialists since they evicted her from the estate where she lived."

"I didn't know women could be samurai."

"It is not without precedent," said Ipokash.

Imagawa spoke sharply and Ipokash gave another small bow and remained silent. Mendeleev gathered he and the native woman must have spoken out of turn. He closed his eyes. He did not pray, but he feared not escaping this situation alive. He reached out to the one invisible being he knew could help. *"Legion, are you still there? Can you still hear me?"*

Components of Legion still occupied Mendeleev's brain, but remained silent. They relayed information about the activities aboard the airship to the rest of the swarm, which found this a fascinating development and turned its full attention to Mendeleev. The swarm analyzed the data from the time Mendeleev first realized the ship had been occupied.

Mendeleev guessed the samurai aboard the airship were mercenaries, but Legion doubted the assessment. In the United States, a scientist called Professor Maravilla had developed a rapport with a former samurai named Masuda Hoshi. Based on the information Legion had, it seemed unlikely the Meiji government would hire samurai as mercenaries. Instead, this seemed like a desperate force's independent action, but Legion was at a loss to know what this small group hoped to accomplish.

Legion almost suggested questions to Mendeleev, but decided to remain silent for the moment and watch. As Ramon Morales suggested, humans must solve their own problems.

Samurai brought the two airmen Mendeleev requested to the command deck. The scientist briefed them. "I think our best chance is to cooperate with these pirates." He whispered in case the Japanese knew Russian better than they indicated. "We might learn their plans and determine if there is a larger plot against Russia."

Legion considered the word pirates. It was accurate since the samurai hijacked a ship. As he considered their motives, Legion calculated a high probability of on-going piracy. If these samurai were exiles like Masuda Hoshi, capturing the ship might allow them to conduct raids on other vessels or villages. Legion found the possibility fascinating and wondered how the introduction of samurai pirates would affect negotiations between Russia and the United States.

Legion calculated ways to use an airship for piracy. He devised schemes such as using knock-out gas, netting, and non-lethal weapons to disable an ocean-going vessel from above without harming its cargo. As Legion calculated these possibilities, he wondered if the samurai would have the materials necessary to modify the ship for this operation. He considered entering the leader's brain to better understand and perhaps help out, but stopped himself. This was no game and humans were not mere toys.

"How many hostiles do we face?" asked the helmsman, named Zolnerowich. His voice seemed familiar. A quick genetic scan revealed Zolnerowich had a high-ranking brother who Legion once interfaced with. "Maybe we could retake the airship."

"I've counted over twenty hostiles," said Krupin, the mechanic. "Over twice as many as us."

"If the army here in Poronaysk gets involved, they may start shooting," said Mendeleev. "They could destroy us, the hydrogen works, and half the town."

"More work, less chatter," interjected the samurai leader from across the gondola. Legion had already built up extensive language banks from observations made around the Earth and understood her before the Ainu woman translated.

The Russians exchanged glances, realizing they'd attracted more attention than they desired.

Zolnerowich took the helm and adjusted the ballast, leveling the ship. Krupin checked the hydrogen pressure. He requested permission to go to the keel and disconnect the gas lines. Mendeleev endeavored to relay the request through Ipokash. Imagawa granted permission and sent Krupin on his errand accompanied by two samurai.

Legion found the Ainu woman fascinating. He registered her tension and the sweat on her brow, despite the cool air. The alien swarm checked data and confirmed that the tattoos on her lips indicated she was of an age to be married. He wondered if she'd left a husband behind.

Legion turned his attention to the airship. The Russians had been preparing to depart for St. Petersburg the next day, so the ship was ready to go. They had plenty of fuel for the engines. The outboard boilers were already stoked and ready to engage. The hydrogen bags were full to capacity as were the ballast tanks.

Zolnerowich cleared his throat. "May I ask what our course will be?"

"South to Lake Tunaycha," came the reply via Ipokash. "It's isolated, level terrain down there. You can train the samurai how to fly the airship."

"Not my ship!" The cry came from the top of the ladder. Mendeleev recognized Captain Yerokhin's voice. The ship's commander aimed a pistol as he climbed down the stairs. He was a fool to consider a weapon discharge this close to the hydrogen. Perhaps he bluffed, hoping to intimidate the samurai.

The captain wore a Navy coat over pajamas. He must have escaped his guard, then made for the bridge. Imagawa and her lieutenant dropped their swords, which lured the captain down the ladder.

Mendeleev tried to indicate a third samurai hidden behind the ladder, but the captain didn't notice. As the captain descended, the hidden man appeared and brought his sword down on the captain's wrist. The hand flopped to the deck, the pistol discharged, and the captain screamed in pain and rage as he crumpled to the deck holding the stump.

Dogs below barked in response.

Mendeleev and Zolnerowich both rushed forward, but Imagawa and her lieutenant intervened. She held her hands out, indicating silence while the animals settled. Meanwhile, Imagawa's lieutenant turned, ripped open the captain's coat and tore a piece of lining free to use as a bandage.

Mendeleev retrieved a handkerchief from his pocket and held it to his mouth, horrified. Zolnerowich calculated whether or not he could use the distraction to attack Imagawa but he failed to devise a workable plan. Imagawa removed her helmet and evaluated the situation.

Legion considered what Ipokash had said about going south while the samurai warriors tended the captain's wounds and carried him up the ladder. Imagawa's plans seemed consistent with the samurai taking the ship for piracy. He tried to imagine other purposes and searched the records of captured enemy vessels. Aside from piracy, two other prominent results appeared—holding the vessel or its crew for ransom, or making mischief.

The Russians would pay a hefty ransom to get their airship or Dmitri Mendeleev back. If true, why would the samurai need to operate the craft themselves? Legion realized the likelihood of a successful ransom attempt would mean taking the airship further than Sakhalin Island, but the Russians already indicated a willingness to fly the ship as far as they could. Ransom didn't compute.

Mischief seemed a higher probability, but what mischief? Again, Legion wanted to suggest questions to Mendeleev, but restrained himself.

Krupin returned to the gondola and stopped short when he saw the disembodied hand laying in a pool of blood. His breath came in ragged bursts as he announced all lines except the mooring tether had been released.

Mendeleev grabbed the man's shoulder to steady him. "Will we be all right without a ground crew?"

Krupin's eyes refused to leave the hand. He broke out in a sweat. The man's pulse increased. "Wind is from the southeast," he said at last. "We should be all right."

Legion suspected Mendeleev could hear the quaver in the man's voice.

Through Ipokash, Mendeleev related what needed to be done. Although an imprecise translation, she conveyed that the scientist would man the engine relays while Zolnerowich steered and Krupin released the mooring line.

"Get underway." Imagawa kicked the severed hand into the shadows.

The men took their stations with samurai keeping careful watch.

Legion continued to calculate reasons for the airship's capture. A mission to discredit the emperor's power and gain popular support seemed a high probability. Usurping the throne directly also ranked high. Either possibility could precipitate further warfare and involve either the United States or Russia.

Krupin signaled the gondola via the speaking tube. "Mooring line released. We are free to maneuver." He sounded steadier now.

Mendeleev opened the valves, then engaged the steam engines. The four propellers spun to life. The sudden noise startled even the stoic Imagawa. The scientist released ballast sending a torrent of water to the ground below. The airship lifted and the winds carried it back, away from the mooring post.

The dogs resumed their barking. This time a cry sounded from below. Guards on the ground pointed upward and called out, looking to officers for direction. By then the airship floated too high to catch. Did they even know someone hijacked it? Zolnerowich took a compass heading and adjusted the vessel's course.

Legion, you have abandoned me. Although Mendeleev remained silent, Legion had no problem hearing his thoughts.

Legion considered and after a moment, decided to speak. *"We have not abandoned you. We have been watching and calculating possibilities."*

"Why didn't you stop the samurai from taking the airship?

Certainly you can see what a disaster this would be for our goal of world unification."

"We could not stop the samurai without taking over their minds and bending them to our will."

"That hasn't stopped you before." Although silent, Legion detected Mendeleev's sharp emotions.

"We were wrong, before."

Waves of surprise and shock buffeted Legion. A deist, Mendeleev believed he could find God through research and reason. As such, Mendeleev saw Legion as a conduit to God. To Legion, that provided sufficient reason to distance himself from humans. He had no desire to be mistaken for the universe's creator and had no more access to the creator than they did.

Legion's own beliefs in such matters were complicated and even contradictory at times. Similarities between life forms and the intricacies of the universe sometimes suggested a grand intelligence to Legion, one even greater than him. Then again, Legion had traveled so far and seen so much he tended to believe any greater intelligence would be like him, something which started mortal and ascended. Legion didn't know if God existed or what God was. All he knew was that he didn't want to be God.

"We will seek help for you." With those words, Legion allowed the components within Mendeleev's brain to fall silent.

Ramon looked out at the dark ocean waters and the stars above from the *Ballena's* bow. His adventures in the last year had accustomed him to travel over land. He wondered if he could get used to ocean travel with its lack of landmarks or even scenery that changed much until the ship came within sight of a new port or coastline.

"I wouldn't have expected to find you out here all alone," said Captain Cisneros.

Ramon turned around and shrugged. "Fatemeh fell asleep. I decided to take a walk. Only so many places you can go on a ship."

"That's true." The captain nodded, then turned to leave.

"I was just curious," said Ramon, "how do you know where we are?"

Cisneros looked over his shoulder, but didn't say anything.

"If it's not a trade secret or something."

The captain laughed and joined Ramon at the ship's rail. "No, it's not a secret." He pointed back at the ship's bridge. "You just have to track the compass heading, speed, and the time. We keep track of our location on charts and confirm it using the positions of the stars."

Ramon absorbed the information, fascinated. "How? I've looked at the stars a lot, but they just move east to west, like the moon and the sun." Ramon also remembered the vision of the universe Legion showed him. Stars were so distant from the Earth and so far apart from each other, he couldn't imagine seeing differences in them as you traveled.

The captain pointed off to the right. High in the sky, the Little Dipper's tail pointed to the North Star. "The further south we are, the closer Polaris gets to the horizon." He pointed overhead, and swept his arm to the south. "In fact, if we go far enough to the south, we would see whole new constellations."

"I hadn't thought of that," said Ramon.

Cisneros smiled. "How far north and south have you traveled?"

"I guess north would be Denver, maybe San Francisco. South…" Ramon shrugged. "Is Hawaii further south than Tucson?"

"By a little ways." Cisneros patted Ramon on the shoulder. "Still, you haven't been through a huge latitude variation." He looked over his shoulder back toward the crew compartments. "At least when you'd be paying attention. I'm not surprised you didn't notice the North Star move closer to the horizon."

"Would you mind if I visited the bridge tomorrow, to see the charts and equipment?"

Cisneros nodded. "Don't let me keep you from your lady, though."

"Well, I think an hour here or there would be fine." Ramon winked. "For that matter, I'm certain she would enjoy the tour as well."

"Knowing Fatemeh, I think you're right." The captain

yawned and excused himself.

Ramon remained at the bow for a time looking up at the stars. As he did, he could almost imagine himself falling into them, much like he did when Legion showed him the vision of his home world. Ramon remembered how the creature from the stars had presented himself as a dust devil, whirling in a vast wasteland.

As he stared at the sky, Ramon could almost imagine Legion's voice in the back of his mind.

"Ramon Morales, something has happened that could have ramifications for the peace being negotiated between the United States and Russia, but we're hesitant to get involved without seeking your council."

Ramon's brow creased. He never remembered Legion seeking advice. It took a moment for him to realize the words were not a memory. Legion actually spoke to him. "I thought you had left." Ramon's heart raced. Legion had promised to leave humans alone, to leave his mind.

"We had ... mostly," said the alien. *"We would not have contacted you if we didn't feel this was important. We would have acted on our own accord if we didn't agree that humans should be left to work out their own problems."*

Fatemeh told Ramon that Legion could affect a person's cells and their very thoughts. Was Legion manipulating him? He couldn't be certain. Even so, the alien sounded contrite. "What's happened?"

"Japanese warriors who call themselves samurai have stolen a Russian airship. We do not know what they intend to do with it."

"Couldn't you enter their minds and find out?"

"We could, but it would be interference."

Ramon snorted. He appreciated the alien's effort at minimizing contact. He considered the samurai. "What about Professor Maravilla? One of his friends is a samurai."

"Maravilla is too dependent on us."

Ramon looked up at the stars. "That may be true, but I want to contact his friend Hoshi. He might be able to give us some advice. Maravilla can be a go-between for us."

"Maravilla is asleep right now. We will contact him when he is next awake."

"Thank you, Legion." Ramon sighed. "Let's hope we can solve this problem." Legion fell silent. Ramon thought about Hawaii and the events leading them onward to Japan. He wondered if this could somehow be a situation Legion engineered. He shook his head, hoping that wasn't true, then walked back to his cabin where he undressed and climbed into bed next to Fatemeh. As he cuddled up against her back, he wondered if Legion watched.

CHAPTER FOUR
COURTROOMS AND JAIL CELLS

Shinriki and Resak traveled overland to the point where the Kamenka River exited the mountains. Scrub brush and rolling countryside made for a slow hike, but two men on foot found the path more direct than following the Poronay River.

The bandits' trail had not been easy to follow when fresh. Shinriki and Resak found numerous false leads, but the path of twenty mounted bandits did not soon vanish in autumn when new growth slowed. Resak pointed out places where people on horseback had sheered low-lying branches and the animals grazed.

The Ainu followed the river along a ridge line until they came to a clearing. There, they found a timber structure. "Did the Russians build this as a hunting lodge?" asked Resak.

Shinriki shook his head. "I don't think so." He pointed to the woods beyond and several fresh stumps. Around the building itself, the ground had been trampled and there were several fire rings, indicating many people had inhabited the area.

Despite that, no one stood guard. No smoke wafted upward from the lodge's roof. Shinriki's heart sank realizing whoever occupied this place abandoned it. They had further to go to find Ipokash.

As they approached, horses neighed. They crept around the cabin and found a makeshift corral which held the village's horses.

"The bandits left our horses behind?" asked Resak incredulous.

"Take heart, we can take them back. That is something." Horses walked up and nickered when the men approached. Shinriki's stomach burned. Although pleased at finding the camp and knowing the samurai had been here, the horses' abandonment angered him. It turned their theft into a waste. A water trough occupied one end of the corral and bundles of hay, no doubt stolen from the Russians, had been broken open. Shinriki guessed the horses had just enough food and water for two or three weeks. Perhaps the samurai intended to return.

Shinriki turned to the lodge and scraped at the dried mud between the logs. He pulled out several pine needles, still green. "This was built recently and quickly."

They passed through the door, covered by a tattered cloth. Inside, they found more evidence of recent habitation. A Poronaysk newspaper sat atop a low table in the room's center. Shinriki did not read well, but he did not need to in order to recognize the woodcut of an airship on the front page.

Resak shrugged. "Why have the bandits abandoned their camp?"

"It's because they found a new place to call home," said Shinriki.

"But where?"

Shinriki pointed at the airship illustration.

Resak snorted. "How can samurai bandits hope to capture an airship?"

"It would take stealth and cunning. They could use help from a Russian speaker." Shinriki ground his teeth and thought of Ipokash. They might guess she spoke Russian from where she lived. When she shouted in Japanese, they recognized her as a suitable translator.

"Is that even possible?" Resak's eyebrows came together as he considered the possibilities.

"A week ago, I would not have believed a ship of the air was possible," said Shinriki. "What concerns me more is where do the bandits plan to take the ship, and is there any chance the Poronaysk City Council will even believe our warning?"

Resak sighed, uncertain how to answer.

Shinriki patted his cousin on the shoulder. He folded up the newspaper and took it with him, then went outside. Searching the area, they found a foot path leading toward Poronaysk, confirming Shinriki's suspicions. He returned to the corral and released the horses.

Masuda Hoshi, a samurai who had left Japan to farm chiles near Las Cruces in the New Mexico Territory, sat next to his friend, Professor M.K. Maravilla, in the Mesilla Federal Courthouse's gallery. Hoshi's farmhand, Billy McCarty, stood trial along with Luther Duncan a reporter for the *Mesilla News.*

"All rise for the Honorable Judge Warren Bristol," called the bailiff.

Everyone stood as a balding man with thick salt-and-pepper whiskers entered from a door behind the bench. "Be seated." The judge's robes swished as he sat, then he shuffled a few papers before lifting one. "William Henry McCarty and Luther Fennimore Duncan, you are each charged with escaping from lawful Federal confinement at the Presidio in San Francisco on or about August 20, 1877. William Henry McCarty is further charged with aiding and abetting enemies of the United States of America on or about August 21, 1877. How do you plead?"

The *Mesilla News,* Hoshi, Maravilla, and even Colonel Wilberforce Johnson who commanded Fort Bliss had pooled money to hire the area's most noted attorney, a former Texas state senator named Albert Jennings Fountain, to defend Billy and Luther. He'd settled in Mesilla five years earlier. Even though he owned a rival newspaper called the *Mesilla Independent,* Fountain had a special interest in the case. He stood ramrod straight and his thick, bushy mustache seemed at odds with his well-groomed black hair. "My clients plead not guilty, Your Honor."

Judge Bristol made notes then asked the attorney for the United States to make his opening statement.

The portly and affable Thomas B. Catron commanded the room's attention when he stood. "On August 19, 1877, several witnesses in San Jose, California, heard Mr. McCarty, Mr. Duncan, and two associates discussing plans to bypass the United States Army force in San Francisco and meet with the Russian force in Sausalito. When army representatives went to question these people, they were met with weapons drawn." He paused and cast a disappointed glare at Luther and Billy. "They were taken into custody for questioning. That night, they escaped custody. Mr. McCarty stole a boat and crossed San Francisco Bay to the Russian side."

Catron did not mention Ramon or Fatemeh Morales by name, even though the trip to Sausalito was their idea. Fatemeh believed the creature called Legion controlled the Russians and pressed the invasion, but didn't think the army would believe her if she told them. Hoshi didn't blame her. He wasn't entirely sure if he believed in this Legion.

Billy and Ramon found the Russians in Sausalito as expected. Soon after, Ramon and the Russian colonel went into some form of trance. According to Billy, that's when Ramon spoke to Legion and convinced him to leave humans alone.

"Soldiers shot Mr. Duncan and remanded him to the Presidio hospital." Luther winced at Catron's words, reminded of the memory. Billy flashed a reassuring smile. The two hoped evidence from their trial would exonerate Ramon and Fatemeh. Even if Billy and Luther went to jail, perhaps Captain Cisneros could help the newlyweds find a good home outside the country.

Catron continued in his Southern drawl—surprising in a Republican appointee. "Army records make it clear that Luther Duncan and William McCarty escaped lawful imprisonment. Testimony at the time makes it equally clear they intended to cross into Russian held territory. Witnesses saw Mr. McCarty unlawfully obtain a boat from the Army's pier at the Presidio and row it toward enemy lines."

At the desk next to Catron sat the first woman appointed as a United States Marshal, Larissa Seaton. She frowned and made notes as the attorney spoke. She was Billy and Luther's friend, but she had brought them in to face charges.

"There can be no doubt their whole expedition's purpose was to betray the citizens of the United States." Catron looked from the jury to the judge. "Thank you, Your Honor." With that, the portly man squeezed into his chair.

Albert Fountain stood to make his opening statement. "Your Honor, Gentlemen of the Jury, my clients had one important reason for crossing San Francisco Bay: to observe Russian forces. My client, Mr. Luther Duncan, was exercising his

duty as a reporter to present information to this country's people about the invaders' actions. The arrest of Mr. Duncan and
his colleagues is a clear violation of his first amendment rights."

Fountain might own a newspaper that competed with
Duncan's, but he believed in the fellow newspaperman's cause.
Besides, the trial would increase both papers' sales and Foun-
tain had no argument with that.

As the defense attorney continued, Maravilla gasped,
drawing several people's attention including Hoshi's. The professor flashed a nervous smile and waved off their concern.
All except Hoshi returned their attention to Fountain's opening
statement. Maravilla covered his face with his hands. When the
professor looked up, a single tear streaked down his face. He
excused himself and left the courtroom.

Hoshi didn't think the attorney's statements would account for such a reaction and he worried his friend had fallen
ill. Even so, he waited until Fountain finished his presentation
and the judge called for a recess.

Hoshi stepped into the courthouse atrium, but Maravilla
had vanished. The samurai continued outside where summer
warmth lingered into early autumn. The professor sat on steps
leading up to the town square's bandstand, whispering to himself.

Hoshi stood in front of Maravilla for almost a full minute
before the professor looked up. "It's Legion," he said. "The being from the stars. He's returned."

Hoshi frowned. Maravilla hadn't mentioned Legion for
nearly a week.

"Legion wonders if you know a samurai named Imagawa
Masako," said the professor.

Hoshi's mouth dropped open and he reached out to the
bandstand to support himself. "I saw Imagawa Masako fall in
battle with the emperor's troops. She was formidable. Her death
convinced me the battle against the Meiji Emperor's army was
futile and my choices were leave Japan or die."

"Apparently Imagawa is still alive." Maravilla spoke in
hushed tones, uncertain how this news would affect his friend.
"She hijacked a Russian airship on Sakhalin Island."

"Sakhalin?" Hoshi's brow creased. "I presume you mean

Karafuto Island, north of Hokkaido."

"I'm not familiar with the geography, but Legion confirms the island is indeed north of Hokkaido and east of the Russian mainland." Maravilla stood and faced his friend. "Legion admits he should not have meddled in human affairs, but he's concerned this could complicate matters. Do you have any idea what Miss Imagawa would want with an airship?"

"What she wants is the Meiji Emperor's downfall and the shogun restored. She lost money, power, and a manor house. Most samurai willing to surrender can make new lives, but in this new order, as a woman, Imagawa has nothing."

"What will she do with the airship?" pressed Maravilla. "Legion wonders if she's turned to piracy."

Hoshi shook his head. "Imagawa would not stoop to life as a simple thief. She understands taking an airship is an act of war. She has something bigger in mind."

"Would she attack Tokyo?"

Hoshi closed his eyes. "I don't know. The Imagawa I knew wouldn't take life without a good reason. She would attack only when it suited her objective, taking as few lives as she needed."

A woman's voice interrupted. "I wondered where you two got off to."

Maravilla and Hoshi looked up to see Larissa Seaton staring at them. She wore a green cap and jacket, and stood with her fist on her hip. "The trial is about to resume. I thought Mr. Fountain made a good case for Billy and Luther."

"We'll be in soon. We just have some business to attend to," said Maravilla.

"At the bandstand?" asked Larissa.

"It allows me to observe the weather," said Hoshi. "I may have to leave early to attend to the harvest."

Larissa glanced toward the courthouse. "You don't think the trial will be finished in time for Billy to help?"

"Chile peppers do not care for the affairs of men. They will be ready when they're ready."

Larissa shrugged, then waved and returned to the trial.

The villagers cheered when Shinriki and Resak returned with the horses. Despite the warm welcome, Shinriki's heart sank when he looked across the river. The airship was already gone. Could the soldiers at Poronaysk even track the stolen vessel? He hoped the theft would cause the mayor to pay more attention to his request. What's more, they found Russian army brands on several horses in the samurai corral.

Although bone weary, Shinriki dressed in his finest robes and combed out his beard, knowing such simple things could impress the Russians and sway their opinion. He rowed across the river and went straight to city hall.

He walked to the mayor's office and encountered the same secretary he had before. "May I speak to the mayor?"

"I'm afraid he's in a meeting with the city council," said the secretary.

Assuming the council met to discuss the ship's theft, Shinriki grunted. "I have evidence the mayor needs to see."

The secretary narrowed his gaze, as he decided whether or not an Ainu could be allowed into such a meeting and uncertain what 'evidence' he may have to present. After a moment, the secretary shrugged. "This way."

He led Shinriki down the hall to a pair of double doors. "There will be an opportunity at the end of the meeting for public comment. Please do not speak until the mayor calls for such comment and only when he calls on you."

"I understand." The simplistic explanation irritated Shinriki, but he tolerated it because otherwise he might be escorted out before he spoke.

Shinriki entered the chamber. Inside, eight men sat at a long table with the mayor at one end. Businessmen in fine suits occupied two of the chairs lining the walls. Shinriki took an empty seat and listened to the self-congratulatory banter. Pleased by Mendeleev's visit, the men expected good things to happen in their city. They seemed unaware of the airship's theft. Instead, they listed items they needed to request from the government, then asked for comments from the businessmen in attendance.

Shinriki cleared his throat but the men ignored him.

One businessman stood up. "If we are to operate as a

hydrogen station for airships, we need to clarify our status. Are we a private facility or a military facility? If we're a private facility, we should expect payment each time an airship docks or anytime we ship hydrogen elsewhere. If we're a military facility, I would expect the military to take over operation and pay me for building the facility."

"We will forward your concern to St. Petersburg, Mr. Abramovich," said the mayor.

Shinriki held up his hand. The mayor ignored him again and spoke to the other businessman in attendance. Once their business concluded, the mayor turned his attention to Shinriki. "May we help you?"

"I came to you when rogue bandits from Japan attacked my village." He retrieved the newspaper clipping from within the robe's folds. "These bandits… I believe they stole your airship." He slapped the article on the table.

The men looked at him and blinked. After a moment, they all laughed.

"The airship's sudden departure surprised us," declared a man in uniform, "but there's no evidence of theft."

Shinriki's hands clenched and unclenched. "The czar protects the Ainu, does he not? My wife is missing and the bandits are still free. They have your airship. We found their hideout along with our horses and some of yours."

The man in uniform turned serious. "I will send someone across the river to investigate."

The mayor shook his head. "You don't believe this report, do you, Major Lopatin?"

"Horse thievery is serious business." The major clicked his heels together, then bowed at the waist. He whirled and left the office, ignoring the newspaper clipping on the table. The other men followed the major. Shinriki wanted to run after them, but knew it would do no good. He grabbed the clipping and stormed out of the building.

Fatemeh rolled over in bed and reached out for Ramon, but found a cold spot where he should have been. She sat up and blinked at the daylight streaming in through the cabin windows. A coffee carafe stood on a stand near the bed. She reached over and poured herself a cup. Although cold, it helped her wake up enough to rise and dress.

Walking through the ship's corridor, several crewman's eyes followed her. Worrisome as Ramon's absence was, it reminded her what she loved about the former lawman. He loved her for who she was, not as someone who would keep house for him. They were partners in their adventures through life.

When she had turned thirteen, her parents had arranged a marriage with a merchant from Shiraz. She had been certain the merchant would want the betrothal annulled when she converted to the Bahá'í Faith. Instead, the merchant said it wouldn't matter. He said Fatemeh would learn the error of her ways once they had been married for a time and would renounce her new beliefs.

Soon after, her best friend wrote a poem about Fatemeh and how no woman should be subject to a man's will. A mob strangled her friend, then pushed her down an abandoned well and heaped stones upon her. Fatemeh stopped, closed her eyes, and steadied her breath. She'd run away from Persia, believing herself responsible for her friend's death.

For the first time in the last year, she wondered about Hamid, the merchant her parents betrothed her to. She wondered if he had married another in her place. She assumed Hamid would be indifferent to her departure, only his pride hurt.

Fatemeh shook her head and continued on to the deck where Ramon paced along the ship's railing. "You're up early," she said.

Ramon looked up, his face haggard and drawn. "Legion is back. He tells me samurai warriors have stolen a Russian airship."

"I thought Legion planned to let humans attend to their own affairs."

"He did, but he feared this could endanger the peace Russia and the United States are negotiating."

Fatemeh could see that. To her, the Russian invasion had been the symptom of an illness. The illness itself proved to be Legion's interference in human affairs. Once Ramon had

convinced Legion to stop interfering, she paid little attention
to the treaty negotiations. To her, the negotiations themselves
demonstrated a healthy relationship. Last she knew, the Russians had left California and Oregon. Although disputed territory, there seemed a good chance Russia would cede Washington back to America, if it could keep oil-rich Alaska.

"Has Legion communicated with you?"

Fatemeh blinked back surprise. "I only spoke to Legion
when he occupied General Gorloff's mind. As far as I know,
he's never been in my mind at all. Why would you ask that?"

Ramon looked off toward the ocean. "This voyage to Japan, which is so near Sakhalin Island, seems a coincidence. I
feel like we're being manipulated somehow."

"I haven't been steered at all," said Fatemeh. "I just thought
Japan seemed more interesting than sitting around for three
weeks on a British plantation in Hawaii."

Ramon smiled at that.

"Maybe we should speak to Captain Cisneros," suggested
Fatemeh. "After all, he's had more experience with Legion than
we have."

"He did offer to show me around the bridge today." Ramon reached out and took Fatemeh's hand. "The question is,
how much do you trust him? He was a pirate after all."

"He came to our aid when we needed it most." She sighed,
wishing there had always been someone to come to the rescue.
She remembered the angry look on her father's face when her
friend had died. He'd said she deserved her fate. At one time,
Fatemeh loved her father more than any other man, but he'd
betrayed that trust. Even now, thousands of miles away, that
betrayal hurt.

Ramon and Fatemeh found the officers hard at work on
the ship's bridge, but no sign of the captain. The first mate, Mr.
Gonzalez, lowered his binoculars. "May I help you?"

"Captain Cisneros offered a tour of the bridge today."

"The captain's down in the lab. Shall I lead the way?" Gonzalez handed the binoculars to a junior officer.

"Please." Ramon and Fatemeh spoke as one. Gonzalez led
them back out on deck and through a hatch. They walked along
an inner corridor until they came to a cabin in the ship's bow.

When Gonzalez opened the door, a fearsome stench assaulted them. Captain Cisneros wore goggles and poured contents from one flask into another. The liquid within turned a bright green. He set the flasks down and lifted the goggles.

"Pleased to see you!"

"We came to take the tour," said Ramon. "It seems there's more to this ship than we imagined."

Cisneros laughed and Gonzalez took his leave. "This is where I can make the chemical reaction fuel rods for the *Ballena* and *Calamar*. I have a limited supply of raw materials aboard, but this lab extends both vessels' ranges." He took a moment to secure the glasswork then turned again. "Are you ready for the tour?"

"We haven't had breakfast yet," said Fatemeh. "We hoped you could join us."

"Most kind." The captain smiled, but shook his head. "I'm afraid I've got too much to do this morning."

"Legion contacted me last night." Ramon whispered the words in case others nearby could hear. "He says samurai have stolen an airship."

The captain's smile vanished. "This place does rather smell. I think I could use some refreshment after all." He walked over to a speaking tube and blew into it. He asked the steward to set out breakfast, then led the way to the crew cabins at the ship's stern. "I thought Legion vanished for good. I never hoped to hear from him again."

"Is that true?" asked Fatemeh. "Why are we going to Japan? Did Legion tell you to?"

"Not at all." Cisneros frowned. "As I explained, Sir Elias has clients who want to consult with me on some designs. I can say nothing more without betraying confidences."

They reached the captain's cabin, where they found the table set and fresh coffee waiting. The captain offered them each a cup.

Both Ramon and Fatemeh accepted. Ramon took a sip. "As I understand, Legion can adjust the chemicals in people's brains to help them work better, solve problems, even move faster and with more precision. Could Legion influence a person without them knowing?"

Cisneros paused, his own cup halfway to his mouth. "I'd never considered that. When Legion... occupied my mind, I heard an incessant chatter as some components spoke to others. It's hard to imagine him being there and not hearing him."

"Legion is a swarm," said Ramon. "What if only one or two components resided in your brain?"

"Would one or two be sufficient to influence a person?" Cisneros sipped his coffee. "I don't know." He lowered the cup. "This news is quite troubling. The emperor outlawed samurai and a few outlaws in an airship could cause big trouble. What is Legion doing?"

"Legion is watching and relaying information to me and to Professor Maravilla," said Ramon.

Cisneros winced as though hurt. "Why Maravilla?"

"Because his friend Masuda Hoshi used to know the samurai who stole the airship. Her name is Imagawa Masako."

Fatemeh leaned forward. "*Her* name. The samurai who stole the airship is a woman?" She lifted her eyebrows. "She used to be a friend of Hoshi's?"

Ramon nodded.

Fatemeh sat back and folded her hands, seeing new dimensions to the current dilemma. Had Imagawa hurt and betrayed Hoshi? If so, it could be a factor in the coming days.

Shinriki awoke to a boot nudging him in the shoulder. He opened sleep-crusted eyes to see a Russian soldier hovering over him in the morning light. The soldier reached down, grabbed Shinriki and hefted him upright. "Come with us," he growled.

"What for?" croaked Shinriki.

"I don't need to answer questions from horse thieves." The guard shoved Shinriki through the door.

The villagers stood outside their huts, watching the soldiers and looking from one to the other. Soldiers collected the horses with army brands and led them toward a barge. "I found the horses in the mountains yesterday," explained Shinriki. "I already told your commander."

"All my commander told me was to investigate a horse theft. It seems I found evidence of one. We'll let the magistrate sort this out."

The soldier shoved Shinriki along behind the horses. He wanted to argue about the clear misunderstanding, but the looks on the soldiers' faces convinced him otherwise. He hoped the magistrate would prove more rational. Resak peeked around his hut's cloth doorway. Shinriki shook his head. Resak ducked back inside, not attracting the soldiers' notice.

The Russians took Shinriki across the river to Poronaysk and led him through the streets. He was grateful he had fallen asleep in his clothes and boots. Still, he wanted to bathe his face and clean the dirt from his hair.

The small procession passed in front of the city hall, then went down a side street. The soldier shoved Shinriki into a small building, then ordered him downstairs. In the basement, a guard took him to a cell and closed the door. The only light came from a small, open, but barred window high in the wall. A wooden bench served as the only place to either sit or lay down, unless one wanted to lay on the stone floor. A chamber pot held vigil in the corner. The room stank of urine and mildew.

"When will I see the magistrate?" asked Shinriki.

"When he feels like it," said the guard. A moment later, the upstairs door clanged shut.

Shinriki dropped onto the wooden bench, which bowed and squeaked, threatening to give way beneath him. He sighed as his stomach rumbled. The Russians could have waited to arrest him until he'd eaten breakfast.

Shinriki tried to comprehend the morning's events. When he spoke at the meeting the day before, the Russians must have become suspicious of his claims. They sent someone across the river and they found their own horses corralled with the Ainu horses. That much was clear. It puzzled Shinriki they would assume he had stolen the Russian horses in the first place. Wasn't he the one who warned the Russians bandits lurked in the mountains? Hadn't they searched for those bandits?

Shinriki ran fingers through his long hair, then sat back against the cold, stone wall. He had lived his entire life on

Sakhalin Island, but his parents were born in Hokkaido. They told stories of the samurai who took what they wanted. If an Ainu man resisted, the samurai beheaded the offender. At least Shinriki still had his head, but he had lost so much. The samurai captured Ipokash and killed many of his friends.

The day wore on. The sunlight's angle shifted through the little window and grew more diffuse as clouds thickened. Around noon, the door at the end of the hall opened and Shinriki thought it might be time to go see the magistrate. Instead, the guard brought a bowl of fish gruel, a chunk of stale bread, and a cup of water.

By that point, the meager and unpalatable meal looked delicious and he gulped it down, even sopping up the leftover gruel with the dry bread. The guard did not linger to collect the dishes leaving Shinriki to wonder how much longer he would have to wait.

The sunlight faded and gave way to night. Shinriki shivered and wished for a blanket. He did his best to make himself comfortable on the wooden bench and fell into a restless slumber. He awoke in the middle of the night when he rolled off the bench and hit the floor with a thud. He might have lingered there except the dust made him sneeze and shadowy figures crept along the walls—mice or rats, he couldn't quite tell and it made little difference.

The next day, the guard brought him a bland, millet porridge. "How long am I to remain here?" he asked. The guard shrugged as he gathered up the previous day's dishes and left Shinriki alone with his poor meal.

At last, around mid-morning, the guard arrived and opened the cell door. "This way."

By this time, Shinriki's beard and hair were a wild, tangled mess. His clothes smelled of stone dust, mildew and urine. Despite the relative chill, he suspected that remaining in the same clothes for two days added to the olfactory bouquet.

The guard led him to city hall, and seated him before a desk. "Wait here." The guard stepped to the back of the room and loitered by the door.

A short time later, a blond army officer with little round spectacles, a black frock coat and hat entered. He removed the hat then sat at the desk and peered at Shinriki over steepled fingers. He smelled of boiled cabbage.

"Would you care to explain why we found army horses in your village's corral yesterday morning?"

Shinriki took a deep breath and let it out slowly. "I found them in the mountains, near an abandoned hunting lodge along with our horses. I warned you people, there are samurai bandits in the mountains. They raided our village and stole our horses. They must have stolen yours as well."

The man opened a folder and reviewed a paper. "Yes, I see you've made quite a pain of yourself with the mayor." The investigator set the paper down. "If there are samurai bandits in the mountains. Where are they now?"

Shinriki retrieved the newspaper clipping from his robes and passed it over before thinking better of it. "They stole your airship."

The investigator took the paper and frowned. He read then shook his head. "The airship left a little earlier than scheduled, that's all. Like seagoing ships, they are concerned with prevailing winds and weather conditions. It's clear they decided not to wait. There's nothing sinister about their departure." The investigator added the newspaper clipping to the file folder.

"Bandits stole your airship and left the horses behind." Shinriki hated to sound desperate, but he plunged on anyway, struggling to find the right words to say 'I planned to return the army horses,' in Russian. The phrase came out, "I wanted to return the horses."

The investigator stood. "I think you invented the bandit story as a way to steal Russian horses. This is a serious offense. I will review the facts and summon you again. Hopefully by then, you will be in a mood to give more sensible answers." The investigator grabbed his hat and left Shinriki in stunned silence.

The guard collected Shinriki and led him back to the dank cell. As the door clanged shut, Shinriki placed his face in his hands, ashamed he could not do more for Ipokash or his village.

CHAPTER FIVE
ELEMENT OF THE RISING SUN

Onofre Cisneros watched from the bridge as the *Ballena* steamed into Tokyo Bay. The harbor reminded him of many ports he'd visited. Weathered, wooden buildings, with somewhat steeper roofs than those in Mexico or California, stood above the docks. Unfamiliar, Japanese script adorned the signs. As they lowered the gangplank, a dockworker came aboard and demanded to know the ship's business. Balderas, the boatswain, handed over a letter. The dockworker opened it with some suspicion, but nodded when he read the letter from Sir Elias and saw the currency enclosed. Balderas then handed him a second letter to be delivered to the Imperial Engineer. The dockworker hurried back down the gangplank and shouted instructions to his coworkers.

Cisneros left the bridge and went to the deck, summoning Balderas. "Everything go as expected?"

"Yes, sir, he seemed quite pleased to deliver your message."

"I'll be in my quarters." Cisneros looked up to the twilight-darkened sky. Ashore, people lit lanterns and even a few gaslights. "I don't think we'll hear a response before the morning, but I wish to be notified in any event."

"Yes, sir." Balderas resumed his duties.

Cisneros stopped by Ramon and Fatemeh's cabin. "We've arrived at Tokyo," he said. "I don't know what to expect, but I will secure lodgings for you ashore, if possible."

"Thanks, Captain," said Fatemeh. "Do you think we could go ashore before then?"

"I'd wait until morning." The captain crossed to the porthole and peered out. "I've never been to a city where the docks aren't at least somewhat dangerous, especially at night." He turned around. "If you do go out tomorrow, be sure to let the boatswain know where you've gone, in case we need to track you down."

"We'll be sure to take care." Fatemeh gave a reassuring smile.

"Has my steward checked on you? Have you had supper?"

"Delicioso," said Ramon. "As always. Gracias!"

"De nada." The captain tipped his hat and left the two alone to enjoy their evening together.

Cisneros returned to his cabin in the vessel's stern, pulled off his boots, and dropped into a large chair by the window. He opened a book and began to read while awaiting supper. Soon his head nodded and the book dropped into his lap. He awoke when someone knocked on the cabin door. Sun streamed in through the window and the crick in his neck caused him to regret falling asleep in the chair.

"Come in," he called.

The steward appeared with coffee and a plate piled high with eggs, ham, and tortillas. "There's a man at the dock. Transportation awaits to take you to the Naval Lord and Imperial Engineer." He collected the meal untouched from the night before.

"Both at once?" Cisneros lifted his eyebrows.

"I gather they're one and the same man."

"I'll be ready soon." The captain stepped over to a basin and splashed water on his face. He paused at the dining table long enough to gulp down a little of his breakfast. After downing a cup of coffee, he pulled on his boots, jacket, and hat, then strode out to meet the visitor.

A Japanese man with a tailcoat, matching vest, and bow tie met him on deck. He bowed. Cisneros returned the courtesy.

"I am Kyozo. Please follow me."

He led Cisneros down the gangplank to the dock where a rickshaw waited. A lean man with a tattered shirt and a wide straw hat stood ready to pull the conveyance. Both Cisneros and the man in the tailcoat climbed aboard. For a moment, the captain wondered if the lean man could pull the cart with both men's weight, but he soon recognized the rickshaw utilized an ingenious application of a lever and fulcrum. The rickshaw driver ran along the pier and up into well-maintained dirt streets.

Although early in the morning, people already bustled about, starting their chores. Most wore belted robes, similar to the rickshaw driver. Men wore leggings over the robe and women wore something which resembled a wide, padded belt around their mid-section. Some carried baskets while others carried nothing at all. Cloth banners decorated with Japanese script or circles and flowers flapped in doorways. Every now and then, the scents of cooking fish or pork wafted out to the street, making the captain wish he'd lingered over breakfast longer.

As they moved further into the city, the wooden buildings near the dockside gave way to stone structures, more like the captain would expect in a western metropolis, similar to structures in Mexico, except for the sloped roofs.

Half an hour later, they reached a gated courtyard. At the far end stood a two-story building with three entryways and arched windows above. To the side were two square towers, and behind them, the building's wings extended further, which made Cisneros think of a European manner house. "The Tokyo Prefectural Office," explained Kyozo. He gestured to a man near the front steps who ran inside.

Kyozo and Cisneros strolled from the gate to the prefectural building. Passing through the doors, they entered a tiled foyer. A door to the side opened and a man in a top hat and tails stepped through. He removed his hat and bowed.

"I am Katsu Kaishū, First Naval Lord and Engineer to the Meiji Emperor."

"Pleased to meet you." Cisneros shook hands with the Naval Lord.

Lord Katsu led Cisneros down the hall and out a back door. They continued past several buildings and across a bridge. The Imperial Palace stood to the captain's right. He admired the grand buildings and the surrounding gardens, but soon realized the palace was not their destination. To the left stretched another large but plain building. Windows near the roof admitted light and enormous doors on one end hinted at what must be stored within.

Katsu and Cisneros entered. Two white and brown airships floated just off the floor. These vessels were much smaller than the Russian craft. As shown in Pennington-Smythe's drawings, a wooden exoskeleton held a large gasbag in place. Disproportionately large, white tail fins emblazoned with a red circle ringed the gasbags' sterns. Cisneros realized the emblem matched the Japanese flag.

An exposed catwalk extended behind the gondola underneath the bag, giving access to the engine system. A steam engine at the stern drove propellers hanging from the sides via an elaborate rod and gear system. Workers climbed along the exoskeletons, inspecting rigging and the gasbags.

Katsu approached the nearest airship. A stepladder led up into the control cabin. "The Russian airships are designed to carry invasion forces," explained Katsu.

"Yours are designed for defense." Cisneros relayed the impressions he already formed from the plans Pennington-Smythe showed him. "They're attack ships in case Russians invade."

"Exactly." Katsu nodded, impressed. "However, in the long run, we see advantages to airships as a means for cargo and passenger transport. These ships are good, but we believe they can be made better. We'd like ideas about how to extend the cargo capacity and create engines which can move a larger ship with less fuel."

"I believe I can help you with that." Cisneros paused and rubbed his chin. "Beautiful ships. If only the lifting gas wasn't explosive..."

"Ah, but we solved that problem," said Katsu. "The French astronomer Jules Janssen discovered a substance he called helium. We call it the gas of the rising sun. It's much more stable than hydrogen, so we do not fear fires or explosions, the way the Russians do."

Cisneros ran his hand over the lightweight paper wall. "Fire would still be a concern."

"Indeed," said Katsu, "but no more than it would be aboard any wooden ship."

Cisneros took a moment to admire the simple and beautiful controls. Two solid wooden wheels stood near the gondola's bow with a compass in a capstan beside them. One wheel controlled the rudder, the other raised and lowered the elevator fins.

"Allow me to show you the passenger cabins." Lord Katsu slid a bamboo and paper panel aside. They walked straight back along the gondola. Six cabins lined the corridor. Each had a simple mat on the floor and a chest of drawers. An almost stylized watercolor on rice paper adorned each cabin's wall. Although Cisneros had limited experience aboard a Russian airship, this craft seemed much more comfortable. A small galley occupied the space behind the passenger cabins. Storage closets took up space underneath the ladder leading up to the exposed catwalk. The sparse design conserved weight.

Lord Katsu climbed the cargo bay ladder and opened the hatch leading to the service walkway. The large engine at the stern served to counterbalance the gondola. In addition to the transmission system, Cisneros noted pulleys which allowed workers to draw the propeller housings close to the catwalk for maintenance.

"Could you imagine this design revised to use your chemical reaction steam engines? If we enclosed the service walkway and vented oxygen into the control cabin, these could be used at quite high altitude. Such craft would be virtually invisible to people on the ground." Katsu's eyes gleamed with pride.

"With the chemical reaction steam engines, you could also increase your cargo capacity." Cisneros's stomach fluttered with excitement. "Sir Elias Pennington-Smythe said you wanted to try a trans-Pacific run soon."

"We have flown the ships throughout Japan, but have hesitated going further because we do not desire international attention." Katsu put his hands behind his back. "You control a friendly, discrete port for us to test our airships' true range."

"Won't sending one across the Pacific leave you undefended?"

Katsu shook his head. "We're not worried. The Russians are still preoccupied in America."

"Very well, then," said Cisneros. "I'd be happy to make arrangements to receive you when I return home in a couple weeks."

"Why wait so long?" Katsu's eyebrows came together. "We're prepared to conduct the test right away."

"Really?"

"You could accompany the ship and experience it first-hand."

When Cisneros didn't answer right away, Katsu retrieved a pair of goggles from his tailcoat's pocket. He removed the top hat, put the goggles on, and smiled. "To show how much faith I have in the design, I'll accompany the ship as well."

Cisneros laughed aloud. He had to admit, it sounded like a grand adventure. "All right, I'll do it on one condition."

"Name it."

"I have friends who wish to stay in Tokyo."

"I will make arrangements." Lord Katsu bowed, then the two men shook hands.

Lord Katsu had invested in a new hotel, which he viewed as an experiment inspired by his time serving in the first Japanese delegation to the United States. The Naval Lord convinced entrepreneurs to build the small hotel near the new Tokyo railroad line, not far from the seaport. The hotel featured the best Japanese food and the most modern amenities. He'd been pleased to offer Onofre Cisneros's friends, Ramon and Fatemeh, a complimentary room while the captain flew to Mexico.

The accommodations pleased Ramon and Fatemeh. They occupied a two-room suite. One room included a bed, the firm mattress just a few inches from the floor. Rice paper panels obscured the light from windows which overlooked the bustling streets below. A short table stood in the other room's center, surrounded by cushions. The hotel's staff gave them privacy, but also helped at a moment's notice.

On the second morning after arriving in Japan, a knock at the door startled Ramon as he buttoned his waistcoat. A strange machine which rolled on continuous track treads, similar to the *Calamar*, stood in the hallway. Above the treads, jutted a broad, cylindrical body, with a round head on top. Gauges where the eyes would be and a serene grillwork smile lent a pleasant demeanor to the machine. Two cylindrical arms stuck out from the side. The strange automaton ticked and whirred, controlled by internal clockworks.

"Who is it, Ramon?" asked Fatemeh from the bedroom, where she finished dressing.

"Some kind of mechanical man."

A click and a thump sounded within the automaton and it thrust out a metallic claw, grasping an envelope. Ramon took the proffered note, tore it open, and read it as Fatemeh emerged from the bedroom. She clapped in delight. "It's like Professor Maravilla's mechanical wolf, only it's designed to deliver messages."

"It's from Captain Cisneros. He wants us to follow the automaton," said Ramon.

Fatemeh stepped back to the bedroom for a moment and retrieved her shoes. They followed the automaton down the hall and through a gate into a hydraulic elevator. The elevator carried them up two levels, where the automaton led them out to a balcony just below the hotel's roof.

The Imperial Palace's grounds spread out below them. One building's roof opened like a clam shell and an airship ascended. At first glance, it reminded Ramon of the Russian craft, but on closer inspection, it proved smaller and more elegant. By Ramon's estimate the gondola was large enough to house several people, fuel for the large steam engine astern, and some cargo.

"It's beautiful," said Fatemeh.

Ramon glanced down at the automaton's note. "It's called the *Bashō*."

"Even better."

Ramon looked at her. "How can more airships be a good thing?" He shook his head. "It's just a path to more warfare."

"I have no doubt it could fight." Fatemeh rubbed her chin. "But it's named for a poet and they asked Captain Cisneros to accompany them to Mexico. That tells me they're more interested in commerce than combat. The Japanese have promised to open their borders. This looks like a grand start."

The airship cleared the hanger and continued upward. An engine chugged to life and the vessel puttered overhead, then turned eastward, toward the bay.

"It still worries me." Ramon rubbed the back of his neck.

"Unfortunately, some people will always find it easier to

justify building something for war than for peace." She smiled. "But tell the truth—aren't you just a little jealous of Captain Cisneros and his journey to Mexico by air?"

Ramon shook his head and pulled Fatemeh close. "He should be jealous of me. I have you and we have a new country to explore, corazón."

The wind increased as Dmitri Mendeleev walked below the *Nicholas Alexandrovich*. The airship strained at the tethers holding it to the ground. Nearby, two samurai stood watch.

"I need to speak to Imagawa," said Mendeleev.

The samurai looked at each other, not quite understanding.

"Imagawa," repeated Mendeleev.

At last, one samurai seemed to comprehend and spoke to the other. The second thought for a moment, then responded. The first man climbed the ladder leading into the *Nicholas Alexandrovich's* gondola and disappeared. A few minutes later, he returned followed by Imagawa and Ipokash.

Mendeleev pointed to the clouds, then pointed to the straining ropes. Waves rippled across Lake Tunaycha. "This airship cannot remain exposed to the storm. It could be damaged."

Ipokash made a halting translation and Imagawa laughed. She spoke harsh words which Ipokash translated as, "We have no hanger and you're a fool if you think we'll try to fly in this weather." She blushed as though embarrassed to have called Mendeleev a fool.

"We might do better in the sky." Mendeleev pointed upward. "We could get above the storm into calmer winds."

He waited for Ipokash to translate and Imagawa's answer. "She says those winds don't blow the direction she wants to go. We wait."

"Where the devil do you want to go, then?" Mendeleev put his hands on his hips. "I've been training your people for a week. Aside from the captain who is just hanging on to life, you have a cooperative airship crew. Where do you want to go?"

Imagawa didn't wait for Ipokash to finish translating. She

spoke low and dangerous. Ipokash swallowed. "That is not for prisoners to know. Question her again and she will order you beheaded along with the captain."

Imagawa turned and shouted orders to the two guards, then spun around and returned to the gondola. Ipokash followed and soon the guards shoved Mendeleev forward.

With a sigh, Mendeleev reentered the airship. Imagawa stood near the wheel, arms folded, staring out at the developing storm. The guards escorted him up the ladder and down the corridor to his cabin. He entered and dropped into a chair.

The airship bucked and rocked in the storm. At one point, the floor dropped out below him. He grabbed the table for support and thought the ship's nose would crash into the ground, but the ship leveled off before anything worse happened.

Someone knocked at the door. "Come in," called Mendeleev.

Ipokash entered, carrying a plate with smoked fish and a roll—a safe food choice for a bucking and rolling ship. The bandits had captured plenty of smoked fish during the raid in which they took Ipokash prisoner. "Thank you," said Mendeleev, "though I'm surprised to see you here. Usually one of the guards brings me food."

Ipokash nodded. "I know, but Imagawa makes me serve her as it allows her privacy from men. When in the kitchen, I asked the guard if I could bring you dinner." She set the plate down on the scientist's desk.

Although grateful for nourishment, Mendeleev had little appetite with the ship twisting and turning on its tethers. A moment later, he realized Ipokash remained in the cabin. "Please be seated." He held out his hand.

She nodded and sat in the room's other chair. "I cannot stay long. I'll be missed."

"You want to tell me something?"

She nodded and looked around, as though double checking the cabin door was closed. "You asked what Imagawa intends to do. I know, but she would kill me if she knew I told you."

Mendeleev frowned. He reached out to take Ipokash's hand, but she pulled it away. He wasn't sure whether he offended her or if she didn't trust him. "I promise I won't tell her I know her plans. If I accidentally tell her, I'll say I overheard the guards."

She thought for a moment, then gave a sharp nod, as though satisfied. "Imagawa intends to attack Japan."

Mendeleev's brow furrowed. "Japan!"

She held up her finger and shot him a panicked glance.

"Japan?" he whispered. "I guessed a Russian target so she could show the samurai's power and have the shogunate reinstated."

"That would not restore the shogunate," said Ipokash. "The Meiji Emperor wishes an end to the samurai. Imagawa wants revenge. She will attack a Japanese target with a Russian airship hoping to start a war between the two countries. She hopes to see Mutsuhito's army destroyed and a shogun rise to fill the vacuum."

"Does she see herself as shogun?"

Ipokash considered, then shook her head. "I do not believe she is so bold."

"Russia would destroy Japan." Despite the bucking ship, Mendeleev cut into the smoked fish and took a bite.

"Don't be so certain," said Ipokash. "I have heard Imagawa say the Turks plan to invade Russia. She also says Russia is at war with a country called America."

"Imagawa tells you these things?" Mendeleev looked up.

"I happen to be near when she discusses these things with her staff."

Mendeleev took another bite. "Thank you for the information. I'm not sure what I can do with it, but I shall think on it." He looked up. "Why do you translate for them?"

Ipokash frowned. "The alternative would be to die. I have a husband and friends I would like to see again. This is an evil place."

Mendeleev didn't agree, but he hated that someone had captured his airship and made him do their bidding. "I will do my best to assure you get home." He lifted his chin toward the door. "You should go."

She nodded, stood, and balanced as more turbulence rocked the ship, then she disappeared through the door.

Mendeleev chewed the roll.

"Do not despair," came a voice from the back of the scientist's mind. *"We will relay this information to those who can help."*

"Legion?" asked Mendeleev. Legion didn't answer, making him wonder if he'd imagined the voice.

CHAPTER SIX
THE BRAZEN SHARK

Ramon and Fatemeh skirted the Imperial Palace on their way to the newly opened University of Tokyo. Lord Katsu encouraged them to contact a good friend who taught physics at the university, Pierre LeFebre. Ramon had been impressed with Fatemeh's talents ever since he met her, but his respect increased with the visit to Tokyo. Less than a week in Japan, she already understood many words and could read some signs. The former sheriff thought a human language must be easy for a woman who could speak to owls.

The University of Tokyo campus was rather small—just a few white buildings topped by tile roofs. Fatemeh did her best to read the door signs. She smiled when they came to the third building. "Sciences," she said.

They climbed the stairs and walked down the hall. Ramon's stomach fluttered. If all went according to plan, he would soon study in halls like this. They passed an open door. Inside, a teacher stood before a blackboard speaking to the class. The students wrote on sheets of parchment. Ramon's heart rate increased.

As a sheriff, if Ramon saw or heard something, he remembered it. Although literate, he found writing uncomfortable and wondered if professors would expect him to take notes.

He looked up. Fatemeh stood down the hall with her hands on her hips, watching him. When he noticed, she walked across the hall and went upstairs. The upper level had more doors. Ramon guessed these must be offices rather than classrooms. A short distance down the hall, Fatemeh came to a door with a sign written in characters Ramon recognized. It read, "LeFebre."

Fatemeh knocked and a voice responded. Ramon thought

he heard "Haitte kudasai." He recognized that as "Please enter."

They entered the office and discovered a man with papers stacked on his desk. He stared at a drawing of a blocky, mechanical device on a blackboard. Ramon thought the drawing looked similar to Captain Cisneros's chemical reaction steam engine.

"Êtes-vous professeur LeFebre?" asked Fatemeh. "Je suis Fatemeh Morales et ceci est mon mari Ramon."

It pleased Ramon to understand that she had introduced them. It pleased him even more when the professor answered in English.

"Ah, Mr. and Mrs. Morales. I've been expecting you!" He turned around and ran up to Fatemeh as though she were an old friend, embraced her and kissed one cheek and then the other. Ramon's jealousy lasted only until the professor came over and did the same thing to him, making him uncomfortable.

"Pleased to meet you," said Ramon, although he didn't exactly feel it.

"Are we interrupting you?" asked Fatemeh.

The professor held up his hands. "Not at all. I'm just reading a journal article by Nikolas Otto. He has been working with a colleague's designs, creating a small and efficient, electrical coal-gas-driven engine." He smiled. "I understand you know the Mexican engineer, Cisneros, and have seen his chemical reaction steam engine. Perhaps this interests you, no?"

"Knowing about new engines is interesting," said Ramon, "but I don't think we can help you determine how they work."

The professor toyed with a chalk stick and shrugged.

Fatemeh smiled. "What would you do with this new engine?" Ramon wasn't certain whether the details interested her or she just wanted to put the physicist at ease.

"Captain Cisneros's chemical reaction steam engine is quite small and weighs little. It also works for undersea or high altitude vessels. This is why Lord Katsu is so interested. The problem is that the fuel is difficult to make in quantity. This would be a problem for building numerous small vehicles for personal use."

"Small vehicles for personal use?" Ramon imagined the

sky filled with ornithopters such as the professor's. That future at once charmed and terrified him.

"Imagine Otto-cycle tractors in place of steam tractors or horse-drawn plows. Perhaps Otto-cycle engines could be mounted in carriages so horses wouldn't have to pull them. Imagine how clean cities could be!"

Ramon had stepped in enough horse manure over the years to appreciate the idea. He liked Mesilla, New Mexico because they had an ordinance which prevented horses on the streets. Would such a town allow horseless carriages? He tried to imagine such vehicles rolling through the old town's narrow streets, or through crowded cities such as Tokyo. His days as a sheriff told him new laws would have to be crafted to make such vehicles safe. Despite his earlier forebodings about note-taking, he wanted to delve into the books and explore the issue further.

"You didn't come here to discuss engines." The Frenchman placed the chalk down in the tray. "What have you seen of Tokyo so far?"

"To be honest, not much," said Fatemeh. "We've been to a few shops and cafés near the Imperial Palace. This is our first time venturing further."

"Well, one of my favorite places in Tokyo is quite close. I'll be happy to show you." The professor led the way out to the hall. They went downstairs and out through the back door. Walking past two more buildings, they came to a wooded, wild area. They strolled along a trail until they came to a lake with a bridge spanning the middle. Ramon listened as hard as he could and just discerned a few distant street noises.

"This is beautiful," said Fatemeh. "A little wilderness in the middle of the city."

"It is called Ikutoku-en Shinjiike. The pond is shaped like the kanji for heart and this is a favorite spot for lovers." The professor winked at Ramon. "This pond has been here for over 250 years. Osaka Castle's shogun built it."

"Osaka's a long way away," remarked Ramon.

"Nearly 200 miles," confirmed the professor. "Nevertheless, the shogun controlled Edo, as Tokyo was known in those days."

"What is a shogun?" asked Fatemeh. "I've heard the word, but I don't know what it means."

"Sort of a samurai general," said the professor. "Until recently, shoguns held more power than the emperor himself."

Ramon considered the situation with the airship on Sakhalin Island. "Is this why the emperor wrested control of Japan from the samurai?"

The professor shrugged. "Politics aren't my forte, much as engines aren't yours. Still, it's a rather medieval system and Emperor Mutsuhito wants Japan to be part of the nineteenth century world. That's why he founded the university..."

"At Tokyo's figurative heart." Fatemeh knelt down by the lake.

"Mutsuhito?" asked Ramon. "I thought Meiji was the emperor's name."

"Mutsuhito is the emperor's given name," explained the physicist. "I gather Meiji is the reign's name, so Mutsuhito is the Meiji Emperor."

Ramon scratched his head, realizing a diplomat needed to understand much. "I'd like to walk over to the bridge."

"You two take your time," said the professor. "I should return to my notes. When you're finished here, please come find me in my office and I'll take you to a good place for dinner." He turned and ambled back through the trees.

Ramon reached out and took Fatemeh's hand. They strolled along the lake, enjoying each other's company. They reached the bridge and walked halfway across. Ramon took Fatemeh in his arms and kissed her. As the kiss went on, a voice spoke in the back of Ramon's mind. *"The samurai plan to attack Japan."*

The sudden voice caused him to bite Fatemeh's lip. "Ow," she cried.

"Sorry. I thought I heard something."

They looked around as a bird made a deep "whook" sound. Up in a tree stood a white-faced owl with ear-like feathers on its head. Fascinated, Fatemeh walked toward it, leaving Ramon in the center of the bridge.

"Couldn't this have waited until a better time?" whispered Ramon.

"We thought you'd want to know as soon as we learned Imagawa's

plan," said Legion. *"Her goal is to start a war between Russia and Japan."*

"Did you make the owl appear?"

"We do not have powers of such magnitude. He was in the tree all along. We simply stimulated his auditory sensors so he would distract your mate."

Ramon snorted at the description of Fatemeh. "Let me consider what we should do. I may have a message for Professor Maravilla soon."

Ramon caught up with Fatemeh. "Legion just spoke to me," he said.

"That explains why you were talking to yourself." She turned to face him. "It also explains who woke this owl."

"Be that as it may, I gather the samurai bandits plan to attack Japan itself. Since it's a Russian airship…"

Fatemeh frowned, not needing him to finish the thought.

"The problem is, who do we tell?" Ramon looked toward the Imperial Palace. "If we just show up and tell them we know an attack is about to occur, they'll want to know how we know."

"We need Hoshi's advice," said Fatemeh.

"I'd feel better if Hoshi were here."

"Why couldn't he be?" Fatemeh shrugged. "Captain Cisneros is on his way to America. He could meet Hoshi in Ensenada and bring him back."

"Do you think he would come?"

"We will be glad to relay the question through Professor Maravilla," said Legion.

Hoshi strolled down a row of chile plants, checking the peppers and picking those he deemed ripe. He worked alone, since Billy and Luther's trial had not concluded. Although he supported Billy and wanted to see the outcome, he found the attorneys' give and take tiresome. Moreover, he had no desire to lose his first crop. It was a miracle the chiles had not withered away during a recent mission he did for the United States Army. They employed him to track the outlaw Curly Bill Bresnahan through Northern Mexico and Southern Arizona and recover a lightning gun he stole from Fort Bliss in El Paso.

Fortunately, the mission had paid well. Even if he lost this harvest, he had money for next year's crop. Nevertheless, he relied on this year's crop to establish his reputation as a farmer and to show he could produce a hot and flavorful pepper.

A horse clomped down the road and nickered, attracting Hoshi's attention. A tall, thin man with a bowler hat rode a brown horse. He realized it must be Maravilla. He adjusted the strap holding the basket around his shoulders and walked back down the row to the house.

Hoshi saw Maravilla as a kindred spirit. They were each exiles from their respective countries. In many ways, Maravilla had lost more than Hoshi. He once had a wife, daughter, and property. He'd advised the Mexican military. During the revolution, soldiers had killed Maravilla's wife and daughter, then abandoned him in the desert. A lesser man would have given up and allowed the desert to take him. Maravilla had resumed his research and sought a new home.

Hoshi had left Japan when he realized the samurai rebellion against the imperialists would fail. Many of Hoshi's fellow samurai had fought until death or they committed suicide. Though loyal to his daimyo and the shogun, Hoshi appreciated Mutsuhito's attempts to end Japan's isolation.

Hoshi had rebelled because he did not believe the emperor had an inherent right to rule. True, many shoguns inherited their titles, but there came a time they had to prove themselves through their swordsmanship. In a democracy a leader may not fight to prove themselves, but they did have to prove themselves capable to lead. Hoshi felt he could live with that system while he attempted to find a path in the modern world.

Unfortunately, New Mexico would never be home.

He set his basket on the porch as Maravilla tied the horse's reins around the rail.

"Have they reached a verdict yet?" asked Hoshi.

Maravilla shook his head. "I'm convinced Mr. Fountain will save the day and they will be exonerated."

"If you are certain, they will be hung for sure."

Maravilla barked a laugh. "I'm never certain when you jest my friend, but I can tell you Mr. Catron sweated during the cross-examination today."

"Cross examination, objection, opening arguments, closing arguments. Why can't these Americans simply make their
statements about what happened and let the jury make its decision?"

"The process is supposed to assure fairness." No humor
brightened the professor's face.

Hoshi scowled but accepted his friend's statement. If anyone had experienced an unfair justice system, it was him. "If
you're not here with news of the trial, you must have something else to tell me." Hoshi held out his hand, inviting the
professor inside.

"I have had a message from Legion. Imagawa plans to attack Japan itself."

"Impossible," declared Hoshi. "Imagawa is loyal to Japan.
She would never attack her own country." Hoshi removed his
shoes, then cleared his throat when Maravilla made no move to
take off his riding boots.

"Imagawa was loyal to Shogun Tokugawa, not the emper-
or." Maravilla bent over to remove his boots. "Just as Mexico
underwent revolution, so did Japan. Today's Japan is not the
one you served."

Hoshi sighed. He went to the kitchen and started a fire in
the cast iron stove. "What does Legion—or Ramon Morales, for
that matter—want me to do? Imagawa will drop bombs where
she will."

"Ramon wonders if you will travel to Japan."

Hoshi turned. "Do you have any idea how much time and
money that will require? If I bought passage back to Japan, all
the money I earned tracking Bresnahan would be exhausted.
What's more, Imagawa's damage would be done by the time I
got there."

"Not so, my friend. All you must do is travel to Ensenada.
Captain Cisneros left Japan two days ago aboard an airship. He
will meet you and take you back to Japan."

"A Japanese airship?" Hoshi's eyes widened. The prospect
of seeing such a thing almost tempted him to agree to the adventure without further discussion. The fire crackled and he
breathed life into the flames. He stood and placed a kettle on

the stove, then looked at the window and the fields beyond. "I must attend to the harvest."

"First of all, I think Billy will be free in just a few days. He can handle the harvest."

Hoshi narrowed his gaze. "Somehow, I doubt the first thing Billy McCarty will want to do after release from prison is attend to my chile harvest."

Maravilla held up his hand, then retrieved a paper from his coat pocket. "You may be right. I've been sketching plans for a chile harvester during the trial." He unfolded the paper and set it on the table. It showed a machine with strong, pistoning legs for support and movement. Notes showed two claws to pluck the vegetables from the stems.

"My crop will be destroyed!" declared Hoshi. "I'd rather let Billy at it in a drunken stupor. It looks like a monster! What will it do, eat my crops?"

Maravilla leaned forward. "You have an opportunity to help your homeland and restore lost honor. You want to see this airship created by your countrymen. It's a new era, my friend. Be a part of it."

"I will consider it," said Hoshi. "As long as you promise not to build your infernal machine and destroy my crop."

Maravilla gave a lopsided smile as the tea kettle whistled. "I'll promise not to destroy the harvest."

Imagawa climbed down the ladder into the airship's gondola. The samurai turned and bowed. She returned the courtesy, then waited for the report.

"The weather is calm. The Russian scientist says this is a good day for travel," reported Nanbu Daisuke.

She grunted and nodded, then stepped to the window and peered out at the sky. High, thin clouds parted, revealing blue strips here and there. The ship stood steady at its mooring. How easy it would be just to sail away in this airship and leave her problems behind, but she had a duty to her homeland. If she didn't act, Japan could become another country where men strove to acquire as many possessions as possible without demonstrating need or worthiness.

Although her stomach burned at the prospect, they must attack Sapporo—Hokkaido Prefecture's capital. She turned and strode to the charts at the gondola's stern. She summoned Nanbu with a flick of the finger.

"At this point, do we need to keep any Russian captives aboard?" asked Imagawa.

Nanbu pursed his lips and considered. "I'd like to keep the two steam mechanics. They have skills our people do not have. Also, I think we should keep the Russian scientist aboard."

"Why?" She agreed, but she wanted to hear Nanbu's reason.

"I don't believe he's passed along everything he knows."

Again Imagawa grunted. Under different circumstances, the masculine sound would amuse her. Even in a light-hearted mood, she wouldn't laugh in front of Nanbu. Masuda Hoshi warned her about ambitious men who exploited any weakness they found. To lead men like Nanbu, she must appear serious and strong.

"I agree," she said at last. "Instruct all but the mechanics and Mendeleev to disembark. Prepare for launch as soon as they're off the ship." She dropped a ruler on the chart, and measured fifteen western miles from their location to the nearest settlement. She performed a quick mental calculation. "We're approximately two hundred chō northeast of Korsakov. On a pleasant day like this, they can be persuaded to make the hike."

"If they make the journey, won't they alert the townspeople to our mooring?"

She leaned in close. "I don't want those men to live long enough to see Korsokov, but the men we keep should believe they have made the journey. What's more, men who believe they are being freed will leave more quietly than men taken before a firing squad. Am I understood?"

Nanbu swallowed, a momentary sign of weakness. "I'll make sure our best snipers are readied." He turned around and called to the bridge crew. "Prepare for launch!"

Nanbu's seamanship pleased Imagawa as she turned to the door leading outside. She climbed down to the grassy field, put her arms behind her back, and strode out away from the airship.

Turning around, she gazed at the Cyrillic letters, which spelled out the airship's name: *Nicholas Alexandrovich.* The name did not fit. A brazen owl adorning the airship's keel near the bow better evoked its predatory nature. Its sleek lines reminded her of a sea predator. A name popped into her head: *Atsukamashī same—The Brazen Shark.*

Within fifteen minutes, samurai lowered ladders from the passenger deck and the Russians descended. Half-dressed and sprouting stubble, they cursed in their native language. The Russian captain descended last—his wrist bandaged and his face pale. She wondered if he could actually survive the walk to Korsakov.

The men looked around, some smiling, others perhaps suspecting a trap. Imagawa frowned at her own subterfuge, but an open confrontation would put her men at risk. She couldn't afford that now. If the Russian airmen warned their superiors, her plans could fail. She glared at the men and forced herself to see them as the enemy. If they'd had honor, they should have felt shame at the airship's capture. They should already be dead inside.

She climbed the ladder into the gondola and studied the charts while her men continued their departure preparations. She gathered this brazen shark would only be able to make a few trips to Japan before it would need its hydrogen stores refreshed. That didn't seem an insurmountable problem. She hoped two or three raids would be sufficient to convince her countrymen Russia had declared war. Once the Japanese army attacked, she would no longer need the airship.

She walked to the window and watched as samurai released tethers from the ship's side. Once done, the ground crew had sufficient time to run for the rope ladders and climb aboard. The helmsman released ballast water drawn from the nearby lake and the ship ascended faster. At this point, the mechanics would be engrossed in their engines and Mendeleev would be in his cabin. Imagawa gestured toward Nanbu who barked a one-word command into the speaking tube.

Imagawa strode to the windows and looked to the ground. Her snipers picked off the Russian airmen as the ship rose. Her knuckles turned white as she gripped the railing before her. The men falling to the ground had families and homes, but so did the men behind her. The samurai she led pledged their lives to the people and the land, only to be tossed aside like garbage.

Nanbu ordered the engines engaged. The Russians lay on the ground, their blood soaking into the soil—soil that should belong to Japan. The Russians called the island Sakhalin, but the Japanese knew it as Karafuto.

She left the gondola and strode back through the ship, past the passenger cabins into a large hold situated between four large gas bags. Bombs stood in racks along the walls, ready to drop out through large doors below. According to Mendeleev, the Russians set out to test the ship and dedicate a hydrogen plant. She considered the reasons why the ship would be so well armed for a ceremonial mission. Perhaps the Russians wanted it ready to change missions at a moment's notice. Perhaps Mendeleev lied about the mission to make her worry about the time before discovery. It didn't matter. The armaments suited her purpose.

She continued toward the airship's tail, pleased to have time alone. She had not asked for power or responsibility. She had not asked to command men. Despite that, those traits defined her and she could not give them up because the emperor preferred an army of commoners to loyal samurai. She knew samurai who found powerful positions in the army, navy, and the imperial court, but those positions were reserved for those close to the emperor. Those positions were denied women altogether.

At forty-years-old, Imagawa had no desire to marry, nor did she want to leave her home to become a peasant. Her samurai would be wasted as soldiers, merchants, or common laborers. This left few options.

A sniper appeared from a small chamber and bowed.

"You did well." She bowed, projecting more confidence than she felt. She continued without awaiting a response. Reaching the tail, she frowned. Even if she succeeded in this quest, could she reclaim her home? In her home, she could disappear into her rooms, meditate, read, or practice sword forms without disturbance. She longed for such peace and solitude, but doubted she could reclaim them. In the Japan of her youth, a woman of skill could become samurai. Losing that home was unacceptable.

With a sigh, she returned to the gondola and did her best to enjoy the three hour flight south by southwest. *The Brazen Shark* reached Sapporo with the sun high in a blue sky. She allowed a shark-like grin. The horizontal red, white, and blue bars of the Russian imperial flag on the airship's tail should be clear. She looked out at the small village, nestled between the mountains and the Ishikari River.

"Make three turns around the city. Identify targets. I prefer we attack government buildings and coastal warehouses, places with fewer people, targets the Russians would attack. Let's minimize civilian casualties."

"Yes, ma'am," came the response from around the gondola. Men went to the windows with spyglasses and plotted an attack plan. As they made their sweeps, the men approached and consulted her. Once satisfied, she looked to the bombardier, Kanbei.

"You may fire when ready," she said.

He opened the hatch in the *Brazen Shark's* belly and coordinated with the helmsman and the navigator. When they gave the signal, he let the first bombs fall along Sapporo's waterfront. Imagawa watched the buildings erupt in flame, then wiped away a tear before anyone could see. She loved Japan, but it had taken a disastrous course. Nothing hurt worse than correcting the one she loved so much.

CHAPTER SEVEN
THE NAME OF STORM

General Mikhail Ivanovich Dragomirov stared at a Russian map. The Empire stretched across three continents: Europe, Asia, and North America. At this point, the North American holdings were concentrated in the Alaska and Washington Territories. A few months ago, Dragomirov imagined the Russian Empire stretching all the way to Texas. Now, even Washington was just a bargaining chip—something they could give up so they could keep Alaska.

A decade ago, they sold Alaska to America for a pittance, but that was before the Russians knew about oil under the ground and recognized its value.

The general marveled at the thought of a worldwide Russian Empire. It seemed possible in the days when the voice spoke to him. Under normal circumstances, he'd dismiss hearing voices as madness. However, this voice spoke to every important Russian from the czar to his ministers to the generals. Moreover, the voice spoke to many lesser Russians, including peasants and soldiers. Almost everyone he knew had heard the voice.

"The voice" was a poor name for the presence because it did more than speak. It gave men greater agility and assured every plan or machine devised worked the first time. The presence called itself Legion and the name fit well. Like a legion of elite troops, the presence assured victory no matter where the Russian army went. Legion not only spoke to Russians, but spoke to all it encountered and convinced them the Russians were benevolent.

Unfortunately, shots still had to be fired. Something limited how far and how fast Legion could spread. Dragomirov imagined Legion as a spirit of some sort, who could stretch out and talk to different minds at the same time. The general understood an army could spread itself too thin when it moved. He wondered if that's what happened to Legion. Had it not anticipated how far it would have to go to cover the globe? Somehow that didn't make sense given everything else Legion understood.

After spreading itself thin, whatever Legion was, it vanished. The Americans who accepted Russian influence began to have second thoughts. Some still welcomed the Russians, but most took up arms and drove the Russians from California and Oregon.

Dragomirov sighed as he stared at the map. If he had mounted an invasion, he would have grabbed and held British Columbia so he could maintain a steady supply line to Washington and Oregon. Legion argued the Russian airships made such a strategy unnecessary and would have added Canada and England to the list of Russia's enemies. It seemed like a sound argument at the time.

When Legion vanished, Russia had one functioning airship with another under construction. The functioning airship had been destroyed over San Francisco and the second one had just come into service.

The general's adjutant entered the room and saluted. He handed the general a report which turned Dragomirov's attention from America to Western Asia. There, oblivious to Russia's objectives in America, Turkey and Austria vied to control Bosnia and Herzegovina. Austria fared poorly against the Ottoman Turks and screamed for Russia to honor its treaties and send forces. Russia had sent a few volunteer forces, but this report showed they had just been rebuffed when they attempted to cross the Danube.

There was a real danger Russia would lose significant territory around the Black Sea, where all of its warm water ports were now located. Just a few weeks ago, Russian forces were poised to occupy San Francisco—not just a warm water port, but an outstanding Pacific port as well. Dragomirov pushed the unproductive regret from his mind.

He could use an airship to drop bombs on Turkish troops, but Mendeleev pulled strings and took the only ship available to inspect a gas production facility on Sakhalin Island.

"Where the hell is the *Nicholas Alexandrovich?* Is Mendeleev still out on that God-forsaken island?"

"He's due back in four days, but no one has seen the airship since it departed Vladivostok, bound for the island," reported the adjutant.

"What do you mean no one has seen it? Did it arrive at Poronaysk or not?"

"As far as we know, sir. We have no telegraph lines out to Sakhalin Island. It should be on its way back."

Rage simmered within Dragomirov. Mendeleev convinced the czar that showing off the airship in a cross-country flight would improve the people's morale after the recent defeats in America. The general imagined those spirits falling anew when the people learned Russia had become landlocked. Surely someone had seen the airship. "Telegraph all stations, I want to know where the *Nicholas Alexandrovich* was last sighted and when. Bring me the news as soon as you have it," said the general.

The adjutant saluted, spun on his heel and left.

The general sighed and considered other options. He consulted with tacticians and checked the supply status. He brought over a secretary and drafted a memo to the admiral who commanded the Black Sea fleet to ask for a meeting to devise strategy. It was familiar and necessary work to the general, but he missed Legion all the more when he had to coordinate with others. When Legion spoke in everyone's head, he could move troops and ships with a mere thought. He would know where Mendeleev's airship was just by asking.

Ramon and Fatemeh discovered Lord Katsu's mechanical man did more than deliver messages. The concierge at their hotel could dial instructions commanding the automaton to pull a rickshaw to destinations around the city. After a week in Tokyo, Professor LeFebre suggested they visit the new National Museum in Ueno Park.

The mechanical man rolled through the streets at a speed

which rivaled running horses. Men and women carrying bundles jumped out of its way. Several times, Ramon thought the mechanical man would run into a wagon or a horse-drawn streetcar, but somehow he could evade such obstacles—often at the last possible moment. By the time they arrived at the museum, Ramon's heart pounded and he wiped sweat from his brow. He stepped from the rickshaw and offered a trembling hand to Fatemeh.

She stepped off the rickshaw and smiled at the mechanical driver. "Arigato," she said.

"He can't understand you." Ramon shook his head and laughed. "He has to be programmed with those dials and levers in his chest."

"It never hurts to be polite." Fatemeh shrugged.

"Dōitashimashite," said the mechanical man in a scratchy voice.

Ramon and Fatemeh both turned to look. The mechanical man stared straight ahead unblinking, waiting for Ramon to flip the lever commanding it to start the return trip. They looked at each other and shrugged, then turned around to face the gates to a park containing artfully trimmed trees and bushes. A short distance down the path a fountain sprayed water high into the air. The museum sat further back—a red brick building with a grand entryway surrounded by two domed towers.

The newlyweds walked through the park, lingered for a moment to admire the fountain, then continued inside. All the signs were in Japanese, but Professor LeFebre told them an impressive display of Edo period paintings awaited in the museum's north wing on the bottom floor.

They turned and found a room filled with folding screens and hanging scrolls showing everything from fierce samurai warriors in battle to colorful depictions of trees to a calm, gray tiger licking his paws. The paintings were on paper instead of canvas and many seemed to be made with ink and water colors instead of oil paints, which gave them an ethereal quality. Some paintings included flecks of gold leaf, which shone in the sunlight streaming in through the windows.

Fatemeh sighed and squeezed Ramon's hand as she lingered first before one painting and then another.

They admired a painting which depicted a man in a gray hat and brown robes decorated with flying birds. Fatemeh pointed to Japanese words printed in the corner. "I wonder what it says."

Ramon had to admit he was curious as well. As he looked at the painting, the words shifted and blurred. He removed his glasses and cleaned them, then slipped them back on. When he did, instead of Japanese, he saw English. "Gust of wind carries leaves from the trees, giving the name of storm to the mountain wind."

"That's beautiful," said Fatemeh. "Did you just come up with that?"

Ramon shook his head. "No, that's what it says." He pointed at the painting.

"Your Japanese is coming along much better than mine!"

"The poet's name is Funya no Yasa'hide."

"Legion?" Ramon blinked at the voice within his mind.

"What about Legion?" Fatemeh took a step back and placed her hands on her hips.

"I hear him in my mind. He says the poet is Funya no Yasa'hide." Ramon smirked and looked up at the painting. "I never considered it before, but Legion could be a great help in this whole diplomatic business. He could translate and help promote understanding."

"We fear it would bore us to be little more than a servant to humankind."

"Why do you hear Legion now?" asked Fatemeh.

Although she couldn't hear the reply, Legion responded. *"Imagawa's airship has attacked Hokkaido. Dozens have died, although an analysis of the attack indicates she avoided the most populated areas."*

Ramon's shoulders slumped as he relayed Legion's report. "I suspect we should get back to the hotel," he added.

"Why?" Fatemeh's eyebrows came together.

"News is sure to reach Tokyo soon. I suspect there could be trouble for people from outside Japan until they sort out who is responsible and are certain they've routed out any spies."

Fatemeh huffed a sigh, but nodded. "I see what you mean. Where is Captain Cisneros?"

"*The* Bashō *should reach Ensenada tomorrow,*" reported Legion.

Ramon relayed the information, then thought: "*Will Hoshi arrive in time to meet him?*"

"*If Maravilla's report is accurate, and presuming he met no unexpected delays, he should be there.*"

Ramon looked around the museum. Even if news reached Tokyo right away, it would be a while before they came to the authorities' attention. "*Would you mind translating a few more poems for me?*" asked Ramon.

"*Certainly,*" said Legion.

"I want to walk around a little more before we get back in the automaton's rickshaw." Ramon stepped close to Fatemeh and wrapped his arm around her shoulder. "Besides, I feel in the mood to read some more Japanese poetry."

She smiled at him and they stepped over to the next painting.

Onofre Cisneros's back hurt. He sat on the deck of his cabin aboard the *Bashō*. He loved the light-colored wood which framed the paper interior walls. He loved the gentle sunlight streaming in through the porthole. He wished the ship came equipped with chairs as he knew them.

He stretched his back and looked down at plans he labored over. The Japanese airship impressed him, but he already saw numerous ways he could improve on the design. The *Bashō's* steam plant sat in the ship's stern with the stack jutting out like a tail. If he replaced the alcohol-burning steam engine with a chemical reaction steam engine, he could halve the weight.

He lay flat on his belly and drew netting which would allow men to climb up to the superstructure where a promenade deck with large windows could be installed. Airmen could use the area as a defensive platform or as a place to maintain a lookout.

He paused. The Japanese built these craft to defend against other dirigibles, but he now envisioned a sky filled with airships from many nations battling each other through smoke-darkened skies. Onofre Cisneros shuddered.

"This is why men like Ramon Morales who want to be diplomats are so important." Legion's voice resounded in Cisneros's mind. The captain rolled over and sat bolt upright. During the year when Legion had lived inside his mind and chattered non-stop, the entity seldom startled him. He grew used to sharing his thoughts. No matter how well he knew the alien, its presence now felt intrusive.

"How long have you been here?" Cisneros whispered the words so they wouldn't travel too easily through the paper walls.

"We are always nearby. We just entered your cerebral cortex a few minutes ago."

Cisneros nodded. "Do you have news from Ramon or Maravilla?"

"We have news from Mendeleev. The hijacked Russian airship attacked Sapporo. The ship then traveled north, back to a new hiding place on Sakhalin. Ramon has asked whether he should seek authorities to tell them what he knows."

Cisneros shook his head. *"That would raise suspicion. Ramon and Fatemeh should be as discreet as possible and make sure they carry their papers with them at all times, especially their letter of introduction from Lord Katsu."* The captain didn't speak the words aloud, but rather thought them clearly and distinctly, hoping Legion would hear.

"Of course I understand," said Legion. *"You used to speak to us like this all the time. We don't understand why your attitude toward us has changed."*

"Years ago, when I owned a mine, I had a mistress. I used to tell her everything. Then one day she left," thought Cisneros. *"She broke my heart and I found it difficult to trust another woman for a long time."* The woman had been a spy for Benito Juárez while the French controlled Mexico. She passed information to the government which allowed them to take everything he owned.

"Is there anything Ramon and Fatemeh can do to help with the situation in Sapporo?"

Cisneros looked down at his drawings. *"How many people are aboard the Russian airship?"*

"Mendeleev believes there are twenty-three. Aside from the bombs

dropped on Sapporo, the ship is fully armed." Cisneros wondered if the alien swarm already anticipated what he considered. How well could Legion read his thoughts?

The captain stood and left the cabin. He entered the gondola where Lord Katsu looked out over the water. The minister turned and smiled. "Isn't the view fantastic? I have to tell you, it's been great to get away from the hustle and bustle of Tokyo."

Cisneros nodded. "While you're away, do you have anyone to read your mail and attend to your correspondence?"

"Of course," said Katsu. "Otherwise I'd find my desk piled high with a mountain of papers when I return. My secretary sorts through the correspondence, answers what he can and leaves the rest for me to attend to when I get back."

"Can your secretary sign for you?"

If Lord Katsu thought the question strange, he gave no hint. "Absolutely. In fact, I think he has more business sense than I do. What's more, I have my automata to deliver messages. Those mechanical men are far more trustworthy than any human helpers."

"Very clever," said Cisneros. He stepped over to the window with his back to Katsu, just in case his lips moved while he communicated with Legion. *"One of Katsu's automata looks after Ramon and Fatemeh at the hotel, right?"*

"Yes," affirmed Legion.

"Do you think you could instruct Ramon how to operate its controls?" A wind gust caught the ship, causing Cisneros to reach out for the railing in front of him.

"It's quite simple. Yes."

"Stand by, I'll have a suggestion for Ramon soon."

"Something catch your eye?" asked Katsu.

Cisneros turned around and shook his head. "No, just enjoying the view." He winced and grabbed his back. "If the Japanese build another airship, I recommend installing a few Western-style chairs."

Imagawa sat on the captain's bed aboard *The Brazen Shark*. She still didn't find European chairs comfortable and preferred to sit on the floor, but despite the cabin's size, it offered little floor space. She moved into the cabin after the captain's eviction. She didn't like it, but her warriors expected it. Even though the bedding had been changed, the room still smelled of sickness and infection. Killing the captain had been merciful. Even if he'd survived the overland hike, his disability would have forced him into a disgraceful retirement.

"The way of the samurai is found in death." She reflected on Samurai Yamamoto Tsunetomo's words. As soldiers, the Russian airmen should have expected to die in combat. Still she experienced a guilty pang at ordering their deaths.

Many expected a woman to have a soft heart, but she viewed it as a weakness. Even as a child, she'd preferred her father's weapons and armor to dolls and flowers. She never wanted children to care for. At times her old mentor, Masuda Hoshi, would hold a kitten to his face to hear it purr, or gaze across a field at peasant farmers. She supposed some of his compassion rubbed off on her.

Imagawa's father had led the daimyo's guard. Hoshi had been his lieutenant. When he'd seen Imagawa's interest in weapons, she'd pleaded with him to train her as a samurai. Most women trained as samurai learned to fight as foot soldiers with polearms. Hoshi trained her to do so as well, but he also trained her in swordsmanship and marksmanship. "A samurai must be well rounded in order to take any position on the battlefield."

When not fighting, Hoshi had liked to cook or garden. Such skills seemed effeminate for such a strong, wise warrior, but perhaps that's why he had no problem training a girl to fight. In the years to come, she'd proven her skills in personal challenges and when her father died, the daimyo had offered the guard's leadership to Hoshi. He declined, but recommended Imagawa.

Eight years ago, the daimyo turned his lands over to the emperor. For a time, the emperor let the samurai keep their houses and he'd paid them a stipend. After four years, the emperor cancelled the stipend and soldiers ordered Imagawa, Nanbu, and Hoshi to vacate their homes. Imagawa would not give up without a fight. Hoshi had been right there—until the emperor's forces proved too strong, then he fled like a dog.

A gentle tapping at the door interrupted her thoughts. "Come in."

The Ainu woman entered carrying a food tray. Her black, tattooed lips drew Imagawa's attention. She wondered how a woman could allow such a thing to be done. She reached up and touched her own lips. "Does it hurt?"

Ipokash gave a sad smile and shook her head. "Not now. It did when it was done. I couldn't eat solid food for days."

"Why did you do it?"

"Without the tattoos I could not marry. They show I am an adult."

"I have no tattoos. I was married, but he died."

"You are not Ainu."

That much was true. Imagawa noticed the Ainu woman still held the tray. "Please set it down on the desk. I'll eat in a little while."

Ipokash bowed and set down the tray.

"Do you miss your husband?" asked Imagawa.

Ipokash's eye glistened and her lips trembled. She gave a sharp nod, then turned around and bumped into a man standing at the door—Nanbu. He smiled and leered. "A pleasure to feel a woman's touch, even if it is accidental."

"Let her pass," growled Imagawa.

Nanbu stepped back and gave a slight bow. Ipokash hurried around the warrior, who then entered the room. "Tethers are holding. Guards are assigned. We're secure for the night."

The airship sat in a small depression on Karafuto's southernmost tip, a stretch of land a mile long and a half mile wide. A lack of settlements lowered the risk of discovery. "What troubles you, Nanbu?"

He looked over at her dinner plate, cooling on the desk. "There's only so much dried fish a person can eat. We could use some fresh fruit and vegetables while they're available. Rice would be appreciated as well. Water sustains us, but a little sake would improve morale."

Imagawa grunted and nodded. "One attack against Japan will cause consternation. I suspect a second attack will be necessary to induce them to declare war. We will wait four days and then make a second attack. This time we will conduct a raid wearing Russian uniforms, so there will be no doubt in their minds who is attacking. We'll get the supplies you and the men desire."

Nanbu bowed. "Yes, ma'am." He turned to leave.

"Nanbu," she called.

He stopped in the doorway, back rigid.

"I want you to leave the Ainu woman alone. You have a wife and the Ainu are not fit consorts for warriors."

Nanbu turned around again and gave another bow. "As you wish, my lady."

She frowned, sensing sarcasm, but let it pass rather than risk a fight. He backed out of the room and slid the door closed. She sighed, glad to be alone again with her thoughts. The smell of dried fish masked the smell of sickness.

CHAPTER EIGHT
COURIERS

Masuda Hoshi arrived in the Mexican port city of Ensenada the day before the airship *Bashō* was due, presuming no delays. Captain Cisneros recommended a hotel and a stable via Maravilla.

Getting around Ensenada proved easy enough. Many people in the town spoke English and Hoshi had picked up some Spanish from Billy and his neighbors in Las Cruces. Ensenada's people seemed somehow less suspicious of his Japanese heritage than people in America. Hoshi supposed that could be because colonial-minded Europeans posed a greater threat than a poor "Chinaman."

In truth, Hoshi was far from poor. Samurai were not known for their wealth, but Hoshi practiced frugality and saved money during his long years in the daimyo's service. Arriving in America, he'd had enough money to buy land, seed, and support himself for the three to four years he needed to establish the farm. Of course, abandoning the farm twice in its first year on missions for others was not the way to assure success. Some days his desire to serve others felt like a character flaw.

At least the first time he'd abandoned his farm, it had been with a promissory note from the United States army. This time, he just had Maravilla's word that an airship traveled to meet him and his presence had been requested.

What did it mean that Imagawa lived? The last he'd seen her, she lay face down in the mud, bleeding from a bullet wound. The sight had convinced him she'd died and his heart broke. He wondered what happened after he left the field. He should have stayed and helped.

He'd met her when he was twenty-two. She'd been his master's precocious, twelve-year-old daughter. Most boys well into their teens weren't as strong as her. He'd trained her and as she grew into adulthood, he supposed he'd fallen in love with her.

They'd shared a brief romance when she'd reached her twenties, but she'd loved a man closer to her age. That man had loved duels, though, and died young.

What could it mean if Imagawa commanded an airship? It meant somehow she lived, a dangerous prospect indeed. Over the years, she'd taken many violent samurai teachings to heart. She loved fighting and swordplay more than helping those in her care as the Code of Bushido dictated.

Hoshi wondered if an emperor controlling an army could, in fact, live by the code of Bushido. The Meiji Emperor said he wanted to bring Japan into the modern age. Was that for the people or for his own power and ambition? Not enough time had passed for Hoshi to be sure.

The little seaside port of Ensenada, tucked between the ocean and the mountains reminded Hoshi of similar places in Japan, though less green. In a small seaside tavern he ordered a dish called ceviche, not unlike sashimi from home. He wanted tea to drink, but in a tavern, he felt compelled to order a beer, which soothed his road-weary nerves.

After dinner, he returned to the hotel and fell into an uneasy sleep.

The next day, he awoke, gathered his belongings and went to the docks to await the *Bashō*. A solitary gray cloud hung over the ocean in an otherwise clear blue sky. As the morning wore on, the distant "cloud" proved to be the Japanese vessel.

He cursed, hating to admit Maravilla had been right. Deep down, he hoped he would spend three or four days waiting, then go home with an excuse to toss the Mexican inventor off his land. Despite his better judgment, he liked Maravilla. He appreciated the ways he could use his mind to understand and manipulate the natural world. However, the murder of his wife and daughter had damaged Maravilla to the point Hoshi wondered if the thing called Legion was just an imaginary friend created to fill the void left by their absence.

Others had confirmed this creature called Legion existed, but Hoshi still harbored doubts. Was it really a creature from the stars? Or was it an evil spirit? Did westerners not know their own Bible well enough to remember the demonic entity called Legion?

As the airship drew closer, dock workers dropped their tasks and gathered on the pier. They laughed, jumped and cheered as the airship descended and hovered over a long pier jutting out into the bay. Hoshi noticed a sign at the end of the pier which indicated a ship called the *Ballena* normally docked there.

A ladder unfurled from the airship and several men in Japanese navy uniforms descended. Hoshi bristled at the sight. He hung back, keeping his comfortable seat for the time being.

Those gathered on the docks also recoiled from the armed men. Murmurs went up in Spanish. The people feared an invasion like those which had happened up North, only now Japan invaded Mexico instead of Russia invading the United States.

The murmuring increased as a man in a black frock coat, blue silk vest, canvas trousers and knee-high black boots descended the ladder. Hoshi recognized him from Ramon and Fatemeh's wedding—the pirate captain, Onofre Cisneros.

Cisneros seemed to recognize many of the people who gathered on the dock. He pointed and gave instructions, sending them on errands for supplies. He turned and shook hands with two men who had descended after him. One wore the uniform of a naval captain. The other wore a tailcoat and top hat. Hoshi clenched his jaw. He thought he recognized the man as the emperor's upstart Naval Lord, Katsu Kaishū.

Katsu was just as unhinged as Maravilla.

"Masuda Hoshi! Is Masuda Hoshi here?" Onofre Cisneros called.

Hoshi looked up. The man in the captain's uniform also called out, this time speaking in Japanese.

Hoshi stood and walked over to those gathered on the pier. He pushed through the crowd and bowed to Cisneros and the other gentlemen. "I am Masuda Hoshi," he said.

Cisneros's eyes widened, revealing both surprise and pleasure at finding Hoshi so easily. The captain introduced the men on his left and right. As Hoshi suspected, the man in the top hat was Lord Katsu. Cisneros introduced the other man as Captain

Sanada. Hoshi bowed, greeting the men with courtesy.

"As soon as you're ready, you may board the ship and settle in," offered Sanada in Japanese.

"I'm afraid I didn't know when to expect you, so my belongings are still at the hotel." Hoshi spoke in English for Cisneros's benefit—and he hoped the captain did not find him rude. "It will take me about half an hour to get ready."

"Outstanding," said Cisneros. "I could use some time to refresh myself with some home cooking and gather up any accumulated paperwork." He gave a cursory bow to Hoshi. "Please take your time. Although we hope to start the return voyage today, we'll be a few hours."

Hoshi excused himself and returned to the hotel. He needed just a few minutes to gather his belongings into saddlebags. He visited his horse at the stable and confirmed she was well tended. Once satisfied, he returned to the dock where he found the crowd had thinned, but not dispersed entirely. He bowed to the guard on duty and introduced himself. Another man came down from the airship and led him aboard.

The former samurai marveled at these men's youthfulness. He wondered where they had been ten years ago. Had they tended crops for a daimyo? Were they the children of merchants? In America, one could never look at a person and know the answers to these questions. He would have to get used to that being true in Japan as well.

Hoshi smiled when he entered the airship. It reminded him of a small, floating Japanese house. An officer led him to his quarters. He thanked the young man, then closed the door behind him and did his best to make himself at home.

As the afternoon wore on, people shuffled down the corridor outside the room. He peeked out and watched as crewmen stowed materials in side rooms and cubby holes. Looking back toward the command deck, he saw Captain Cisneros approach. "It's a pleasure to see you," said the captain. "Frankly I wasn't sure..."

"...whether I'd really be here." Hoshi completed the thought. "Tell me what you know about this Legion."

Cisneros looked from one side to the other then held his hand forward, indicating they should enter Hoshi's quarters.

The captain slid the door shut behind him and the two settled down across from each other on cushions. "I sometimes wonder whether or not I believe in Legion. Ever since I helped Fatemeh and Maravilla destroy the Russian airships over Denver last spring, ideas came easier to me than before, I was more dexterous than I thought possible, I heard voices in the back of my head. Sometimes I saw visions. None of that is proof of a being from the stars is it?"

"No," said Hoshi. "But if it's madness, it's the same madness which afflicts Professor Maravilla."

Cisneros snorted and nodded. "What can you tell me about Imagawa Masako who I'm told has stolen a Russian airship?"

"If anyone could do it, she could. She is ruthless and will do anything to win a fight."

The corner of Cisneros's mouth lifted—a sly grin. "Well, we have that in common."

"Maravilla tells me you walked away from your mines in Northern Mexico."

Cisneros nodded.

"She would have descended into those mines and made the Mexican army pay for every inch with a life. That is the kind of opponent we face." Hoshi looked at the ground and sighed. "And what do we have? A pair of dreamers, a mad pirate, and a paper airship."

"Two paper airships." Cisneros flashed a wry grin. "And a submersible."

Hoshi looked up. "Every advantage we can muster helps."

Ramon paced the suite's sitting room. "It's only been a day, but it feels like I've been trapped here forever."

Fatemeh looked up from the book she read and sighed. They weren't exactly trapped. They just decided to stay in familiar neighborhoods near the hotel so they didn't attract undue attention. She focused on something else he said. "Forever? Aren't you enjoying our honeymoon?"

He dropped onto an adjoining cushion. "In a way, I'm having the time of my life. We've seen Japan and Hawaii. I

even kind of enjoyed swimming in that skimpy bathing suit."
He paused and noticed her distant gaze. "Aren't you having a
good time?"

Her eyes snapped back into focus. "I'm having a great
time. I'm just thinking about other times and places. You're
going to college when we get home. Now I'm thinking about
my own future."

"You're a healer." Ramon said it with conviction.

"I know herbs and roots. I have some common sense
knowledge, but I have a feeling people would respect me more
if I had a degree in medicine or pharmacology."

"What's stopping you?"

She rolled her eyes. "I traveled to the United States because
I hoped there would be better opportunities there for me than
in Persia." She sighed. "Although I still believe that's true, it's
not easy for a woman to get into college."

"And when have you ever turned away from a challenge?
I'll be studying. I assumed you'd be working as a healer, but
there's no reason you can't study right alongside me." He slid
closer and kissed her. Fatemeh's arms enfolded Ramon, but before they grew more involved, a knock sounded at the door.

Ramon looked up through fog-shrouded and tilted glasses. He straightened them, ran fingers through his hair, then
answered the door. The automaton ticked, whirred, and held
out a letter.

"Please come in," said Ramon.

"No tip required." The automaton spoke in a scratchy,
sing-song simulation of Lord Katsu's voice.

Ramon reached out, pushed a button, and the automaton
rolled into the room. Ramon stepped behind it and flipped a
switch, which deactivated its dry cell battery, then flipped a
small lever which disengaged its clockworks. The letter it held
fluttered to the floor.

Fatemeh hopped off the cushion and swept up the letter.
"It says Lord Katsu is unavailable and cannot grant us an audience until next week. His secretary sends his regrets."

"Just as we hoped he would."

She turned the paper over. "The letter is in English, but it's
addressed in Japanese."

"Do you think you can copy his writing?"

"I'm good, but I'm not that good. I do have a plan." Fatemeh stepped into the hall and put on her shoes. "I'll be back soon." Ramon stuck his head through the door and kissed her, then watched her stride down the hallway.

Ramon closed the door and opened the automaton's chest cavity. There, he found a perplexing series of dials, gauges, knobs and buttons. He retrieved a map of Tokyo from the bedroom and unfolded it, then did his best to remember the instructions Legion had given him for programming the mechanical man.

From Mendeleev, they learned Imagawa would return to Sapporo in three days. From Cisneros, they learned the Army Lord's name and that he was on good terms with Katsu Kaishū.

Ramon dialed instructions into the automaton. Fatemeh returned an hour later. Engrossed as he was, Ramon looked up for a brief kiss. Another hour passed and Fatemeh lit a gas lamp for Ramon to see. Once finished, he sat back and wiped his forehead. "Where did you go?"

"The bookshop around the corner. I told the owner I was writing a novel about Japan and needed to know how a letter from Katsu Kaishū's secretary to the First Lord of the Army would be written. I told him the letter should suggest that rogue Japanese attacked Sapporro and it should cite reasons such as the attack's limited nature and lack of ground forces."

Ramon arched an eyebrow. "The bookshop owner was willing to help?"

Fatemeh grinned. "He said young ladies shouldn't write such things, but I told him I wrote the story in the interests of peace, which is true. He thought Lord Katsu would recommend placing a naval force and soldiers in strategic locations to try to capture anyone who landed. I then asked him to suggest that it would be a tragedy if Japan went to war against Russia."

"Will the handwriting match?"

Fatemeh shrugged. "Does it need to? How many calligraphers do you suppose the army and the navy departments employ?"

"Quite a few, I suspect." Ramon looked at the letter and nodded. "I think it will pass."

"It just needs to be convincing enough for the military to act on it," said Fatemeh. "If the army requests, Katsu's secretary can order more ships stationed at Sapporo."

Ramon folded the letter and placed it in the automaton's pouch.

Fatemeh nodded agreement. "So, do you suppose it's safe enough for us to go to the little ramen place around the corner? The smells were heavenly as I passed and I'm starving."

"I'm willing to risk it if you are." Ramon grabbed his jacket, then stepped back to the desk and extinguished the lamp.

CHAPTER NINE
HAIKU

A courier wearing a palace guard uniform ran into the map room at Army Headquarters in St. Petersburg and spoke to a captain, who led the guard over to General Dragomirov. He saluted. "Sir, I've been sent over from the palace. The Japanese Ambassador has just filed a formal complaint about an airship attacking the city of Sapporo. The czar personally assured him no such attack has been authorized." He paused for a moment and chewed his lip. "The czar demands to know if you issued any such orders."

Dragomirov puffed out his chest and sneered at the mere suggestion that he would do such a thing. He pointed to the palace guard. "No such order was issued from this office." He turned to the captain. "Draft a letter to that effect and bring it to me for signature and seal."

The captain saluted and set about his task.

The general turned to his adjutant. "The *Nicholas Alexandrovich* is due back in St. Petersburg today, if I'm not mistaken."

The adjutant heaved a weary sigh. "We've received preliminary reports from several cities along the ship's expected flight path. No one has seen it."

"I have a feeling we've had a sighting." The general ran his hand over his bald head. "Has Mendeleev lost his mind? Is it piracy? Are the Japanese just trying to start something?" Dragomirov held his hands out, inviting the adjutant to add another suggestion. When he received no reply he continued. "Get a courier over to the admiralty right away. I want a ship patrolling Sakhalin Island's waters looking for the ship or signs of wreckage."

The adjutant saluted, spun on his heel and left.

Ramon listened to Fatemeh as she read from a book of poems by Bashō she'd purchased from the bookseller around the corner from their hotel. They had little else to do while they waited to see what came of the message they sent via Lord Katsu's automaton. Fatemeh pronounced the Japanese words slowly, trying to translate as she went.

"None is traveling this road but I, this autumn evening."

Ramon's brow furrowed for a moment as Legion's words resounded in his mind. He realized it was a translation of the poem Fatemeh read. "Legion…" The word came out as a hiss.

Fatemeh looked up, concerned. "Is there a problem?"

"The situation is unchanged." Only Ramon could hear Legion's answer to Fatemeh's question. *"We just thought you would enjoy more translations."*

Ramon sighed and nodded. "No problems." He removed his glasses and thought for a moment. He hated excluding Fatemeh every time he communicated with the alien swarm. "That poem you read could almost be about Legion." He repeated the translation and Fatemeh nodded. Although Legion remained silent, Ramon felt his presence, like a figure looming over his shoulder. He knew he'd caught Legion's attention.

"Please explain how the poem describes us."

"I think I can best explain with a story," said Ramon. "Fifteen years ago, my father served in the Federal Army at Fort Union, near a town called Watrous. One day in spring—I think it was about mid-April—a soldier came to our home in Socorro to tell us papá had been killed defending the Union at Glorietta Pass." Ramon's voice grew thick.

"We have seen this much," said Legion, *"and understand your hatred of warfare stems from this event."*

Fatemeh reached out and took Ramon's hand. She squeezed, silently urging him to continue.

"I hated the Confederates. I wanted to join Colonel Canby and slaughter them as they returned to Texas."

Fatemeh winced and Ramon worried he might have revealed something a little too dark about himself. "Go on." Her voice was soft and held no judgement.

Ramon swallowed and pushed ahead. "The parish priest in those days was named Father Patricio. I don't remember how I ended up in the parsonage talking to him or how the subject came up, but I told him about my papá and how I hoped to go to war. Mamá wouldn't sign the papers which allowed me to join the army while under age. I hoped the padre could help me."

"*Did he?*" asked Legion.

"He wouldn't," gasped Fatemeh.

Ramon shook his head. "He told me I would damage my own soul if I sought to avenge my father. Those words didn't help, but the fact he refused to sign the underage permission form kept me from running off and gave me time to consider those words."

"*Your memories tell us it would have done no good if he had signed those forms. You were just thirteen. The army wouldn't have taken you.*"

"He sounds like a wise man," said Fatemeh.

"You're peeking." Ramon meant the words for Legion, but realized he spoke them aloud when he noticed Fatemeh's confused expression. "Legion's peeking. He's looking into memories without invitation." He folded his arms. "Even so, Legion is right. The army wouldn't have taken me. I was too young. I think the priest and my mamá must have been worried and they spoke to a local farmer. I spent the summer working. I don't remember many details. I just remember getting up early and feeding the animals, tending the crops, and coming home exhausted."

Fatemeh's brow creased. "Did the farm work help take your mind from your father?"

Ramon shook his head. "I still grieved for my father, but the experience showed me I needed to work to care for the living. By the time school came around, the classroom felt restful."

"So why do you get so anxious sometimes about returning to school?" Fatemeh's mouth ticked up in a mischievous grin.

"School's a place for boys and I'm a man. It's scary going back." Ramon shrugged, but thought of a better answer. "My teacher worked me quite hard and I worry about whether or not I can still do the work."

"I know you can do it, Ramon."

Ramon leaned over and kissed her, then remembered he had an audience. He returned to the story. "He gave lots of homework which engaged me. I found when I didn't throw myself into it, I would start to dwell on my father's memory and the anger would build. Being a student calmed me. It was a road, like the one in the haiku. Each person in these stories taught me through their choices and by letting me do the work myself."

"*None travels this road but I...*" repeated Legion. "*Must you travel the road alone?*"

"At times, we all have to figure things out for ourselves," said Fatemeh, as though she heard Legion's silent question. "A good teacher is the one who shows us the best road to take."

In his cabin aboard the *Bashō*, Hoshi stared at a sheet of paper, struggling to find the kireji, or cutting word for a haiku about flight. Flying aboard a Japanese airship named for one of the all-time great haiku poets, he wanted to write something to document the experience, even if he never showed it to another person.

The smooth voyage amazed him. From time to time, the airship encountered turbulence, but if it dropped ballast and gained altitude, the ride smoothed out again. The one thing Hoshi did not like was the cold. Even the sunshine filling the pleasant stateroom failed to warm him.

Cisneros explained that air grew colder the higher they flew. He also explained about the new lifting gas the Japanese ships used and how it made open flame less of a concern than on Russian ships. Still Cisneros seemed nervous about the Japanese ship's construction. Hoshi admitted wood and paper provided little protection for those aboard, but as someone used to fighting on foot or horseback, it worried him less than the prospect of falling from the sky.

Hoshi abandoned the haiku and went over to his saddlebag. He retrieved a cozy sweater he'd purchased in Las Cruces and put it on under his kimono, then he stood and walked to the back of the gondola and climbed the ladder to the walkway underneath the balloon. Out here, the engine noise and the wind almost deafened him.

He found several men congregated outside by the boiler. Open flame may be unwelcome inside, but it posed few problems out here on the metal catwalk and the boiler generated heat, even as cold air blew through the lines surrounding the crew. The men, who shouted to hear each other, grew silent when Hoshi approached.

He warmed his hands and tried to flash a pleasant smile. He stopped when a crewman stepped back, startled. "Please don't mind me," he called. "I'm just aboard as a passenger."

The men looked at him, then cast surreptitious glances at one another, but remained silent.

Hoshi finished warming his hands, then returned to the gondola. As he reached the deck, he encountered Captain Sanada, who nodded. "I'm about to dine. I wondered if you would care to join me."

Hoshi bowed. "I would be honored."

The officer's galley was smaller than the crew's mess where Hoshi typically dined. A steward set out three food trays, then bowed and left the two men alone. Hoshi's mouth watered at the sight of grilled fish, a meat and potato stew, and good, sticky rice. The rice in New Mexico was coarse and expensive, brought by train from the southern states. Most went to Chinese railroad workers, but he had convinced a general store owner to stock a few bags now and then. Although a few Mexican cooks experimented with rice, it was a novelty in the western United States

"What brings you aboard my ship, Mr. Masuda?"

Hoshi served himself some rice and a piece of fish. "I thought Captain Cisneros would have told you. I have been asked to consult about some matters on Karafuto Island."

"Karafuto belongs to the Russians," said Sanada. "They even call it by a different name—Sakhalin, if I remember correctly. Why would the imperial government wish to discuss such matters with a samurai?"

"Samurai, Captain Sanada? I am merely an American farmer."

"If the emperor wanted a farmer's opinion, there are many in Japan." Sanada snorted and helped himself to food. "It's obvious you're a samurai. It's in your bearing, the way you move, the way you expect men to respect you." He took a bite and leaned forward. "You are no peasant farmer, nor a rich land owner."

Hoshi nodded. "That is true, but it is also true I love the feel of soil in my hands more than the feel of a sword. This is why I'm content to be a farmer in America."

"Many samurai hated to lose their stipends and their positions." Sanada poured a cup of tea and offered it to Hoshi, who accepted. "Many have killed themselves rather than give up their rank. A few have joined the Imperialist army as officers." The captain poured a cup of tea for himself. "Do you oppose the emperor?"

"I do not return to Japan to mount a coup, if that's what you wish to know." Hoshi sipped the tea, then set the cup down. "I think suicide is a waste unless the cause is honorable, and I have no desire to become a peasant."

Sanada narrowed his gaze. "Aren't you a farmer now? Haven't you become a peasant?"

"In America, the farmer owns his own land. I suppose I am a peasant, but I am also a daimyo."

"A daimyo without samurai?" Sanada swallowed a bite of fish followed by some tea. "Then what is going on at Karafuto that you have been asked to consult with?"

"If Captain Cisneros has not told you..."

"To Hell with Captain Cisneros. He is not Japanese. This is a Naval Airship under the emperor's command. If something is happening I may become involved in, I want to know."

"Understandable." Hoshi savored the stew, then followed it with some rice.

Captain Sanada sat back and folded his arms, expectant.

"A former samurai of my acquaintance is suspected of piracy," said Hoshi. "It's possible a Russian airship is involved."

Sanada's eyes went wide. "Why hasn't Cisneros confided this in me?"

"I suspect it's because we're dealing with secondhand information and rumor at this point. We have few facts."

"I would like to be prepared."

"We have some time on the voyage back to Japan," said Hoshi. "I suggest we meet with the captain in the morning."

Sanada finished his rice, then poured more tea. "How did you know to meet us in Ensenada? This flight was not announced."

"A messenger told me of plans for the test flight. I was not entirely certain you would arrive until you did." Hoshi hoped the captain would not press for more details. British agents in Hawaii brought Cisneros and the Japanese together. They could conceivably have sent a message to Hoshi.

Sanada nodded. "Now that ten years have passed, what do you think of the Meiji Restoration?"

"I think it's admirable the emperor wants Japan to join the world rather than sit alone." Hoshi sipped his tea. "What do you think of it?"

"As a sailor under the shogunate, I was confined to coastal waters around Japan. I have now flown across the great Pacific Ocean and I expect I may do so again, if my ship is not destroyed by these pirates you describe. I like this new world and I have a hard time even describing it."

"Have you ever tried haiku?"

The captain laughed. "Haiku is for nobles, not for men like me."

"That's the real beauty of the Meiji Emperor's restoration. He has created a world where poetry is for everybody."

Sanada narrowed his gaze. "What if I told you I don't want to write poetry?"

Hoshi shrugged. "In a world where peasants may write poetry, nobles may be exempt."

"But I am neither peasant nor noble."

"I foresee a time for Japan when no one will be." With that, Hoshi sipped his tea, then excused himself.

CHAPTER TEN
CONVERSING WITH OWLS

A loud rapping on the door sounded just as the clock struck noon. Ramon stood and gestured for Fatemeh to remain seated. He cracked the door and peered out. Lord Katsu's automaton clicked and whirred, holding up a sealed envelope. Ramon grabbed it. "Thank you," he said.

The automaton turned, then rolled down the hallway. Ramon pushed the door closed, then examined the envelope. An official seal held its flap closed.

"Who's it from?" asked Fatemeh.

Ramon shrugged and put his finger under the flap to break the seal.

Fatemeh grabbed his arm and shook her head. "We may not want whoever sent that to know we've read it."

"It's addressed to us," said Ramon.

Fatemeh narrowed her gaze. "Better be careful anyway."

Ramon nodded and retrieved a knife, heated it in the flame of one of the gas lamps and carefully ran it under the seal to preserve it. Taking out the parchment he read, eyes widening. "It's from the Lord of Home Affairs, Ōkubo Toshimichi. He requests our presence at dinner tonight. He says he'll send Lord Katsu's automaton to retrieve us at four o'clock."

"Is it a request or an order?"

"Sounds like an order to me." Ramon considered the note. "I also think we should dress suitably. This guy sounds pretty important."

"He is," said Fatemeh. "He was one of the architects of the Meiji Restoration. He's probably the most important man in Japan aside from the emperor himself."

"Why does he want to see us?"

"I guess we'll find out."

That afternoon, Ramon and Fatemeh assembled the finest wardrobe they could from the clothes they had brought. Ramon wore a gray jacket and purple bow tie while Fatemeh wore an elegant black ruffled jacket with matching skirt. The automaton knocked at four o'clock, then led them downstairs. Before climbing in the rickshaw, Fatemeh crossed the street to a curio shop. Ramon took out his pocket watch, and checked the time. Just as he replaced it, Fatemeh returned with a bundle wrapped in brown paper.

"What's that?" asked Ramon.

"I've heard a gift is expected when visiting people," she said.

Ramon bent over and kissed her, pleased at her forethought. They climbed in the rickshaw and took another frantic ride, narrowly avoiding collisions with merchants and carts.

Soon the automaton turned down a less crowded, tree-lined lane a short distance from the palace. It stopped in front of a house set back from the lane which embodied both Japanese and western elements. A sloping, tiled roof topped a two-story wooden structure. A porch surrounded the building. Built of dark wood and surrounded by pines, the house reminded Ramon more of a mountain cabin than the manor houses built by rich Americans.

The newlyweds climbed up the steps to face a hinged door, similar to those at their hotel and at a few public buildings they'd visited. A woman in a kimono and obi opened the door and bowed to them. Ramon and Fatemeh returned the courtesy. Without speaking, the woman pointed to Ramon and Fatemeh's feet and indicated a neat line of shoes to the side.

Ramon and Fatemeh slipped their shoes off and then followed the woman into the main room. Ramon blushed looking down at his dirty socks.

Right away, the room's simplicity struck Ramon. Although he had never traveled in elite circles, he knew the homes of the wealthy and the powerful were huge. He imagined them filled with the finest things money could buy.

A few watercolors hung from this home's walls. A table against one wall had a few paper sculptures on it. Enchanted, Fatemeh walked over and peered at them.

"Origami," said a man who entered the room. "It's a hob-by. It takes my mind off the complex affairs of state." The man wore a western-style suit with a black bow tie. A ribbon held his long hair in a ponytail. His neat mustache exploded into bristling mutton-chop sideburns. He stepped forward and bowed. "Ōkubo Toshimichi." He indicated the woman who answered the door. "My wife, Lady Hayasaki Masako."

Ramon blinked, but realized that Lord Ōkubo's wife merely shared a given name with the samurai Imagawa. He recovered quickly and introduced himself. "Ramon Morales." He grasped Toshimichi's hand and felt immense power in the grip. Ramon wouldn't want to arm wrestle this man. He let go and held his hand out to Fatemeh and introduced her.

"Charmed." She held out the brown-paper parcel. "Thank you for inviting us into your home."

Lady Hayasaki took the parcel and unwrapped it. She and her husband both smiled at the little wooden owl. Ōkubo took the carving and set it among the origami.

Ramon hoped they had made a good first impression. "I'm afraid we know very little Japanese."

Ōkubo held up his hand. "Please don't worry yourself on that account. I learned English years ago and taught Masako. We are pleased for the opportunity to practice your language."

Ōkubo led them into an adjoining room where chairs surrounded a table. The Lord of Home Affairs indicated his guests should sit. Lady Hayasaki left the room for just a moment, then returned followed by two girls who carried serving trays. The upper class in Japan did reserve some luxuries for themselves.

"I hope you'll forgive the sudden, informal invitation to dine," said Ōkubo, "but I thought you would prefer to keep a low profile given your surreptitious letter to me."

"Surreptitious letter?" Ramon swallowed hard and looked around seeking an escape should this prove a trap.

"Please don't play coy." Ōkubo leaned forward. "It was easy enough to determine the letter's origin, especially since Lord Katsu's automaton delivered it. He left one of the automata at your disposal and Lord Katsu's secretary is quite adept at figuring out who sent a machine on a given errand." Ōkubo reached out and took a plate. Using hashi sticks, he helped himself to fish, then handed the plate to Ramon. "Why did you feel you had to resort to such a ruse to get information to me about the Russian airship in Hokkaido?"

"We feared you might waste time trying to find out how we got the information," interjected Fatemeh. "We felt it was more important you should act."

Ramon took the dish and grasped his hashi. Although he had practiced, the sticks teetered and rolled in his fingers. He managed to push a piece of fish onto his plate.

"Why do you suspect renegade samurai stole a Russian airship?" pressed Ōkubo.

"We've been living through Russia's invasion of America." Ramon appreciated having a moment before attempting to use the hashi sticks. "The Russians don't hit and run. They drop troops and take over. They have a way of... influencing people." Ramon hesitated explaining about Legion or how Legion could influence their behavior. Ramon wasn't even certain he could do justice to such an explanation.

Ōkubo grunted and gave a sharp nod, then reached for a small plate. "You've made a case these are not Russians, but why samurai? Why not say, Chinese or Koreans?"

"According to yesterday's newspaper, the casualties were quite light." Fatemeh lifted a morsel of fish to her mouth.

Ramon nodded. "That's right." He grimaced, then composed himself. Such a hasty answer could reveal he possessed more knowledge than he could account for. "Whoever conducted the attack wanted to avoid hurting people."

"Interesting conjecture," remarked Ōkubo, "though I have known samurai who are ruthless when trying to achieve an objective. What do these samurai hope to accomplish?"

"I gather the restoration of the emperor's power displeased many samurai." Ramon's stomach grumbled, but he resisted the urge to dig into his food. "Perhaps these samurai wish to see a popular call for the shogun's return."

"Again, an interesting conjecture." Ōkubo lifted a finger. "However, I might suggest it's just as possible the Russians test our resolve, sending a minor strike to see if the emperor's army has teeth before launching a larger assault."

Ramon had to admit the idea sounded plausible, but

Fatemeh raised the doubt he harbored. "Why exactly would the Russians attack Japan?"

If a woman's question offended the Lord of Home Affairs, he gave no indication. Instead, he countered with a different question. "Why did the Russians invade America?"

"They wanted oil and America's resources."

Lady Hayasaki broke her silence. "Japan has many farms. It's closer to Russia. Sapporo is a fine warm water sea port."

Ōkubo grinned. "My wife states the case well. It's clear the Russians will lose much of the territory they gained in America. Perhaps they'll get to keep Alaska, but it's land much like they already possess. I think it's possible they're testing to see if there's a battle they can win."

Ramon looked to Fatemeh, then down at his plate. He grabbed his hashi and lifted a bite of fish, holding his hand under the morsel to prevent it falling on the floor. Lady Hayasaki gave a sharp intake of breath and Ramon realized he must have committed some faux pas, but wasn't certain what he'd done. The fish dropped. He stabbed at it with the hashi and popped it in his mouth, then swallowed it down.

Ōkubo poured tea in Ramon's cup. "Thank you." Ramon took a drink. "If I may be so bold, what do you plan to do about the airship attack?"

"I am the Lord of Home Affairs and will do what I must. I have already asked the army to send troops and the navy to send ships to defend Hokkaido."

"Then you don't plan to attack Russia?" Ramon dared to hope.

"That is more than I can discuss with an outsider," said Ōkubo, "even one who appears to have Japan's interests at heart."

Ramon frowned even though he appreciated the lord's position. They were outsiders and this audience was remarkable. It pleased Ramon the Japanese believed in the possibility of a new attack and planned to send troops to Hokkaido. Perhaps if Imagawa attacked again, the Japanese would see the threat wasn't Russian.

"In our travels, we've heard of a samurai called Imagawa Masako." Fatemeh took a new tack and allowed Ramon a chance to eat with the awkward hashi sticks while he thought. "I didn't know women could be samurai."

"There have been many notable women samurai," declared Lady Hayasaki. "The Tale of the Heike celebrates Tomoe Gozen, a remarkable swordswoman and archer. Lady Hangaku was another powerful samurai. Any bushi class noble may take up the sword whether male or female, especially in times of need."

Both Ramon and Fatemeh looked at her, then blinked and turned their attention back to their food when they realized they were being rude.

"Like many westerners, you equate samurai with European knights," explained Lady Hayasaki. "Samurai are landless soldiers a daimyo pays to protect the peasants who farm his land. It is a sacred calling and I am proud to be married to a samurai."

Fatemeh inclined her head. "I thought the Meiji Restoration meant the samurai were outlawed."

Ōkubo's eyes glistened as he nodded. "The Meiji Restoration is a time of transformation for the samurai. We no longer fight for daimyos under the shogun. Instead, we pledge our fealty to the emperor and pursue other functions in society besides warfare." He lifted a hand, and summoned one of the serving women. He spoke to her in Japanese, then continued. "I see a future where samurai head businesses and command industry. Samurai will no longer be mere soldiers. We will lead the world."

"Then what about this Imagawa? Who is she? Does she have a place in this new Japan?" Fatemeh leaned forward.

"Throughout history, there have been women who have inherited leadership positions," explained Lady Hayasaki. "Tachibana Ginchiyo ruled her clan after her father's death. Yamauchi Chiyo assumed her husband's mantle after his death, and led her clan to many victories."

"Then why does Imagawa rebel against the government?" asked Fatemeh. "It sounds as though she would retain her title."

"It is not so simple," said Ōkubo with a shrug. "Samurai are expected to transform into new roles, they cannot expect to retain the old roles and be paid for service that is no longer required."

"Transform or conform?" Fatemeh narrowed her gaze.

"Perhaps a little of both," suggested Ōkubo. The serving girl returned and placed a bottle and two glasses in front of Ramon and the lord. Ōkubo poured milky liquid for himself and Ramon. "Imagawa would have to find a new way to make a life. I believe that's what she truly fears."

Ōkubo lifted his cup. "I drink to our new friendship and our new understanding."

Ramon lifted the cup and took a cautious sip. He fought not to cough as he swallowed the strong rice wine.

Lady Hayasaki stood and beckoned Fatemeh.

Lady Hayasaki led Fatemeh outside where the pine trees cast long shadows in the setting sun's orange light. "I would prefer to leave the men to their nigori."

"They won't get too drunk will they?" Fatemeh looked over her shoulder, somewhat worried about hauling a drunken Ramon back to their hotel room.

Lady Hayasaki Masako smiled. "No, but Toshimichi hopes to loosen your husband's tongue just a bit more to find out what he knows. I prefer a more direct approach."

"We've told you what we know." Fatemeh folded her arms.

"I believe you," said Lady Hayasaki. "However, you have not told us how you know it."

Just then, an owl hooted from a nearby tree. Fatemeh squinted and looked for the bird. She walked down the steps into the soft grass, heedless of the pine needles poking her feet. She hooted back at the owl. The owl responded and fluttered its wings. She smiled and stood straight, then hooted again.

The owl responded and flew off.

"There are some who say I talk to owls." Fatemeh's gaze followed the retreating bird.

"What did this one say?"

"No one can speak owl as readily as you or I speak English." Fatemeh turned around and faced Lady Hayasaki. "I know the owl likes life in the city because there are plenty of mice for her to catch. There are trees for her to build nests in. I know the owl is happy by the timbre of her voice." Fatemeh took a step toward the porch. "Ramon used to be a sheriff in America. He needed to know the townspeople. He was in the army and he fought the Russians, who took him captive. We were both aboard one of their airships." Fatemeh took a deep breath and released it as she put her hands behind her back. "We have no reason to deceive you. It's just that everything points to the airship being controlled by Japanese who wish to foment problems."

"And your questions about Imagawa," pressed Lady Hayasaki, "you think she's the samurai behind the attacks?"

Fatemeh considered the question and how best to answer it. "A friend named Masuda Hoshi told us about Imagawa."

Lady Hayasaki sucked in a breath. "He is a great samurai indeed. His departure was a loss for Japan."

"He came to America to be a farmer," said Fatemeh.

"That's a waste." Lady Hayasaki looked up to the darkening sky. "He could be so much more."

Fatemeh's jaw tensed. "In America, farmers have risen to lead the country. Perhaps he did not wish to be looked down upon for his choice." As soon as she spat the words, she regretted them. She wasn't in a position to judge another culture.

Lady Hayasaki nodded. "That would be Hoshi's way. I suspect you're correct about him." She walked down the steps toward Fatemeh. "You are not American are you? Why did you move there?"

"I wanted to be a healer and I could not be one in my homeland." A partial truth. Fatemeh could have been a healer, but it would have required marriage to a man she didn't love. Now she was a healer and a wife, but by choice rather than decree.

Lady Hayasaki nodded and Fatemeh noticed the gray strands in her hair and the small lines around her eyes. To Fatemeh, those features enhanced the woman's beauty and power. "Never forget, Fatemeh, homelands change and sometimes they only change when we stay there and fight for it."

Fatemeh frowned, wondering whether she could ever return to her homeland, but she nodded.

Lady Hayasaki held out her hand. "You should take your husband back to the hotel before he or my husband drinks much more."

Fatemeh followed Lady Hayasaki inside. There, Ramon and Lord Ōkubo sat at the table, eyes bright. "Why didn't you say so to begin with?" asked the Lord of Home Affairs. "You know a samurai stole the Russian airship because spirits told you."

Ramon blinked at Ōkubo. "I never said…"

"You didn't have to. It's obvious from your description."

Lady Hayasaki looked at Fatemeh. "I'll summon the automaton."

CHAPTER ELEVEN
THE POWER OF GODS

Ipokash roused Dmitri Mendeleev, left him a breakfast of dried fish and stale bread, then told him to dress right away. As soon as he'd finished his morning ablutions, a sharp knock on the door heralded the arrival of Imagawa's lieutenant, Nanbu. When Mendeleev opened the door, Nanbu reached in and yanked him out into the corridor. Without words, the samurai pushed him forward to the gondola where the crew prepared for departure.

Mendeleev strode to the window and blinked at the sight outside the ship. Men in Russian uniforms loosened the cables tethering *The Brazen Shark* to the ground. On closer inspection, the scientist realized the men were disguised samurai. They climbed aboard as Imagawa ordered ballast released. The autumn air had turned chill, allowing the ship to rise rapidly and high. Sparse cumulus clouds dotted an otherwise deep blue sky. Imagawa called an order and the compass needle drifted southward.

Imagawa's understanding of airship operations impressed Mendeleev. She watched Shichoroji at the helm for a moment, then stepped over and checked the ballast readings. Satisfied, she turned to Nanbu and asked a question. Mendeleev caught her eyes darting toward him and she spoke the word "Ipokash." Apparently she had some questions.

Nanbu turned and gave orders to a nearby samurai, who scurried up the ladder. A few minutes later he returned with Ipokash. Imagawa continued to scan the horizon through a spyglass. From their altitude, Mendeleev doubted she could see much detail below. Perhaps she admired the clouds.

She collapsed the telescope, turned, then addressed the Ainu woman.

"Imagawa worries the Japanese Navy may be stationed at Sapporo now. She wants to be seen, but she would also like to get away if they open fire. What is the best strategy?"

Mendeleev nodded as he considered the problem. In normal flight, the airship took in air, which is heavier than hydrogen, to descend. It released air to rise. Both took time. The airship rose fastest if it released water ballast, but it had a limited supply. To Imagawa's advantage, most sea-going vessels were not equipped with cannon that fired overhead.

"Descend now and take on water," suggested Mendeleev. "This will force us to fly low as we arrive, but if navy ships are waiting, you can release the water and air from the forward tanks. This will lift the nose." He mimed the action. "Then apply full power to the engines while you empty the tail tanks. We should shoot upward as fast as we're able." Ipokash tried to follow along. She stopped a few times and corrected herself.

Imagawa frowned but nodded, then turned around and explained the plan to Shichiroji with no pantomimes. He swallowed hard, then gave a sharp nod and said, "Hai!"

The ship began a slow descent toward the ocean. When it reached the water's surface, the crew deployed hoses and pumped water aboard. Once the ballast tanks were full, the ship began a long laborious ascent.

Soon, Hokkaido came into view and Imagawa barked orders. Her hands lifted skyward and Mendeleev guessed she ordered the crew to gain altitude.

They flew low enough the cries of startled fishermen reached Mendeleev's ears. *The Brazen Shark* just cleared the tree line a mile inland.

Imagawa looked from the clock to the ground. From time to time, she focused the spyglass on something below, then consulted the charts. At last, she looked up with grim determination and made a chopping motion. The helmsman shouted orders. *The Brazen Shark* tipped forward and Mendeleev stumbled a few steps before he recovered his balance.

The scientist dared to take a few more steps toward the gondola's forward window. Nanbu barred his teeth, but allowed him access. As Mendeleev reached the window, Imagawa handed him the spyglass.

Just ahead, Japanese Navy ships floated in Ishikari Bay. Imagawa allowed the dive to continue until Mendeleev could make out people on the decks. At that point, she gave a command and held out her hand for the spyglass. The scientist passed it to her, then looked over his shoulder to see crewmen opening the airship's bay doors.

A few minutes later, several bombs splashed into the water near the warships and explosions sent water plumes skyward. Imagawa barked orders and *The Brazen Shark* shuddered as the forward ballast tanks opened. The nose shot skyward and Mendeleev grabbed the rail in front of him to keep from tumbling. The ship shuddered as the mechanics revved up the engines and released more ballast.

Mendeleev worked his way to the gondola's stern to get a better view. Sailors on the ships below rolled mortars—the cannon that could lob shot highest—onto the decks.

"Release the remaining ballast," called Mendeleev. He mimed water falling and said "sploosh."

Imagawa shot him a look, then turned to the crewmen and gave them a sharp nod. They did as instructed and emptied the aft ballast tanks. The ship lurched upward even faster. Mendeleev's stomach dropped and he fought the urge to vomit.

Two mortars launched shells, but they fell far short of *The Brazen Shark.*

Imagawa gave another order and the airship leveled off. Mendeleev released a breath he didn't know he held. The scientist summoned Ipokash. "Did we achieve anything with those stunts?"

Imagawa laughed when Ipokash translated. A few minutes later, the Ainu woman relayed the samurai's short reply. "She accomplished exactly what she set out to do." Ipokash shrugged, not understanding the objective any better than Mendeleev.

The samurai leader strode through the gondola and issued orders. Soon the compass needle shifted just to the west of north. The elevator men opened the ballonets and took in air. The ship began a slow descent as it traveled over Hokkaido.

Two and a half hours after bombing Sapporo, Imagawa handed Mendeleev the spyglass. Before them lay a peninsula and a bay, which opened onto the straight between Hokkaido and Sakhalin.

When Imagawa turned away, Mendeleev handed the spyglass to Ipokash. "Can you tell where we are?" he whispered.

She looked and frowned, thinking about it for some time. She looked again, then returned the spyglass to Mendeleev. "I think it might be Wakkanai, but I'm not sure."

Imagawa whirled around and smiled. She spoke to Ipokash, then laughed. The Ainu woman blushed and lowered her eyes. "She says I have a good sense of geography."

The airship descended toward the docks. Imagawa walked back to the chart table. Curious, Mendeleev followed. No one made a move to stop him, so he beckoned Ipokash. Imagawa stared out the stern windows and Mendeleev followed her gaze.

The Brazen Shark's bay doors opened again and this time the scientist didn't recognize the objects which tumbled out. "What are those?"

"Simple smoke bombs." Ipokash translated Imagawa's words.

Perhaps a dozen people on the docks fled the wafting, black smoke. A few minutes later, ropes uncoiled and the samurai dressed in Russian uniforms, now wearing gas masks, climbed down.

"The smoke is safe," said Imagawa, "but the masks will make Wakkanai's people think it's poison. The peasants will have exciting stories to tell."

The gas masks will also obscure the faces of the samurai, thought Mendeleev.

Dogs barked, but no one fired shots. Mendeleev examined his pocket watch, then sat on the chart table's edge. He glanced over his shoulder at the gondola's door. They floated low enough, he entertained a fantasy of kicking it open and jumping out, but soon dismissed it. He might just get away, but where would he go? He would be a Russian in a village which thought it suffered a Russian raid. Such an escape would just play into Imagawa's plans.

Within the hour, the warriors returned to the airship carrying small bundles. Mendeleev recognized rice bags and liquor bottles. He almost rejoiced at the prospect of something to eat besides dried fish.

"*Legion, can you hear me?*" asked Mendeleev silently. "*If so, please let Morales and Cisneros know about the raid on Wakkanai. Have them ask why the mighty Russian army is reduced to stealing rice and sake.*"

Onofre Cisneros sat up from the plans he worked on and leaned against the wall. It provided his back much-needed relief. He closed his eyes and as his mind quieted, he witnessed a battle in progress. He opened his eyes again and looked around, then checked his pocket watch. Not enough time had passed for him to have fallen asleep or dreamed.

"*We are relaying images,*" came Legion's silent voice. "*Aboard the Russian airship, Mendeleev watches samurai raid Wakkanai.*"

"*Who else is seeing this?*" asked Cisneros.

"*Ramon Morales sees the images. He told the Lord of the Home Affairs samurai hijacked the airship. Based on Ramon's initial warning, the Home Affairs Lord convinced the navy to mount a defense in Sapporo.*"

Cisneros closed his eyes and continued to watch the scene as it unfolded. He noticed the samurai dressed in Russian uniforms and wearing gas masks. He groaned. Even if the Home Affairs Lord believed these were samurai, many ordinary people would not. If that were true, how many in the Cabinet of Lords would believe?

"*Can you pinpoint where the samurai take their airship between raids?*" asked Cisneros.

"*Not precisely. Mendeleev does not have regular access to the charts and tools necessary to determine that.*"

"*Why not enter a samurai's mind?*" pressed Cisneros.

Legion remained silent for a long time while Cisneros continued to watch images. If not for the pictures, the captain might have thought Legion departed.

"*What you propose is … problematic.*" Cisneros noted Legion's reticence.

Keeping his eyes closed, Cisneros focused on the view

through Mendeleev's eyes, trying to determine how he could help. *"How is it problematic?"*

"The experiment Ramon Morales proposed is to see if humans can solve their own problems. As it stands, our current involvement taints this experiment, but we are willing to proceed within these limits. We will show you what Mendeleev knows, but no more. You must find a solution to this crisis yourself."

Cisneros heaved a deep sigh. If they knew the Russian airship's location, Cisneros thought he could convince Katsu Kaishū and Captain Sanada to divert *Bashō* and stop the samurai, but did the little ship have sufficient manpower or weaponry to take such action?

Cisneros's thoughts turned to Hoshi. He knew Maravilla. Perhaps he also knew something of Legion and would understand the images he'd seen. The captain rose and knocked on the door across the way.

"Come in," called Hoshi.

The former samurai consulted the farmer's almanac. Cisneros's thoughts flashed to the season and he wondered if Hoshi had left the harvest.

"How well do you know Professor Maravilla?" Cisneros turned and closed the door.

Hoshi closed the book and set it on the low table next to him. "He is rude like you and not a little mad."

Cisneros smiled at the description. He sat cross-legged on the floor and faced Hoshi. "You've heard of Legion?" When Hoshi nodded, Cisneros pressed on. "What do you think it is?"

Hoshi's brow furrowed. "Gods or demons, if real. Perhaps you should tell me."

Cisneros shrugged. "Perhaps Legion is a little of both. You doubt its existence?"

Hoshi shrugged. "I believe whatever Legion is, he provides the professor insights and allows him to see things the professor alone could not see. It's unclear to me whether Legion is any less mad than the professor."

Cisneros suppressed a snort. "I don't think he's mad, but he is very ancient and perhaps a little bored. His personality is fragmented."

"Perhaps you could tell me more about why I'm here. All I

know is that Imagawa Masako has stolen an airship and plans to use it against Japan."

Cisneros nodded. "She has already attacked. She dropped bombs on Sapporo and her forces raid Wakkanai as we speak."

"I see." Hoshi folded his hands and looked down. After a moment, the samurai met Cisneros's gaze. "I gather there are two objectives. We must prevent Imagawa from wreaking further havoc and we must discourage Japan from attacking Russia."

"It sounds like Ramon Morales has convinced the Lord of Home Affairs to focus on defense rather than attack," said Cisneros.

Hoshi snorted. "The choice to send more defensive troops was not a difficult one for the Lord of Home Affairs who is concerned with keeping Japan safe. The people who must be convinced are the Lords of the Army and Navy."

"The Lord of the Navy is on this ship and I plan to meet with him today to discuss plans for strengthening the Japanese airships."

Hoshi nodded. "These ships are visible from miles away. Their primary offensive advantage is that few guns can fire high enough to destroy them."

"That's true." Cisneros's brow creased. He'd seen cannon fire destroy two airships, but they'd been grounded first. "Of course, it also means the airships can get close to a target and use little energy to strike."

"That is true, but I think it's a short-lived advantage." Hoshi brought out a piece of paper and dipped a brush in ink. He painted a jagged line. "To destroy airships, you must summon the gods of lightning. The Americans have done this and it dissuaded the Russians from pursuing their attack. Convince Katsu Kaishū he can summon lightning if he is patient. It may stay his hand."

A sly grin crept across the captain's face. "I can do you one better. I can show him how to summon the gods of thunder and although it's a power almost useless against a ground target, it will devastate a hydrogen-filled airship."

"Summoning thunder gods is easy. All you need is a drum," said Hoshi. "I don't see how that helps us."

"I speak of something which will produce a much larger bang than a mere drum, my friend."

Hoshi narrowed his gaze. "Interesting."

Cisneros nodded. "I just wish finding Imagawa was as easy."

As soon as he finished speaking with Hoshi, Cisneros returned to his quarters. He understood electromagnetic principles well enough to make some guesses about the gun Hoshi mentioned, but he had a simpler idea. He sketched a drawing and placed it underneath the stack he planned to show Captain Sanada and Katsu Kaishū.

He walked forward to the captain's quarters and knocked. The captain bade him enter. They both sat at the table. Katsu had dispensed with the western suit in favor of a kimono, white shirt, and hakama. Although the attire looked more casual at first glance, the one-time samurai seemed more menacing and ready for action than he had before.

Cisneros laid the plans on the table. "The fundamental advantage of airships is their ability to travel at altitude and their range. As you've seen, we have just crossed the Pacific and approach Japan in less than two weeks and in considerable comfort." Although his back twinged, he felt little irony, though chairs would make him a little happier. He presented a few ideas for improving the gas bags and engines. "In the long run I think airships are better suited for commerce than war. When used in war, I see them less as vehicles and more as floating fortresses."

Captain Sanada nodded, but Lord Katsu folded his arms. "They do have the ability to attack other airships on their own terms, at the same elevation."

"Indeed." Cisneros anticipated the question. He pulled out designs for enhanced ribbing around the gasbags which could hold soldiers behind shields. This airship resembled the flying fortress he described. "From such structures, soldiers could fire rifles or even crossbows."

"Crossbows?" asked Katsu, at once indignant but with curiosity piqued. "We use non-flammable gas aboard our airships. Why would we want such an ancient weapon?"

Cisneros   pulled   out   another   drawing.   "Imagine phosphorus-tipped crossbow bolts."

Sanada and Katsu studied the plans. Katsu looked up and nodded to Cisneros. "A fine idea and Japan produces phosphorus in good quantity. The Russian airships would indeed be vulnerable, but we'd have to be well within rifle and cannon range for phosphorus crossbow bolts to be effective."

"I have one more idea." The merchant captain's voice held an apologetic note. "It's so simple, I almost hesitate to show it." He withdrew a drawing of a simple rocket stand like those used to launch fireworks. "You could deploy simple rockets right away. Breech a Russian ship's outer skin and send a rocket inside, you'll blow it to kingdom come, as though you'd summoned the god of thunder."

"I like it," said Lord Katsu. "We will implement this soon."

Captain Sanada rubbed his chin. "I have heard the Americans have a lightning gun."

Cisneros sighed, wondering if everyone had heard about this weapon besides himself. He flipped the paper over and sketched batteries, spinning magnets, and electrodes. "I could develop a weapon like this, but it would take a few months, perhaps a year."

"Only a year…" Lord Katsu stood and walked to the window. "Spring departs. Birds cry. Fish eyes filled with tears."

"Beg your pardon?" Cisneros's eyebrows came together.

"Pardon me. It's a poem by Bashō. I see great power in the weapon you propose, but it also strikes me as terrible and frightening. I supported the Meiji Restoration because I thought Japan could benefit from contact with the outside world, but this would take Japan beyond learning. It would give Japan real power—power of conquest." Katsu turned around and shook his head. "I confess I fear such a weapon and pray we would have the wisdom to use it when necessary and not in vain attempts at conquest."

The subdued response took Cisneros aback.

"Develop this idea, but you must share it with no one besides myself." Katsu turned to Captain Sanada. "Never speak of this to anyone."

Sanada lowered his eyes to the table and spoke solemn words in Japanese.

Katsu retrieved small, flat-bottomed bowls and a bottle of sake. He poured three drinks, then held up his bowl. "I pray for the day when airships open up an exchange of ideas between Japan and the rest of the world. I pray for the day when we gain enough wisdom to appreciate each other rather than the vanity to destroy one another."

Cisneros lifted his bowl and drank. The wine soon left him light headed. He gathered up the plans and returned to his quarters.

"*If I may intrude,*" said Legion. "*I think I understand what disturbs Lord Katsu. Please be seated.*"

Cisneros lay the drawings aside, sat down and closed his eyes. Legion showed Cisneros a distant star, bloated and red. The star soon exploded. Cisneros attempted to blink, even though his eyes were already closed. The force of the stellar blast caused dust and gas clouds to collapse on themselves. They began to form a new star system surrounded by planets.

"*Destruction of this magnitude is a prelude to the power of creation,*" explained Legion. "*Lord Katsu is wise to eschew a power which could make him like a god.*"

"*And you?*" asked Cisneros. "*Have you ever been tempted to be a god?*"

"*We have been tempted and we have learned we do not have enough knowledge or wisdom for such a solemn responsibility.*"

Cisneros nodded, realizing even alien swarms deluded themselves.

Ramon's head pounded the day after visiting Lord Ōkubo, exacerbated by the visions Legion showed him of the raid on Wakkanai. Despite that, he felt as though a great weight had lifted. Before leaving the lord's home, Ōkubo drafted a letter they could present to any officials who stopped them, explaining they were the Meiji Government's guests. This allowed Ramon and Fatemeh freedom to explore again. Fatemeh decided she wanted to visit a Shinto shrine.

"Is it quiet there?" Ramon held his head as he asked the question.

"It's a good place for meditation," said Fatemeh.

An hour later, Lord Katsu's mechanical man pulled the rickshaw through Tokyo's streets until houses gave way to a rolling, grass-covered landscape. Thick, white clouds hung overhead. Green leaves still clung to many trees, but a few turned vivid reds, oranges and yellows. The rickshaw stopped at the base of a hill. A pathway led to a two-story building. Sloping roofs overhanging both the first and second floor extended into points. A wind chime sang a gentle melody. Almost two weeks after they arrived, Ramon began to fall in love with Japan and wished he could remain long enough to grow comfortable with the language.

"I've been reading about Japan's religions," explained Fatemeh, as they walked up the hill. "Shintoism is Japan's native religion and involves the worship of the local gods who help with the harvests, trade, war, whatever." Near the Shinto shrine, visible through pine trees stood a Buddhist temple. "The Buddhists, on the other hand, don't even seem to have a god. They believe self is illusion and if we live a noble life, we'll be reincarnated in a higher station than the one we occupied as mortals."

"A higher station?" asked Ramon. "You mean like if we were miners, we'd come back as mine owners."

She shrugged. "That's one interpretation, but they seem to believe in other planes of existence as well, also other worlds."

"You seem troubled."

"Only because this idea resembles what you've told me about the vision Legion showed you." She sighed. "The idea that self is an illusion scares me a little."

Ramon's eyes widened. "You? Scared?"

She shivered and stepped closer to Ramon. "I've been scared and running for years. You're the first person who has made me want to settle down and find my own place."

Ramon looked up the steps toward the temple. "This place seems more peaceful than scary."

"They say ghosts haunt the temples and keep the gods company."

Ramon reached out and gave her hand a discrete squeeze. "Ghosts can't harm us." With that he led her up the steps.

At the top, a priest greeted them in Japanese. Fatemeh

asked if they could pray. The priest bowed and indicated where they should go. They removed their shoes and walked through the entranceway where they reached a stone basin. "We should wash our hands," explained Fatemeh.

She retrieved a dipper and poured water over Ramon's hands, then poured water first over her left, then her right hand. Once done she poured some water into her cupped hand and brought it to her mouth. She offered the dipper to Ramon again.

Fatemeh tilted her head back and gargled. Ramon laughed and nearly spit the water at her. She glared at him as they proceeded through the door into the main hall. Three other people knelt in silent prayer or contemplation. One stood up and left, bowing as he passed Ramon and Fatemeh.

Fatemeh reached up and rang a bell hanging by the door, causing Ramon's head to pound anew.

"Why'd you do that?"

"It makes sure we have the attention of the kami—the gods."

"It sure got my attention."

She placed some coins in a wooden box next to the door, then went inside and knelt down.

"What do you plan to pray for?" asked Ramon.

"Peace." The way she hissed the word, Ramon wasn't sure if she meant to answer the question or requested him to shut up and leave her alone. Ramon thought he might as well pray too, though he had to admit he felt more than a little sacrilegious praying to pagan gods.

As Ramon knelt down, a strange sensation washed over him, as though something transported him from the temple. At first he blamed the hangover, then he looked down and saw a diagram of a machine with strong hydraulic rear legs which raised and lowered it. Gears and pulleys manipulated claws which could reach out and grasp things and place them into a maw. A storage basket awaited in the machine's belly. Voices discussed the force necessary to pick chile peppers and whether hopping optimized the device's locomotion. The voices belonged to Legion, but other voices resonated in the background as well.

"Have you reached a verdict?" A judge posed the question. "We have," came another voice.

The view shifted as though Ramon looked up for a moment. He recognized the courtroom in Mesilla. Billy McCarty and Luther Duncan sat at a table with a lawyer. From the ramrod straight demeanor, bushy mustache and short, dark hair, Ramon gathered the lawyer must be Albert Fountain. They were in good hands.

The view shifted back to the paper for a moment while the clerk retrieved the written verdict from the jury foreman. Hands sketched a battery and a few more linkages and gears.

"What am I seeing?" Ramon asked.

"We thought you wanted to know Mr. McCarty and Mr. Duncan's fate. You see the end of their trial as witnessed by Professor Maravilla," explained Legion.

"Couldn't you have picked a more focused person?"

Someone shushed.

Ramon remembered, he actually knelt in a Shinto temple on Tokyo's outskirts, even though he "saw" a courthouse in Las Cruces, New Mexico.

"We stay with those already familiar with us," explained Legion. *"To do more would be to interfere more."*

"I understand." Ramon thought the words instead of speaking them aloud.

"Mr. McCarty, Mr. Duncan please rise," said the judge. They did and Fountain stood alongside them. "The jury has found you not guilty of aiding and abetting enemies of the United States of America."

Billy let out a loud whoop and Luther shook Fountain's hand.

The judge banged his gavel to restore order to the proceedings. "You gentlemen did, however, escape lawful confinement from the Presidio and the jury has found you guilty of that offense. I sentence you to thirty days at the territorial prison in Santa Fe."

Luther deflated and fell back into his chair. Billy dropped beside him and patted him on the back. Ramon caught words to the effect, "That ain't so bad. It'll be over in no time."

Maravilla's attention drifted back to his drawing and the

view faded. The courtroom voices merged into Fatemeh's. "Ramon, are you okay?"

Ramon blinked and realized he lay on his back, staring up at the ceiling. "I'm fine," he breathed as Fatemeh helped him sit up. "Legion just gave me a look at Luther and Billy's trial."

She indicated the others present, then helped him stand. The two walked outside the prayer hall and he led her into the woods where they could speak privately. "What happened?"

"Not guilty of treason," said Ramon, "but they have to serve thirty days for escaping the Presidio." Looking at Fatemeh, Ramon sighed. He didn't want to spend thirty days separated from her just as their life began to settle down.

She reached out and took his hand. "It's a good outcome … far better than we expected."

Ramon nodded. If Billy and Luther had been found guilty of treason, they could have been executed. To live, Ramon and Fatemeh would have needed to seek permanent exile. Ramon wasn't sure he could have lived with the guilt.

"One thing's for certain. I did encounter spirits in this shrine." Ramon pulled Fatemeh close and held her until he stopped trembling.

CHAPTER TWELVE
SHIFTING TIDES

Shinriki sat in the cell's perpetual twilight chanting an old song. The song held no particular meaning. It just filled the inactive void which came from days on end doing nothing. He knew he had committed no crime, but he had heard stories of Russians seeing crimes where none existed and punishing those people they believed had committed them.

An outside doorway creaked open and heavy boots marched down the hall. It seemed early for supper, but late for a trial. Perhaps the guard marched another prisoner to an adjoining cell. He shuddered at the possibility that a prisoner might be placed in the cell with him. Although he would appreciate the company, he couldn't help but think such a person might be a real criminal.

Keys rattled and Shinriki looked up. The guard wrenched the door open and tossed in a pouch. Shinriki hesitated, then stepped off the bed and approached the bundle. It contained the few things the guards had taken from him when they first threw him in the cell—his knife, his necklace, his coin pouch.

"You're free to go," called the guard. "The magistrate doesn't believe you could have stolen the horses and the time you've served is sufficient for disturbing the peace."

Shinriki blinked. "What if the samurai bandits return?"

The guard laughed, but it contained no malice. Rather it was the laugh of a parent confronted with a child's musing. "Then deal with them." The guard's expression turned cold. "If you value your freedom, don't come back to Poronaysk."

Shinriki sighed and gathered his belongings. The guard escorted him outside, then turned and locked the outer door before he marched back toward his office. The cold wind made Shinriki shudder. He looked up at the orange-streaked cirrus clouds above and thought perhaps another storm would be approaching within two or three days. Returning to his hut where he could build a fire would be good, but it would be just as lonely as the cell.

He trudged through town, back to the river. Late as it was, the fishermen had returned to the village leaving him with no easy passage across. Some Russian boats stood on the river banks. He could just take one and return it with help in the morning. He worried the Russians might use such a temporary theft as an excuse to throw him back in the cell.

He considered seeing if one of the Poronaysk Ainu would help him. Shinriki had two cousins who worked in the factories. Perhaps they could put him up for the night. As he contemplated the possibilities, he caught a distant thrumming sound. He looked up. The first stars twinkled through gossamer clouds in a darkening sky. Among them, a dark form drifted toward the samurai's highland camp. It was the airship! Was Ipokash aboard? He knew deep down in his bones she must be. Would anyone help him seek her? He doubted that.

At last, Shinriki reached a decision. He pushed a Russian boat into the water, climbed in, and rowed across. He would find no help in Poronaysk.

Japan spread out like an inviting green and brown blanket atop still waters. The reddening sun sat on the horizon, streaking the sky orange and white. Lights winked on around Tokyo. All around the *Bashō's* bridge, the crew kept watch. Captain Sanada called out slight course corrections to the helmsman.

As they drifted over Tokyo Bay, Onofre Cisneros sighted the *Ballena* and his heart beat double-time. Accompanying this ship had been a privilege and a thrill, but he missed his own ship and was glad to see it safe and sound.

He turned his attention back to the city. The sun dropped below the horizon in a twinkling and the city lights began to swirl. Dizzy, Cisneros excused himself and returned to his cabin. He sat down and closed his eyes. A scene of forest and low hills played before him.

"Mendeleev knows where he is." Legion's voice echoed within his mind.

"Can you show me?" whispered the captain.

Legion showed the captain an image of the Earth. They zoomed in to an island just north of Japan. A small, industrial town perched near the point where a river emptied into a large bay. Legion expanded the view to show an inland mountain range near the town. An orange dot blinked on and off, like some obscene demonic eye.

"The location is approximate, but Mendeleev said the airship flew over these mountains on the way to Poronaysk. The airship is moored at a clearing near a lodge. Imagawa is angry because she expected to find horses and a supply cache. The supplies were there, but the horses are gone."

"Bandits must have taken the horses." Cisneros folded his arms. "Do you know how long they plan to stay?"

"Unknown," said Legion. *"Mendeleev thinks Imagawa planned to take the horses and leave the airship behind. Her plans require adjustment now that they must travel by foot."*

"Thank you, Legion. I think speed will be essential." The captain considered the necessary steps to reach Sakhalin Island. "Contact Ramon. Tell him to pack and meet us aboard the *Ballena*. Ask him to relay a message to my first mate to ready the ship for immediate departure."

"What do you hope to accomplish?"

"I hope to find a way to prevent Imagawa from causing more damage." Cisneros sat on the floor until his vision cleared. A slow, sinking sensation told him the airship dropped toward a mooring. The captain walked across the hall and knocked on Hoshi's door.

The samurai looked out. "Will we land soon?"

"Almost." Cisneros leaned in close. "Be ready to leave as soon as possible, Legion has just determined Imagawa's location."

Hoshi gave a curt nod. "I'm already packed."

Cisneros returned to the bridge. The palace grounds lay below. The hangar roof opened and bright lights illuminated the interior. Captain Sanada ordered the engines shut down and an eerie silence ensued. The ship took on air and descended. Sanada called for mooring ropes to be lowered. Soon the ground crew in the hangar leapt for the ropes and pulled. Cisneros held on to stabilize himself against the ride's sudden jerkiness.

As the airship neared the hangar floor, Japanese naval officers approached. The gondola door opened and the ladder dropped out even as the ground crews tied off the ropes.

An officer wearing gold epaulets and a sash strode forward. As he climbed aboard the airship, the boatswain snapped to attention and piped him aboard. Cisneros smirked at how the Japanese Navy had adopted this western custom.

"Lord Katsu," said the admiral. "We've been anxiously awaiting your return. May I have a word?"

Katsu Kaishū nodded and stepped close to the admiral. The two spoke in low tones. While they did, Cisneros slipped back to his cabin and threw his belongings into a duffel bag. When he returned to the bridge, the admiral had departed and Katsu wore a worried frown. "There you are," he said. "I fear I must depart right away. A … situation has arisen."

Cisneros had to remind himself the Naval Lord could not know about the attack on Sapporo and Wakkanai or that Ramon and Fatemeh had already discussed matters with the Lord of Home Affairs. It would take too long to explain all that, not to mention explaining why he hid his knowledge during the flight.

Cisneros reached out and shook Katsu's hand. "I must depart as well. Work has piled up in Ensenada during my absence. The sooner I return, the sooner I can make progress on a hangar and the designs we discussed."

"Then you're interested in continuing to work with us?"

"I wouldn't miss the opportunity." Cisneros spoke without irony but hoped he didn't seem too anxious to depart. Now that things proceeded so well, he had no desire to let Imagawa start a war. He had to capture her and bring her back to Japan for justice before her plans escalated further.

"I am delighted to hear it," said Katsu. "I look forward to working with you."

"Until we meet again."

Cisneros and Katsu each bowed. The Naval Lord climbed

down the ladder and followed the officers from the hangar. Masuda Hoshi appeared at the control room door. Cisneros gave him a brief nod, then turned to the captain. "Sir, I must take my leave. Thank you for allowing me to accompany you on this first Japanese trans-Pacific airship voyage."

"It was our honor," said Sanada. The two captains exchanged bows.

Cisneros excused himself long enough to retrieve his duffle bag, then he followed Hoshi down the ladder. Once outside, they paused to let their eyes adjust to the dark night, relieved by just a few gas lamps. This late, finding transportation to the docks seemed hopeless. The two shouldered their bags and began to walk.

"Yesterday, when Legion showed me the end of McCarty and Duncan's trial, Maravilla sketched a machine. Normally he builds machines to study animal behavior but this one looked like no animal I recognized."

Hoshi groaned. "I'll be ruined for sure."

"What do you mean?"

"With Billy in prison for thirty days, there's no one to look after my crops. Maravilla has clearly decided to be helpful and build a mechanical harvester. It no doubt subsists on chiles."

"I could always ask Legion to watch over him, make sure the machine works as it's supposed to."

Hoshi considered for a moment, then shook his head. "No thanks. I'll have enough losses if Maravilla is involved. I can't imagine the mess we'll create if we let that devil get involved as well."

"I suppose this means the honeymoon is over." Ramon stood next to Fatemeh at the *Ballena's* stern rail, watching Tokyo's lights recede behind them.

"The honeymoon doesn't have to end." She reached out, took his hand, and brought him close. "We just have to enjoy what we're doing."

He embraced her and they shared a long kiss. Ramon moved to her cheek, then kissed her neck when he noticed a presence in the deckhouse's shadows. Ramon glanced up. "May I help you?"

A Japanese man emerged from the shadows, holding up a hand. "I apologize. I did not mean to intrude. I was out for a stroll and saw you. I wanted to speak, then realized you were... otherwise engaged. I was about to leave."

"No, no." Fatemeh held up her hand. "It's okay. You're Mr. Masuda, correct?"

The man bowed. Ramon and Fatemeh returned the gesture.

"We've wanted to speak to you as well," said Ramon. "We should find Captain Cisneros and see if he's available."

The three exchanged glances, then entered the deckhouse and descended a level. They knocked on the captain's door. The steward answered. "It's all right," called the captain from within. "We need to make plans."

The steward stepped aside and Cisneros invited them to join him at the table. "Bring us coffee," ordered the captain.

"If it's all the same to you, I would prefer tea," said Hoshi.

Cisneros nodded to the steward, who disappeared. "I don't know about you two, but I've missed chairs."

Ramon and Fatemeh smiled to one another. Hoshi folded his arms. "Chairs weaken the back," he said. "They're bad for a warrior."

"Well, I don't intend to be a warrior." Fatemeh leaned forward.

"You are perhaps the best warrior here." A faint smile appeared as Hoshi spoke. "You are, after all, a healer. What is a healer but a warrior against disease and injury?"

Fatemeh nodded, accepting the definition.

Hoshi continued. "Japan has been healing itself after a civil war. Unlike the one in the United States, a new order took over. The difference is the old order, the Tokugawa regime, resembled your confederates with power distributed among separate houses. The new order, the Meiji regime, is more like the Union, with power consolidated in the emperor. Imagawa is perhaps like a Confederate general in that she is disappointed in the loss and cannot accept the outcome. She sees the new order as disease and wants to correct it by forcing the Meiji army into a conflict they cannot win."

Cisneros leaned forward. "We know that. The problem is, how do we stop her?"

A knock sounded, heralding the steward's return. He set a tray down on the table with both a teapot and a coffee carafe. Assorted empanadas—Mexican fruit pastries—also covered the tray.

Ramon took a pastry. "What happens if we prove to the Russians Imagawa has taken the airship?"

Hoshi shook his head. "Russians would see a Japanese force on Karafuto Island as an incursion. It would start the very war Imagawa desires." He poured a cup of tea. "I fear the Russians may not distinguish between rebels or the army stealing their airship. The result may well be the same."

"I see no choice but to capture the airship," said Cisneros.

"I don't think the answer lies in force." Fatemeh stood, poured a cup of coffee, and handed it to Captain Cisneros. "With all due respect, I don't think you have the manpower aboard this ship to fight the samurai." She poured coffee for Ramon.

Ramon took the cup and sipped. "We could get a message to Dmitri Mendeleev through Legion. Maybe he could invent an emergency which would force the samurai to leave the ship, like a hydrogen leak or something."

Cisneros considered that. "Yes, it doesn't take a large force to fly the ship."

"I fear Imagawa would not be deceived and take steps to prevent the capture, unless…" Hoshi set the teacup down and stared off into the distance.

"Unless?" pressed Fatemeh.

"She would fight me if I challenged her to a duel. It might blind her long enough for the ruse to be effective."

Fatemeh opened her mouth to protest, but Ramon placed a gentle hand on her forearm. "Would you prevail in such a fight?" he asked.

Hoshi took a deep breath and released it. "I don't know."

Fatemeh pushed Ramon's hand aside. "You wouldn't kill Imagawa, would you?"

"Only if I had no choice." Hoshi looked down at the table,

as though afraid to meet Fatemeh's eyes.

Ramon suspected the emotion wasn't fear, but something closer to regret. Either way, they needed to focus on the mission. "Okay, then, how do we get there? If we don't want to attract the Russians' attention, we can't just sail up to Poronaysk in the *Ballena*."

Cisneros stood and walked over to his desk. He opened the drawer, retrieved a map and laid it out on the table. He pointed. "We're sailing east now. At midnight, I intend to order a course change north by northwest. It'll take about two days to reach Poronaysk at *Ballena's* top speed. We can take the *Calamar* into the bay. Depending on how deep it is, perhaps we can go a ways up the Poronay River."

"How many people will fit in this *Calamar*?" Hoshi leaned forward and studied the map.

"Six." Cisneros leaned back and folded his arms.

"Six? How do we manage this with six people?" Ramon's brow furrowed.

Hoshi nodded. "If I distract Imagawa, that leaves five to pilot the airship, some of whom will need to release the mooring lines."

"It only leaves four crewmen to help pilot the airship," corrected Cisneros. "One will stay with the *Calamar*. I won't leave it behind, and it could come in handy to have someone meet the airship somewhere." He tapped his forehead. "It's not hopeless, though. There are three experienced Russians aboard the ship and the Ainu woman who translates. If those who release the mooring lines can get aboard, Mendeleev will have eight people. I hope that will be enough to lift the ship. If not, the person who stays with the *Calamar* can bring reinforcements."

"I don't like this plan," said Ramon. "Too much can go wrong."

"Too much has already gone wrong," said Fatemeh. "I just hope we can make it better."

"If we're agreed, I'll make arrangements," said the captain.

The group around the table exchanged glances, then after a moment, they all nodded.

"Take these next two days to catch up on some rest," suggested the captain. "By my estimate, we'll be ready to launch the *Calamar* at seven in the morning day after tomorrow."

Hoshi, Ramon, and Fatemeh stood and left the captain's cabin. As Ramon and Fatemeh reached their cabin, Fatemeh reached out and grabbed Hoshi's arm. "What exactly is your relationship to Imagawa? I've heard she was your student, but I see hurt in your eyes whenever someone says her name. Is there something more?"

Hoshi put his hands behind his back. "To me, being a samurai is a matter of service. I served my shogun and the daimyo. I served the peasants who farmed the land. I thought I'd instilled these virtues in Imagawa." He looked down and his eyes glistened with unshed tears. "She fell in love with warfare and the idea that samurai must fight to the death. In a way, the Meiji restoration proved a dream come true for her. It gave her war and death."

"Did you love her?" Fatemeh's question was gentle yet urgent.

"I thought she had died." Hoshi shook his head. "I saw her lying as though dead, but it turns out she's alive. I worry I betrayed her. I also wonder if she did it to deceive me."

"Why would she do that?" Ramon narrowed his gaze.

"Perhaps she thought my presence was… cumbersome."

"I'm sorry." Fatemeh grabbed his arms and stared into his eyes. "Just don't let your hurt lead you into something foolish."

"I'm more of a warrior than that, Mrs. Morales." He gave a curt nod and turned away. "Good night."

Ramon and Fatemeh entered the moonlit cabin. Ramon undressed without bothering to light the lamp. "Are you angry the plan involves Hoshi challenging Imagawa?"

Cloth rustled and laces whispered. "I can't say I like it, but neither am I angry." He startled as she wrapped her arms around him, but enjoyed her naked flesh against his back. "All I know is that I want to know love. This honeymoon is far from over, Ramon Morales."

As the first Japanese officer to take an airship across the Pacific, Captain Sanada expected a triumphant return to Tokyo. He thought there might be a parade or a ceremonial dinner. At least, he expected a few days off to relax and spend time with his family.

Instead, he found the city in an uproar. Aids swept Lord Katsu into meetings and the morning after his return, engineers began attaching a new assembly to each side of the *Bashō's* catwalk. Horrified, Sanada saw the same structure on the *Bashō's* sister ship, the *Bonchō*. Bombs lined the new structure.

Captain Sanada approached an engineer. "What is the meaning of this?"

"Orders from the Imperial Palace." The man reached into his back pocket, retrieved a folded up newspaper and thrust it at the captain.

Sanada unfolded the newspaper and read about the attacks on Sapporo and Wakkanai. His knees threatened to give way and he looked around for someplace to sit. He dropped down on a chair in front of a nearby workbench. According to the article, the Lord of Home Affairs possessed intelligence suggesting rogue samurai conducted the attacks, but several navy officers reported the ship had Russian markings. Even more damning, the airship dropped gas on Wakkanai and Russian soldiers raided the city.

He looked up at the *Bashō*. Lord Katsu had convinced the emperor to fund the airships based on the idea they could defend Japan, but Sanada knew the Russians would never be so foolish as to invade. He expected many peaceful journeys carrying cargo to Mexico and perhaps the United States.

He folded up the newspaper and left it on the workbench, then walked out to the street. He waited for a horse drawn streetcar and climbed aboard. A few minutes later, it passed near his neighborhood. He climbed off and trudged home.

Opening the door, his young daughters' shouts cheered him for a moment. His wife gasped. "I didn't expect you home so soon."

"There is little for me to do until I receive orders," said the captain. "It looks like I may have to leave again soon. I want to spend time with my family."

"Why would you leave?" She looked down. "Not that business with the Russians?"

Sanada nodded, then gave his daughters an extra squeeze. "Let me get you dinner." His wife stood and retrieved another plate. She brought it to the table and the captain ate.

Soon after dinner, a knock sounded at the door. Sanada answered. A man in a navy uniform saluted, then handed the captain a sealed packet. He took it, opened it, and read. "I am to depart first thing in the morning."

Each cabin aboard the *Ballena* came equipped with something Captain Cisneros called an "alarm clock." The simple device could be adjusted to ring a bell when the clock reached a certain time. It was still dark outside when the alarm clock went off. Fatemeh rubbed her sleep-crusted eyes and silently cursed the Frenchman who gave Cisneros the idea for this infernal device. She climbed out of bed, then prodded Ramon before dressing.

Knowing they planned to trudge through scrub brush in uncertain weather, Fatemeh selected a pair of canvas pants she'd sewn for herself. Although she'd resented the implication she should learn to sew so she could attract a husband, she had to admit the skill came in handy as an adult.

Ramon and Fatemeh were ready by the time Captain Cisneros's steward arrived with breakfast. They ate then made their way to the deck. There, crewmen attached hooks from a crane to the *Calamar*. Hoshi joined them on deck and put his hands behind his back as he eyed the submersible. He wore a katana at his waist.

Two crewmen approached. Fatemeh recognized Jorge Apodaca who had been an owl rider in the Battle of Denver. She shook his hand and introduced him to Ramon. Apodaca introduced his companion, Carlos Rodriguez. "The captain owes us a little shore time. After all, we've been minding the store while he's been gallivanting around in airships."

"Hey!" the captain pointed at Apodaca. "You were granted all the shore time you wanted as long as you completed your duties. Mr. Gonzalez would have granted more if you hadn't been slacking off."

Fatemeh smiled at the banter, pleased to have some of the owl riders reunited for this venture.

Cisneros summoned those assembled and they climbed aboard the *Calamar*. The undersea vessel had two seats up front for the pilot and co-pilot. The other four seats sat against the outer walls, angled slightly, so the occupant could turn their head and look outside. From their earlier tour, Fatemeh realized this was less to allow sightseeing and more because the captain could use help watching for obstacles.

Piping and control cable ductwork ran overhead. Clearly, the captain chose function over luxury when he designed the submersible. Cisneros took the pilot seat and Apodaca sat next to him in the co-pilot's chair. Rodriquez took a seat in the back and, at the captain's command, activated the chemical reaction steam engine. The engine began a rhythmic whosh-whosh as the water in the boiler heated.

Cisneros stood and poked his head out through the hatch. "We're ready."

The deck crane hoisted the *Calamar* off the deck, then lowered it down the side. The craft swayed from side to side until they reached the water with a lurch. As the crane cable slackened, the craft bobbed in the turbulent water beside the ship. Cisneros and Apodaca climbed out and released the hooks, then closed the door. The captain engaged the propeller and the boat tumbled away through the rough waves. Cisneros reached over and turned several valves in rapid succession and soon the little boat dropped below the surface.

Fatemeh wanted to enjoy the underwater sights, but thoughts of confronting Imagawa absorbed her. She turned and faced Ramon. His eyes were closed and at first she thought he napped. Then she noticed his lips moving. A moment later, his eyes popped open.

He looked around, as though confused. "I just spoke to Legion. Mendeleev says he can distract the samurai. We should let him know when we're near."

Fatemeh wondered what it would be like to have such intimate first-hand contact with her husband's thoughts. Was Legion privy to thoughts about her she didn't even know? She tried to brush those concerns aside as she reached over and squeezed Ramon's hand. He smiled back at her. She loved the kindness behind his smile. Ramon boarded this submersible because he cared about her and about the Japanese who he'd just met. He cared about people around the world who could be affected by Imagawa's selfish actions.

She turned and looked out at the fish swimming beside the *Calamar*. She wondered if they were curious about the alien craft in their midst. If so, they gave no indication.

"I see where the Poronay River flows out into the bay," announced Cisneros. He shook his head. "There's a shelf there and the river bed appears shallow. I think I can get us to shore though."

As they progressed, the ride roughened. Fatemeh grabbed onto the seat's armrest and wished some kind of restraint existed to hold her in. She thought she would tumble to the deck at any moment. Soon, the submarine scraped bottom and ground to a halt. "We're on the shelf, not far from shore," he said.

"Will you be able to get the *Calamar* out of here, Captain?" asked Apodaca.

"No problem. It's low tide. We'll get some more water under us in a few hours. At worst, I'll lower the treads and roll to deeper water." While making plans the day before, they decided Cisneros should remain with the *Calamar*. He and Ramon could communicate over long distance via Legion. This allowed them to adjust meeting times and locations as needed.

The passengers climbed the ladder. When Fatemeh reached the top, she gritted her teeth and feared they'd have to swim for shore. Then she looked at Ramon, and remembered he couldn't swim. She climbed back down. "If you can lower the treads and roll into deeper water, can't you lower them and roll to shore?"

"And risk the army spotting us?" Cisneros shook his head. "I'm proud of the *Calamar*, but there's little she can do against an airship in the hills and I don't want soldiers shooting at us."

As they spoke, Rodriguez retrieved a gutta-percha parcel. Fatemeh followed him up the ladder. He disconnected a hose near the hatch and attached it to the parcel, which soon inflated and proved to be a small boat.

Those going ashore climbed aboard and rowed to the

beach. Apodaca and Rodriguez consulted a map while Fatemeh took in the landscape. A small village, recently ransacked and rebuilt stood nearby.

"This is Ipokash's village," mused Ramon.

"Ipokash?" asked Fatemeh.

"She's an Ainu woman, who has been translating for Mendeleev."

"We should avoid attention," suggested Hoshi.

A shout rose from the village. An arrow struck the ground at Hoshi's feet.

"Too late for that," said Fatemeh.

A man knelt near the closest hut and nocked a second arrow. Another man held a spear and strode toward them.

CHAPTER THIRTEEN
SHARK HUNT

Hoshi drew his sword. Apodaca aimed a revolver.

Fatemeh stepped between and called out in Japanese. "We're here to help."

The older man, who held the spear, took a step forward. "Samurai have done plenty to 'help' us." He spoke halting, broken Japanese as though long out of practice.

"We are not samurai." Fatemeh cast a fleeting, guilty glance back toward Hoshi. "We seek to stop samurai who are out to hurt people." She cringed, hoping the men understood.

The older man lowered the spear somewhat. Ramon gestured for the men around him to follow suit.

"He is samurai." The man with the spear gestured to Hoshi.

"I *was* samurai." Hoshi spoke in his native Japanese. "I am now a humble farmer. I seek to stop those samurai who have turned to banditry."

Ramon spoke one word. "Ipokash."

The spear-wielding man took two more steps forward. "Ipokash? What do you know of Ipokash?"

Fatemeh's brow furrowed at the familiar word. A moment later, she remembered what Ramon said before people started waving weapons around. "Was Ipokash taken from this village?" asked Fatemeh in Japanese.

The spear-wielding man looked back at his companion, then rested the spear's haft on the ground. "Is she all right?"

Fatemeh repeated the question to Ramon, who nodded.

The older man took several wary steps forward. He wore a thick beard and a robe similar to Hoshi's kimono but it bore a more abstract, geometrical pattern. "Ipokash is my wife," he said. "The bandits captured her almost three weeks ago. I fear for her."

148

Hoshi looked over to Ramon. "How has she been treated?" He whispered in English. "We must be as straightforward and truthful as possible."

Ramon considered what he knew via Legion. "She's been treated well—for a servant. A few men have wanted... to have their way with her, but Imagawa has stopped them."

"She would," affirmed Hoshi. He turned and spoke in Japanese.

The older man approached the group. He beckoned his companion, whose beard was little more than a light fuzz. "My name is Shinriki." The spear-wielding man gestured over his shoulder. "This is my cousin, Resak. The airship the samurai stole flew to a lodge in the mountains. We are going to free Ipokash."

Hoshi looked to Ramon. "Didn't they go there two days ago?" Ramon nodded and Hoshi addressed Shinriki in Japanese. "Why did you wait? Are you sure they're still there?"

Shinriki's face crumpled in pain. "The Russians jailed me for asking too many questions. They just released me two days ago. When I returned, I found no one but Resak would help. They feared going to prison as I did. I wanted to leave right away but Resak persuaded me to rest and gain my strength. I am ready to fight."

He did not answer Hoshi's second question. The expedition would be futile if the samurai bandits left. Fatemeh reminded herself Ramon would know if they departed because Mendeleev would tell them. "We go to take the airship from the samurai. Would you lead us to their camp?"

Fatemeh approached Hoshi. "We can't involve them. They don't know what they're up against."

Hoshi shook his head. "They know better than anyone." He pointed to the huts and the recent repairs. "The samurai took Ipokash in a raid on this village. Shinriki here must have survived through luck. It appears many men were killed in the raid."

"What do you know of the..." Fatemeh struggled to find a word. She mimed a large object moving through the sky.

"I have seen the airship. A Russian called Mendeleev brought it here. I found a newspaper article in the samurai camp. I believe they stole the airship." Shinriki spoke the words with a forced conviction, as though he expected not to be believed.

Hoshi turned to Fatemeh and Ramon. "These men could lead us right to the samurai. No doubt they know the mountains far better than we do."

"They'll get themselves killed," hissed Fatemeh.

Ramon squeezed her shoulder. "We might get ourselves killed. Hoshi's talking sense. If we go crashing through the mountains without knowing where the lodge is, there's a good chance we'll be seen and lose the element of surprise. These men are going anyway. We could use more help."

Fatemeh sighed and looked down. "You're right."

Hoshi asked the question again. "Would you lead us to the samurai camp? We will help you free Ipokash."

Resak spoke sharp words, but Shinriki held up his hand. The younger man lowered his bow and his arms trembled as he relaxed. "Resak is young and hot-headed," explained Shinriki. "He worries about trusting you. I don't blame him. The Russians have told us to come to them in times of trouble, but they have proven unworthy of my trust. You are, however, the first who have believed me when I say samurai took the airship. Why?"

"We were in Japan when the samurai attacked Hokkaido." Fatemeh tripped over the words, but she thought she made herself understood.

Shinriki nodded, accepting the statement. He looked back at the gutta-percha boat on the shore. "You should hide your boat before we depart." He cast a glance toward Poronaysk. "If they're on their guard, the Russians will not appreciate strangers landing on their shores."

Hoshi translated the words for Apodaca and Rodriguez. They holstered their revolvers and nodded to each other. "Agreed, we should hide the boat. The gutta-percha can get brittle if it's left out," said Apodaca. He returned to the boat, unloaded the supplies, then withdrew a plug. The boat shrank down and Apodaca folded it into a small parcel one man could carry.

The group from the *Ballena* gathered up the supplies, then

followed Shinriki to his hut where they stashed the boat. When they emerged, several villagers stood in front of the huts. An old man asked Shinriki a question in the Ainu language. Shinriki answered and the old man looked worried for a moment, then smiled, nodded, and raised his hand in a gesture of blessing and goodwill.

Shinriki gestured for the group from the *Calamar* to follow him back to the river.

Captain Sanada thought the ten-hour flight across the Sea of Japan was all too brief after having crossed the Pacific. The *Bonchō's* presence out the starboard window reassured him. He still didn't know what to think. Had the Russians really been stupid enough to attack Japan?

The airships arrived over Vladivostok in the afternoon. Sanada ordered airmen out to the catwalk. He scanned the city with a spyglass and found the small naval base. The Russians had acquired Vladivostok from the Chinese less than twenty years before. The seaport village's wooden and block structures on rolling hills looked almost Japanese to him.

"We have a signal from the *Bonchō*," called Sanada's first officer. He handed a paper to the captain.

The captain eyed the recommended targets and nodded. He trusted Captain Himura's judgement. "Move us into position and drop us to one-thousand feet."

"Yes, sir," said the first officer.

The dirigible drifted over the naval base. Ironclad ships anchored in the harbor. Men ran along the decks, implying alarms sounded, though the distance was too great to hear. He took the speaking tube and called to the men on the catwalk. "Drop the bombs."

A moment later, dark objects plummeted toward the first ship. Several struck together near the bow, sending up a shower of sparks, metal, and wood in a great smoke plume.

"This autumn, why am I aging so? To the clouds a bird." The haiku by the poet Bashō captured Sanada's melancholy over the destruction. The target tipped, bow downward. The captain didn't need to watch any longer to know it would sink into the bay.

They drifted inland and dropped another salvo on the naval base itself. The first officer shouted and Captain Sanada whirled around with his spyglass. The *Bonchō's* first target ship had not sunk after all. They whirled a deck cannon toward them.

"Drop ballast, give us some altitude!"

"But, sir, what cannon can fire even this high?" asked the first officer.

"Don't argue, just do it!"

The first officer turned to issue the commands, but too late. A smoke plume issued from the cannon. Soon after, a shell tore through the balloon above the captain's head. Sanada ordered the engines revved up to full power, to try to get some distance from the naval base, but the ship plummeted as the gaping hole expelled helium. The captain dropped to his knees and grabbed the railing. "Try to steer out to sea. It's our best chance to survive."

The captain wished he'd taken time to visit the temple and pray to the gods. He hoped they heard his prayer now. He wanted to make it home and see his wife and daughters again. He prayed this attack on Russia would not be in vain. Just then, the ship hit the water and all became a roar as darkness engulfed Captain Sanada.

A courier delivered a telegram to General Dragomirov in the map room of Army Headquarters in St. Petersburg. The general opened the telegram and read. As he did, the room's temperature seemed to rise. "Major Zolnerowich!"

The adjutant stood, marched to the general, and saluted.

The general thrust the telegram at the adjutant's chest. He read, eyes growing wide.

"This news disturbs me on more levels than I care to think about." The general wore a calm veneer as he spoke. "Why is it we had no intelligence of a Japanese attack on Vladivostok? For that matter, I never saw any reports the Japanese were developing airships much less had actually built any."

"There is some good news," ventured Zolnerowich. "Our new high-elevation cannon have demonstrated their effectiveness."

"Yes. They shot down one airship." Dragomirov spoke through tightened lips. "The other airship flew eastward, presumably on course for Japan."

"They fished prisoners from the water," added the adjutant. "The captives will be interrogated."

"I expect so," said the general. "Do we have a report from Sakhalin Island?"

"The *Nicholas Alexandrovich* has not been found. Parties plan to go ashore today to question soldiers at the base garrisoned at Poronaysk. If necessary, they will march overland to look for signs of the airship or its wreckage."

"Very good." The general frowned. The hand he clutched behind his back trembled with the rage he refused to express. "I want our intelligence agents in Japan recalled and... questioned. I want them replaced with new intelligence agents who can provide me information about their military capabilities. Am I understood?" He breathed those words close to Zolnerowich's ear. The general could smell the adjutant's sweat.

"Yes... yes, sir." He snapped a salute, turned, and left.

A second courier arrived at the map room, looked around, and made for the general. He wore a court official's finery—a red-breasted jacket with black sleeves and gold buttons. A large imperial crest and a tall metallic brush adorned his hat. At first glance, it would be easy to assume this courier outranked the general himself.

The courier snapped a crisp salute. "Sir, His Excellency Czar Alexander II requires your presence. Please accompany me."

Dragomirov had expected this from the moment he read the telegram. He held out his hand indicating his readiness. As they reached the door, the general retrieved his hat and coat, then followed the courier across Palace Square and past the Alexander Column. The general looked to the ground as they passed, feeling he had not lived up to Russia's greatness.

Dark and heavily laden skies hung over St. Petersburg.

Dragomirov expected the first snowfall soon. He smiled. Things always got better for Russians in poor weather. The courier led Dragomirov inside the Winter Palace and through the corridors to an anteroom, just outside Czar Alexander's beloved Amber Room.

Raised voices exploded from within. A few minutes later, the doors flew open. A Japanese man in a black suit and cravat appeared. A footman stood and presented the man's top hat. Dragomirov assumed this must be the Japanese ambassador. The ambassador snatched the top hat from the footman, then gave a cursory bow to Dragomirov. The general resisted the urge to return the bow.

"Is Dragomirov here?" bellowed the emperor from within.

The general did not wait. He strode into the amber room's eerie golden light, stopped a respectful distance from the emperor and fell to one knee, removing his hat.

The emperor stepped over to him and eyed him as though he were a dead mouse on the floor before extending his hand with the imperial ring. Dragomirov kissed the ring and the emperor turned around, giving the general leave to stand. The footman closed the doors and Dragomirov's mouth went dry.

Czar Alexander spun on his heel. "I did not order an attack on Japan and if I did, I would certainly not order one on such an unimportant hunk of rock as Hokkaido. I see no strategic value in it."

"Quite right, Your Excellency," said Dragomirov.

"What I want to know is why the Japanese ambassador demanded an explanation for a Russian attack. I want to know why the Japanese sunk a Russian Imperial Battleship in retaliation for this fictional attack."

Two possibilities occurred to Dragomirov. He took a chance with the one least likely to incur the emperor's wrath. "I suspect the Japanese have been planning this for some time. The invasion of Hokkaido is a fiction they invented as an excuse for their attack."

Czar Alexander snorted a laugh. "That sounds more like Russian than Japanese cunning. The ambassador claims there is photographic proof. I have demanded to see it, of course."

"Of course," affirmed Dragomirov. "Photographic proof

can be faked though. Using double exposures, a Russian air-ship could be superimposed on another photograph. Actors in facsimile uniforms may be positioned to resemble invaders."

"Can you prove such fakery is possible?"

Dragomirov bowed at the waist. "Absolutely. I can have such proof within the day."

"Excellent. Have it sent here as soon as possible." The em-peror strode to his desk and sat down, then indicated a chair opposite. "I don't think the Japanese would claim an attack if nothing happened though. Do you have another theory?"

"Someone aboard the airship—possibly Mendeleev him-self—went mad. They have taken the ship in a misguided at-tempt at piracy. It would explain why they stole such trivial items as food and drink in Hokkaido."

"How do we lose an airship, Mikhail Ivanovich?" The czar reached into a box for a cigar. He lit it, but did not offer one to the general. Without waiting for a response the czar pressed on. "I presume you have men searching for the airship. If you had a report you would have already given it to me. I want up-dates every morning and afternoon until it's found." The czar leaned forward. "Am I understood?"

"Yes, Your Excellency. I understand perfectly." Drago-mirov wondered if a firing squad commander's eyes would seem as icy as the emperor's.

Shinriki tried to understand the strangers who trudged through the woods up the mountainside with him. He spoke little Japa-nese and they spoke no Russian or Ainu. The latter didn't sur-prise him. No one aside from Ainu bothered to learn Ainu as far as he knew.

Most of the strangers had no personal stake in helping him free Ipokash or stopping the samurai bandits. As best as he could determine, the one who called himself a former sa-murai—Masuda Hoshi—knew the leader of the bandits who captured Ipokash, but facing the woman seemed to break his heart.

A woman led the samurai bandits. Shinriki found the fact

incredible, but not altogether surprising after his initial encounter with them. Something had seemed different about that warrior, but he hadn't placed it at the time. Now he understood, though her strength still surprised him, not unlike the woman who accompanied them. She spoke almost as much Japanese as he did and had no problem matching the intensive pace he set.

"We should wait until night to approach," said Hoshi when they stopped for water. "Imagawa will have guards who can spot us. Also, I suspect Mendeleev's distraction will work best when the samurai are tired. They'll be more inclined to seek shelter and sleep than mill around watching for people to attack."

Shinriki nodded, though he didn't understand how Mendeleev would know to create a distraction. He looked toward the sun, still high in the western sky. "Let's go a little further, then we can pause until nightfall."

As they continued up the hillside, crows called to one another. Shinriki worried their cries might alert the samurai on the airship. Crows made noise at the slightest disturbance.

They came to a small depression in the hillside, less a cave than a place they could huddle out of the wind and out of easy sight. They broke out rations. Shinriki and Resak shared dried fish. The strangers had a peppery dried beef and hard biscuits. Neither appealed to Shinriki. Resak tried the dried beef, then nearly drained a water skin to put out the fire in his mouth. They all laughed and Shinriki realized it was the first time he'd shared a genuine laugh since the samurai raid on his village.

Shinriki stepped away from the group and said a short prayer of thanks to the sea god for sending these strangers to him in their odd boat which could be folded up and hidden away in a hut.

The sun set and the skies grew dark. There would be no moon this night and clouds obscured the stars. They had a short distance to travel, but it would be slow going.

They packed up and moved on, doing their best to avoid rustling lest there be a patrol. When Shinriki indicated they were near, Hoshi told them to wait. He ran ahead and scouted. By the time he returned, a few breaks appeared in the clouds and the wind had eased.

"The airship is there," reported Hoshi. "I see one entrance and two guards stand at the bottom. I suspect someone patrols the camp's perimeter, but I didn't see them. If Mendeleev is to create a distraction, this is the time."

Ramon nodded after Fatemeh repeated the report in their language. He sat back and closed his eyes. His lips moved and for a moment, Shinriki thought he prayed. Another minute passed and Ramon's eyes opened. Hoshi swore in Japanese and the strangers spoke among themselves.

Shinriki tapped Hoshi on the shoulder. "What has happened?"

"We hoped to entice Imagawa's crew out," explained the former samurai. "Imagawa doesn't believe there's a reason to leave. We must figure out another plan."

"Why not sneak aboard, free Ipokash and the Russian, then sabotage the airship?" suggested Resak.

Hoshi and Fatemeh turned and looked at him. The solution was elegant and simple. Again the strangers spoke among themselves in their strange language.

"We still must get past the guards." At last Hoshi again spoke Japanese.

"Leave that to me." Fatemeh unslung her pack and removed two rags and a bottle. She instructed Hoshi in their other language.

Hoshi looked up at Shinriki. "Which of you is the more silent tracker?"

Shinriki pointed to Resak.

Hoshi explained a cloth saturated with the bottle's contents would suffice to knock out a guard with no noise. All they had to do was place the cloth over the guard's mouth and nose.

Resak nodded.

The two disappeared in the dark. Shinriki moved forward to a tree where he could watch the airship. Although he had seen the craft during the day in Poronaysk and flying overhead, this was the closest he'd approached. Cold, wan starlight, illuminated the giant gray mass. It hovered over the clearing like a low, ominous cloud with ropes tied to the ground to keep it from floating away. Any lower, trees would puncture the airship's rippling skin. Between the gentle movements and the undulating skin, Shinriki thought for a moment the enormous ship might be imbued with a life all its own.

The men called Apodaca and Rodriguez came up behind him. One of them hissed words and touched himself on his head and shoulders, almost as though he drew a cross shape in the air. The other frowned and nodded. Shinriki motioned them over behind another tree.

Long minutes ticked by and Shinriki's heart pounded so loud he thought sure the guards must hear. Just as he thought Hoshi and Resak must have been captured, they appeared. Cloth went over the guards' noses and the rogue samurai dropped to the ground.

Hoshi waved. Apodaca and Rodriguez scurried from their hiding place and ran to the ladder. Shinriki gave a signal to Morales and Fatemeh, then moved forward himself. Hoshi and Resak wasted no time climbing up to the floating vessel.

By the time Shinriki reached the ladder, Apodaca and Rodriguez were already halfway up. Ramon and Fatemeh ran across the field behind him. Following their lead, Shinriki did not wait, he started to climb. At the top, he found a strange room lined with windows and machines.

Hoshi motioned to them and they fell into the shadows and waited for Ramon and Fatemeh to reach the strange room. Each creak and groan startled Shinriki and he looked around. He believed someone would appear and they would have to fight. He reached for his knife and felt the hilt's reassuring solidity. He cast a glance toward the windows, glad it was dark outside. He didn't want to think about how high off the ground they were, even if tethers held the airship.

Ramon and Fatemeh reached the control room and took in the scene. Without waiting for their comrades to emerge from the shadows, Ramon proceeded to the ladder near Shinriki's hiding place. He pushed open a hatch and disappeared above.

Without a word, Hoshi, who left his wooden geta behind, emerged from the shadows and followed Ramon and Fatemeh up the ladder in silence. Ramon passed several doors, as though he knew the way. He stopped before one and summoned Shinriki forward.

Shinriki approached conscious of the plink-plinking his

boots made on the metal deck. At that moment, he wished he wore soft tabi, like Hoshi's. Ramon indicated Shinriki should enter the room in front of them.

Heart pounding, Shinriki tried the door. It wooshed to the side. Snuggled under a blanket, Ipokash slept. Unable to restrain himself, he rushed forward and touched her shoulder. She rolled over and blinked a few times, then gasped.

"Shinriki, you're alive!" The words sounded loud in the quiet airship.

Shinriki held his finger to his lips then sat down on the bed's edge and hugged her close. "I'm sorry it's taken me so long to get here." Tears streamed down his cheeks into his beard. He sat back and brushed them aside, angry at his weakness, both in crying and in being unable to save Ipokash without help.

"You're here now and that's what matters." She hesitated and her brow furrowed as though the Ainu language had grown unfamiliar. Shinriki wondered if she'd had many opportunities to speak it.

The six people with Shinriki crowded into the cramped little cabin. The deck canted just a little toward the window. Again, the fisherman's heart pounded, certain they would be discovered.

Rodriguez slid the door shut and Hoshi whispered something in their language. Ramon and Fatemeh each responded, but a bright light flashing through Ipokash's cabin window interrupted them.

An unnatural, loud voice boomed out in Russian. "We have this ship surrounded! Attempt to launch and we will open fire!"

Shinriki dared to peek out the window. Russian soldiers emerged from the woods. They flashed strange, almost magical lights at the ship. Shouts in Japanese sounded from the corridor outside.

On edge, ever since Mendeleev suggested a hydrogen leak, Imagawa pulled on her haori. She wondered why he tried to lure the crew outside. The ship listed ever so slightly to starboard and stayed there, as though extra weight had been added. A bright light shone from outside and a voice boomed in Russian just as she prepared to enter the corridor. Nanbu ran down the hall shouting, "Alarm!" Warriors clambered from bed and rushed to their posts.

Imagawa whirled around and looked out the window. Russian soldiers had surrounded the airship. A small group rushed toward the ladder. Where were her guards? If they'd evacuated the ship, they would have been easy targets for this force. How did Mendeleev know?

She rushed from her cabin, sprinted down the hall, and shot down the ladder into the gondola. "Marksmen on the door, now!"

Two men with rifles ran to the door and aimed. "Hostiles on the way up," called one of the riflemen.

"Knock them off and raise the ladder," called Imagawa.

The marksmen did as commanded, then pulled the ladder up, beyond reach.

A Russian officer stepped forward and shouted something through a megaphone.

"Shall I get the Ainu woman?" asked Nanbu.

"I don't need her to know he's calling for us to surrender." Imagawa sneered. "Cut the mooring ropes. We need some distance. Stoke the engines, I want us under power as soon as possible."

"Mistress Imagawa, if we cut the ropes, we won't be able to moor the ship at the next harbor," said Nanbu.

Imagawa planted her hands on her hips and stood straight. Even though Nanbu stood a full foot taller than her, he cowered. "If we don't leave right now, we may not possess a ship to moor."

As if to emphasize her point, a lookout called, "Russian soldiers are climbing the mooring lines. They'll try to breach the hatches."

Nanbu whirled around and grabbed the speaking tube. "Clear the mooring lines now. Engineering, stoke the boilers." He nodded to the man at the ballast controls, who understood he should be ready to drop ballast as soon as possible.

Screams sounded in the night as the samurai cut ropes. *The Brazen Shark* floated almost twenty feet off the ground, over the treetops. If the climbers knew what to do in a fall, they would be fine, though some might suffer broken limbs. Imagawa hoped at least one or two suffered a broken neck.

She walked over to the window. The Russian soldiers raised rifles. "Drop ballast!"

Water splashed on the ground lifting rocks and mud. Despite that, the Russian soldiers held their ground and fired. Two windows in the gondola shattered and the warriors dropped to the deck.

Imagawa turned around. The helmsman, Shichiroji, lay on the floor, head punctured by a burbling bullet hole. She ground her teeth. He was a good, loyal man. She climbed to her knees, found Nanbu, and pointed to the dead helmsman. "Get him out the door. He's almost one hundred fifty pounds worth of ballast."

Nanbu nodded, then stood and drug the helmsman to the door and shoved him out.

The Russians fired again, but this time, the airship had climbed beyond their range.

"Engaging the engines," called a voice from the dark.

Nanbu took the helm. "What's our course?"

"Southwest, toward Korea." Imagawa walked to the window and considered. The Russians now knew someone had stolen one of their airships. There were Japanese bodies behind. She wondered if this would be enough to make problems for her. "Belay that order, swing back around over the lodge. Let's drop a few bombs on those Russian soldiers, make them pay."

"Yes, ma'am," said Nanbu. He swung the wheel around, hard. Another warrior called for men in the bomb bay to stand by.

Imagawa took the wheel from Nanbu, the uneasy sensation of unfinished business gnawing at her gut. "Gather every man not otherwise engaged and search this ship. I think there are Russians aboard."

"Yes, ma'am." Nanbu bowed, then pointed to two men and summoned them to follow.

CHAPTER FOURTEEN
THE WAR IN THE AIR

When Mendeleev failed to convince the samurai to evacuate the airship, Hoshi worked out a plan with Ramon and Fatemeh. With intelligence from Legion, they would find the fisherman's wife first and get her to safety. They would then find Mendeleev and do as much damage to the airship as possible. To that end, Hoshi had allowed Ramon to take point as they proceeded to Ipokash's cabin while he took up the rear.

As a result, in the cabin, Hoshi stood closest to the door. From the whispers of those near the window, he learned Russian troops surrounded the airship. A confrontation ensued. Muffled shouts echoed through the halls. From time to time, footsteps clanged down the hallway outside. The ship tipped and swayed as Russian soldiers grabbed onto the lines. Soon afterwards, a loud popping heralded the tether lines' release. Hoshi's stomach fluttered as the ship lifted into the air.

"We should take the engines," whispered Hoshi. "There will be fewer guards than in the gondola. It will give us a tactical advantage and we might sabotage the ship as we'd hoped."

Cisneros's men nodded to each other. Fatemeh placed her hands on her hips, as though poised to argue.

"He's right, corazón. The only other option is to sit here and wait to be captured."

She thought for a moment, then nodded.

"Are there enough of us?" asked Apodaca.

Hoshi lifted his chin toward Shinriki and switched to Japanese. "Will you and Ipokash help?"

Shinriki gazed into his wife's eyes. After a moment they both gave a sharp nod.

Hoshi smiled, eased the door open and stepped into the

hall. Having some room, he took a deep breath, then drew his katana. He stepped gingerly down the hall all too conscious of his heartbeat and his tabi susurrating against the metal deck. At the end of the hall, he threw open a door. A guard, on edge from the earlier excitement, whirled around to confront them. Hoshi thrust with his sword and the man collapsed in a gagging groan. Hoshi withdrew the sword and shoved the body to the side.

He continued on, just noticing Fatemeh's quiet disappointment and Ramon urging her forward. Like the Japanese ships, a catwalk ran toward the tail, but the ship's envelope enclosed this one. Large gas bags billowed and undulated just above and to each side, like some gigantic beast's organs.

Hoshi visualized the ship from the outside. The first pair of engines were amidships, just outside the cargo holds. Hoshi took a moment to whisper over his shoulder. "Will we have to go through the hold to reach the forward engines?"

Apodaca shook his head. Although he had fought in the Battle of Denver, he hadn't boarded either airship. "I remember looking at plans. I think there's access to the stub keel ten meters further up."

Hoshi didn't know metric units well, but noted a door about thirty shaku ahead and pressed on. A moment later, he came to the doorway and a ladder that led to a lower catwalk against the starboard hull. A similar catwalk stood opposite. He pointed to Apodaca and Rodriguez and indicated they should take the port side. He'd take starboard. Once the two sailors disappeared, Ramon, Fatemeh, Ipokash and Shinriki approached. "Stay up here and watch for trouble."

Hoshi disappeared down the starboard ladder. He walked along the stub keel catwalk and came to a wide spot where two men watched dials and turned valves. A Russian wore coveralls and a tool belt. The other man wore a kimono and a hakama.

An alarm bell sounded and the men looked up. Hoshi struck at the Japanese man, who dodged long enough to draw his own katana. Hoshi jumped back, raised his weapon and struck downward, catching the man in the neck. He fought to stay upright, but collapsed to his knees.

"I have come to take the ship from the pirates! Will you

help us?" Hoshi spoke the words in English, then in Japanese. The Russian mechanic shook his head and backed away, confused. Hoshi needed Ipokash.

He patted the air in a "stay put" motion, then ran back along the catwalk and climbed the stairs. There, a samurai held a wakizashi knife to Ipokash's throat. Shinriki lay on the ground. Ramon stood, revolver drawn.

"Masuda Hoshi, I never would have expected to see you again," said the samurai.

Hoshi's brow furrowed. "Nanbu?"

"Come with me. Imagawa will want to see you."

Rodriguez appeared behind Nanbu. "Drop the knife, friend!" He spoke Spanish, but distracted Nanbu just enough for Hoshi to deliver a sword thrust.

Nanbu dropped the knife and jumped backwards. Hoshi pushed past Ipokash, which gave Nanbu enough time to draw his own katana and thrust. Hoshi knocked the sword aside and jumped back. As he did, warriors ran in from fore and aft surrounding the group.

The narrow catwalk gave Hoshi an advantage as he pressed forward. He could take on each man one at a time, but he feared for his friends. As he considered surrender, Nanbu thrust. Hoshi countered it, knocking the katana from Nanbu's hand. The warrior screamed. Hoshi thrust his elbow into Nanbu's face, knocking him backward into the arms of the warrior behind.

"I will speak to Imagawa."

"Take these people to the hold and watch them." Nanbu held his bleeding nose and struggled to stand. "Accompany me to the gondola."

Hoshi nodded and sheathed his katana. Imagawa's lieutenant pushed past the men who lined the catwalk, clearing a narrow path. Hoshi followed. He cast a backward glance long enough to see Ipokash helping Shinriki to his feet.

When Hoshi arrived in the gondola, Imagawa peered out the window through a spyglass. She looked much as he remembered: fierce, strong, proud. She turned, casting eyes from Nanbu and the cloth he held under his bleeding nose to Hoshi. Her widened eyes betrayed surprise.

"I never thought I'd see you again," she said. "Though I must admit, when I asked myself who could sneak past my guards and get aboard this ship, yours was the name that kept coming to mind."

"I thought you were dead, Imagawa." Hoshi took a step forward. Nanbu raised an arm to block him but Imagawa waved him aside. "Why do I find you commanding a Russian airship?"

"Because a Japan which insists I serve men has swallowed the Japan where I was a warrior." She snorted. "Why do you attempt to destroy my airship?"

"Because I still love Japan and its people even if I cannot live in the new regime." He fought to free his voice from emotion. He came close to saying, 'Because I still love you and don't want to see you throw your life away.'

She narrowed her gaze and studied him, as though she heard the unspoken part.

Hoshi frowned and fought to return to matters at hand and not ones abandoned long ago. "Give up this vessel. Admit to the government you're the one who attacked Japan."

"This vessel is all but finished now." Imagawa shrugged. "An admission implies I committed a crime. I fight to free our country from those who would destroy our culture and traditions."

Before Hoshi could respond, the ship jolted to the side.

"What the hell!" Imagawa ran to the window and opened her spyglass. Hoshi looked around. No one opposed him, so he joined her. A Japanese airship's silhouette blocked out cold starlight. Was it the *Bashō*? He couldn't tell.

Sparks showered from the Japanese airship's upper rim. They fired a rocket, just as Cisneros had proposed. Hoshi gritted his teeth.

"Hard to port, now! Full power on the starboard engines!" Imagawa fanned her arms out. "I want spotters around the gondola."

A man standing before a bank of dials shook his head. "The first attack damaged the propeller on starboard engine number one." Hoshi gathered the man must be acting engineer.

"Cut power on the port side. Swing around now!"

The second rocket missed, but sparks flew from the Japanese

airship again. When Hoshi rode across the Pacific, he never sensed airships were agile craft. The Russian airship's long, shuddering turn confirmed his guess.

"Third rocket bounced off the skin!" Hoshi couldn't tell who called out in the darkened gondola. The voice came from near the chart table.

Imagawa continued to watch. She beckoned Nanbu, who pushed Hoshi aside. "I think the rockets are just basic fireworks," she said.

Nanbu nodded. "Devastating if they hit a gas bag."

Imagawa pointed out the window. "There are two men mid-way up the enemy's gas bag. They're shielded, but they expose themselves when they fire. Get marksmen up to our gun ports. Pick them off."

"Fourth rocket missed," called the spotter.

"We have two nine-pound cannon aboard. We could try to punch a hole in their ship," suggested Nanbu.

Imagawa pursed her lips. "Don't waste time. Get the snipers in position. If you have extra men, you can try the cannons." She cast a meaningful look at Hoshi.

Nanbu left to carry out the orders. Hoshi tried to guess how many people Imagawa still had left. The Russian airship was much bigger than the *Bashō*. He guessed it could carry at least fifty crewmembers, maybe even a hundred. Thirty samurai fought for their daimyo at its height.

She whirled on Hoshi. "What do you know about that craft out there? Where's it from?"

Hoshi played dumb and shrugged. "If they're shooting fireworks, maybe they're from China."

Imagawa sneered and took a step toward Hoshi. "I'm guessing they're Japanese and somehow the emperor's men convinced you to sabotage this ship. If you failed, then their job was to shoot us down."

Hoshi sighed and put his hands behind his back. "I did come aboard to try to stop you. I have no love for the emperor, but I have no desire to see Russians overrun Japan because of your stupidity."

Aside from the distant, sputtering engines, silence ensued on the bridge. The enemy launched a rocket and the ship lurched and listed over to the side again. Hoshi reached out and grabbed the rail with one hand. With his other he caught Imagawa's wrist. When the ship righted itself, she shook her hand free. Staccato popping accompanied a subliminal shudder as the snipers returned fire.

"I've lost helm control," called the man at the wheel.

"They hit the rudder," called the spotter. Imagawa sprinted across the gondola and grabbed a speaking tube. "Is there fire astern?"

Hoshi strained to hear the response. "No fire, but we have a mess of broken cables."

A whistle sounded from another speaking tube. Imagawa opened it. "This is the commander."

"Sniper thinks he destroyed a rocket launcher. Nine pounder is loaded. We're going to try."

"Fire!" called Imagawa.

A faint boom preceded the ship tilting to the side again. Hoshi turned and peered out into the darkness, the lightweight cannonball missed its target.

A bearded man appeared at the top of the gondola's ladder. He wore a black jacket thrown over a nightshirt. He spouted gibberish that might be Russian. Was he the scientist Mendeleev? He locked eyes with Hoshi and blinked as though he'd seen a phantom. The Russian captive must have met all the samurai. He spoke again. This time Hoshi caught the word "Ipokash." He must be asking where she was.

Imagawa called to the spotter by the chart table. "Get Professor Mendeleev astern with the other prisoners. We may have to use them if we need to jettison ballast."

The spotter came forward, grabbed Mendeleev's arm and led him back up the stairs.

"You can't be serious about dropping prisoners from the airship," barked Hoshi.

Imagawa stormed across the deck. "You know something about that ship!"

"You already guessed it's Japanese. Their ships were unarmed as far as I knew, but they equipped them for a mission last I saw."

"Them? Are there others? And just why would you have

permission to see an imperial airship if such a thing existed?"

"Because a guest of Katsu Kaishū invited me aboard."

"That traitor!" Imagawa spat on the deck. She looked up. "Did Lord Katsu put you up to this?"

Hoshi shook his head. He hadn't betrayed any secrets. Many people in Japan and Mexico had seen the airship and Lord Katsu was known to have been aboard, but Imagawa had been hiding out, away from any news sources.

The Russian airship shuddered from the recoil as the nine-pounder fired again. The Japanese vessel made a slight turn. Did they feel they'd inflicted sufficient damage? Were they running? Had they learned what they wanted?

"Why have you turned up?" Imagawa's gaze bored into Hoshi. "No more evading my questions. You knew how to find my airship. The Russians found my airship." She pointed a trembling finger at the window. "These imperialist pigs knew where to find my airship. I want to know how!"

"Ipokash's husband led me here. I would guess the Russians have been looking for their missing airship for some time." He glanced out the window. "As for the imperialists..." He shook his head. "I have no idea. They seemed more interested in commerce than warfare. That's all I'll tell you. If you harm my friends, I will kill you myself." Sparks flew from the imperialist airship—another rocket.

"You may not have the chance," sneered Imagawa.

Hoshi and Imagawa each grabbed the rail. "Release more ballast, give us some altitude," she called.

Helpless, the elevatorman backed away from the controls. "Tanks are dry."

"Drop the bombs, do anything to get us up higher!"

Hoshi shot a meaningful look toward her.

"Have the passengers help." Her voice held a bitter note.

The rocket hit, ripping through the ship's skin. A moment later, an explosion rocked the ship, sending Hoshi to the floor.

"The hydrogen!" Imagawa rushed to the stern for a better view.

"Negative," said the spotter. "The rocket exploded after it passed through."

"We're venting hydrogen," called the elevatorman. "We're

losing altitude fast."

"The imperialists are moving off."

"Where are we?" called Imagawa.

"Land ahead," called the navigator. "Our course was south by southwest before the turn. Must be Russia."

"Damn!" She looked around the gondola. "I guess the Russians are getting their airship back. Everyone brace for impact." She pointed to the elevatorman. "Level off. Try to ease us down."

Hoshi stood and looked up the stairs, worried about his friends.

CHAPTER FIFTEEN
POWER STRUGGLES

As the airship bounced and jostled, Ramon tried to get his bearings and learn something about the large bay. He barely remembered the bomb bay from the airship destroyed in the Battle of Denver, but the rough ride made him think a similar fate awaited this craft.

Apodaca and Rodriguez sat nearby and studied the surroundings. The samurai guarding the doors wore guns. Before the airship began its tumultuous ride, they had discussed strategies for breaking out, convinced the guards didn't understand Spanish. Then things started hitting the airship and they fell quiet and listened, trying to figure out what happened and how to react.

Fatemeh knelt down and examined Shinriki's wound. The fisherman leaned his head against his wife's breast, a contented smile on his lips despite the situation. The fisherman's cousin, Resak sat nearby, eyes darting between Fatemeh and Ipokash, eager to help but uncertain what to do. Fatemeh removed some herbs from her pouch and had Shinriki chew on them, then sat next to Ramon.

"I'd like to put some cold water on that bump, but I think our options are limited," she said.

Ramon nodded. Samurai escorted a bearded man wearing a jacket over a nightshirt into the hold. Ipokash waved. Unhindered by the guards, the bearded man approached.

"*Is that Dmitri Mendeleev?*" Ramon hoped Legion listened.

"*It is.*"

"*If you're in both of our minds, can you make us understand each other?*"

Legion's components whispered among themselves, as though they considered the idea. "*It verges on the interference you discouraged me from."*

"I know," thought Ramon, *"but this is an emergency. We need to coordinate our efforts."*

"As you wish."

"Professor Mendeleev," called Ramon. "What's going on?"

The Russian scientist's eyes widened at whatever he heard. He spoke Russian, but Ramon understood him nonetheless. "The guard tells me we've been attacked. It seems we're descending rapidly."

"Over water or land? Do you know where we are?"

"I don't know." Mendeleev shook his shaggy head. "I got a look at the compass though. From the heading, I have a pretty good idea we'll land on the Russian mainland, somewhere north of Vladivostok."

"Legion, does Mendeleev have enough information to relay to Cisneros? If the captain could get close, I could light a signal fire."

"Or, as this is an emergency, I can act as a homing beacon for him."

Mendeleev narrowed his gaze. "You speak to Legion, too?"

Could Mendeleev hear Ramon's unspoken conversation? Legion answered Ramon's silent query. *"In this proximity, yes, Mendeleev can hear your conversation with me."*

Ramon nodded, then stumble-stepped across the bucking floor to the scientist. "You asked Legion for help. We're the ones he sent."

"It took you long enough to get here." The statement stung, but Ramon sensed Mendeleev intended no rebuff.

A voice called out in Japanese.

"Brace for impact." Ipokash translated the words. Ramon noticed he could understand her just the same as Mendeleev. Having Legion as a friend could prove useful for a diplomat.

"Your best chance of surviving the impending crash is to open the doors and jump when you approach the ground," said Legion.

Ramon and Mendeleev looked at each other and nodded. Mendeleev pointed out two winches, one on either side of the floor's large hatch. Mendeleev ran for one, Ramon the other. A samurai guard shouted at them, but refused to release the support pillar he gripped with white knuckles.

Mendeleev nodded to Ramon and the two men cranked.

As they did, wind whooshed in through the open hatch. The ground below flew past in a gray blur lit by morning twilight. The ship bucked again and Ramon's grip on the winch slipped, smacking his hand. He yelped in pain, and Fatemeh ran over to join him. She took up where he left off.

"Gather anything we can. We'll have to jump for it soon," said Ramon.

Apodaca and Rodriguez donned their packs which the samurai had searched and returned. Ipokash, Shinriki, and Resak blinked at Ramon. Although Mendeleev understood him, they did not. Mendeleev realized the problem and called out. They exchanged a few words and the scientist barked out a laugh. "She doesn't think these gentlemen will let us return to our cabins for supplies."

"I think she's right," said Ramon, "but have her tell them to get ready to jump."

"We're saving them, too?"

"Do we have a reason to let them die?" countered Ramon.

"It's far from certain they will." Despite that, Mendeleev relayed the request to Ipokash who in turn shouted to the warriors. They looked at each other with uncertainty, then reached a decision and nodded. Soon, all the bay's occupants gathered around the open hatch and waited.

As the light increased outside, trees became clear. They moved slower than Ramon first thought, but he still didn't want to jump. He reached out, pulled Fatemeh close, and gave her a long kiss. She melted into him.

"*By my calculations, this is the optimal time to escape,*" said Legion.

Ramon clung to Fatemeh longer than he should, but finally broke the embrace and looked over the edge, gritting his teeth. They now traveled ten to twenty feet over a grassy field. They still moved faster than Ramon liked. Across the way, Mendeleev pointed, then went over. Fatemeh swallowed, gave Ramon a quick kiss, then jumped. Apodaca pushed Rodriguez, then followed. Shinriki looked unstable, and Ramon wondered how he would do with the jump, but he could not help. While he considered this, the two samurai warriors also jumped.

Ramon swallowed and willed himself to drop over the

edge. The turf came up and smacked him in the face and he rolled several times.

He struggled to find breath, but a fierce crash caused him to sit up and suck in air along with a salty, coppery tang. The airship drifted onward and the gondola struck the ground. Several people jumped out the door before the wind caught the airship and hefted the tail high in the air. A moment later, it crashed down on its back. The wind pushed it further along the ground until it hit the tree line, where the fabric fluttered and flapped like a discarded circus tent.

Ramon struggled to stand and looked around in a blur. He searched for his glasses before his vision cleared and he realized he still wore them. "Fatemeh!" he called.

"Over here!"

He looked around the unfamiliar terrain until she stood and waved.

He ran toward her, but six steps later his legs gave out and he dropped to his knees. Fatemeh ran up to him, "How in the world did your glasses stay on your face?"

He took them off. The first thing he noticed was blood splattered on the lens. Then he realized the impact flattened the nosepieces. It would take some work for them to be serviceable again. A rip sounded and Fatemeh produced cloth from somewhere. Had she ripped it from her blouse? She poured liquid on the cloth and dabbed at his numb face. Pain awoke and he cried out.

"You're okay, I think you just cut your lip," she said.

He nodded. "We need to find the others and some fresh water."

Mendeleev limped up. He'd ripped his jacket and lost a slipper. "We should go to the airship. See if there are any supplies we can scavenge."

"Do you know where we are?" asked Ramon.

Mendeleev shook his head. "Not precisely." He pointed over his shoulder. "The ocean's that way. If your help travels by sea, that's the direction they'll come from. Given the terrain, I don't think we can be more than five or ten miles from the coast."

Ramon nodded and Fatemeh helped him to his feet.

They stood up and came across two people together on the ground. Shinriki lay curled in a broken heap. Ipokash hovered over him. Fatemeh knelt down and opened one of his eyes. "He's in shock," she said. "Try to keep him warm."

Resak ran up. Fatemeh looked him up and down, then mimed drinking from a bottle. Resak blinked as if stunned, then took off his water skin and handed it over. She lifted Shinriki's head to see if he would drink. He sipped a little water. Fatemeh handed the water to Ramon next. He was tempted to swish the water around in his mouth and spit it out, but he swallowed it instead, glad to feel no broken teeth go down his throat.

Apodaca and Rodriguez joined them. Rodriguez sported several scrapes and cuts. Apodaca had weathered the fall better, though his pack had a big rip in it.

"Something's happening near the airship." Apodaca pointed.

Ramon heard shouts in Japanese. A moment later, steel clanged. Ramon looked over at Fatemeh, and they ran toward the sound. Someone else called out and steel clashed a second time.

Hoshi and Imagawa faced each other, swords drawn. Hoshi shouted and thrust, knocking Imagawa's sword from her hand. She reached for a dagger at her belt, but Hoshi allowed the follow-through from his strike to carry him full circle. He kicked her in the ribs, sending her sprawling on the ground. He pressed the sword to her side.

She sneered and spoke clear and calm. Ramon thought he caught the word seppuku. Hoshi grunted and nodded, then backed up, pointing his sword at Imagawa.

"What's going on here?" called Fatemeh.

"I challenged Imagawa to a duel. I said she had no right to call herself samurai if she resorted to piracy. She accepted and lost. She will now commit seppuku rather than suffer the shame of defeat. I have granted this wish to honor our shared history."

As Hoshi spoke, Imagawa struggled to her knees. She withdrew her tanto and held it high.

Fatemeh lunged and grabbed the knife's hilt. "You will not do this!"

Ramon looked up at Hoshi. "You would let her commit suicide, when you believed it to be a foolish choice."

"It was not the right choice for me," said Hoshi.

"It's not the right choice for anyone." Fatemeh wrenched the knife from Imagawa and tossed it far away. Imagawa looked up, teeth barred and hissed angry words at Fatemeh.

Hoshi shook his head. "She says not to interfere."

"I know what she said." Fatemeh looked into Imagawa's eyes. "I don't like how women are treated in Japan. I don't like how they're treated in America. Their treatment in Persia is even worse." She struggled to find words in Japanese but Imagawa blinked, not comprehending. She turned to Hoshi. "Translate it."

Hoshi turned his back.

Fatemeh worked through her anger and hurt to try again. The warrior gazed into Fatemeh's eyes. She remained silent for a long moment. At last she responded in subdued tones.

Fatemeh nodded and spoke words which caused Hoshi to sigh. He turned around. "Allow me to translate."

"Japan may not be perfect," said Fatemeh. "Under the Tokugawa regime, there were strict classes: peasant, samurai, daimyo. The Meiji regime has problems, but blurred social lines mean life is less regimented. People can make their own dreams. Be such a person. If you don't like the roles women assume, make your own role and demand people follow it. You can't return to the old ways, even if you start this war."

Hoshi translated and Imagawa's expression softened a little. Fatemeh released her wrists and Imagawa let them drop to the ground. She spoke.

"She thinks she's done with airships for now," said Hoshi.

Imagawa looked up and sighed. She spoke to Hoshi, then looked at Fatemeh whose eyes shone with unshed tears.

"She says she made her statement against the Meiji regime and you're too late. It doesn't matter whether she lives or dies. She will fight no longer. Lead where you will."

Hoshi stood, walked some distance away and hung his head. Fatemeh remained next to Imagawa and Ramon walked over to Hoshi. "What's the matter?"

The samurai-farmer shook his head. "This is what I didn't

want to see, a broken Imagawa surrendering to fate. Letting her commit suicide would have broken my heart. I fear this has broken my soul."

As the morning wore on, *The Brazen Shark's* survivors gathered near the wreckage. Fatemeh liked Imagawa's name for the airship, which suited the craft's sleek lines and power before the crash. The name *Nicholas Alexandrovich* made her imagine an overblown portion of male anatomy.

Admittedly, she had come to enjoy that portion of the male anatomy when utilized by Ramon, but didn't think an airship deserved to be named after it.

Twenty people survived *The Brazen Shark's* crash. Of those, seven had invaded the ship with Fatemeh. Mendeleev and Ipokash made it out along with a Russian mechanic who held on through the airship's wild slow-motion summersault. That left ten from Imagawa's crew. Two samurai had been left behind. Hoshi killed two more. The rest had fallen from the ship or tumbled within and died.

Fatemeh treated the wounded throughout the morning. As supplies ran low in the small pouch she wore at her hip, Apodaca ran up with a black medical bag he found in the wreckage.

Treating the wounded allowed her to hear their stories, though she didn't understand them all. They told their stories in at least five languages, but, people translated. She learned a Japanese ship had attacked *The Brazen Shark*. Hoshi guessed after the *Bashō* left him in Tokyo, it must have departed on a hunting expedition with its sister ship. One of the Japanese ships found its quarry and brought it down.

Fatemeh found Ramon straightening his glasses with plyers salvaged from the wreckage. When he finished, they still sat crooked on his face, but they were more stable. "Did we accomplish too little too late?" she asked.

"Why do you ask, corazón?"

She shook her head. "It seems Imagawa accomplished what she set out to do and the Japanese stopped them. Did we accomplish anything?"

Ramon put his arm around her. "Would the Japanese airship have been in the area if we hadn't made contact with Lord
Ōkubo? Would Mendeleev and Ipokash have survived the
wreck? What would Imagawa have done next? It's impossible
to know these things, corazón, but I think we helped make the
situation better."

Fatemeh looked over at Imagawa, sitting by herself. She
looked old and frail—exposed in her kimono and hakama. She
helped the samurai, but her spirit held no fire. She needed time
to heal and Fatemeh hoped she could help.

After a lunch of dried fish, the survivors examined the
gear. Discussions ensued about what to do. Imagawa's lieutenant, Nanbu, suggested they travel east to China, then south
to Korea where they might find safe refuge. "We should go to
the coast," ventured Ramon. "We can find help there." Fatemeh noticed he avoided specifying where the help would come
from.

Hoshi translated for the samurai. Nanbu stabbed his finger
at Hoshi, and Fatemeh feared another duel would break out.
Hoshi made a suggestion which placated the warrior.

"He accused us of leading them into an imperialist trap,"
said Hoshi. "I reminded him we're not imperialists and, in fact,
imperialists shot us down. I told him help would arrive soon
and they stood their best chance with the imperial government if they returned voluntarily." He cast a glance to Ramon.
"You've told me the coast is no more than ten miles to the east.
For your sake, I hope you're right."

"Why won't they just leave and go their own way?" asked
Fatemeh.

Hoshi pursed his lips. "Because we need each other and
they know it. They need your skills as a healer. We need their
fighting ability if we should encounter Russian forces and want
to avoid a protracted stay in prison."

Fatemeh nodded understanding.

That afternoon they packed what they could carry and
hiked due east. During the walk, they encountered no villages or people. Fatemeh wondered how long it would be before
the Russians discovered the airship's wreckage. She tried to remember her geography. If she remembered right, Vladivostok

occupied this Russian province's southern tip. Where were the roads? Further inland perhaps.

She fell back to speak with Imagawa as they walked. "How do you feel today?"

Imagawa remained silent for so long, Fatemeh thought she wouldn't answer. "Confused," Imagawa admitted at last. "I feel I accomplished what I set out to do. I lost my battle with Hoshi. Why are you not content to let me die?"

"Because your death would be a waste."

Imagawa looked at her. "My life as it stands will be a waste. I have no power unless I marry."

"Will they take all your money?"

Imagawa laughed. "What money? The imperialists refuse to pay my stipend. I have some money saved, but it won't last long... presuming the government hasn't seized it already."

"There are ways to turn a little money into a fortune," suggested Fatemeh. "People may not listen to a poor woman, but they will listen to a rich one who funds industrial growth."

"Even if I could fund such growth, I have little desire to waste my life manipulating money."

Fatemeh smiled. "Neither do I. I used what little money I had to travel."

"I have no desire to flee Japan like Hoshi, either." She frowned. "If I return to Japan, I will be jailed, perhaps killed."

This time Fatemeh turned silent for a while, as she considered how much to say. After a moment she met Imagawa's gaze. "Back in America, Ramon and I tried to stop the Russians. However, we violated our government's trust. When we go home, we face a prison term." Fatemeh reached out and put her hand on Imagawa's shoulder. The warrior flinched. "Once that term is complete, we will move forward together. The threat of punishment does not deter our dreams. The point is, there are many possibilities open to you, if you open your mind."

Imagawa scowled but nodded. "I shall consider your words."

Fatemeh returned to Ramon and walked beside him. As she did, Imagawa's gaze fell across her back.

After a three-mile hike, they came to a vast flood plain. The river hugged the lowest point, just to the north. If not for the mountain valley's remote location, Fatemeh thought this could be good farm country. They followed the floodplain for three more miles until they reached the Sea of Japan. The survivors made camp and ate more dried fish. The samurai pulled out a sake bottle they'd scavenged from the wreckage and passed it around until empty. Imagawa made her own lean-to, well away from the others.

In their own lean-to, Ramon and Fatemeh held each other through the night. "According to Legion, Captain Cisneros should be on the beach in the morning."

"Legion, Legion… I wish I never heard the name Legion," grumbled Fatemeh.

"He's been quite helpful."

"He also got us into this whole mess. I wonder what the world would have been like if he hadn't involved himself." Soon after she uttered the thought, fatigue caught up with her and she drifted off to sleep.

She awoke to squawking seagulls. The birds reminded her of San Francisco and she shuddered. She remembered bullets firing and blood splattering as Luther Duncan collapsed on a pier. Back in New Mexico, Luther spent thirty days in jail, just for helping her. She faced the same fate. She put her arms around Ramon and squeezed him, glad for this start to their marriage. Aside from facing death on an airship, it had been quite pleasant.

She sat up and recognized the *Calamar* bobbing in the waves. A hatch opened and Captain Cisneros emerged and waved. She climbed out from among the blankets, threw on a coat and waved back.

All around, in the camp, the samurai warriors groaned from their night of revelry, but most milled around and packed their belongings, preparing for whatever awaited them.

Ramon emerged from the bedroll and joined Fatemeh. Hand-in-hand, they strolled to the beach. Apodaca and Rodriguez joined them. Captain Cisneros disappeared into the *Calamar*. A few minutes later, the submersible rose from the water and rolled onto the shore. Startled cries rang out and the samurai gathered around to see the strange craft.

Cisneros opened the hatch and considered all those assembled. He climbed down the ladder and shook Ramon's hand. "I only have room for five."

Ramon shrugged. "So make multiple trips, or go back to the *Ballena* and get launch boats."

Cisneros shook his head. "I won't risk the launches to these seas." He pointed out to the white-capped waves and the ship rocking well off shore. "The *Calamar* may have enough fuel for one more trip after this one. There's no way I can get everyone.

Fatemeh brought Cisneros and Ramon into a close huddle. "Can't you make fuel aboard the *Ballena?* You have the lab."

The captain shrugged. "It's a matter of time and raw materials. I have a batch in process, but it'll take at least three more days. Once the new batch is gone, I'll have exhausted my raw materials."

"Can you get more in Tokyo?" asked Ramon. "I want to return, tell them what's happened."

Cisneros rubbed his chin, then nodded. "I can. It's a two-day trip, though."

"That's fine." Ramon looked back to those nearby. Apodaca and Rodriguez craned their necks trying to hear what the three discussed in secret. "Mendeleev should accompany us as well as Hoshi. If they'll listen to reason, maybe we can present our case to the Russian ambassador. Besides, it's either three days waiting for you to make fuel or a four-day round trip. It doesn't seem like much difference either way."

Cisneros nodded. "That makes sense. Who else should I take? Fatemeh, I presume?"

Ramon nodded, but Fatemeh interrupted. "Some people are wounded," she said. "You should take Shinriki, Ipokash and Resak back to their village."

"Sakhalin Island's far side is out of the way." Cisneros folded his arms. "And that makes six people."

"They'll be better off on the *Ballena* than staying out here in the weather," argued Fatemeh. "Someone can sit on the *Calamar's* floor until you get back to the ship." She lifted her chin, toward the *Ballena.*

"Corazón," Ramon grabbed Fatemeh's hands. "I need you. Why should you have to wait while I go?"

"These people need me and this is a job you can do yourself."

"What about my crewmen?" Cisneros cast a glance toward Apodaca and Rodriguez who now looked glum and muttered among themselves as though they'd heard the plans.

"I'm impetuous, but I'm not stupid," said Fatemeh. "They're my insurance we'll be here when you return. Aside from Shinriki, most suffer superficial wounds. I should stay and help, but most will be better in three or four days."

Ramon glanced around at the wild terrain and the dark grey clouds lingering above. "Will you be okay out here? It feels like you could get snow."

Fatemeh stepped over to Imagawa. She spoke a few halting Japanese words. Imagawa nodded and spoke. Fatemeh returned to the men. "She's prepared to stay. Her men have camped in worse conditions than the Russian wilds in autumn."

"Are you sure you want to do this?" asked Ramon.

"They need me," said Fatemeh. "I think I can help Imagawa."

Ramon cast a dubious glance her way, then nodded. "I'll miss you, corazón."

"It's not the first time we've been apart."

"Just the first time since we've been married." He brought her close and kissed her. They parted and Fatemeh helped Ramon pack, then watched as the six people clambered aboard the submersible.

Captain Cisneros waited until the others boarded before he climbed the ladder. He waved and closed the hatch. A few minutes later, the *Calamar* chugged and churned, then rolled into the water. A short distance out, it began bobbing with the waves, then disappeared below.

Imagawa watched as Captain Cisneros's strange submersible boat disappeared under the waves and she thought this new world might be stranger than she first imagined. She returned to her lean-to and decided the men would need to build better shelter if they were to wait four days in this wild place. Before doing so, she sat down to meditate on the last few days.

She thought about flying in the airship she called *The*

Brazen Shark. She had freedom and power unlike any she had ever known. What's more, she had succeeded in her goal. She set Japan on a course for war with Russia. If that course continued, there would be a place for her in the new society, she could achieve her old station after all.

If Hoshi and this Morales succeeded in stopping the war, promise remained. Fatemeh suggested she could carve a path for herself in this new society. She considered what the path might be. She liked nothing more than a sword in her hand, and how it became an extension of her arm, which forced her to focus. Perhaps she could open a dojo and teach girls swordsmanship. She liked the future such a generation might bring.

Prison time did not frighten her. If the Japanese deemed she must be executed for her acts, so be it. She had been prepared to die. Fatemeh may have done her no favor sparing her life. The strange woman may have accomplished nothing more than delaying her fate, but Imagawa conceded value existed in having options.

A man yelled out. Imagawa grabbed her katana and ran from the lean-to as Kanbei withdrew his sword from Rodriguez's chest. The sailor looked down at the seeping wound in disbelief before his knees gave way and he crumpled to the ground.

"What are you doing?" Fatemeh's voice trembled with hurt and rage as she started toward the fallen man. As she passed Nanbu, he snatched her around the waist and pulled her toward him with one arm. The other hand withdrew a revolver from his kimono.

"Miss Fatemeh!" Apodaca looked from his fallen comrade to Fatemeh and rushed toward her, drawing his own revolver.

Nanbu fired. The bullet struck Apodaca between the eyes, whipping him backward onto the hard ground.

Fatemeh struggled in Nanbu's grip, but stopped when she felt the hot barrel of his pistol near her forehead.

"Let her go!" called Imagawa.

"No," growled Nanbu. "You are welcome to wait here for the imperialists to return, Imagawa, but we are leaving."

Imagawa barred her teeth. "Go if you must, but leave Mrs. Morales behind."

"We travel through rough terrain without a guide. We need a healer," he said.

Imagawa took a step forward and lifted her katana, but Nanbu pushed his pistol barrel into Fatemeh's head for emphasis and she bit down a yelp at the seering heat. "I don't intend to fight you with a sword," said Nanbu. "You're deranged. All the men see it. We will wait, watch, and see what happens in Japan."

"It's okay," croaked Fatemeh. "I'll go with them. I'll find my way back, I promise."

"I fear it's a promise you won't keep."

Imagawa considered a direct confrontation, but calculated no way to win. That didn't mean she couldn't help. For now, she would let them go, no matter how painful. Nanbu didn't give her tracking skills enough credit.

CHAPTER SIXTEEN
THE MEIJI EMPEROR

Ramon found Dmitri Mendeleev by the *Ballena's* forward rail. The wind blew through the scientist's shaggy, gray beard and hair. Ramon cleared his throat and Mendeleev turned and gazed at him through half-lidded eyes. "You've repaired your glasses."

Ramon snorted a half-laugh. As before, Legion adjusted his brain chemistry so he understood despite the language barrier. "Captain Cisneros has some good mechanics aboard the ship. They fixed them up for me." He stepped forward to stand next to the scientist. "May I ask what you're thinking about?"

This time the scientist snorted. "We'll be in Tokyo tomorrow. What do you think I'm considering? Will they execute me because I conspired with the pirates who attacked Hokkaido or will they execute me because they see me as a Russian who attacked them?"

"Rebel samurai held you captive. They have no reason to execute you at all." Ramon placed his hands on the rail and looked out at the vast ocean.

"Perhaps they will just make me a prisoner," mused Mendeleev. "I'm getting rather used to that."

Ramon turned and narrowed his gaze, trying to understand what the scientist meant.

Whether Legion translated the idea to Mendeleev or the scientist just wanted to talk, he continued. "Before the samurai, Legion and his dreams of world unity held me captive."

Legion's surprise blossomed clear in Ramon's thoughts. He echoed the alien's question. "You saw yourself as Legion's prisoner?"

"Wasn't I?" Mendeleev shrugged, eyes forward. "Legion dictated everything I did. I insisted on taking the airship to

184

Poronaysk so I could conduct experiments on air density and hydrogen. It gave me a chance to fly in the airships I designed. I hadn't been allowed to do that during Legion's regime."

"*What about the dream of world unity?*" Ramon detected hurt in Legion's silent query.

"It is a nice dream," agreed Mendeleev, "but unity means little if people are not free to dream their own dreams and pursue their own goals."

"*I would have granted freedom, once unity had been achieved and the chance of humans destroying one another had been eliminated.*"

"Czars and emperors everywhere have long made the same promise." Mendeleev shook his head and closed his eyes.

Ramon considered Legion's words and remembered his days as Socorro County Sheriff. Miners, farmers, and ranchers, all had their own uses for the land. Ramon didn't believe those conflicts would end unless Legion controlled the people forever. "I think you've had it backwards, Legion. You thought unity would bring peace, but I think humans have to find peace first on their own, then unity has a chance to follow. That's what I tried to convey in Sausalito." That seemed ages ago, but it had occurred right before he returned to New Mexico and married Fatemeh.

"*Indeed, I left and then Imagawa stole an airship and you implored me for help again.*"

Ramon and Mendeleev looked at each other. "Thank you for your help. I'm not sure if we could have stopped her otherwise." Ramon shivered and folded his arms. "I'm worried because Imagawa said she had completed her mission. Russia and Japan may yet go to war."

"*Do you think I should have intervened more?*"

"It could have saved much trouble, yes," conceded Mendeleev, who had been silent, "but now there is an opportunity for Russia and Japan to talk and work out differences, perhaps come to a stronger agreement than we would have if you just told Imagawa what to do."

Legion remained silent for a long time. Ramon thought the alien had left, although where he'd go, he had no idea. "*The universe is infinite,*" said Legion at last. "*I have never lost my capacity to learn. Everywhere I go, I discover new things. I should know intelligent beings have the capacity to learn as I do."*

"A good teacher guides, but does not provide the answers," said Mendeleev.

"In answer to your question, Ramon Morales, I have many places yet to go. I am not bound to your world, but the truth is, I am somewhat lonesome. I see potential in humans to become like me, if they survive long enough. May I remain and observe a little longer?"

Ramon lifted his eyebrows. "Do we have a choice?"

"I grant you one."

"Then remain," said Mendeleev, "and we will try not to call on you too soon this time."

Ramon's head spun and he grabbed the ship's rail to steady himself. As he recovered, he considered Legion's comment about being lonesome. Just then, it struck him the swarm usually referred to itself as "we." When had it started referring to itself in the singular? He filed the thought away and would consider it again later.

He looked over to Mendeleev. "The Japanese are good people. I will do everything in my power to keep them from executing or imprisoning you."

This time Mendeleev's brow knitted. He nodded as though he understood some, but not all Ramon said, then he spoke a few words in Russian. Ramon caught the gist of the scientist's meaning and thought he understood one or two words. He believed he could learn the language in a few days if he applied himself. He wondered if Legion had done something to him or if the understanding was a side effect of Legion's earlier translations.

The two looked at each other for a moment, then Mendeleev patted Ramon on the shoulder and walked away, beckoning for him to follow. The scientist led him below decks and knocked on a door. The Ainu woman, Ipokash, answered. Mendeleev spoke to her. She looked back at the bed, where Shinriki lay with a cloth on his forehead, his eyes closed, then stepped into the hall, pulling the door closed behind her.

Ramon turned around and knocked on Hoshi's door. The farmer answered and bowed. "I want to assure Professor Mendeleev I will do everything possible to return him home."

Hoshi pursed his lips. "The Japanese Lords may have a

different opinion."

"I've met two of them. They are good men as you are. Please tell him."

Hoshi spoke the words in Japanese and Ipokash translated them into Russian. Mendeleev smiled, patted Ramon on the shoulder and said, "Spasibo." The gratitude on the scientist's face clarified the word's meaning for Ramon.

Upon arrival in Tokyo, Captain Cisneros summoned a dock worker and gave him a message for Katsu Kaishū. He then gave a list of chemicals to Boatswain Balderas. "I want everything you can manage aboard by lunchtime."

Balderas grinned. "Getting ready for a round-the-world voyage?"

"Just about," said the captain.

By mid-morning, Lord Katsu's mechanical man rolled across the gang plank and handed a letter to the boatswain, who carried it to the captain. Cisneros read it, nodded and looked up. "Round up Morales, Masuda, and Mendeleev. Lord Katsu has agreed to see them."

Fifteen minutes later, the captain strode to the deck and found the men gathered around Lord Katsu's automaton. The mechanical man rolled across the gang plank and led them to a coach with no horses. All marveled at the sight except for Ramon, who cringed. The mechanical man opened the coach door and the four men climbed aboard.

The automaton closed the door, then grabbed the shaft and rolled through the streets. Cisneros studied the men in the coach. Ramon gazed out at the streets. Mendeleev sat deep in thought—whether contemplating the mechanical man or concerned about his own fate in the hands of the Japanese, Cisneros could not tell. Like Ramon, Hoshi stared outside, but with less longing and more wonder.

They soon rolled up to the Tokyo Prefectural Offices where two guards met them, issued curt orders in Japanese, then made a smart about-face and marched forward. Hoshi, Mendeleev, Ramon, and Cisneros followed them inside, down a hall, and into a room with a long table. Cisneros recognized Katsu Kaishū, but not the other man.

Ramon bowed. "Lord Ōkubo. It is a pleasure to see you again."

Cisneros swallowed as he recognized the Lord of Home Affairs' name.

Lord Katsu invited them to sit, then began. "We stand at the brink of war. As you know, a Russian airship attacked Sapporo and Wakkanai. Lord Ōkubo tells me you have reason to suspect pirates controlled the ship."

Ramon held out his hand to Mendeleev. "This man is Dmitri Mendeleev. He's a Russian scientist from the airship in question. He can confirm a samurai named Imagawa Masako hijacked the ship."

Lord Katsu barred his teeth and both Cisneros and Hoshi shot Ramon a warning glance. "Prince Yamagata convinced the emperor to order an attack on Russia before either Lord Ōkubo or I could investigate further. The airship *Bashō* was lost with all hands during the attack."

Cisneros gasped and leaned forward. "Captain Sanada?" he whispered, but realized his place.

Katsu's gaze softened. He cleared his throat. "Captain Sanada is believed dead. *Bashō's* sister ship, the *Bonchō* shot down a Russian airship leaving Sakhalin Island."

"We know." Ramon pointed from Mendeleev to himself. "We were aboard when it happened. What we want to know is whether or not we can stop a full-scale war."

"Perhaps you can, if you can maintain your manners, Mr. Morales." Lord Ōkubo leaned forward.

Ramon's jaw tensed for a moment, then he relaxed, put his hands together and made a respectful bow. Cisneros forced himself to stifle a laugh. The gesture reminded him of Fatemeh, but it also proved just the thing to placate the two lords.

"The emperor will grant you an audience and listen to your story, then decide what to do," explained Lord Ōkubo. "You will bow low in his presence and will not speak unless invited to. Am I understood?"

Ramon swallowed, then nodded. "Yes, sir. Absolutely."

Cisneros turned to Lord Katsu. "Has the emperor requested

my testimony?"

Katsu and Ōkubo exchanged glances, then Katsu shook his head. "No, but you may attend."

"Thank you, but I hoped to get underway as soon as possible. We required minimal provisions and my crewmen stayed behind in Russia guarding Imagawa and her men."

Katsu half rose. "She still lives?"

"You left her behind?" Ōkubo narrowed his gaze.

"I beg your pardon, my lords," interjected Hoshi. "Many factors contributed to the captain's decision. The captain acted in the interests of international peace and goodwill. Also, Imagawa requests a trial for her and her men, rather than summary execution."

"Of course, of course." Ōkubo granted permission as though it should have been obvious.

"Hurry and get her." Katsu leaned forward. "Bring her back as soon as possible."

"Unless there is anything else, I will make a request for an imperial audience." Ōkubo stood and left the chamber.

"I also have business to attend to," said Lord Katsu. "I suspect the audience will happen within the hour, but if it will take more time, I will arrange quarters for you."

Once Katsu left the room, Ramon looked at Hoshi. "I don't remember Imagawa requesting a trial."

Hoshi sighed. "I know you of all people understand love, Mr. Morales. I had to assure she had a chance to make a new start."

Cisneros faced Ramon. "I'll be back with Fatemeh as soon as I can."

Ramon stood and shook the captain's hand. "I know. Godspeed, my friend."

Hoshi also stood.

"Where are you going?" asked Ramon.

"With the captain." Hoshi made the statement as though it should be obvious. "You don't need me here. I agreed to come along because I thought you could use my help in matters of etiquette and protocol, but I see you already have made friends in high places." He leaned forward and spoke in a low tone. "I may be able to help with Imagawa and her men."

Ramon shook Hoshi's hand and wondered if the prospective audience with the emperor spooked him.

Soon after they left, a young woman brought in a tea pot. She poured tea for Ramon and Mendeleev. The Russian scientist appeared baffled and perhaps a bit nervous. Ramon tried a Russian phrase. "Drink up." He brought the cup to his own lips. In English he said, "It helps calm the nerves."

Mendeleev nodded and sipped the tea.

The Japanese serving girl smiled and backed out of the room.

Soon afterward, a sleepy-eyed man entered and introduced himself as Itō Hirobumi. "I am a member of Lord Ōkubo's staff, but I speak Russian." He introduced himself to Mendeleev. The two conversed in hushed tones. Ramon followed somewhat and inferred Itō informed the scientist about the coming meeting.

"Have you ever met the emperor before?" asked Ramon.

Itō nodded.

"Is there anything I should know?"

"Be respectful. He will have the power of life and death over you."

More than two hours later, a young man in an army uniform with gold piping on the sleeves and the trouser legs appeared in the doorway. "Follow me, please," he said in Japanese.

Itō looked to Ramon. "I believe it's time for our audience."

They followed the young officer from the room, through the Tokyo Prefectural office's back door, and across a bridge spanning a moat. Trees obscured the Imperial Palace. The scents of flowers and greenery tempted Ramon to stay. He'd grown to love Japan. The officer led them past gates and across a courtyard into a long, two-story building with a sloping, slate-tile roof.

They marched through a long hallway, then the officer held up his hand indicating they should wait. He opened one side of a double door and entered. A moment later, he returned and beckoned them forward. As they entered, the officer stated their names.

Emperor Mutsuhito, known as the Meiji Emperor, sat in

a golden, padded chair. He wore an elaborate western military-style uniform, with gold braid swirled around the arms. Ramon thought the gold braid on his chest resembled railroad tracks. The emperor wore enormous epaulets which looked like giant brushes. They seemed as though they should weigh the emperor down.

Katsu Kaishū and Ōkubo Toshimichi knelt on the floor below the throne. Ramon, Mendeleev, and Itō joined them.

The emperor studied the men for several moments. "Professor Mendeleev tell me your story," he commanded.

Itō translated for Mendeleev. The scientist nodded and began to speak in Russian. Ōkubo's man did his best to follow along and render the words into Japanese. Mendeleev told how Imagawa captured the Russian airship and how she made him teach her samurai how to operate the craft. He took care to mention the Ainu woman Ipokash who translated. The emperor sniffed at the mention, as though a woman had little relevance to the tale.

Mendeleev told how Imagawa held the Russian crew and noted their eventual release. He gave his best account of the raids on Sapporo and Wakkanai. He concluded the account by describing Ramon and Fatemeh's daring raid on the airship, the Russian attack, and how the *Bonchō* thwarted Imagawa's escape.

"You did nothing to stop Imagawa?" asked the emperor.

"I was but one man," translated Itō. "I looked for ways to escape and ways to sabotage her plans, but in my opinion, she would have killed me if I tried anything."

The emperor sniffed, then asked for Ramon to tell his story. Again Itō translated.

Ramon told how he honeymooned with his wife and how they traveled to Japan. He said once they knew about the attack on Sapporo, they worked to alert the authorities about the samurai pirates. Once Cisneros returned, they decided to try to stop them.

The emperor leaned forward. "You decided to stop an airship filled with samurai on your honeymoon?"

Itō translated and Ramon answered with a simple "yes, sir."

The emperor didn't wait for the translation before he sat

back and barked out a laugh. "You are either the bravest man I've met or the stupidist." Itō translated the part about Ramon being the bravest man and omitted the second part. "Lord Ōkubo tells me the spirits like you and he trusts you even if you are an ill-mannered American."

"Arigato gozaimasu." Ramon bowed low.

The emperor smiled. "Wait outside. I will confer with my ministers."

Lord Ōkubo's man held the door while Itō, Ramon, and Mendeleev left the chamber. The officer led them down the hall to a small sitting room and told them to wait. Ramon's stomach began to rumble and he hoped they would be excused soon. He hoped for the chance to find a good beef stew.

He didn't have long to wait. Lord Katsu entered and bowed. Ramon and Itō stood and returned the gesture. "The emperor is anxious to prevent war with Russia. You have convinced him a misunderstanding occurred and he has commanded you to go to St. Petersburg to work with our ambassador there to prevent a war."

Ramon took a step forward. "What about Fatemeh?"

"I'll be happy to provide hospitality when she arrives in Tokyo. She'll be here when you return."

"When do we go?" asked Itō.

"This afternoon," said Katsu. "The *Bonchō* prepares for departure. My assistant will show you the way and accompany you on the journey."

Just then, Ramon noticed Lord Katsu's mechanical man whirring and ticking nearby. "Fine with me, as long as he doesn't fly the airship."

CHAPTER SEVENTEEN
OWL TRAIL

Captain Cisneros stood on the *Ballena's* bridge and watched the horizon. Soon land appeared in the distance. He retrieved the spyglass and checked their position. "Land ho," he said, half to himself. He pulled out his pocket watch. "Round trip to Tokyo in eighty-two hours. Not quite a record, but not bad. Well done."

"We've got a problem," called the first mate. "Ship off the starboard bow."

Cisneros swung his spyglass around and swore. He couldn't see the ship's colors, but he guessed it must be a Russian cruiser on patrol. "Keep going," he ordered the helmsman. "We're just a friendly merchant ship on business."

The captain strode outside and leaned on the rail, watching the ship. As it drew close enough for him to see the people on deck, he waved.

Someone on the other ship lifted a speaking trumpet and called out in a language Cisneros didn't recognize, but from the Cyrillic letters on the ship's bow, he knew the man spoke Russian.

Cisneros turned around and opened a locker and retrieved his own speaking trumpet. "No comprende! Vladivostok!" He suspected the Russians would know English better than Spanish. Even if they didn't understand the words, he hoped they would interpret them as a lost Mexican merchant ship bound for Vladivostok.

The man on the other ship gestured to the south
Cisneros looked ahead and pretended not to see.

The man on the Russian ship shouted at them and continued pointing southward. The helmsman followed orders and continued straight ahead.

The two ships drew close enough together Cisneros could see the infuriated scowl on the other man's face. He lowered the speaking trumpet and shouted over his shoulder. A moment later, guns on the ship's deck turned toward the *Ballena*.

The captain swore under his breath. "Mierda." He turned around and ran back to the bridge. As he reached the door, the Russian ship fired across *Ballena's* bow. The hairs on the captain's neck stood on edge as he called out orders. "Turn southward!"

The helmsman nodded and turned the ship.

"Throttle down a bit. I don't want to outrun them... yet. Let's see what they do." Cisneros glanced toward the first mate. "Ready the *Calamar*, but don't bring her on deck until I give the order."

"Aye, aye, sir."

Cisneros returned to the deck and strolled to the stern. He watched the Russian cruiser for a good thirty minutes. He had hoped the *Ballena's* course change would satisfy them and they would return to their patrol station closer to shore. Instead, they remained right on their tail, bound and determined to follow the *Ballena* into port at Vladivostok, where they would check their papers and discover nothing destined for a Russian port, then take everything that wasn't nailed down.

Cisneros returned to the bridge. "Course due east," he said. "Open up the engines to full speed!"

The engines revved up and the ship shot forward. He loved the raw power. Returning to deck, he watched the Russian ship fall farther astern until they vanished. Even then, he gave it another ten minutes, returned to the bridge and ordered them to turn north, dropping to two-thirds speed.

He hoped the Russian captain would assume he'd chased off pirates. Cisneros figured the Russian captain was too shrewd to just continue southward to Vladivostok with no prey. He'd probably turn around and try to cut off the *Ballena* before it reached shore.

At this point, the *Calamar* now had a full supply of fuel rods and his crew worked on more. He could make a few round trips of over twenty miles or more if he needed. However, he hoped it wouldn't prove necessary. He suspected the

Russian ship would patrol the area where they first intercepted the *Ballena* and unless they detected any suspicious activity, they would resume their regular patrol.

A whistle sounded from the speaking tubes. Cisneros answered. "*Calamar* is ready to go."

"Go ahead and bring her on deck and summon Mr. Masuda. I don't want our men to have too much time ashore. They'll get lazy!"

Legion watched Ramon Morales as the airship *Bonchō* traveled over Asia. At forty-five miles per hour—fast by human standards—the airship sped high over barren, rocky, and wild land, which Legion knew to be Mongolia. Morales delighted in standing on the catwalk behind the gondola, wearing goggles and sticking his head through the safety lines. The wind rushed through his hair and he laughed.

Legion allowed components of himself to ride the ship's wake, only performing sufficient calculations to avoid destruction. The ride exhilarated him. The airship passed birds in flight and Ramon smiled and waved. Invisible, Legion swirled around the birds, admiring their colors and elegant, organic wings. Morales loved the airship just as Legion's organic ancestors had fallen in love with machines.

For millennia, Legion had traveled the universe, content to explore and learn all he could. Although Legion's many parts spoke among themselves, he had forgotten how stimulating other voices could be—voices which expressed both dissent and meaningful agreement. Ramon reminded him what good conversation could be like.

Watching Ramon and Fatemeh, Legion observed the power of two people working together to achieve a common goal. One person's strengths often compensated for the other's weaknesses. Despite that, Ramon's energy seemed little diminished as he traveled to the Russian capital. He did seem to miss Fatemeh, especially at dinner and bedtime when he expected someone beside him. At night, he said quiet prayers to his deity and asked for Fatemeh's safety.

Ramon prayed and spoke those words, even though he sometimes doubted the deity he invoked. Despite being an invisible force with vast powers and knowledge, Ramon never once envisioned Legion as a replacement for a deity. Legion appreciated that about Ramon.

Invigorated from the fresh air, but somewhat chilled, Ramon returned to his cabin within the gondola. Legion gathered his components and followed. Ramon washed up, then went across the hall where Itō Hirobumi sat with Dmitri Mendeleev.

Itō helped Ramon learn Russian. The former sheriff threw himself into the studies and proved a natural. When the alien translated the conversations with Mendeleev, he altered chemicals and rerouted neural pathways. When he left, he never bothered to undo what he'd done. Ramon had already picked up more Japanese than he admitted and he now demonstrated an aptitude for Russian.

Ramon believed Fatemeh possessed superior gifts to him—and in some ways she did. Because of that belief, he didn't apply himself to language until forced to. Legion found it interesting he allowed his talents to shine more in her absence.

The *Bonchō* would arrive in St. Petersburg in a little under three days. Even with Legion's meddling, it seemed doubtful Ramon would master the language in such a short time, but he would be able to present formal greetings, make simple requests, and sense what people said even when no one directed comments toward him.

The scientist explained court etiquette to both Itō and Ramon. Although he feigned little interest in such things, Mendeleev proved a skilled tutor. He spent considerable time in the Romanov's palace and scientists relied on funding from the rich and powerful. Mendeleev might see himself as above etiquette, but he would use it to get what he wanted.

Feeling proud, Legion reevaluated his relationship with humans. They started as the subject of an experiment to see if he could influence a culture's development. They now transcended experimental status, but what were they now? Pets? That implied he assumed responsibility for humans, something he never intended. He believed he could move on whenever he wanted.

The problem was, he didn't want to move on. He wanted to stay at least a little while longer and see if these humans worked out their differences.

Ramon took a break from his lessons with Mendeleev and Itō. They called for supper. As they ate, they swapped stories of the places they had been and the things they had done. Ramon told how Fatemeh had angered the mine owner Randolf Dalton in Socorro and how he convinced people she practiced witchcraft so she would be eliminated.

Itō told about a prank he played while a student at the University of London and Mendeleev laughed and told how his mother took him across Siberia to get an education. Ramon understood the scientist's youthful poverty and admired how he persevered to improve himself.

As stewards cleared the dishes and the men returned to work, Legion longed for jovial banter. When Ramon returned to his quarters and turned down the blankets, Legion chanced to ask Ramon a question. *"May I tell you a story from my travels?"*

The question surprised Ramon and Legion feared the sheriff would tell him to leave. Instead, the swarm registered the increase of electro-chemical activity in Ramon's brain.

Ramon posed a counter-suggestion. *"As long as you let me form my own pictures while you tell the story."*

"I shall endeavor to restrict myself to words." With that, Legion began a tale of a large, shaggy animal herd living on a small Earth-like planet orbiting a red star. It pleased him to share his observations, even though the story had little action and perhaps no point. Legion took no offence when Ramon's brain activity indicated he'd fallen asleep. He chanced to peek at Ramon's thoughts, pleased the former sheriff dreamed of distant worlds.

Onofre Cisneros piloted the *Calamar* toward the Russian coast. Masuda Hoshi sat next to him, eyes closed and hands folded. At one point, a faint chugging resonated through the hull, which Cisneros recognized as a ship's propeller in the water above. From his vantage, he couldn't tell for sure, but he guessed the

Russian Navy ship patrolled the coast, looking to see if the *Ballena* returned.

Soon, Cisneros reached the shore and surfaced. Throwing the hatch open, he smiled—just for a moment—when he saw the camp's lean-tos. Wind stripped the roofs off several shelters already. No smoke wafted from campfires. No one milled around the makeshift structures. "It looks like they left," he said as he climbed back inside.

Hoshi narrowed his gaze, but remained silent, waiting to see what they would find.

Cisneros took on ballast to lower the *Calamar* to the sea floor, then extended the tractor treads. Once the submersible trundled ashore, the captain disengaged the fuel rods and climbed out. Hoshi followed a moment later.

They found a few food scraps and some empty sake bottles. The captain's stomach burned when he found Apodaca's and Rodriguez's packs abandoned in a lean-to. If they'd left, why hadn't they taken their supplies with them? He turned around and studied the camp with care. Hoshi approached another tattered lean-to surrounded by footprints. Hoshi lifted frayed rope. "I believe the samurai tied someone up and threw them in to die."

"Who?"

Hoshi didn't answer. Instead he studied the footprints. "Imagawa," he said at last.

"How do you know?"

"She and Fatemeh have the smallest feet. If the captive had been Fatemeh, she would have waited."

Cisneros appreciated the logic as he followed the footprints

Whoever had been left to die had not been content to do so. Footprints led to a place where flies congregated on brown-stained grass. Blood—and lots of it—had spilled.

A little further up the hill, the captain found two mounds. He swallowed, but lifted a few rocks. Within the grave, he found Apodaca, a bullet hole between his eyes.

It had been many years since Onofre Cisneros had stepped inside a church, but he removed his cap and made the sign of the cross, then reburied his shipmate. Imagawa respected the men enough to make it difficult for animals to get at them.

Buried in a flood plain, rushing waters would carry them out to sea one day. A fitting end for sailors.

Cisneros followed Imagawa's footsteps to the camp, where she must have scavenged for supplies. "Where did she go? South to Vladivostok or west toward China?"

Hoshi walked the camp's perimeter. Cisneros found few clues, but Hoshi pointed to some broken twigs and scuffed earth. "They followed the river valley inland. They hope to reach China."

The captain removed his hat and ran fingers through his hair. He hated to lose the samurai, but Fatemeh concerned him most. Just to be certain, he checked the other grave. As he suspected, it belonged to Rodriguez. "Why did they take Fatemeh?"

"They must have wanted her skills as a healer to treat the injured. Their progress will be slow."

Cisneros shook his head. "It doesn't make sense. Why did they restrain Imagawa? Wouldn't she want to go with them?"

"Imagawa achieved her objective. She accepted she must return to Japan and meet her fate. The others were not so sanguine to face punishment."

The captain narrowed his gaze. "Then why did she follow? She knew we'd be here soon."

"Her men turned against her. Imagawa seeks revenge."

The captain spat on the ground. Gonzalez aboard the *Ballena* would begin to worry if he lingered too long ashore. The first mate might even do something foolish like try to come ashore himself. The *Ballena* wouldn't last long if the Russian ship returned.

Despite that, Cisneros didn't feel he had a choice. The *Calamar* had a full fuel supply and the samurai had as much as a four-day head start on foot. He checked his weapons and returned to the submersible with Hoshi close behind. They climbed aboard and activated the chemical steam engine. "Hang onto your seat. This will be a rough ride," he said.

The captain engaged the clutch and the *Calamar* rolled forward, flattening the flood plain's grasses and scrub brush. He hoped wounded samurai chose to follow the river as long as possible. Near the coast, the flood plain was a mile or more wide. The *Calamar* couldn't follow long if they turned into the woodlands surrounding them on each side. He swallowed and opened the throttle.

Imagawa followed Nanbu's trail as it disappeared into the forest. Anger and disgust seethed within her. She would have welcomed a duel, but the coward ordered her own men to bind her and leave her behind for Cisneros to discover. She wouldn't let the insult stand. What's more, Fatemeh held insights into this new era she found useful. Nanbu could have stayed put until more men could travel. Simple impatience dictated Fatemeh's abduction, which in turn violated the code of Bushido.

A bitter smile formed as she thought of Hoshi's devotion to the code. The samurai steeped Bushido and swords with idealism. She treasured her sword, but preferred a pistol or rifle in battle any day. She reached down and felt the shark skin sword handle. Despite her preferences, Imagawa smiled at the thought of hacking Nanbu to pieces for his betrayal. Nanbu proved himself both a coward and an idiot. He should have taken her sword. Instead, he left it stuck in the ground near Apodaca and Rodriguez's bodies.

She hiked through the spruce and fir forest. Although the others had a day's head start, she believed she could catch up. She didn't believe Fatemeh could maintain a forced march, and at least five others were wounded. Their path through the flood plain had been clumsy and easy to follow. She faced little additional difficulty among the forest's trees.

Ominous, dark clouds formed overhead and a chill wind blew, causing her to pull her Haori closed around her neck. She wished for a proper coat or cloak, but appreciated her boots. Her lips grew parched and she realized she needed water and the river had grown distant.

An hour later, she heard a trickling. She paused for a moment and listened. The path to the water diverged from the trail she followed. Ten men could be loud and boisterous. Perhaps they hadn't heard or perhaps they didn't need water yet. She barred her teeth and stripped some bark from a tree on the

trail, so she could find her way back, then pursued the sound
to its source.

She knelt beside a small stream and lifted icy water to her
lips. As she did, snow began to waft down from the sky. She
took another drink then stood up with a curse. Her stomach
rumbled, but she hated to take time to eat lest snow obscure
the trail. She grabbed a piece of dried fish from her pack and
chewed as she walked.

The cloudy skies made it difficult to tell time. The snow
remained light, but the clouds grew darker. Either the storm
threatened to worsen or night prepared to fall.

With no way to light her path, Imagawa followed the trail
a short distance further, then sat down at the tree's base. The
branches overhead kept the ground snow free. She removed a
blanket from her pack and wrapped up in it as best she could,
hoping it would not grow so cold she would freeze to death.

As she drifted off to sleep, a hooting sounded. Her eyes
popped open and she looked up into a birch tree's branches.
An owl gazed down.

"Go bother someone else, bird. I'm no prey for you."

The owl launched itself from the branch and flew off
through the trees. As her eyes drifted shut, she envied the owl
and its power of flight. She wondered what the bird would do
if it could no longer fly.

Fatemeh carried a light pack compared to those the samurai
hefted. It contained the medical supplies salvaged from *The
Brazen Shark*. Several times she looked for ways to escape, but
didn't feel she could disappear far enough into the dense forest
to elude recapture.

Relief washed over her when they came to a small river
and Nanbu ordered them to make camp for the night. She
dropped her pack and tried to rub some feeling back into her
shoulders. Nanbu ordered the uninjured men to gather fire-
wood. Fatemeh had no reason to expect Imagawa to follow.
The smart plan would be to stay put and wait for Cisneros.
Even if Imagawa did follow, Fatemeh couldn't decide if it

would help her own situation.

The most wounded samurai's leg suffered a serious cut. She leaned over and reached for the bandage. He gasped air and shouted in Japanese. Nanbu overheard and shouted a response. She didn't understand well enough to tell for sure, but she gathered Nanbu ordered him to let her do what she needed.

She unwrapped the crusted and brown bandages, revealing an angry red infection. She could have prevented it if they'd stopped more often. Fatemeh found a cloth in her pack, took it to the water, soaked it, and brought it back. When she applied the icy water to the wound, the samurai yelled again. "That's nothing," she said as she retrieved an iodine bottle from the pack and poured it on, hoping to slow the infection.

The warrior squinted his eyes shut, but grabbed his sword. Despite the implied threat, Fatemeh found a slim bandage roll and wrapped the wound anew. By the time she finished, she smelled smoke. The samurai had started a fire. Her stomach rumbled as she anticipated even a meager meal.

She moved on to the next man, whose arm had several lacerations. He no longer bled and she saw no infection. Conserving the bandages, she washed the wound and left it uncovered.

As she finished tending the wounded men, snow dusted the ground. She pulled out a slim blanket from her pack and moved close to the fire. Nanbu handed her a plate. "Arigato," she said.

He grunted and nodded.

The slim piece of dried fish seemed to mock her. She determined to take her time and make it last, but the flavor almost made her gag. She swallowed it down with some water and her stomach rumbled again. She wondered how much progress Ramon made as she watched the snow fall toward the flames and evaporate.

As the darkness deepened, Nanbu shooed her away from the fire so the most wounded could have warmth. She had no argument. She did her best to cover herself with the blanket and despite shivering, drifted off to sleep.

Later, a fluttering in a nearby fir tree awakened her. An owl's orange, glowing eyes peered down at her, and it hooted.

She understood at least one person followed. She sat up and looked around. All the samurai slept. Had they bothered to post a guard?

She hooted at the owl. It flew off a short distance. Nanbu reached out, grabbed a rock, and pitched it. She didn't understand the words, but gathered he hoped to shoo away the owl. The warrior rolled over and released a loud snore.

Fatemeh counted bodies. All lay around the fire. She decided to take a chance. She slung her blanket over her shoulders and eschewed her pack for one with food. As she followed the owl toward the nearest trees, her foot landed on a twig and it snapped. She froze.

"Where are you going?" came Nanbu's sleep-thickened voice.

"I need to pee." She hoped she'd used the right words in Japanese.

It must have been close enough. He grunted and rolled over. The owl hooted again. Fatemeh needed no further encouragement. She followed it into the woods.

CHAPTER EIGHTEEN
GIANTS AND THEIR NEIGHBORS

The sky lightened somewhat with twilight's arrival. The sparse dusting of snow brightened the terrain just enough for Fatemeh to backtrack the samurai's trail. Although grateful the snow didn't drift, she left clear footprints. If the samurai chose to pursue her, they would have an easy job. She hoped the sun would come out and melt the snow, but the looming overcast kept her hopes low. Perhaps they would delay a search, trusting she would need to return for food or water.

She looked up when the owl hooted.

She had strayed off the path and the owl chastened her. Although she told people owls didn't speak, she understood the owl's meaning better than she understood some people. She found it more difficult to articulate why the owl chose to help her. Bahá'í teachings focused on human interaction, but they also taught progressive revelation. They taught that God manifested himself through the ages and revealed more and more of his teachings as humanity grew.

If true, it stood to reason progressive revelation must comprise Buddhist teachings. Buddhists taught that self was illusion and all life was connected. It seemed the spirits of owls and other animals must be connected to the spirits of humans. She looked forward to the day she could speak to those Bahá'í teachers close to Bahá'u'lláh, the manifestation of God, to see what they thought.

As Fatemeh approached a wide spot in the path, a figure leapt out from behind a tree, katana held high.

Fatemeh stood, foggy breath bursting from her mouth in discreet clouds. Imagawa lowered the blade, sheathed it, and gave a respectful nod. "You escaped," she said in Japanese.

204

"I'm impressed." Imagawa's breath also came out in little white puffs.

Fatemeh looked at her in the kimono, haori, and hakama. She must be freezing. "We should return to the coast and meet Captain Cisneros." Fatemeh thought she mangled some of the words, but pointed down the trail. Imagawa looked where she pointed. Impatient, the owl stood on a tree branch and hooted.

After a moment's consideration, Imagawa shook her head. "I will kill Nanbu for what he did."

Fatemeh's sigh manifested in a thick cloud. "Leave them." Her sleep-deprived mind struggled to find words. "Fighting them does no good."

"My soul is damaged," said Imagawa. "I have suffered too many defeats of late. I cannot let Nanbu's betrayal stand."

"Killing Nanbu won't restore your honor. You regain honor by returning to Tokyo to face justice and contribute to a new, healthy Japan."

Imagawa frowned, but considered Fatemeh's argument. In the silence which followed, Fatemeh noticed a crunching sound and a faint glow through the trees. Imagawa heard it too and summoned Fatemeh into the trees' shadows. The owl fluttered away. Fatemeh had assumed it hooted because it wanted her to follow. Did it warn of impending danger? Sometimes her understanding proved less than perfect.

The man who ambled into the clearing wore trousers and a frock coat. He hitched up his pants and lifted a lantern, studying the tracks in the soil. As he glanced around, Fatemeh recognized Onofre Cisneros. She emerged from the tree cover. "Captain. It's good to see you." Imagawa appeared beside her, but stopped short when Hoshi appeared, also holding a lantern.

The captain smiled. He set the lantern down and grabbed Fatemeh in a hug. The impropriety set her teeth on edge, but his body's warmth felt so good, she reached around and returned the hug anyway. He let go and looked ready to hug Imagawa as well, but she stepped back with her hand on the sword's hilt. The captain made a wise choice and let her be.

"You seem delighted to see us." Fatemeh's foggy brain worked to speak English again after thinking in rudimentary Japanese for the last few days. More than anything, she wanted a good, strong cup of coffee.

"I feared you'd been killed or I wouldn't be able to find you," said the captain. "I hated to leave you the other day, but didn't have another choice. The *Calamar* allowed me to catch up. It took just four hours to cover the ground you covered in three days."

"What about Ramon? Is he with you?"

Cisneros gave a sly smile. "He's traveling to St. Petersburg to see if he can negotiate a peace between the Japanese and the Russians."

"Without me?" The emotions washing over Fatemeh startled her. Pride at him taking this step warred with jealousy that he made the trip without her.

Hoshi stepped up. "I presume the other samurai are ahead and do not wish to join us."

"No." Fatemeh pursed her lips. She wanted to get back to the *Ballena* and discuss things in a warm cabin, but a sense of responsibility prickled at her. "Do the Japanese expect us to bring the samurai along?"

"Do you really think we could persuade them to go if they don't want to?" Cisneros shrugged. "What will happen to them anyway? This far into autumn, they'll either die out here in the woods or they'll make it to China. Either way, I doubt they'll make much more trouble for Japan."

Fatemeh turned to see what Imagawa thought, but she had vanished.

Cisneros scanned the trees. "Where'd she go?"

"No doubt she's gone to confront Nanbu," said Hoshi.

Fatemeh cursed under her breath. "We should follow her."

Cisneros shook his head. "I have no intention of tangling with samurai warriors. If they have differences to settle, we should let them."

"I won't just let Imagawa throw her life away if I can avoid it. I disagree with her, but I think she and Japan need each other." Fatemeh picked up her pack and turned. Like Imagawa, Hoshi had vanished.

Cisneros reached out and grabbed Fatemeh's arm. "What will you do when you catch up with her? You can't force her to go with us. She'll overpower you."

"I hope I'll be able to talk some sense into her." Fatemeh set out. The owl hooted. A minute later, Captain Cisneros's boots crunched on the frosty ground.

Ramon fell asleep to a tale of warriors on a distant planet. The warriors looked human—almost. They had orange skin and large black eyes. Writhing and wriggling purple mustaches hung under their noses. Despite their differences, they built tools, loved, fought, and lived lives much as humans did. One day, a woman moved into town who could build machines like no one else had seen. Her machines could lift heavy objects with ease and manipulate matter to form new materials. Some called her a witch and threatened to drive her away until a warrior stood up for her.

Ramon awoke with a start, half expecting to find himself on the distant world, but he found himself aboard the Japanese airship. After getting his bearings, Ramon considered the story's veracity as he pondered its resemblance to the story he shared with Fatemeh.

"*I have seen millions of worlds,*" said Legion within Ramon's mind. "*The story happened, but I did pick it because it resembled your story.*"

Ramon's anger threatened to take control. He threw back the blankets and sat up on the bedroll, but then stopped. He looked around at the sunlight streaming into the simple, clean cabin of wood and paper. He shivered and hoped the Japanese would figure out a way to heat their airships without risking fire.

Calmer, Ramon whispered, "You're still in my mind?"

"*I have not pried. I simply observed your sleep patterns. You seem troubled.*"

"I hope Fatemeh will be all right."

"*I could find out if Cisneros knows.*"

Ramon shook his head. He climbed from blankets, poured water in a basin and splashed it over his face until he awakened more. Thinking of the lightweight, thin walls, Ramon closed his eyes and thought the next words. *Why did you stay in my mind?*

Why did you watch me?

"Fatemeh stays with you. She sometimes watches you when you sleep."

Ramon snorted and sought his trousers. *Do you remember the story I told you about the adults who helped me overcome the pain of my father's death?*

"Of course."

Have you ever been a teacher? Ramon grabbed a shirt and walked over to the porthole and looked out.

Legion remained silent for so long, Ramon thought he had left. A moment later, he felt more than heard a response in the negative.

The *Bonchō* drifted over an expansive blue lake. Ramon thought Fatemeh would love the sight and wished she were there to see it with him.

You've seen the harm which comes from manipulating people, and when I feel you're close to doing that it upsets me. Ramon sighed and spoke aloud. "You have good insights. Please tell me if you think I'm making any mistakes."

"I think leaving Fatemeh behind was a mistake," said Legion. *"She is your best teacher and best advisor."*

"I know she is."

A soft knock sounded at the door. Ramon walked over and slid it aside to reveal Lord Katsu's mechanical servant. It held out a coffee carafe. Behind him stood Itō. "Sorry to disturb you, but I heard you speak. I gather Americans prefer coffee to tea."

Ramon's cheeks flushed and he nodded. "Thanks, just thinking aloud. Are we still on for Russian lessons?"

Itō nodded. "Starting in half an hour."

The mechanical man closed the door and words formed in Ramon's mind. *Is he the future you see for man?*

"Oh, no." Although silent, Legion empathized. *"He is far too fragile. In fact he is far more fragile than you."* Legion paused. *"We were speaking of advisors."*

Ramon nodded as he put on his shirt and suspenders. "Until Fatemeh's beside me again, will you be my advisor? Don't tell me the answers. Just help me see the right road to travel."

"I would be delighted to." Pleasurable waves emanated from Legion. *"It allows me the opportunity to see how this all comes out."*

Another silence ensued and Ramon tossed on a waistcoat and prepared to find Mendeleev and Itō to start the day's lessons. *"Can you ever forgive me for what I've done to humanity?"*

Ramon stopped, surprised. "Why does a creature like you need my forgiveness?" He didn't bother to lower his voice.

"You're correct I do not need your forgiveness, Ramon Morales, but I desire it." During the next silence, Ramon pictured clockworks whirring and ticking. *"I will outlive you, but I might not outlive your kind. I hope your children will look on me with fondness and seek me out as a friend."*

The clouds started to break up as Fatemeh and Captain Cisneros walked through the woods. Their footfalls sounded all too loud. "If they're looking for me, they'll have no trouble finding me."

"If the samurai are camped where you left them, Imagawa must have their attention by now."

She looked up at blue slices peeking through the clouds. Despite her exhaustion, it gave her hope. She also suspected her fatigue kept her brain from shutting out the captain's actions in the grove. She needed to address the issue in order to clear her head. "Why did you hug me?"

The captain stopped and cocked an eyebrow. "Did I do something wrong?"

"Well, it's just not proper," said Fatemeh. "After all, I'm another man's wife." The words sounded strange to her and she knew people in some other cultures were less reserved about touching, even when the other sex was concerned.

A thorough gentleman, the captain refrained from laughing, but his smile showed great amusement. "Fatemeh, I've come to think of you as a dear friend. You set me on a good course in life. You called on me in an hour of great need. I worried when I found you'd disappeared from the camp. You're like a sister to me." He paused for a moment, then inclined his head. "I hope it wasn't wrong to hug someone who is like a sister."

She closed her eyes against a tear which formed as she

considered her own family. "Not wrong at all." She hated the quaver in her voice. "I just wish my own family had been so kind."

He stepped closer and put his arm around her shoulder. "You're trembling. We should turn around and return to the *Calamar*. You need to get warm."

Fatemeh thought the plan sounded excellent, but she forced herself to shake her head. "Imagawa reminds me of you when we met. Bad circumstances damaged her, but she has potential. I see her as family, too."

Cisneros chuckled. "All right, my sister. Let's go get our cousin and find some place warm."

They walked a hundred more yards when raised voices became clear. They spoke so fast, Fatemeh had a hard time understanding their words. Despite her weariness, Fatemeh sprinted ahead with Cisneros close on her heels.

When they broke into the clearing where the samurai had camped the night before, Fatemeh stopped in her tracks. Hoshi corralled the samurai into a wide semi-circle. At the focus stood Imagawa and Nanbu.

Imagawa held her sword overhead. Nanbu held his across his body. Imagawa thrust downward, but Nanbu caught the thrust on the flat of his blade and swung out. The move threw Imagawa off balance and gave Nanbu a chance to reposition himself. Imagawa recovered just in time to evade Nanbu's thrust. They each scrambled to new positions. Imagawa crouched low and Nanbu stood with his sword before him. Imagawa feinted, then thrust upward, driving her katana in between two ribs as Nanbu sliced the wrong way, attempting to block. Four samurai looked among themselves, then bolted for the river's opposite bank. Hoshi let them go.

Nanbu's knees gave way, but he held onto his sword. Imagawa pulled her sword free and took a step back. On his knees and panting, Nanbu clutched his wound. From the blood gushing around his fingers, Fatemeh guessed Imagawa struck his liver. Despite the injury, Nanbu struggled to regain his feet. Imagawa took another step back and held her sword in front of her.

Cisneros cocked his pistol. Fatemeh looked from him to the

remaining samurai. He didn't aim, just kept the weapon ready.

Nanbu reached his feet and gripped his sword in quavering hands, but even Fatemeh realized he held the sword too low to block a blow. Fatemeh ran toward the fight. "No!" she shouted.

The distraction allowed Nanbu to get in a half-hearted thrust. Imagawa dodged and raised her sword. She brought it down in a clean arc which stuck in his neck. Nanbu dropped to the ground. A gurgling filled the still forest. Imagawa lifted her blade and brought it down again, severing Nanbu's head.

Fatemeh turned and clamped her eyes and mouth shut to stifle a scream which contained more anger than horror. Cisneros had called her family and indeed, Fatemeh had begun to think of Imagawa that way, but all at once, she seemed more like the Persian family she abandoned than the American family she adopted.

Murmurings sounded behind Fatemeh. She turned and Imagawa wiped her blade and sheathed it. Hoshi barked commands and the men pledged their allegiance to Imagawa.

"I am ready to go with you, now," she said.

Fatemeh struggled to find words in Japanese. She could call them up in Persian, French and English, but she couldn't put enough Japanese words together to tell Imagawa she was a barbarian. Imagawa represented the world Fatemeh rejected. Her world could burn to ashes, and Fatemeh would help set it alight.

The healer turned and stalked back to Cisneros who said something she didn't hear. She continued into the forest.

When she breathed easier and blood no longer pounded in her head, she listened. The owl hooted. She sought it out and followed its voice. It led her back to the trail. She walked along, oblivious to the pain in her feet and her stomach's growling. She longed to be in Ramon's arms and wished circumstances had not sent him as far away as St. Petersburg.

She struggled atop a rise, then her legs wouldn't move any longer. She dropped to the ground and sat there, out of energy. She tried to stop the tears, but they came anyway. It had been almost two years since she felt this lonesome, since before Ramon came into her life.

Crunching snow and twigs heralded Cisneros tromping up the trail. Loud as the one-time pirate could be, more than one person marched up with him. She suspected Imagawa, Hoshi, and the others as well. She tried to rise but failed.

Imagawa knelt down beside her. She shifted a pack from her back. Fatemeh recognized it as Nanbu's. Imagawa took out a piece of dried fish and handed it to Fatemeh, then handed her a suitou bottle filled with water. Fatemeh stared at her for a moment, then took the bottle and drank some water. She ate the fish in a few bites, then drank a little more.

With a sigh, she allowed Imagawa to help her stand.

"I am ready to face my fate," said Imagawa. "Thank you for not allowing me to end my life."

Fatemeh looked at her and wondered if she'd made the right choice after all.

The *Bonchō* passed into Russian Turkistan at night. Their course carried them near the Golden Mountains of Altai. Despite the idyllic name, Ramon spent a fitful night as winds poured off the mountains and buffeted the little Japanese airship. At one point, the floor dropped out from below Ramon, but it took a few seconds for him to smack into the tatami mat on the floor. The moment of floating reminded him of the time Legion showed him the distant reaches between the planets. Legion called it weightlessness.

Ramon thought he must have been asleep and dreamed the sensation, but a sudden shudder ran through the walls and made him sit bolt upright. He peered around the darkened cabin. A few minutes later, the winds lessened to a gentle swaying rhythm and Ramon drifted off to sleep.

A gentle knock on the cabin door awoke him later and he padded over, tried to push it open, then remembered it slid sideways. Lord Katsu's automaton stood on the other side holding a carafe and a coffee cup. "Thank you," muttered Ramon as he took the proffered items. The automaton trundled away.

Ramon slid the door shut, poured some coffee and tried to wake up. Once dressed, he walked forward to the bridge. The officers stood by the forward windows in quiet consultation. One looked through a spyglass, then lowered it.

Ramon looked down at the chart table and noted their position—about halfway across Russian Turkistan.

Perhaps less than a thousand miles south stood Persia—Fatemeh's homeland. She'd described it to him as a desert land with palm trees, beautiful and harsh all at once. He sensed she missed it in much the way he missed Socorro. The scent of hot oil or distant church bells ringing would remind him of the place he once called home. They both left because people wanted to use power to dominate and control them rather than use their strengths to be good neighbors and help.

He left the bridge and climbed the steps at the gondola's stern. The view from the catwalk took Ramon's breath away. A white field of puffy clouds lay below them, so thick, he could almost believe a giant's castle lay somewhere below. If he did encounter such a thing, would he be Jack and attempt to take what he could before the giant crushed him, or could he and the giant find a way to be friends? It occurred to Ramon there are two choices when you smell blood, help or attack.

Ramon felt a presence nearby. He looked up to see Dmitri Mendeleev. "Beautiful is it not?"

Ramon was pleased to understand the Russian phrase without Legion's help. "Yes it is," he shouted to be heard over the engine's roar.

"This is why I wanted to build airships," called the scientist. "I wanted to see sights like this, see new places and experience new things. I did not build them for war." His eyes glistened. "It seems like there's always a war and soldiers will take any advantage they have."

"Why must there always be war?" Ramon grabbed the lines before him and peered out at the blue sky. The petty concerns of humans below seemed far away.

Mendeleev shrugged. "Russia is so large and we have neighbors all around. Sometimes they want what we have, sometimes we want what they have." He shook his head and turned around, leaning back on the railing. Ramon feared he might topple over backwards. "We can't afford a war with Japan right now. We already have a war with the United States and I hear the Ottoman Turks swarm over Bosnia."

Ramon considered the analogy with Jack and the Bean-stalk. "Neighbors are happier when they share with each other."

Mendeleev grunted. Ramon sensed the scientist agreed, but didn't know how to convince others of such a simple principle. "Rough night last night?" Mendeleev changed the subject.

Ramon nodded.

"I feared this airship would crash. It's not as strong as Russian airships."

Having been aboard a Russian airship, Ramon had to agree. More than Russian pride fueled Mendeleev's sentiment. Ramon looked down at the clouds beneath the walkway's metal grating. Vertigo washed over him. His heart skipped a beat, his stomach lurched, and he reached out and grabbed a rope to stop the sensation of falling. He closed his eyes and lifted his head to face the distant horizon. His vision settled. "Do you think the Japanese could be taught to build more ... robust airships?"

Mendeleev frowned but nodded. "The czar wouldn't approve. It takes many people a long time to build an airship. Four Russian craft have now been destroyed. We're building a fifth, but it isn't finished yet."

Ramon filed the information away as a chill sent a shudder rippling over his skin. "What if Japan had something to offer Russia?"

"Japan's main value is its sea ports."

Ramon sighed. "You know, airships reduce the need for warm water sea ports when it comes to trade."

Mendeleev nodded. "The thought has occurred to me, but it doesn't answer what Japan could offer Russia."

"Let me think about that." Ramon looked at his pocket watch. "It's getting late. We should meet with Itō. Perhaps he will have some ideas."

Mendeleev nodded and the two walked back down into the gondola. Ramon sighed at the relative quiet of the interior. They gathered in Itō's quarters. Lord Katsu's automaton set out cups and poured tea. Ramon watched it and remembered the frightening rides, pulled through Tokyo's streets. Though the automaton had moved at breakneck speed, it never crashed and it always arrived at its destinations. It had the strength to pull a rickshaw with two people, and yet it handled the delicate china with grace and ease.

"I have a feeling Japan may have something to offer Russia in exchange for better airship technology."

Itō looked up with interest.

Mendeleev followed Ramon's gaze and nodded, appreciating the idea. "Tireless automata welding, riveting, building. Indeed, they could build airships much faster than humans."

"And they could be used for far more than airships," suggested Ramon. "They could operate factories, build houses, harvest crops. In exchange, Russia could show Japan how to improve its airships."

"You propose a trade?" Itō narrowed his gaze. "One technology for another to prevent a war?"

"I propose Russia and Japan must learn to be good neighbors." Ramon folded his arms. "Good neighbors share and cooperate rather than fight."

Itō nodded. "I like the way you think, Mr. Morales, but the mechanical man is one thing I cannot allow you to trade. We will be neighborly in other ways, but not this one."

"Not everyone wishes to be good neighbors," cautioned Mendeleev. "Some just want to own everything."

"Which inevitably leads to someone falling down a beanstalk." Ramon folded his arms. "Fee fi fo fum."

Fatemeh, Cisneros, Hoshi, Imagawa, and the four men who remained loyal to her trekked back through the forest to the flood plain. They found the *Calamar* at the forest's edge and climbed aboard. Cisneros seemed too weary to complain about eight passengers. Hoshi sat cross-legged on the floor for the rough ride back to the beach.

Fatemeh took a seat at the stern and huddled by the engine, absorbing its heat. They rolled down the river valley in just a few hours and reached the Sea of Japan a little after noon.

In the distance, a ship moved toward the shore. Cisneros lifted a spyglass, then spat out a curse.

"It's the Russian patrol ship we saw earlier," he explained. "We can't let them get their hands on the *Calamar*." He dropped below, sealed the hatch, and opened the throttle. The craft shot forward and Hoshi tumbled over backwards. A whistle followed by an explosion sounded nearby.

"Are they trying to destroy us?" asked Fatemeh. "I'd think this craft would be more valuable to them in one piece."

Cisneros shrugged as he turned valves and threw a lever forward. "If they even recognize it as new technology, I suspect they'd be happy to blow it to bits and sort through the pieces to understand it."

The *Calamar* continued into the waves. When it bobbed and bounced, Cisneros turned a valve to fill the ballast tanks while throwing a lever to retract the treads. Cisneros leaned across Imagawa to throw another lever forward engaging the screw propeller. In shallow water, the small craft eased forward at too slow a pace for Fatemeh's taste.

Another explosion sounded much closer. Fatemeh stood and walked forward. She climbed the ladder to the hatch and looked out the forward windows. They rode along on the surface. From her vantage, she couldn't see far enough to spot the Russian ship.

She breathed a relieved sigh when water splashed over the upper windows. From behind, samurai fought to suppress terrified gasps and groans as water rushed by the windows. The fright soon gave way to wonder as they descended below the tidal water's turbulent wake and could peer into the undersea world revealed.

Cisneros faced forward and refused to relax. Another explosion sounded from behind, close enough to rock the submersible. The Russians had fired where the craft had been, but Cisneros acted fast enough the Russians misjudged. The captain took the submersible even deeper. As they traveled, a chugging noise resounded throughout the small boat.

"What's that?" asked Fatemeh.

"We're passing below the Russian destroyer," explained the captain.

After a few minutes, the ride smoothed out and all became quiet save for *Calamar's* own engine chugging away. Fatemeh's muscles tensed as Imagawa's gaze fell upon her. Fatemeh knew she would have to talk to Imagawa at some point, but this was not the time. She just wanted to absolve herself of the responsibility.

As the undersea voyage wore on, Fatemeh worried the Russian destroyer had found the *Ballena* first and destroyed it. She looked up at the captain from time to time. If he worried, he gave no outward sign.

Cisneros checked the gauges, nodded, then surfaced. When he opened the upper hatch, Fatemeh breathed a relieved sigh to see the *Ballena* standing tall above the water next to them. The captain climbed out and attached hooks to the submersible. Within a few minutes, Boatswain Balderas hoisted them aboard.

Fatemeh didn't wait to see what Cisneros did with the samurai. She went to the quarters she'd shared with Ramon. She didn't even think to ask the captain if she'd been assigned a new cabin.

She entered, dropped onto a chair and unlaced her boots. She undressed just enough to be comfortable as she stretched out on the bed. Imagawa's fight with Nanbu kept replaying over and over in her mind.

When she finally drifted off to sleep, Fatemeh had a nightmare about a young girl who acquired a lamp holding a terrible djinn. The girl thought she could control the djinn and make it a force for good. Instead, the djinn used its power to destroy everything in its path.

Fatemeh awoke sweat-soaked and panting in a jumble of blankets. The *Ballena's* engines rumbled and she knew they were underway. Someone had delivered coffee. Fatemeh poured herself a cup. It had been sitting long enough to grow tepid, but the astringent brew proved welcome nonetheless.

Fatemeh poured a second cup, then strove to make herself presentable. Stepping into the corridor she found a crewman and asked which cabin Ipokash and Shinriki occupied. The crewman gave her directions and soon she knocked on the door.

Ipokash answered. Behind her, Shinriki sat at a table. He looked much better than when Fatemeh last saw him. It seemed the captain's doctor had given the fisherman good care.

"May I come in?" asked Fatemeh in Japanese.

Ipokash bowed and then stepped aside.

"How are you doing?" asked Fatemeh.

"We are well." Ipokash said the words with a deep frown. "We are also worried about our village. There are few left."

Fatemeh took a deep breath and blew it out. "Could your people find another village? Join with them?"

"We would love to go to Hokkaido where there are many Ainu," explained Ipokash, "but the Japanese don't welcome us."

"It must have been difficult during the Tokugawa regime." Fatemeh folded her arms.

"I am not happy the samurai attempted to destroy our village," said Ipokash, "but Imagawa treated me with respect, made sure her men didn't do unmentionable things. With more Japanese like Imagawa, I think we could make a home in Japan."

"Are you serious?" Fatemeh leaned forward.

Shinriki spoke to Ipokash. Fatemeh didn't recognize the words as Russian and suspected they spoke Ainu. Ipokash nodded. "He says the samurai respected us enough to fight us. In some ways, it is better than Russian indifference."

Fatemeh frowned but nodded. Perhaps Imagawa had a role to play after all.

CHAPTER NINETEEN
THE SKELETON AIRSHIP

General Mikhail Dragomirov wondered what had become of the mighty Russian Empire in the last few weeks. He stared at two new disappointing dispatches. That spring, Russia stood ready to dominate the world. Now Japanese airships struck Vladivostok, and Ottoman Turks massed in Bosnia. The only good news was America and Russia had just agreed to a peace treaty. Once the American Congress ratified it, Alaska would be Russian again. The general wondered what the new boundaries would mean for relations with their new neighbor, Canada, who strove to negotiate their own independence from England.

One dispatch the general held said farmers traveling to Vladivostok had come across a huge vessel's smoldering, blackened remains—no doubt the missing *Nicholas Alexandrovich*. The second dispatch he held from the navy confirmed his suspicions. A destroyer had driven a Mexican cargo vessel away from the coast. A few days later, they encountered a boat near the shoreline. The destroyer fired and the boat sank. Clearly pirates had seen the airship go down and wanted to salvage what they could.

Dragomirov handed the latest dispatches to Major Zolnerowich who pinned them to a cork board with other recent dispatches. The general walked up to the board and tried to understand the information presented. He cast a brief glance at Zolnerowich, whose brother had served aboard the airship. Was he dead, or a prisoner somewhere? They could not know at this point.

The general turned around and studied a map spread across a table. At the czar's orders, the navy positioned itself to blockade Japan. Dragomirov sent troops to Vladivostok by train. He gritted his teeth as he looked at Japan. He didn't have the resources to invade, not without airships and not while trying to better support their Austrian allies. At best, he could defend against the Japanese.

The major approached the map table and cleared his throat. When the general looked up, the major handed him another paper. "A Japanese airship has just been sighted crossing the Volga River near Saratov. Its course is northwest."

"Damn." Straight for either Moscow or St. Petersburg itself. His mind raced through the possibilities. There had been no further reports of Japanese naval or ground action and no one reported downed telegraph lines. "How soon will they get to Moscow, or here for that matter?"

"We estimate St. Petersburg in about twenty-four hours." The timing implied twelve hours to Moscow. "I should point out, the sighting came from an inexperienced telegraph officer, and we're assuming they travel the same speed as our ships."

"Telegraph Moscow, order garrisons to stand by. If the navy can shoot one down, then so can we."

"I'll alert our men here, as well." The major turned to leave, but paused. He turned around and cleared his throat again.

The mannerism annoyed the general.

"Sir, the *Alexander Alexandrovich* is almost finished. I've been trained in flight and a crew stands ready. I request permission to launch the ship and confront this new threat."

The general rubbed a hand across his bald head. "I inspected the ship just yesterday. It has no skin. It's still just a large framework."

The major had been along as well. "That's all she lacks along with some heavier armaments. We can mount light cannon right away. The outer skin just streamlines the ship. In good weather, the wind will sing through the girders." He shrugged, then flashed a self-conscious grin before turning serious. "We can still use her to mount a defense."

The general rubbed his chin. "Very well. See to it. Send word when you're ready to launch."

The major saluted, snapped his heels together, and turned.

Before he strode off, the general cleared his throat. The major stopped and blushed as he looked over his shoulder and caught the general's smug grin. "Major, do be careful and also consider, they may not be here to attack us."

The major eased around to face his superior. "Why do you say that?"

"Perhaps wishful thinking." The general walked over to the cork board. "I'm also looking at the way things add up. Our airship disappeared. A Japanese officer says a Russian craft attacked them." The general waved his hand through the air. The major knew the story same as him. "It's possible someone hijacked the ship in an effort to start a war between Japan and Russia."

The major gave a sharp nod. "You've been over that with other generals. It's also possible the Japanese army hijacked the airship to create a pretext for invasion."

The general accepted the possibility. "The problem is this, why would the Japanese send a lone airship right into Russia's heartland when they know we can shoot them down? Why would Japan invade Russia at all? The main thing we have in common is an interest in Sakhalin Island—maybe Korea. Why not just invade and take the island? It would be far easier than sending an airship here."

The major frowned, but didn't answer.

"Don't let your anger over your brother's loss blind you to the possibility they may seek a truce. I would welcome someone who prefers peace right now. We can't afford another war, and the czar is running out of family to name airships after."

The major looked down at the ground and sighed. After a moment, he looked back up. "Anything else, sir?"

Dragomirov shook his head. "As you were."

The major saluted and this time the general let him leave.

Fatemeh stood in the *Ballena's* bow. A smoke trail from Poronaysk's factories betrayed Sakhalin's position on the horizon. She scanned the blue-black ocean for battleships or destroyers. Despite the recent clashes with Japan, it seemed Sakhalin Island concerned the Russians less than the mainland.

As they approached the island, mountains grew visible. Soon, Poronaysk appeared—brick buildings huddled together against the ocean's onslaught. Fatemeh pulled her cloak tight.

Shinriki and Ipokash joined her a few minutes later. Their robes reminded her of Japanese kimonos, except for the geometrical patterns on the tattered and ragged cloth. They had utilized the shipboard facilities and cleaned the robes, making them bright and vibrant, even on a gray and dismal day.

The robes' long sleeves failed to hide Ipokash and Shinriki holding hands. The simple gesture reminded Fatemeh how much she missed Ramon. She prayed for his safety and she wanted to discuss her own conflicted feelings about Imagawa. Unable to reconcile her respect for Imagawa's strength with disgust at Nanbu's senseless murder, she had avoided the renegade samurai ever since boarding the ship.

Fatemeh could just make out the Ainu village's distant huts as the anchor clattered from its well. Captain Cisneros stepped up behind Shinriki and Ipokash. "Are you packed?"

The Ainu couple blinked at the captain, not comprehending. Fatemeh translated the words into Japanese.

Ipokash shrugged. "We had nothing with us besides the clothes we wore." Her voice held an apologetic note.

Fatemeh translated for Cisneros, then turned to Ipokash. "You have nothing to apologize for."

Cisneros led the way to the ship's stern. Instead of the *Calamar*, sailors prepared a standard launch boat. Nearby Shinriki's cousin, Resak, watched the sailors with interest. "We depleted several fuel rods taking the submersible overland," explained the captain, "and the lookouts see no reason for us to hurry or use stealth to get ashore."

As the captain helped Ipokash aboard, Imagawa appeared on deck. Resak's hand flew to his knife hilt. Fatemeh couldn't help but notice how tattered her kimono had become. Like Ipokash, she'd laundered it, but its wear still revealed the past weeks' trials. "May I come ashore with you?"

The captain turned to Fatemeh for help understanding the request. Fatemeh tensed, but looked up to Ipokash, who nodded. "Imagawa wants to know if she may accompany us."

The captain frowned, but nodded. "I have no objection."

"The captain says you may come along." Fatemeh wondered if the hesitant Japanese words conveyed the coldness she felt. She turned her back on Imagawa and climbed aboard the boat without assistance. Imagawa followed, and sat across from Ipokash.

Cisneros climbed aboard along with three other sailors and Resak, then ordered the boat lowered into the water. At first, Fatemeh thought the men would take up the oars in the boat's bottom and row to shore, but Cisneros clambered into the stern and lowered a propeller assembly into the water. A chemical reaction steam engine, similar to those used aboard the *Calamar* topped the assembly. The captain opened two valves, starting the reaction. Soon, the propeller spun to life and the boat zoomed to shore.

Fatemeh joined the captain in the stern. "I thought you'd depleted your fuel rod supply."

"It's a matter of weight and surface friction," explained the captain. "The *Calamar* is heavy and runs under water. It takes a lot more power to propel it to shore. Plus, we can row this boat if it runs out of fuel."

The explanation made sense to Fatemeh, so she sat back and fell silent.

Imagawa and Ipokash spoke in hushed tones. Their words seemed almost trivial, unless someone knew the history these women shared.

"How are you?" asked Imagawa.

"Well and glad to return home," said Ipokash.

Shinriki eyed Imagawa for a long time. When he spoke to his wife, he laughed and slapped his knee.

"He says something seemed strange about you when you raided the village. He thinks you're much more attractive without armor."

Shinriki blushed as Ipokash translated the words into Japanese.

Fatemeh wondered whether the assessment offended the warrior. Her mouth tipped up a little, indicating more amusement than offense at the words.

The boat soon reached the shore and the passengers disembarked. Several Ainu men and women stopped work to eye the new arrivals. When they realized who came ashore, several rushed toward the beach and embraced the three returning villagers.

An older man hung back and watched the *Ballena's* crew with suspicion. His gaze narrowed as it fell across Imagawa, as though he tried to decipher the reason for her presence.

Shinriki, Ipokash, and Resak beckoned Fatemeh and Cisneros to follow them up to the village. Imagawa followed as well, even though the Ainu had not invited her.

Shinriki led the group into a small hut. A blackened fire pit lay before them. To the left stood two water tubs. Two beds lined one wall. Shinriki lifted a bear pelt and patted a recent repair with pride.

Imagawa turned to Ipokash. "Did the Russians do nothing to help?"

Shinriki shook his head. "No, in fact I found Russian horses along with ours and the villagers arrested me as a thief."

Imagawa scowled and stormed from the hut. Curious, Fatemeh followed. The samurai stood outside, arms folded, glaring at Poronaysk. "Why are you so angry?" asked Fatemeh. "After all, you and your men ransacked this village."

"I saw the village as an extension of Poronaysk. I watched both the city and village some time before I struck and I knew Ainu lived in the city. I never thought the Russians would be so indifferent to their own citizens."

"Why not?" The sharp words surprised Fatemeh even as she spoke them, but she plunged on. "The Japanese have at best tolerated the Ainu and at worst treated them as second-class citizens. In fact, there's nothing about the Ainu at all in any Tokyo museum I visited. At least the Americans treat Indians as attractions worth showing off at carnivals." Fatemeh stepped closer to Imagawa. "You pity yourself as a woman in the Meiji era. Try being an Ainu."

Imagawa whirled on Fatemeh, her hand grasped empty air where her sword would have been if she'd been armed.

Fatemeh continued. "Must you kill all your critics?"

Imagawa sneered and allowed her arms to hang akimbo. "Your Japanese has become quite good."

Fatemeh's anger kept her from laughing at the lighthearted

remark. "Why did you kill Nanbu?"

"I killed Nanbu because he betrayed me. Worse, he had threatened violence on Ipokash. He tied me up and left me for dead, and he kidnapped you."

Fatemeh turned and walked away several steps. "Not every argument should be settled with the sword. Words can hurt, but those hurts can be healed."

Imagawa looked around at the village. Empty, blackened spaces revealed sites where huts used to be. An empty drying rack stood outside a smoke house. Fatemeh wondered how the village would fare during the winter after Imagawa's attack.

"The emperor's swords and guns turned me into what I am," said Imagawa. "I was content learning swordsmanship and studying history under the Tokugawa regime."

Fatemeh scowled. "The emperor didn't turn you into a killer. You turned yourself into one. You must find another path. No one can do it for you."

"I require no assistance finding a path." Imagawa turned and stared off to the mountains. "'We suffered severe casualties, our forces withered to nothing, and we fled.'"

Fatemeh shook her head, not understanding the second statement.

"It's a line from Samurai Tsuchimochi Nobuhide's history. Defeated, he fled because he had something to live for. I once believed a samurai found their way in death, but perhaps it is found in life after all."

"That's what Hoshi believes," said Fatemeh.

"And you think Hoshi exemplifies samurai culture?" Imagawa grimaced and walked away.

Captain Himura steered the *Bonchō* well to Moscow's north, which added time to the journey, but he noted the Russians had shipboard cannon which could shoot down airships. This suggested land garrisons would also be so equipped. Ramon, Itō, and Mendeleev accompanied the captain at the chart table in the bridge's stern. They discussed the best way to approach the city.

"I suggest we circle around St. Petersburg and approach from the bay," said Mendeleev. "There's room to maneuver and it puts us close to the Winter Palace. There's even a mooring mast near the airship hanger at the docks."

Captain Himura shook his head after Itō translated. He noted the Japanese ship's design meant it couldn't be moored at a Russian tower.

"What's more, this ship is large enough to be a good target," said the captain.

Pleased and surprised, Ramon followed the discussion with ease. He had to agree with the captain. "We could land outside the city near the main road. Lord Katsu's automaton could pull a cart. Professor Mendeleev could dial in the path."

Itō scowled. "It would place the automaton at unnecessary risk."

"I'd still like to hear what Professor Mendeleev thinks."

After Itō translated, Mendeleev held up his hands. "The route through the city is complicated. I'm not sure if I could program it into the mechanical man."

The captain traced out the path through the city streets. "It also allows time for troops to figure out where you're going and set up a barrier."

Given the automaton's speed, Ramon questioned the second concern, but he voiced a different thought. "Does it even matter if we're captured?" He shrugged. "As long as we're given a chance to explain why we're there." He repeated his idea in Russian, both for practice and for the scientist's benefit.

"Captured is fine," said Mendeleev. "Shot before we explain ourselves would be a tragedy."

The Russian bore such a somber expression, Ramon had to laugh. "We could approach during the predawn hours and land in the Winter Palace's courtyard."

Itō explained the suggestion to Himura. The captain nodded. "Our ship is small enough we could pull it off." Itō switched to Russian and addressed Mendeleev. "Is there heavy artillery near the palace?"

The scientist shook his head. "Not facing into the courtyard that I know of."

Ramon leaned forward. "Is it possible there's artillery you

don't know about?"

Mendeleev shrugged. "Of course. Russians have a talent for keeping secrets."

"Airship incoming ahead!" cried a lookout from the forward window.

Itō, Himura, and Ramon all looked at Mendeleev. He shrugged. "We started building another airship before I left, but it shouldn't be ready so soon."

They all moved to the bow and the ship listed forward just a bit with the extra weight. The captain took the spyglass and frowned, then handed it to Mendeleev.

"Choknutyj!" The scientist passed the spyglass to Ramon.

An airship did indeed approach in the clear, blue sky. However, a dark steel skeleton enclosed inflated gas bags. Stripped of its sleek, outer skin, this airship seemed more threatening than its kin. Like a lion with exposed ribs, it looked fierce and hungry, ready to take chances to capture its prey. Naked cannon aimed toward the *Bonchō*. Marksmen balanced on the girders. No skin hid this ship's teeth. The exposed vessel looked dangerous, much as Russia could be if stripped of too much pride or forced into a desperate position.

Itō's mouth hung open, his eyes wide. The abject fear echoed shivers traveling down Ramon's spine. Captain Himura set his jaw and straightened his back, as though he prepared for a fight.

Mendeleev shook his head. "What the hell are they thinking? They can't make good speed without a skin and if the winds increase too much they'll rip the interior bags wide open."

Ramon remembered how Professor Maravilla's ornithopters had to seek a safe path inside the airships that attacked Denver. No such difficulty presented itself with this ship, but he knew the men aboard must recognize the vulnerability and be on guard as a consequence. Ramon stepped away from the group and glanced out a window. The airship passed over undulating, tree-covered plains. At least they had room to maneuver if needed. No mountain peaks stood nearby and the weather seemed calm with just a few clouds.

He caught snippets of conversation from the bow. They

discussed evading the skeleton airship—either turning wide or doing their best to shoot past it. Mendeleev noted the Japanese airship would be faster than even a finished Russian craft.

"We should see if they have anything to say," said Ramon. The others looked up at him.

"What if they fire on us?" Captain Himura placed his hands behind his back.

"Then have your men prepare to put on extra speed and evade." Ramon shrugged. "We're here to make peace. That airship is the first test. They sent it out here unfinished because they're scared and have nothing else able to challenge us. If they talk, we'll get off on the right foot."

"If they fire, we'll know they want war," said Itō.

Ramon shook his head. "If they fire, they just confirm they're scared. We get away from these folks and try to find more rational people at the palace right away."

"And if those at court aren't rational?" asked the captain.

"Then I suppose this mission is a lost cause after all." Ramon stepped up to the captain. "Sir, I recommend you raise the white flag, or whatever you do to demonstrate surrender, as soon as possible."

The captain scowled, turned and lifted the spyglass to his eye. He watched the skeleton airship for a few minutes, then turned around and barked an order. Two men rushed from the bridge and ran toward the catwalk behind the gondola.

As the ships approached one another, Ramon pondered the guns within the girders. He wondered if the ships they'd confronted in America had been so well armed. He remembered gun ports, but had there been so many? Dmitri Mendeleev's wide-eyed expression made Ramon suspect the number of weapons surprised him as well. Or, perhaps something else caught his attention.

Signal flags appeared outside the Russian ship's gondola. The first mate turned around. "They're ordering us to land."

The captain strolled back to the chart table. He moved a marker, which indicated the airship's current position and took some measurements. He looked up. "Signal we'll comply." He pointed ahead. "We'll drop to the ground by the Volkhov River, five miles ahead."

The first officer opened the speaking tube and issued the necessary orders. A few minutes later, more signal flags appeared. The captain scowled. "They're ordering us to descend now." He folded his arms. "I don't like the trees below us." He turned to the crew at the helium valves. "Take us down, but keep us moving forward. Let's get as close to the river as we can and hope they can't shoot downward."

"They have sharp shooters," said Mendeleev after Itō whispered to him.

"Rifles scare me less than cannon." Captain Himura folded his arms.

The *Bonchō* drifted downward, but continued forward. The Russian airship slowed and began a shuddering turn. By the time the *Bonchō* settled to the ground, they had reached the river valley just as the captain requested. Looking around, Ramon couldn't see how the larger ship could have even come close to the ground before this. Then he remembered the stolen airship on Sakhalin Island, which stood tethered and swaying over the treetops.

Captain Himura ordered tether lines deployed. The ship was secure when the skeletal Russian airship appeared overhead. It descended next to the *Bonchō*, but remained above it. Ladders descended from the superstructure and Russians climbed down, jumping over to the Japanese airship's rigging.

An even longer ladder unfurled from the gondola to the ground. Three men descended. Ramon swallowed as he watched the ladder tilt and sway in the breeze. When the men reached the ground, one held his hands up and a man in the gondola tossed down a speaking trumpet.

The man who caught it lifted it to his mouth. "We control your ship. Come out and tell us what you want."

Ramon looked over to the captain and waited for his permission. Himura gave a brief nod, then Ramon opened the door. They were only two feet above the ground. He jumped out and Mendeleev followed.

The Russian officer dropped the speaking trumpet.

The last person Major Andrei Zolnerowich expected to see aboard the Japanese airship was the missing scientist Dmitri Mendeleev. The major drew his sidearm and pointed it at the brown-skinned man with battered glasses. "You will turn over your hostage at once."

Mendeleev stepped forward, hands in the air. "I am no hostage. I am with the Japanese delegation of my own free will."

"And the man with you? He is not Japanese."

The man with the battered glasses pushed them further up his nose. "I am Ramon Morales, an American, acquainted with the being called Legion who wanted to unify the world. I have a unique perspective and I'm here to help." The man called Morales used poor grammar and was hard to understand, but the reference to the creature called Legion caused an unexpected longing to well up within the major.

Not long ago, Russians had a strength, unity, and purpose unlike any in history. For a time, they understood each other's thoughts and the military could influence those they wanted to conquer, rather than firing weapons. Then Legion vanished and the empire began to collapse again.

Zolnerowich lowered the pistol. He knew snipers overhead had Mendeleev and Morales in their sights. If the strangers rushed him, they would be gunned down. "What do you want?"

"We wish to speak with the emperor," said Ramon.

"Pirates hijacked the *Nicholas Alexandrovich*," added Mendeleev. "The Japanese wish to apologize for the attack on Vladivostok and will discuss reparations."

Zolnerowich pursed his lips and studied the Japanese airship—frail, even compared to the skeletal craft above him. A well placed shot could sever the undercarriage from the balloon. If the balloon carried hydrogen, one shot could obliterate the craft. "My brother served aboard the *Nicholas Alexandrovich*. Helmsman Zolnerowich. What happened to him?"

Mendeleev's brow creased, as though trying to remember the man in question. "I believe the samurai released him near Ozerskoye on Sakhalin Island."

Zolnerowich found the explanation convenient. They had

no way to confirm the statement's veracity in short order, but he saw no reason Mendeleev should lie to him, unless the scientist had turned traitor. The scientist and the czar were rumored to be acquaintances who corresponded. "I cannot allow you to fly your airship into St. Petersburg."

"You can take us to the city in your ship," suggested Ramon.

"I must leave soldiers here, aboard your vessel," countered Zolnerowich.

Ramon nodded. "May I propose this to the captain?"

"Yes." Zolnerowich gestured toward the ship with the pistol. "If you try to ascend, we'll shoot you from the sky."

Ramon swallowed. Perhaps the American understood how tempting it would be to destroy the Japanese vessel and be done with it. The major allowed a thin smile to appear, enjoying the power he held. If he played his cards right, perhaps this assignment could land him a promotion.

"Understood." Ramon disappeared into the craft.

Mendeleev put his hands behind his back and studied the Russian vessel. "It's dangerous to fly an airship without its skin. It's not streamlined. Air gusts can catch it and blow it around."

The mini-lecture prickled Zolnerowich. "I'm well aware of that, sir. This is an emergency mission."

A moment later, an air pump whirred to life and the Japanese airship dropped a foot lower. Zolnerowich lifted his pistol again. Ramon appeared at the door and stepped out. A strange cylindrical device on continuous track treads followed him and rolled off the edge, dropping to the ground with a thud. The device almost resembled a man with two arm-like cylinders ending in claws and two eye-like gauges above a grillwork smile.

Ramon spoke to Mendeleev in hushed tones, then pointed to the ladder leading into the Russian ship. Mendeleev shook his head, then opened the mechanical man's front compartment. He flipped switches and turned dials. At one point he looked up, rubbed his long white beard, and muttered to himself.

While the scientist worked, Ramon approached the major. "Our delegation is almost ready."

As he spoke, a Japanese man appeared at the door and

stepped to the ground.

"What is that machine?" asked Zolnerowich.

"A loyal companion, but he requires periodic maintenance." Morales turned and presented Itō Hirobumi, the emperor's special representative. "He represents Japan and will
accompany you along with Mendeleev."

Itō shot a questioning glance at Morales, which Zolnerowich found odd. Morales spoke to the ambassador in Japanese.
Itō lifted an eyebrow but nodded.

Zolnerowich believed something strange transpired,
but Americans and Japanese had such mysterious ways, he
couldn't be certain. The major crouched down and grabbed
the speaking trumpet. He shouted orders up to the ship. Soon,
hatchways opened and ropes descended. Two squads climbed
down and took up positions around the Japanese airship. Even
though Legion no longer controlled them, they displayed discipline and coordination, making the major proud.

Zolnerowich summoned the sergeant of the guard and
gave him orders, then ordered Mendeleev and Itō into the
Alexander Alexandrovich. Zolnerowich holstered his pistol and
followed. Once they reached the gondola, he gave orders to
return to the city. As the airship ascended, it began to pirouette
on its axis. The major wore a smug grin as he noted Itō's admi-
ration.

Rifles popped below.

Zolnerowich ran to the window and looked out.

The mechanical man zoomed away from the Japanese
airship. Several Russian soldiers dropped to their knees, rifles
raised, but the mechanical man soon outdistanced their range.
He thought a figure stood atop the platform between the mechanical man's treads, hugged close to its barrel-shaped body.
Was it Morales?

He whirled on Mendeleev and Itō. "What is that abomina-
tion doing?"

The Japanese ambassador's mouth dropped open and he
shrugged.

"It would seem the mechanical man had an errand to run,"
said Mendeleev. "I think automata will prove quite handy in
the future."

Hoshi found Imagawa on the *Ballena's* afterdeck practicing sword strikes with a wooden practice blade.

For a moment he envisioned her as a youth, ponytail down her back, wearing a flowered kimono and obi, face set, strong as any boy. Hoshi drew his sword and fell into step beside Imagawa, lifting the sword high, then stepping forward and bringing the sword down in a single fluid motion. They practiced ten strokes together, then Imagawa turned, sword held ready to thrust. Hoshi turned, stepped backwards and brought his sword into a defensive position.

Imagawa smiled, stood straight, and bowed. Hoshi followed suit. "What do you think of my form, Sensei?"

Hoshi folded his arms and evaluated her as he did when they were both younger. "You have much improved, but you are stubborn and that will be your undoing."

"You once told me my stubbornness was my strength." She turned and faced the ocean, watching the white water roll away behind the ship.

"I am no fortune teller. I had no way to know the world would change so much." He turned and faced the sea as well, hands behind his back. "I hear the police no longer allow swords to be worn on the streets. No such prohibition exists in the United States."

"You're the one who taught me the sword is just an ideal. Practice with it hones our focus, but its effectiveness is limited against a man in armor." She snorted. "I lost my armor when *The Brazen Shark* crashed."

"Armor is readily forged, though it has limitations in the world of guns." He sighed. "There are many guns in the American west."

"Are you asking me to come to America with you?"

Hoshi considered the question. He hadn't intended to ask, but he wondered what she would say if he welcomed her. It would be nice to have a companion from his homeland, though he suspected she would be difficult to live with in other ways. "You would have a place to stay." Not an outright invitation, just a suggestion to see how she responded.

"I face prison time, or even execution when I return." She spoke without strain, just stating facts.

"I do not intend to leave this vessel when we dock in Tokyo." Hoshi questioned his motives for avoiding Tokyo. Was he afraid? He tried to brush the thought aside, but found it difficult. Imagawa saved him from the effort by responding.

"Tell me of the Americans, Sensei." Her voice assumed a childlike quality, as though she requested a bedtime story.

"They are an independent lot. Even the poorest peasants possess an emperor's pride. Many own land, like small daimyos. Because they are small, they must learn to defend it themselves like samurai."

"Daimyo, samurai, and peasant all in one package," she mused. "I am told Americans have no discipline. Many are drunken louts who pick fights for no reason."

Hoshi considered the rumor. "There are terrible and reckless people, but such people exist in Japan as well. Also, there are people such as the Apache, who are brave and disciplined warriors. I fear those who came from Europe have forced them onto small plots of land and they may die out."

"They sound like the Ainu—proud and brave, but endangered." She turned and faced Hoshi. "This is how I see women in the Meiji era. Unless we are suited to be a wife, mother or servant, we are useless."

"In America, women fight to be heard. Some, like Fatemeh, are healers. Some teach. There's an astronomer in Massachusetts named Maria Mitchell who discovered a comet. I even know a woman who has become a federal marshal."

Imagawa turned back toward the sea. "That is all well and good and Mrs. Morales has given me some things to consider." She leaned on the ship's rail and she grew wistful. "This Fatemeh is a mystery to me. She talks of fighting for things she believes in, but yet grows angry when a villain dies. If you see a mosquito, you slap it. If you see a dangerous spider, you step on it."

Hoshi nodded. "Where you saw a man reduced to a mosquito, Fatemeh still saw a man." He dared to reach out and take her hand. "I fought to stop you, but couldn't kill you because I still saw a woman, not an insect."

"I wanted to die because I failed." She squeezed Hoshi's hand. "She saved me because she believes one can reinvent oneself." She let go and stood straight again. Hoshi couldn't quite read her expression. It held neither regret nor hope.

"The Tokugawa regime made us what we are," mused Hoshi. "We believed a person's honor and class determined their value. In the new regime, there is potential for all humans to be equal and find their place based on their abilities."

"I'm not sure if I believe all humans are equal, even now." Imagawa folded her arms and Hoshi feared she might close mental barriers against him.

"I'm not sure if I do, either," admitted Hoshi, "but a mere girl once rose through training and perseverance to become a strong warrior. In this new era, everyone has such potential, not just a warrior's daughter."

Imagawa lifted her chin. "I tried to kindle a war so a shogun would rule Japan because I think imperialists have no honor. I now welcome an audience with the emperor. I will learn whether or not there is a place in this new regime for me."

"If you came to America, you could make a place for yourself, without having to rely on the emperor's verdict."

"If I understand your lesson, fighting injustice is honorable in this era as in the past, but all have potential in the new era. This includes women, peasants, even the Ainu. If I leave Japan, who will fight for the women? Who will fight for the Ainu?"

"If you are executed, the questions remain unanswered." His voice caught on the words.

"If your lesson is true, I will not be executed," she countered. "If your lesson is false, then it doesn't matter, for my original conjecture is correct. There is no place for me in this world." With that, she turned and walked away. Hoshi watched her, at once proud and angry. He wished he possessed her brave heart.

CHAPTER TWENTY
GUERILLA DIPLOMACY

A knock interrupted Fatemeh mid-poem. Annoyed, she placed her finger in the book she read and looked up. "Come in," she said.

Hoshi entered and bowed. Fatemeh used a ribbon to mark her place, then held her hand out to the room's other chair. "What can I do for you?"

Hoshi sat and folded his hands. "I am concerned about Imagawa. I believe you could advise her how a woman can lead a constructive life in the modern world."

Fatemeh set the book aside and frowned. "Why did you help her murder Nanbu?"

Hoshi's brow furrowed. "A duel for honor is not murder."

"A duel need not be fought to the death." Fatemeh leaned forward. "You showed that when you dueled her. Did he deserve to die? How many other deaths did she cause when she bombed Sapporo and when she captured the Russian airship? Do we have any idea?"

"Many samurai become obsessed with death."

"Not just samurai," mused Fatemeh. "No one leaves this life alive, but we all have something to contribute. Killing is evil because we have placed our goals ahead of all other human goals."

"You prevented her from committing seppuku. You must feel her life has value."

Fatemeh sat back and nodded. "I did, but I fear she has become so obsessed with death, she can see no other path." Her gut twinged, but she proceeded anyway. "I'm not sure I see her value in this new world."

"Perhaps it is not your responsibility to find her path," suggested Hoshi. "Nevertheless, I think she could benefit from speaking to someone who sees life's value."

Fatemeh didn't want to speak to Imagawa much less see her again. Imagawa reminded her too much of her father and one-time fiancé—inflexible and obsessed with rules—death, the penalty for those who strayed from even the stupidest rules. She wondered what it would take to heal the world of Imagawa's evil. She folded her arms. "Let me think about it."

"Please don't take too long," said Hoshi. "Captain Cisneros says we'll be in Tokyo tomorrow. I don't know what fate awaits Imagawa, but I fear her return to a destructive path if she's presented no alternative." Hoshi stood to leave. He looked at the book Fatemeh read and smiled. "You do realize Bashō was a samurai."

Fatemeh looked down at the haiku book next to her, then met Hoshi's gaze. "According to the biography, Bashō gave up samurai status."

"Nevertheless, he trained and understood Bushido. You have spent time in Japan, but I wonder if you understand all the nuances of Japanese culture." With that, Hoshi excused himself and left Fatemeh alone with her thoughts. She leaned forward and rubbed her face. Had she made an effort to understand samurai culture, or had she dismissed it when she discovered she didn't approve?

Fatemeh picked up the book and read the next haiku, then stared at it dumbfounded. She stood and looked out at the blue skies over the ocean. The light snowfall on Sakhalin Island seemed a distant memory.

Aboard the *Ballena*, one cabin disturbed Fatemeh and she always quickened her pace a little when passing. It had no place on a civilian cargo vessel and Fatemeh feared Cisneros might return to piracy.

She walked to the door marked "armory" and tried it, not surprised to find it locked. She proceeded to the deck where she found the boatswain discussing a maintenance job with his crew. She cleared her throat.

Balderas turned around. "May I help you ma'am?"

"I fear I locked my key in my cabin, you wouldn't happen to have a master key I could use to retrieve it?"

Without question, he retrieved a key ring from his pocket,

took off the master key and handed it to her. "Bring it right back, please, Mrs. Morales."

"I will." She smiled, took the key, and went to the armory. Once inside, she chose a derringer, checked to see if it was loaded, then concealed it in a pocket sewn into her skirt. With a sigh, she returned to deck and handed Balderas the key.

She squared her shoulders, walked to Imagawa's quarters, and knocked. When beckoned, she entered and found Imagawa staring out the window. Fatemeh drew the derringer. "I have been considering the last few days' events and I realized I should not have let you live. You are not a person to compromise and the only way you win is by destroying your opponent. The only way to heal this situation is with your death."

Imagawa eased around to face Fatemeh, wearing an unreadable expression. "I grew up in an ordered world. People knew their place and did not deviate from their assigned paths. As a samurai, I trained with sword, pistol and fists. It made me strong so I could protect those who raised the crops to feed a country. I engaged in a campaign to restore order because I thought the alternative was Japan's death."

Fatemeh shrugged. "That part is clear and I could forgive it. What I can't forgive is killing Nanbu just because he sought a new life for himself and the men under his command. What's more, I can't help but wonder what happened to the Russian airship crew. Did you kill them as well?"

Imagawa took a deep breath, then blew it out. "A samurai's entire reason to exist is to deal death in order to protect the weak. I was a samurai for over twenty years before I had a reason to take a life—before I had a reason to exist. In my war with the imperialists, I had a purpose, no matter how terrible. It is still unclear to me what my purpose is, if it is not dealing death." She took two steps toward Fatemeh, who lifted the pistol. "What is clear is your purpose is to heal, and if you destroy me, you destroy yourself." Faster than Fatemeh could follow, Imagawa snatched the derringer. She opened the weapon, then met Fatemeh's gaze. The derringer was empty.

"If your reason to exist is to deal death," said Fatemeh, "you would have killed me. Your purpose is to defend the weak."

"You dared to test me?"

"I dared to confront you." Fatemeh folded her hands and looked to the deck. "I once knew..." She hesitated, thinking how much personal detail to give. "I once knew men who harbored no disagreement. They killed those who defied them." Her voice caught as she remembered her friend, strangled and thrown down a well, but she willed herself not to cry. She looked up and met Imagawa's gaze. "When you protect the weak in a free society, many will try to defy you."

"Nanbu did more than defy me. He humiliated me. To return home with that dishonor would be worse than death."

"And the Russian airship crew?"

Imagawa lay the derringer down and folded her hands. "They were destined to fly over their enemy, drop bombs, and slaughter those below without looking them in the eye. If not Americans, it would be Turks, or perhaps Afghans, or perhaps anyone else who chose to defy the czar."

Fatemeh frowned, but nodded. "You can protect the weak without killing. People can learn."

Imagawa studied Fatemeh for some time. "These men you mentioned who harbored no disagreement, did they learn?"

This time Fatemeh failed to stop a tear. She shook her head. "I ran away."

"And they still kill."

Fatemeh turned and walked to the door, then stopped. "Now then, let's go out to enjoy the snow ... until I slip and fall."

"You know Bashō?"

Fatemeh nodded, then turned and faced Imagawa again. "I think we each can learn something from the other."

"There is little time before we reach Japan."

Fatemeh's mouth lifted in a wary smile. "Captain Cisneros has a delightful selection of tea aboard and wonderful hospitality. It is a beautiful day outside. Perhaps we should ask his steward to bring a pot to a table on deck and continue our conversation there."

"You are wise for such a young woman."

Fatemeh bristled at the words, but let the annoyance drift away when Imagawa's mouth ticked up slightly.

Ramon rode through St. Petersburg clinging to Lord Katsu's mechanical man, hoping Mendeleev made no mistakes programming the course. They wove in and around people, caused horses to rear and upset at least one apple cart. Ramon didn't have time to even shout an apology as they whirled by. As the cold wind stung his face and hands, he wished steam powered the automaton rather than a battery so he could get warm.

The mechanical man rolled through an archway past four stunned guards, and took two turns around an enormous red granite pillar before stopping. The guards ran through the archway, rifles drawn. More guards poured from the building adjoining the archway. Dizzy, Ramon climbed off the platform between the automaton's treads and held up his hands.

The soldiers kept their distance and eyed the mechanical man warily.

"My name is Ramon Morales. I'm here to see Czar Alexander II at the request of Emperor Mutsuhito of Japan."

A man in a blue uniform and fur hat approached. He had a salt-and-pepper mustache. Elaborate gold embroidery decorated red epaulets. "I am General Mikhail Dragomirov. Did you ride all the way from Japan on your mechanical friend here?"

Ramon laughed. "No, sir. I came aboard a Japanese airship called the *Bonchō*. A rather frightful vessel met us, but I feared there would be a long delay if we went through official channels, especially since I have a simple proposal."

"And your mechanical friend here?"

"One of a virtual *legion* of wonders I've seen in the last year and a half." Ramon chanced to lower his hands and walked back to the mechanical man and gave it a pat. The general lifted an eyebrow at Ramon's word choice.

A thrumming overhead interrupted them. Both Ramon and Dragomirov looked skyward. The skeletal airship flew toward its mooring a short distance down the Neva River from the palace.

Once the noise from the airship receded somewhat, Ramon continued. "Some from my delegation wish to keep this man a secret, but I think secretiveness and possessiveness are where warfare begins."

The guards around Ramon parted and a tall man with a heavy mustache and thick mutton chop sideburns approached. He wore a fur-trimmed coat decorated with loops of gold braid. The soldiers all stood straighter as they realized who had appeared. Ramon remembered the etiquette lessons and dropped down on one knee before Czar Alexander II.

The emperor passed Ramon and walked around the mechanical man, looking it up and down. From time to time, he paused and leaned in for a closer look. "Is this a gift?" he asked at last.

"No, Your Excellency," said Ramon. "The mechanical man is not mine to give. I brought him to make a point ... and to get your attention."

The czar turned and waved Ramon to his feet. "You have it."

"Your Excellency, I have come on the Japanese emperor's behalf."

"You are not Japanese." The czar wore a bemused expression as he stated the obvious.

"I am American and well acquainted with the being called Legion."

The czar took a step closer to Ramon. "What is your name?"

"Ramon Morales, Your Excellency."

The czar narrowed his gaze. "Come with me."

"May I bring my friend?" Ramon inclined his head toward the mechanical man.

The czar gave a brief nod. Before Ramon could turn the dial to issue a command, Dragomirov approached and put up his hand. The czar remained silent as the general searched Ramon. Satisfied, the general allowed Ramon to proceed. He dialed in the command for the automaton to follow.

They entered the Winter Palace and the czar led them to a comfortable, carpeted room. A wooden desk covered with framed photographs faced a wall decorated with paintings. The czar settled into a red velvet chair and waved his hands toward two chairs arranged for intimate conversation. "Are you the same Ramon Morales who gave Colonel Dvorkin trouble in

San Francisco three months ago?"

Ramon swallowed, realizing every word he spoke mattered. "Yes, Your Excellency. Our meeting was a reunion for the creature who calls itself Legion."

The czar peaked his hands under his nose and studied Ramon. "You know this voice from the stars, this Legion?"

"Yes, Your Excellency."

General Drogomirov cleared his throat. "Excuse me, Your Excellency." He eyed Ramon. "What do you mean by 'reunion'?"

"Legion is a swarm of tiny automata." He glanced back at the mechanical man. "I suppose you could say he's a little like our friend, except there are thousands of him and Legion thinks for himself." Ramon sensed the number was small, but plunged on anyway. "One swarm was with you in Russia. The other remained in America." Ramon chose not to emphasize the war's role in causing Legion's separation.

The czar leaned forward. "Legion has been ... quiet since you met with Dvorkin. Can you explain this?"

Ramon took a deep breath and thought how best to explain what he knew. "As you say, Your Excellency, Legion is from the stars. He saw the great strides Russia made when you freed the serfs. He saw Russia's might. Legion wanted to share everything great and wonderful about the Russian Empire with the United States of America, which you no doubt know has undergone a painful reconstruction."

The czar nodded and spun his finger in the air, indicating Ramon should pick up the pace.

"After the Battle of Denver, Legion separated into two swarms, Your Excellency. The swarm in Russia continued with the original mission. The swarm in America considered more peaceful ways to expand humanity's knowledge. When I made Colonel Dvorkin's acquaintance, the two swarms met." Despite the chill ride through St. Petersburg's streets, Ramon began to sweat. He considered reaching for a handkerchief, but General Dragomirov's gaze convinced him otherwise. "I persuaded Legion to allow humans to solve their own problems, Your Excellency."

The czar snorted. "I should have you shot for that. We

could have won the war if you had not interfered."

Ramon grew light-headed. He worried the czar's men might act on his first statement. He wanted to scoff at the second part. His mouth went dry and he tried to swallow. "With respect, Your Excellency, without Legion's help, Americans developed ornithopters, lightning guns, and motorized bicycles to aid the war effort."

The czar leaned forward, interested.

"I submit, Your Excellency, Legion realized humanity had grown into something he couldn't and didn't want to control."

"Is this why you brought the mechanical man," interjected General Dragomirov, "to show us what Japan has created and intimidate us?"

Ramon shook his head, perhaps too fast. "Not at all, sir." He pointed to the automaton. "This machine is not designed for warfare, but to serve peaceful causes. Admittedly it's a rather sophisticated servant and I cannot even pretend to understand how he works, but he shows what Japanese scientists have achieved on their own without Legion's help. Now imagine what could happen if Japanese and Russian scientists worked together. Imagine what could happen if Japanese, Russian, and American scientists cooperated."

"With such an alliance, we could conquer the world," breathed Dragomirov.

The czar brought his hand up in sharp rebuke, but a twinkle shone in his eye. "Could the automaton work in fields?"

The question surprised Ramon. The machine delivered letters and navigated through streets. Farm chores would be no different than other commands. "I would imagine it could be programmed to do so, Your Excellency. I know it can be programmed to do repetitive tasks in a factory or a textile mill."

"Sixteen years ago, I freed Russia's serfs, but all has not proceeded as I'd hoped. Not all received good land. Many who did have good land didn't have the help to maintain it. We are struggling, but something like this could indeed help."

Ramon sighed and put his hands together. "I'm sorry, Your Excellency, but the mechanical man is not mine to give. He is private property and I have perhaps betrayed a trust to bring him here."

The czar's eyebrows came together. "You betray Japan to aid us?"

Ramon shook his head. "No, sir ... Your Excellency. I respect you and your empire. The mechanical man is no secret. Many have seen him. I trust the Czar of all the Russias to see this as a demonstration of what humans may achieve without Legion."

"You have indeed captured my interest, Mr. Morales." The czar sat back, removed a cigar from the box and lit it.

The czar's casual gesture lightened the room's mood somewhat. Ramon decided to pursue the meeting's primary purpose. "Your Excellency, pirates hijacked the *Nicholas Alexandrovich* and used it to attack Japan. Japan thought Russia attacked, so they launched a counterstrike on Vladivostok." The czar remained silent, listening. "Your Excellency, may I suggest you have more to gain accepting the hostilities between Japan and Russia unfolded from an unfortunate misunderstanding? If I may be so bold, Russia and Japan have more to gain working together than going to war."

A knock interrupted Ramon. The czar removed the cigar from his mouth and nodded to a footman, who opened the door. A household steward entered and approached the czar with a bow. "Your Excellency, the honorable Itō Hirobumi and Dmitri Mendeleev wish an audience."

"Show them in."

The steward stood and left. A few minutes later he returned, escorting the two men. Itō dropped to one knee as did Mendeleev. The czar went to the scientist and indicated he should stand. He kissed the scientist on one cheek and then the other and then inquired after his health. As he did, Itō turned a furious gaze at Ramon.

The czar then gave permission for Itō to rise.

"Your Excellency, I am here to explain the circumstances of the Japanese attack on Vladivostok. It is my sincerest hope to find an understanding between our governments," said the ambassador.

Czar Alexander II waved the ambassador's words aside as though irrelevant. "Yes, yes, Mr. Morales here has already explained what happened. I think we can draft suitable papers soon enough, especially if you'd be willing to discuss a trade agreement."

Itō cast a glance at Ramon. "He didn't give you..."

Ramon stood. His knees threatened to give way, but he forced himself to walk over to the automaton and gave it a pat. "Your Excellency, with your permission, I think I should return the mechanical man to Lord Katsu in Japan as soon as possible."

The czar cast a cold glance at Itō. "Of course. General Dragomirov will see you out."

Ramon knelt before the czar. When the emperor gave his leave, Ramon bowed to Itō, then reached out and shook Dmitri Mendeleev's hand. General Dragomirov led Ramon back to the courtyard. "Do you think these things could fight our wars for us?" asked the general.

Ramon looked at the mechanical man and shook his head. "I hope not. Fearing war keeps us from being too ready to fight. If mechanical men fought, I'm afraid we would always be at war."

Dragomirov nodded. "You may be right." Soon they reached the Alexander pillar at the courtyard's center. "Is Legion gone for good?"

Ramon shrugged. "I don't know. I'm not even sure what I wish for in that regard. He's pushed us in so many good ways, even if he brought war upon us."

"I miss his constant chatter."

"I grew up in a small town. I think silence does a soul good." Ramon reached out and shook the general's hand. "Perhaps we'll meet again someday."

"Do you need a carriage?"

Ramon opened up the automaton's chest and flipped switches reversing its course. He moved a small lever down a notch, which he hoped would reduce its speed. "Thank you, but I have a ride." With that he hopped on the platform between the automaton's treads as it sped off through St. Petersburg's streets.

Upon arrival in Tokyo, Captain Cisneros summoned a carriage. Imagawa and Hoshi appeared on deck.

Hoshi took Imagawa's hands. "It nearly destroyed me to see you fallen on the battlefield. I hope you can find a good path in this Meiji Era."

"I knew you would not give up as long as I lived, Sensei. I pretended to be dead so you would flee and have a new life. You always had a more rounded picture of Bushido than I did. I wish you well in America."

Captain Cisneros and Fatemeh escorted her to the Tokyo Prefectural Office where she turned herself in to Lord Ōkubo. She gave him a full confession under the condition the men who returned to Tokyo with her would be spared. He agreed and his secretary drafted memoranda to that effect.

As their business concluded, Fatemeh approached Lord Ōkubo. "I hope your wife is well and I hope you would present this note to her." She handed him a sealed envelope.

He nodded and said he'd give it to her.

On the ride back to the *Ballena*, Captain Cisneros looked into Fatemeh's eyes. "I'm sorry you had such a poor honeymoon. Here we are, almost six-thousand miles from your home and you're separated from your husband..."

She placed her hand on his forearm and shook her head. "Ramon does what he must and I still have one more job to finish." She laughed and looked out the window at the buildings they passed. "In many ways, this honeymoon turned out far better than I would have imagined."

Cisneros caught his breath. "Better than you imagined? You nearly broke your neck in an airship wreck, samurai bandits kidnapped you, and a new war almost started."

"I also got to swim in Hawaiian waters, spend many wonderful days with my new husband and perhaps even play a small part in improving the world. What's more, once Ramon returns, our honeymoon will continue another week as we voyage to America. How many couples are allowed six weeks together before circumstances pull them into day-to-day routines?"

"I hope your day-to-day routine is a little less exciting than the last six weeks! For that matter, I fear your day-to-day routine may involve some time in jail when you return."

Fatemeh frowned and nodded. "I know and although prison time scares me a little, it's a small sacrifice for the good we've accomplished."

The captain leaned forward. "Do you think the good will be permanent?"

"Without change, an organism stagnates and dies." Fatemeh smiled. "The world will change and shift. People will try things which will prove wrong and some will do things which will make the world better. It's our nature."

The carriage pulled up beside the ship. Cisneros and Fatemeh boarded and went their separate ways.

The next morning, another carriage pulled up on the dock next to the *Ballena*. The driver sent a note aboard for Fatemeh, who appeared five minutes later. The carriage from the day before had hard wooden seats and bounced the riders over ruts and cobbles. This new carriage had red velvet seats and springs, providing a comfortable ride. The carriage took Fatemeh across town to Lord Ōkubo's house. Lady Hayasaki met her at the door.

"Thank you for agreeing to meet with me," said Fatemeh.

"I am delighted to see you again." Lady Hayasaki invited Fatemeh inside and led her to the dining table where a tea service awaited. A servant appeared, poured tea, and then departed again leaving the two women to speak. Fatemeh wondered how many state secrets the servants knew just from waiting in the wings for the opportunity to serve.

"I presume you are here on the behalf of Imagawa Masako, who surrendered herself to my husband, yesterday," said Lady Hayasaki.

Fatemeh sipped her tea, then set the cup down. "Actually, I'm here on behalf of the Ainu."

Lady Hayasaki narrowed her gaze but remained silent.

"The Ainu are a proud people and I believe Japan would benefit by embracing their differences rather than forcing them to assimilate into your culture."

"Do you presume to critique Japan?" Lady Hayasaki lifted an eyebrow.

"Not at all," said Fatemeh, "but the Ainu have experiences

which would disappear if they assimilated. For example, I met a woman named Ipokash who spoke both Japanese and Russian. She got to know the Russian chemist Dmitri Mendeleev quite well and now has experience with life aboard airships." Fatemeh leaned forward. "I propose Japan finds a place where the Ainu are welcomed, but retain their identity."

Lady Hayasaki considered this for a moment. "Some would see that as a threat to their livelihood. What if the Ainu settled on land someone wants to develop?"

"The Ainu would require a strong person on the Lord of Home Affair's staff to work with them and the Japanese government."

Lady Hayasaki gave a shrewd grin. "You did come to speak about Imagawa."

"I can think of no one better for the job."

"I shall consider it and we shall see what happens during her trial." Lady Hayasaki sipped her tea. "If Imagawa is exonerated, I shall speak to my husband."

"Thank you, Lady Hayasaki." Fatemeh put her hands together and bowed from her seat.

"Your Japanese has improved since we last met," said Lady Hayasaki. "I'm impressed."

Ramon watched distant storm clouds from the *Bonchō's* catwalk. He reflected on the visit to St. Petersburg and knew his success relied more on luck than skill. Despite Imagawa's attempts and some tensions, Japan and Russia didn't want to go to war. However, Ramon wanted to go beyond a simple cease-fire and encourage the two countries to work together. He hoped a cooperative spirit would spread beyond those two countries.

As he watched the storm clouds, Ramon wondered how many troubles between nations came from selfishness and pride. Nations went to war when one had something another wanted. They also went to war when people within the borders had conflicted interests. It's what drove the American Civil War and what he feared could start a war within Russia's borders.

Would automata solve Russia's class inequities? Ramon suspected the answer wasn't so simple, but he hoped they might
relieve the pressures for a while.

The sun drifted toward the horizon, streaking the sky in
orange rays. Ramon shivered, wishing Fatemeh accompanied
him. He'd be in Japan soon, then they'd make the trip back
across the ocean to the United States where they'd face their
next challenges.

Ramon entered the airship, ate a simple meal in the crew
mess, then went to his cabin. He added another blanket to
those stacked on the bed, undressed and crawled in.

His eyes drifted closed and he saw himself standing on
a vast plain. An undulating, buzzing black cloud approached.
Ramon retreated several steps and threw up his arms, fearing
bees. As they drew closer, he realized millions of tiny clockwork machines composed the cloud. The buzzing came from
their whirring gears.

"Legion?"

"*Yes, we're here.*" The voice came from the entire clockwork
swarm. "*We wanted to say goodbye.*"

Ramon sought the right words. "Goodbye? As in goodbye
for good?"

"*Goodbye as in we are taking leave of your world for a time. We
wanted to unify humanity, but we see you accomplished more in one
afternoon's efforts than we did in a year. Perhaps we have lived so long
we can no longer see simple solutions.*"

Ramon shrugged. "I'm not sure if my simple solution
would have worked if not for the inspiration you've given people over the last year or so. Would we have airships, submersibles, and automata without you?"

"*It's impossible to say,*" said Legion. "*We merely unlocked those
dreams within a few skeptics and showed them the dreams' worthiness.
Lord Katsu's automaton, Professor Maravilla's wolf and ornithopters,
the lightning gun—humans developed all these things without our
intervention.*"

"You're referring to yourself in the plural again," mused
Ramon.

"*We are many and one, just as humans are many and one. We
are kindred and we hope to meet again.*"

"Is this your true appearance?"

The swarm vibrated with laughter. *"No, this is still just the way you picture us, but the image amuses us. We may build a new generation which looks like this just to honor you."*

"Will I ever see you again?"

Legion remained silent for some time. Ramon sensed the swarm's members communicated among themselves, calculating an answer. *"Human life is brief. You as an individual might not see us again, but your children or your children's children might. Many individuals who comprise my being have died, many have been born in my brief time on Earth. The same will happen to you. You may not see us Ramon Morales, but you will almost assuredly see us."*

Ramon thought he must be growing used to Legion. That last statement almost made sense to him. "I'll be sorry to see you go. I look forward to the day when humans will see you on more equal terms."

"Continue to encourage humans to cooperate, Ramon Morales," said Legion. *"We impart one last gift before we go. It is perhaps the single best thing we can do to see our experiment grow and thrive. Until we meet again. Adieu."*

Ramon watched the swarm fly away. As he did, the view cleared and he stared up at the *Bonchō's* ceiling. Light streamed in from outside. He couldn't tell whether the entire night passed in conversation with Legion or if he'd spoken to Legion for a brief time and then slept until dawn. For all he knew, it could have just been a strange dream.

He pushed the blankets aside and looked around the cabin. Everything appeared as it did the night before. He peered out the window and saw a vast body of water. They must have reached the Sea of Japan. He would hold Fatemeh before long.

As Ramon dressed, he considered humans and their struggles. He recalled the Buddhist teachings about self being an illusion and the Shinto teachings about people having multiple souls. He shuddered as he buttoned his waistcoat. Walking to the window, he looked out and considered the future.

Humanity is Legion, he thought.

Fatemeh read in her cabin when Captain Cisneros knocked on the door. "Mr. Gonzalez has just sighted the *Bonchō*. I suspect it will land soon."

"I'd like to go meet it." She put on her shoes and the captain sent word for a coach. None were available, but a rickshaw driver offered to take Fatemeh to the palace grounds for a nominal fee. She paid him and he ran off through the streets. The journey proved less harrowing than when Lord Katsu's automaton pulled a rickshaw. Even so, she worried he might take too long and she'd pass Ramon somewhere in the streets.

As she arrived at the palace grounds, the *Bonchō* descended into the hangar. She paid the driver another coin and asked him to wait. She walked to the hangar and showed the guard her letter of introduction from Lord Ōkubo. He gave her a strange glance, but allowed her to pass.

Inside, the ground crew tied off the tether ropes and the gondola door flew open. Ramon jumped to the ground and he ran into Fatemeh's arms. "I've missed you so much."

She returned the embrace. "I'm glad to see you. How are you?"

"I think I stopped a war... and Legion's gone."

Fatemeh nodded. "Imagawa faces trial soon, but I suspect her sentence will be light. If so, Japan may face some challenges in the coming years. I think it'll do the country good."

"How soon before we leave for America?" Ramon's question was soft, almost hesitant.

"I think Captain Cisneros plans to depart as soon as you're aboard."

"I thought that might be the case. Wait here." He climbed back into the gondola. A few minutes later he arrived with his bags and Lord Katsu's automaton. Ramon hopped out and the automaton followed, landing on the ground with a thud.

"He's coming with us? Won't the *Bonchō's* captain return him to Lord Katsu?"

"I'm certain he would, but I'm not quite ready to leave Tokyo."

"I already have a rickshaw driver waiting."

"So much the better."

They walked outside to where the driver shuffled from

one foot to the other.

"How much would it cost to rent your rickshaw for the evening? We have our own driver."

The driver blinked, did some mental arithmetic, then named a price. Ramon handed the driver a few coins. "We'll be back in an hour or two," said Ramon.

He programmed the automaton and they climbed in the rickshaw. "You understand that thing pretty well, don't you?" asked Fatemeh.

"I think I'm getting the hang of it."

The automaton zoomed off through Tokyo's streets. It circled around the palace and went toward the university. As the sun approached the horizon, the automaton stopped near the botanical gardens. Hand in hand, Ramon and Fatemeh walked to Sanchiro Pond. They found their way to the bridge.

"Will Legion interrupt this time?" Fatemeh winked at Ramon.

"I think Legion's gone for good. He said farewell during the return journey. I think he meant it."

Fatemeh's brow creased. "I'll kind of miss him. He caused trouble, but he made the world an interesting place."

"I think humans make the world interesting." Ramon leaned in and kissed Fatemeh. The kiss lingered and she pressed into him, pleased with his confidence and his gentle strength which sought justice without bullying others. She had no doubts he was the right man for her.

"Love. So many different ways to have been in love," she mused when they separated.

"A haiku?"

"One of Bonchō's. It seems appropriate."

"There may be many ways to be in love, but in truth, I love just one woman." He leaned over and kissed her again.

EPILOGUE
THE JACKALOPE

R amon and Fatemeh rested and enjoyed each other's company during the week-long voyage to Ensenada, expecting to be apart for thirty days once they arrived home.

They often took their evening meals with Hoshi and Captain Cisneros. Ramon sensed a certain tension between Hoshi and Fatemeh. When he asked about it one night, she waved it off and said, "Some people react to things based on old ideals. Hoshi is a just man, but he still believes it's okay for some to die to fulfill justice. That makes me uncomfortable."

Hoshi had offered to let them stay at his farmhouse in Las Cruces on their return trip to central New Mexico. "Do you want to decline Hoshi's invitation?"

Fatemeh shook her head. "What's important is Hoshi's working to find his way in this new world. It's just taking me a while to learn different people adapt in different ways."

"Like Imagawa?"

Fatemeh fell silent and stared off into space for a while. Just as Ramon thought she'd chosen not to answer, she nodded. "Yes, like Imagawa. I admire her strength, but I worry about those who might use strength to hold power over others."

Ramon didn't pursue the conversation further. They could not resolve the complex topic through discussion. They would just have to see how things developed in Japan.

Ramon considered the marvels he'd seen in the last year: airships, mechanical wolves and men, owl ornithopters people could ride around in, and submersible vessels. He knew men developed most of those things on their own, but he wondered if any would have happened if Legion had not been involved. If not for Legion, Maravilla's experiments with

253

owl ornithopters might have been a brief footnote in history. Airships and submersibles might be relegated to Jules Verne's *Voyages Extraordinaire*. Would anyone see the need for mechanical men if human labor remained cheap?

The *Ballena* arrived in Ensenada during the second week of November 1877. Ramon realized they'd missed Dia de los Muertos—the Day of the Dead celebration he loved so much. He first encountered Legion as it passed through Mesilla, New Mexico on the Day of the Dead. Soon afterward, the swarm encountered General Gorloff and the war with Russia began.

Captain Cisneros arranged for a coach to carry Hoshi, Ramon, and Fatemeh across the border to Los Angeles. From there, they would take the train to Mesilla. Captain Cisneros presented them with tickets, which included a stable for Hoshi's horse aboard the train.

Fatemeh embraced Captain Cisneros. "Thank you for the wonderful honeymoon."

Ramon lifted an eyebrow at that, but the captain didn't say anything. Instead, he returned the embrace and helped Ramon and Fatemeh load the coach. Hoshi left to retrieve the horse he'd stabled.

When the samurai returned, Cisneros shook Hoshi's hand. "Thank you for joining us. Please give my regards to Professor Maravilla. If he's willing to return to Mexico, I'd be happy to offer him a job."

"I'll let him know." He frowned, but sounded more thoughtful than angry. "We have all spent much time in the last few months confronting our demons. Some of us might find solace at home. Others may be at a point to start new lives elsewhere."

Hoshi rode behind the coach as it pulled out, giving the newlyweds a little more privacy. The driver snapped the reins and they began the long overland journey up into California. Cisneros waved until they disappeared from view.

After crossing the ocean and continents with ease via airship and Cisneros's *Ballena*, the ten-day overland journey to Mesilla wore on their nerves. They all sighed relief when the conductor came down the train's aisle and announced they approached the Mesilla Park station.

They picked up their baggage and Hoshi retrieved his horse. Hoshi waited with the bags while Ramon and Fatemeh went to a livery stable and found horses to buy for the trip north to Estancia. An hour later, they rode up the small road to Hoshi's farm. The former samurai gnashed his teeth. All the chile plants remained, but had grown brown and withered. What's more, all the pods had vanished.

"Someone must have harvested them for you." Fatemeh shrugged.

"That's what I'm afraid of."

Two people lounged in chairs on the porch. As Ramon, Fatemeh, and Hoshi rode closer, they discovered Professor Maravilla and Marshal Larissa Seaton. "It's about time you got here," said Larissa.

"You expected us?" asked Ramon as he dismounted.

"Captain Cisneros wired us a few days ago and told us you'd be here soon," explained Maravilla. "We came by to get the house ready for you."

"I appreciate the sentiment," said Hoshi, "but what the hell happened to my chile plants?"

Maravilla opened his tailcoat and removed a black box from the inside pocket. He turned a knob and flipped a switch. From behind the house, hopped a large, mechanical rabbit. In addition to ears, two antlers stuck above its head. "I built this mechanical harvester. I chose a rabbit's form since they harvest vegetables for their own consumption, but I understood your concerns about damaging the crop. In San Francisco, I used electromagnetic energy to allow the lightning wolf corps to speak to one another. I just refined the idea to control the harvester's behavior as it worked, hence the antelope-like antennae on its head. I call it a jackalope since it possesses both jack rabbit and antelope features."

Hoshi sputtered. "Yes, but... what happened to my chiles?"

Maravilla shrugged. "They went to market and made you quite a profit."

Hoshi paced back and forth, opening and closing his mouth as if he prepared to launch into a tirade. After four circuits, he smiled. "Thank you." He walked up to Maravilla, took his hands and bowed. "Thank you, my friend."

Ramon tipped his hat at Larissa. "Miss Crimson." He referred to the name she used as a bounty hunter.

"It's Seaton now. Larissa Crimson is long behind me."

"How are Billy and Luther?" asked Fatemeh.

"They'll be home in time for Thanksgiving." Larissa smiled.

"That soon?" asked Fatemeh. "I guess it has been almost thirty days since they'd been sentenced."

Larissa's brow creased. She didn't understand how Ramon and Fatemeh could already know the sentence's length.

Ramon's gut churned. "So, I suppose you're here in an ... official capacity." He thought he'd have more time before they were arrested and taken to trial.

Larissa smiled. "I suppose you could say that. It seems you've made friends in some pretty high places." She opened her black coat and removed a letter from the inside pocket. "This is a letter from President Hayes."

She handed it to Ramon, who took it, then dropped down to take a seat on the front step. He read the letter. The president explained he'd received visits from both the Russian and Japanese ambassadors extolling Ramon's excellent work and recommending him to a diplomatic appointment once he established his credentials. "In light of your extraordinary service to this great nation, I extend a full pardon to you, Mr. Ramon Morales and your wife, Mrs. Ramon Morales." He read that part aloud, his hands feeling so weak, the letter threatened to flutter to the ground.

He handed the letter to Fatemeh pointing out another line which read, "It would be a disservice to this country to delay your education any further and I have written a letter to my alma mater extolling your virtues."

"I brought some other mail with me from your house in Estancia. Maybe they should have made me a mailman instead of a marshal." She laughed at her own joke, then passed a letter to Ramon. "I thought you'd like this one first." She handed him a small parcel from Harvard Law School.

Ramon opened the letter with trembling hands. "I've been admitted to Harvard for the Spring Semester, and they've given me a grant for my studies. It won't cost anything. We just have to get there."

Fatemeh sat down next to Ramon and pulled him into a tight embrace. He wrapped her in his arms until he found the strength to stand. When he did, he leapt to his feet, punched the air, and whooped with joy.

"This gives you time to stay for a nice Thanksgiving dinner with us here in New Mexico," said Larissa. "Billy and Luther should be back by then. They'll want to see you before you go."

At one time, Larissa Crimson tracked Ramon across New Mexico to collect a bounty. Now Ramon surprised himself and gathered the former bounty hunter into his arms and danced around. Dizzy, she almost toppled over when he released her a minute later.

He reached out and shook Maravilla's hand, then Hoshi's, after which he had to turn and walk away. He strolled down the road to the edge of Hoshi's property. He shivered in the chilled November air and looked up at the deep blue autumn sky. Again, he wondered where Legion had gone and he considered what the alien had said about a parting gift.

Fatemeh stepped up behind him. He took her in his arms and kissed her.

"Can you stand a little more good news?"

He lifted an eyebrow, half afraid his voice would crack if he tried to speak.

"I think we're about to become parents."

The blood rushed from Ramon's head. He grabbed Fatemeh into another embrace to steady himself. A chirping made him look around. A burrowing owl stood on a fencepost and danced from one foot to the other. Ramon smiled and took Fatemeh's hand and grabbed her around the waist. "I think he has the right idea. I feel like dancing." With that, Ramon twirled Fatemeh in a waltz to unheard music down the lane and toward the future.

ABOUT THE AUTHOR

David Lee Summers became a steampunk in 1987 when he used a nineteenth century telescope on Nantucket to examine the evolution of distant pulsating stars. Since that time he has published a dozen novels and numerous short stories and poems spanning a wide range of the imagination. *Owl Dance* and *Lightning Wolves* are the first two novels of the Clockwork Legion series. His other novels include *The Solar Sea* and *The Astronomer's Crypt*.

David's short stories have appeared in such magazines and anthologies as *Realms of Fantasy, Cemetery Dance, Gears and Levers, Zombiefied: An Anthology of All Things Zombie,* and *These Vampires Don't Sparkle*. In 2010 he was nominated for the Science Fiction Poetry Association's Rhysling Award.

In addition to writing, David has edited five science fiction anthologies including *A Kepler's Dozen, Kepler's Cowboys* and *Space Horrors*. When not working with the written word, David still spends time operating telescopes at Kitt Peak National Observatory. Learn more about David at **davidleesummers.com**